The Confusion of Worlds

The Confusion of Worlds

*Resurrection, the Kingdom of God,
and Otherworld Experiences*

Heiner Schwenke

Translated by Sarah Kühne

Abridged and revised by the author

☙PICKWICK *Publications* · Eugene, Oregon

THE CONFUSION OF WORLDS
Resurrection, the Kingdom of God, and Otherworld Experiences

Copyright © 2019 Heiner Schwenke. All rights reserved. Except for brief quotations in critical publications or reviews, no part of this book may be reproduced in any manner without prior written permission from the publisher. Write: Permissions, Wipf and Stock Publishers, 199 W. 8th Ave., Suite 3, Eugene, OR 97401.

Pickwick Publications
An Imprint of Wipf and Stock Publishers
199 W. 8th Ave., Suite 3
Eugene, OR 97401

www.wipfandstock.com

PAPERBACK ISBN: 978-1-5326-5602-6
HARDCOVER ISBN: 978-1-5326-5603-3
EBOOK ISBN: 978-1-5326-5604-0

Cataloguing-in-Publication data:

Names: Schwenke, Heiner, author. | Kühne, Sarah, translator.

Title: The confusion of worlds : resurrection, the kingdom of God, and otherworld experiences / by Heiner Schwenke; translated by Sarah Kühne.

Description: Eugene, OR: Pickwick Publications, 2019 | Includes bibliographical references and index.

Identifiers: ISBN 978-1-5326-5602-6 (paperback) | ISBN 978-1-5326-5603-3 (hardcover) | ISBN 978-1-5326-5604-0 (ebook)

Subjects: LCSH: Jesus Christ—Resurrection | Near-death experiences | Experience (Religion) | Psychology and religion | Future life | Religion—Controversial literature | Religion and science | Eschatology

Classification: BL53 S394 2019 (print) | BL53 (ebook)

Previously published in German by Verlag Karl Alber, 2017.

Scripture quotations marked (ESV) are from the ESV® Bible (The Holy Bible, English Standard Version®), copyright © 2001 by Crossway, a publishing ministry of Good News Publishers. Used by permission. All rights reserved.

Scripture quotations marked (NKJV) are from the New King James Version®. Copyright © 1982 by Thomas Nelson. Used by permission. All rights reserved.

Scripture quotations marked (NETS) are from *A New English Translation of the Septuagint*, © 2007 by the International Organization for Septuagint and Cognate Studies, Inc. Used by permission of Oxford University Press. All rights reserved.

Scripture quotations from the Greek NT are from *Novum Testamentum Graece*, 28th revised edition, edited by Barbara Aland and others, © 2012 Deutsche Bibelgesellschaft, Stuttgart.

Scripture quotations from the Latin Vulgate are from *Biblia Sacra Iuxta Vulgatam Versionem*, 5th revised edition, edited by Roger Gryson, © 2007 Deutsche Bibelgesellschaft, Stuttgart.

Scripture quotations from the Greek Septuagint are from *Septuaginta: id est vetus testamentum graece iuxta LXX interpretes*, edited by Alfred Rahlfs, 2nd revised edition, edited by Robert Hanhart, © 2006 Deutsche Bibelgesellschaft, Stuttgart.

Manufactured in the U.S.A.   12/20/18

Contents

Analytical Table of Contents | ix
Preface | xv
Abbreviations | xvii

Introduction | 1
1. Otherworld Experiences: The Key to Belief in Resurrection and the Kingdom of God? | 6
2. Resurrection and the Kingdom of God in Zoroastrianism | 18
3. Resurrection and the Kingdom of God in Judaism | 28
4. Resurrection and the Kingdom of God in Jesus of Nazareth | 47
5. Resurrection and the Kingdom of God in Christianity after Jesus | 78
6. The Lakota Ghost-Dance Movement: Otherworld Experiences Stimulate a Belief in a Future Kingdom of God | 119
7. Did Jesus Have Transcendent Experiences That Might Explain His Eschatological Belief? | 122
8. The Great Disappointment | 129

Epilogue | 146

Appendix: Miracles and Science | 157

Bibliography | 163
Ancient and Medieval Writings Index | 185
Author Index | 205

Analytical Table of Contents

Preface | xv

Abbreviations | xvii

Introduction | 1

    The mystery of belief in resurrection and the kingdom of God (1) • Transcendent experiences (2) • Effects of transcendent experiences on worldview (2) • The neglect of transcendent experiences in the history of ideas (4) • The hypothesis of this book and the course of the investigation (5)

Otherworld Experiences: The Key to Belief in Resurrection and the Kingdom of God? | 6

    Otherworld journeys (6) • Paradisiacal, earth-like landscapes (7) • Shining otherworldly persons (10) • Otherworld landscapes as earthly paradise (14) • From existing paradise to utopia (14) • Resurrection (15) • Belief in a soul vs. belief in resurrection (16)

Resurrection and the Kingdom of God in Zoroastrianism | 18

    The eschatology of Zoroastrianism (18) • History and tradition (19) • Gathas: an eternal earthly life? (19) • Zamyād Yasht: resurrection and Frashokereti (20) • Greek sources (21) • Resurrection in middle Persian Zoroastrian scriptures (22) • The recovery of the physical body from its components (22) • The eternal afterlife (23) • The risen are in the prime of life (23) • Luminous resurrection bodies (24) • Renewed paradisiacal earth, eternal spring (25) • Further otherworldly characteristics of the post-mortem earthly life (26) • Conclusion (27)

ANALYTICAL TABLE OF CONTENTS

Resurrection and the Kingdom of God in Judaism | 28

Fading in Sheol (28) • Minor importance of the resurrection idea in the Tanakh (28) • No clear distinction of body and soul (29) • Ezekiel's resurrection vision (29) • Apocalypse of Isaiah (32) • Individual resurrection in Daniel (33) • Book of the Watchers (35) • Book of Parables (36) • Second Book of Maccabees (38) • Further deuterocanonical and apocryphal texts from pre-Christian times (39) • Fourth Book of Ezra (40) • Second Book of Baruch (Syriac Apocalypse of Baruch) (41) • Fourth Book of Baruch (Paralipomena of Jeremiah) (43) • Fourth Book of the Sibylline Oracles (43) • Later developments (44) • Conclusion (45)

Resurrection and the Kingdom of God in Jesus of Nazareth | 47

Methodological questions   48

Physical resurrection   49

Linguistic indications of the doctrine of a physical resurrection (49) • Physical resurrection implies physical afterlife (52) • Physical movement after resurrection (52) • Eating, drinking and satiety in the kingdom of God (53) • The risen and the not yet deceased together in the kingdom of God (54) • Entering the kingdom of God mutilated (54)

Earthly kingdom of God   55

The kingdom of God and its synonyms (55) • Physical afterlife points to an earthly localization of the kingdom of God (55) • Judgment on earth (56) • "On earth as it is in heaven" (57) • "To inherit the land" (57) • Restoration of Israel with Zion as its center (57) • General resurrection (59) • Contextual indications (61)

Objections to the preceding reconstruction of the teachings of Jesus   61

Afterlife of the person without the physical body? (61) • Afterlife without a physical body in the otherworld (63) • Physical resurrection to an eternal life vs. eternal life that believers already possess (64) • Return of the soul into the light (66) • No earthly-spatial conception of the kingdom of God (67) • Presence of the kingdom of God (69) • Afterlife in heaven (70) • "Heaven and earth will pass away" (71) • Conclusion (73)

Otherworldly elements of the afterlife 73

    Eternal life (73) • A life without poverty, hunger or tears (74) • Shining bodies (75) • Seeing God (75) • Conclusion (77)

RESURRECTION AND THE KINGDOM OF GOD IN CHRISTIANITY AFTER JESUS | 78

Overview (78)

The physical resurrection of Jesus as a paradigm 79

    The apparitions of Jesus after his death in the New Testament (79) • Physical resurrection or physical post-mortem manifestation? (80) • The physical resurrection of Jesus and the empty tomb (83) • The physical resurrected body of Jesus in early Christian scriptures (85)

Physical resurrection as Christian dogma 87

    Resurrection of the physical body in Christian creeds and doctrinal documents (87) • Miraculous revivifications as proof of the possibility of a physical resurrection (89) • The unsolvable problem of the reassembly of body parts (91)

The transformation of the resurrection body for the eternal life 93

    The necessity of transformation (93) • No clear time distinction in Christianity between resurrection and transformation (94) • Transformation of the resurrected body in Cyril of Jerusalem (94) • Adapting to afterlife environments: Can flesh burn forever? (95) • How will the resurrected survive world conflagration? (95) • Transformation into a non-physical body according to Thomas Aquinas (96) • Paul's seed metaphor: resurrection as transformation (96) • A combination of a physical resurrection and the seed metaphor (98) • Resurrection with another body without transformation (99) • Superfluousness of the physical resurrection (99)

The transferal of eternal life to the otherworld 100

    Fundamentals (100) • Jesus' expectation of a kingdom not communicable in the Hellenistic arena (101) • Heaven as the abode of the blessed in Hellenism (101) • The instability of the sub-lunar world (102) • The great heaven and the small earth (102) • Heaven as the space for development and the ascent to God (103) • Where shall the immortal soul go? (105) • Contempt for the earthly (107) • Problems with a physical heaven (108)

Afterlife on earth: resurrection, judgment and an intermediate kingdom 108

> Resurrection and the Last Judgment take place on earth (108) • The millennial kingdom in the book of Revelation (109) • Irenaeus and Lactantius: a very earthly intermediate kingdom (110)

An eternal life on an unearthly earth after the end of time 113

> Jesus' silence on the transformation of the cosmos (113) • New earth without the end of the world: book of Revelation (113) • New earth after the end of the world: Second Epistle of Peter (114) • Theological perplexity with regard to the new earth (115) • Descriptions of an unearthly, new earth (117) • Conclusion (118)

THE LAKOTA GHOST-DANCE MOVEMENT: OTHERWORLD EXPERIENCES STIMULATE A BELIEF IN A FUTURE KINGDOM OF GOD | 119

> Otherworld journeys during the ghost dance (119) • Black Elk (120)

DID JESUS HAVE TRANSCENDENT EXPERIENCES THAT MIGHT EXPLAIN HIS ESCHATOLOGICAL BELIEF? | 122

> The search for a specific explanation (122) • Otherworld journeys or encounters with the deceased? (123) • Do miracle experiences hold the key? (124) • Miraculous revivifications as experiential basis for Jesus' belief in resurrection? (124) • Miracles as flashes of the reality of God's kingdom? (125) • Miracles and Jesus' self-conception (126)

THE GREAT DISAPPOINTMENT | 129

> The inevitability of disappointment (129) • Jesus' role in the eschatological process (130) • The two cries of Jesus on the cross (134) • Historicity of the cries of Jesus on the cross (135) • Weakness or disappointment? (136) • Mitigation and omission of the cries of Jesus on the cross (137) • Removal of other embarrassments of the crucifixion scene (137) • Disappointed eschatological expectation as a motif for Jesus' cry to God (139) • Crying out to God and the eschatological divine intervention in Lactantius (140) • Did Jesus expect God's intervention in his lifetime? (140) • The imminent eschatological expectation of Jesus in the sources (141) • Jesus to be carried away on Passover night? (143) • The Son of Man does not die but will be carried up to heaven (144) • Jesus' death on the cross and the tragedy of the confusion of the worlds (145)

Epilogue | 146

Appendix: Miracles and science | 157

> Introduction (157) • It cannot be proved that an experience contradicts science as a whole (157) • Causal closure of the physical world not scientifically provable (158) • Is no extraordinary influence of the non-physical on the physical possible? (159) • Miracle accounts as anecdotes (160) • Do miracles not exist because they are not reproducible using an intersubjective method? (161)

Bibliography | 163

Ancient and Medieval Writings Index | 185

Author Index | 205

Preface

IN THIS BOOK I endeavor to employ knowledge about so-called otherworld experiences to illuminate two enigmatic, interlinked religious ideas: the ideas of the resurrection of the physical body and of a paradisiacal, earthly kingdom in which the resurrected will live eternally with these same bodies. The book emerged from the research project *Transcendent Experiences—Phenomena, Ideas, and Judgments*, conducted at the Max Planck Institute for the History of Science in Berlin. In the context of the project, transcendent experiences are understood as experiences that transcend ordinary reality or familiar categories of explanation. Examples are the just mentioned otherworld experiences, or experiences of a seemingly extra-ordinary influence of the mental upon the physical. Transcendent experiences can strongly influence the lives and thoughts of those experiencing them. Until now, their phenomenology, their impact on the history of ideas, and the ways of cognitively dealing with them have been neglected by scholarship. Addressing transcendent experiences seems to be demanding in terms of judgment, both for experiencers and outside observers. A diligent and circumspect evaluation of the experiences in question often seems to fall victim to the need for cognitive closure. On the one side of the spectrum, we find the habit, particularly among non-experiencers, to block out and to debase transcendent experiences *a limine*. On the other side, there is a tendency both of experiencers and outside observers towards premature interpretations and explanations. And it would seem that misinterpretations of transcendent experiences can also have serious, far-reaching practical consequences, as this study shows.

The book is a slightly abridged and revised English version of the original German edition (*Die Verwechslung der Welten: Auferstehung, Reich Gottes und Jenseitserfahrungen*. Freiburg i. Br.: Karl Alber, 2017). I am deeply grateful to Dale C. Allison, Jr. for encouragement, discussion, and many valuable suggestions and questions. He undertook the most generous effort not only to comment on a previous German version of the manuscript, but to read through the entire English version and to provide linguistic assistance.

I thank Sharokh Raei for checking the retranslations of his German versions of Zoroastrian texts. I am indebted to Sarah Kühne, the competent translator, for the smooth, effective, and agreeable cooperation.

I dedicate the book to my wife, Anne Peters, and to our children, Charlotte and Johannes.

Abbreviations

General

a.	articulus
ad	responsio ad obiectum
arg.	argumentum (= obiectio)
BCE	before the Common Era / Christian Era
CE	Common Era / Christian Era
cf.	*confer*, compare
co.	corpus articuli ("respondeo dicendum")
D	Paragraph in Denzinger, *Compendium*
e.g.	*exempli gratia*, for example
ed(s).	editor(s), edited by, edition
et al.	*et alii*, and others
etc.	*et cetera*, and so forth, and the rest
fn.	footnote
i.e.	*id est*, that is
n.	note
n.d.	no date
p(p).	page(s)
q.	quaestio
s.c.	sed contra
s.l.	*sine loco*, without place (of publication)
s.n.	*sine nomine*, without name (of publisher)
Suppl.	supplementum
vol(s).	volume(s)
vs.	versus

Classical Greek and Latin Authors
Aristotle
Cael.   *De caelo*

Cicero
Rep.   *De republica*
Tusc.   *Tusculanae disputationes*

Diogenes Laertius
Vit.   *De clarorum philosophorum vitis*

Herodotus
Hist.   *Historiae*

Hesiod
Op.   *Opera et dies*

Homer
Od.   *Odyssee*

Plato
Phaedr.   *Phaedros*
Resp.   *Respublica*

Plutarch
Is. Os.   *De Iside et Osiride*

Zoroastrian Scriptures
Y.   Yasna
Yt.   Yasht
GBd.   Greater Bundahishn
Pahl. Riv. Pahlavi Rivāyat
WZ   Wizīdagīhā Zādspram

Hebrew Bible / Old Testament

Gen	Genesis
Exod	Exodus
Lev	Leviticus
Num	Numbers
Deut	Deuteronomy
Josh	Joshua
Judg	Judges
1–2 Kgs	1–2 Kings
Ps	Psalm
Isa	Isaiah
Jer	Jeremiah
Ezek	Ezekiel
Dan	Daniel
Hos	Hosea
Joel	Joel
Amos	Amos
Mic	Micah
Zech	Zechariah
Mal	Malachi

Deuterocanonical Works

2 Macc	2 Maccabees
Sir	Sirach / Ecclesiasticus
Tob	Tobit
Wis	Wisdom of Solomon

Other Ancient Jewish Sources

As. Mos.	Assumption of Moses
2 Bar.	2 Baruch (Syriac Apocalypse)
4 Bar.	4 Baruch (Paraleipomena Jeremiou)

1 En.	1 Enoch (Ethiopic Apocalypse)
4 Ezra	4 Ezra
Jub.	Jubilees
LAB	Liber antiquitatum biblicarum (Pseudo-Philo)
Pss. Sol.	Psalms of Solomon
b. Sanh.	Babylonian Talmud, Sanhedrin
m. Sanh.	Mishnah Sanhedrin
Sib. Or.	Sibylline Oracles
T. Ab.	Testament of Abraham
T. Benj.	Testament of Benjamin
T. Jud.	Testament of Judah
T. Levi	Testament of Levi
T. Sim.	Testament of Simeon
T. Zeb.	Testament of Zebulun

New Testament

Matt	Matthew
Mark	Mark
Luke	Luke
John	John
Acts	Acts
Rom	Romans
1–2 Cor	1–2 Corinthians
Eph	Ephesians
Phil	Philippians
Col	Colossians
1 Thess	1 Thessalonians
Heb	Hebrews
1–2 Pet	1–2 Peter
Rev	Revelation

Other Ancient Christian Sources

1 Clem.	1 Clement
Ep. Apos.	Epistle to the Apostles
Gos. Pet.	Gospel of Peter
Gos. Thom.	Gospel of Thomas
Ign. *Smyrn.*	Ignatius, *To the Smyrnaeans*
Inf. Gos. Thom.	Infancy Gospel of Thomas
Syr. Apoc. Dan.	Syriac Apocalypse of Daniel
Treat. Res.	Treatise on the Resurrection

Ancient and Medieval Christian Authors

Athenagoras
Res.   *De resurrectione*

Augustine
Civ.   *De civitate dei*
Cur.   *De cura pro mortuis gerenda*

Bede
Hist. eccl.   *Historiam ecclesiasticam gentis anglorum*

Cyril of Jerusalem
Catech. illum.   *Procatechesis et catecheses ad illuminandos*

Eusebius
Hist. eccl.   *Historia ecclesiastica*

Gregory the Great
Dial.   *Dialogi de vita et miraculis patrum Italicorum*

Irenaeus
Haer.   *Adversus haereses*

Josephus
A.J.   *Antiquitates judaicae*

Justin
1 Apol.   *Apologia maior*

Lactantius
Epit.   *Epitome divinarum institutionum*
Inst.   *Divinarum institutionum*

Methodius of Olympia
Res.   *De resurrectione*

Minucius Felix
Oct.   *Octavius*

Origen
Fr. Ps.   *Fragmenta in Psalmos*
Princ.   *De principiis*

Tertullian
An.   *De anima*
Res.   *De resurrectione carnis*

Thomas Aquinas
S. Th.   *Summa Theologiae*

Modern Christian Sources

CCC   *Catechism of the Catholic Church.* Popular and Definitive Edition. London: Burns & Oates, 2000 (Numbers are locator numbers, not page numbers.)

Versions, Translations, and Lexica of Zoroastrian, Jewish, and Christian Sources

ANF	*Ante-Nicene Fathers: The Writings of the Fathers down to A.D. 325.* Edited by Aleander Roberts and James Donaldson. Revised by A. Cleveland Coxe. 10 vols. Buffalo, NY: Christian Literature, 1885–97.
BDAG	Bauer, Walter, Frederick W. Danker, William F. Arndt, and F. Wilbur Gingrich. *Greek–English Lexicon of the New Testament and Other Early Christian Literature.* 3rd ed. Chicago: University of Chicago Press, 2000.
ESV	English Standard Version
EZIQ	Sharokh Raei. *Die Endzeitvorstellungen der Zoroastrier in iranischen Quellen.* Göttinger Orientforschungen III. Reihe: Iranica. Neue Folge 6. Wiesbaden: Harrassowitz, 2010.
LXX	Septuagint
NETS	Pietersma, Albert, and Benjamin C. Wright III, trans. *A New English Translation of the Septuagint and the Other Greek Translations Traditionally Included under That Title.* New York: Oxford University Press, 2007.
NKJV	New King James Version
NPNF[1]	*A Select Library of the Nicene and Post-Nicene Fathers of the Christian Church*, Series 1. Edited by Philip Schaff. 14 vols. New York: Christian Literature, 1886–90.
NPNF[2]	*A Select Library of the Nicene and Post-Nicene Fathers of the Christian Church*, Series 2. Edited by Philip Schaff and Henry Wace. 14 vols. New York: Christian Literature, 1890–1900.
NTApoc	*New Testament Apocrypha.* 2 vols. Revised ed. Edited by Wilhelm Schneemelcher. English trans. ed. Robert McL. Wilson. Cambridge: Clarke, 2003.
OTP	*Old Testament Pseudepigrapha.* Edited by James H. Charlesworth. 2 vols. New York: Doubleday, 1983, 1985.
TH	Theodotion

Introduction

*The mystery of belief in resurrection
and the kingdom of God*

RELIGIOUS CONCEPTS ARE OFTEN enigmatic. The doctrines of a physical resurrection[1] and an earthly kingdom of God take a leading place in this regard. They can be found in Zoroastrianism, Judaism, Christianity, and to a certain extent in Islam.[2] Once resurrected, the risen, with their physical bodies restored, will go on to live an eternal, peaceful life under God's reign without disease or old age, catastrophes or hardships, in wonderful surroundings and on earth, but an earth from which violence and decay have disappeared. This idea, however, contradicts everything we know about this cosmos. Ageing and death are essential components of biological life. No living organism lives forever. The lifespan of higher life forms is even more insignificant in comparison to the age of the stars and planets. All animals, including humans, live depending on the destruction of other lives, many from the extermination of other animals. Lions cannot live on grass. Catastrophes such as floods, droughts, storms, fires, earthquakes, volcanic eruptions and impacts from meteorites, asteroids, and comets are a result

---

1. "Resurrection" is often broadly understood as the "postmortal renewal or glorification of a previous existence" (Ahn, "Resurrection"). However, I use this term more specifically for the beginning of the postmortal existence of a person with a physical body. The term "physical resurrection" would thus be a pleonasm, but I use it to assure greater clarity. Typically, the resurrected body is the revived physical body. Resurrection can be thought about monistically or dualistically. Seen monistically, it is the idea that, with the death of the physical body, the whole person dies and is brought back to life through resurrection. In contrast, a dualistic understanding of resurrection implies that, following the death of the physical body, a non-physical part of the person, for example, the soul, lives on and is reunited with the reanimated physical body through resurrection (see also Ringgren, "Resurrection," 7762).

2. I will not explore Islam in any more detail because, to my knowledge, it has never taught an eternal, blissful afterlife *on this earth*. In the Qur'an, the postmortem paradise appears to be in heaven. For Islamic eschatology in general, see Hagemann, "Eschatologie im Islam," for Islamic paradise, see Gardet, "Djanna."

of the nature of the earth and the cosmos. They inevitably bring death and destruction to living beings on earth. Life, as such, will not exist forever on earth because even celestial bodies are transient. The evolution of the sun into a red giant in the distant but certain future will eventually result in all forms of life on earth being extinguished.[3]

Transcendent experiences

How could a belief that so utterly contradicts our knowledge about this cosmos come to be? I suggest that by taking transcendent experiences into account we will come closer to the solution. By transcendent experiences I mean those in which the ordinary limits of the physical world are transcended, that is, exceeded. This can happen, for example, in otherworld experiences. These are experiences of a world other than the one familiar to us. But it may also consist of experiencing perceptions and effects that seem to transgress the boundaries of what is possible according to the usual worldview. This includes perceptions of things not currently present to the physical senses or macroscopic physical events that appear to be caused by an unusual mental influence such as the healing or food miracles of Jesus of Nazareth.[4]

Effects of transcendent experiences on worldview

Until now, research on religious and philosophical ideas has given transcendent experiences little attention, despite the fact that they can heavily influence not only the life but also the worldview of the experiencer. Paul of Tarsus's Damascus-road experience[5] is paradigmatic here in that he mutates from Christian hunter into the most significant missionary of the gospel

---

3. See Ward and Brownlee, *Planet Earth*, 101–65.

4. For the miracles of Jesus, see below, pp. 125–27. For more detail on my concept of transcendent experiences and for the distinction of related terms such as religious, spiritual, mystical, anomalous, exceptional, or paranormal experiences, see Schwenke, "Transzendente Erfahrungen."

5. According to Acts, Paul was on his way to Damascus, to arrest followers of the late Jesus Christ: "[S]uddenly a light from heaven shone around him. And falling to the ground, he heard a voice saying to him, 'Saul, Saul, why are you persecuting me?' And he said, 'Who are you, Lord?' And he said, 'I am Jesus, whom you are persecuting. But rise and enter the city, and you will be told what you are to do.' The men who were traveling with him stood speechless, hearing the voice but seeing no one" (Acts 9:3–7 ESV). See the full account in Acts 9:1–21 and the slightly different versions in Acts 22:3–16; 26:9–20.

in early Christianity. Recently, the effects of transcendent experiences on the experiencer have been examined in greater depth.[6] For example, in the case of near-death experiences[7] it has been shown that they have a massive and long-lasting effect on the worldview of the experiencers.[8] They say, for example: "It had such a profound effect on the rest of my life: the timelessness that I experienced; the knowledge that my consciousness will survive outside my body. It was enough to destabilize my life."[9] Or: "I used to think that I knew what was what. But my worldview underwent a radical transformation."[10] Out-of-body experiences that occur in situations which are not close to death can have a similarly strong influence.[11] William Buhlman wrote of his first experience of this kind:

> Suddenly, everything I had ever learned about my existence and the world around me had to be reappraised. I had always seriously doubted that anything beyond the physical world existed. Now my entire viewpoint changed. Now I absolutely knew that other worlds do exist and that people like myself must live there. Most important, I now knew that my physical body was just a temporary vehicle for the real me inside[.][12]

---

6. See the overviews in Noyes et al., "Aftereffects of Near-Death Experiences"; Greyson, "Near-Death Experiences and Spirituality"; see also Greyson and Khanna, "Spiritual Transformation After Near-Death Experiences." For examples of prospective studies on the effects of near-death experiences, see van Lommel et al., "Near-Death Experiences"; Schwaninger et al., "Prospective Analysis of Near-Death Experiences."

7. By near-death experiences I understand primarily experiences in physiological proximity to death, e.g., during cardiac arrest. See below, p. 6–7.

8. van Lommel et al., "Near-Death Experiences," showed that the effects are triggered not only by the physiological circumstances surrounding a near-death experience. They compared two groups of patients where the people in one of the groups had "only" suffered a cardiac arrest, the others, in addition, retained memories of a near-death experience. From a medical perspective no differences could be ascertained between the two groups. See also Parnia et al., "Qualitative and Quantitative Study"; Greyson, "Incidence and Correlates of Near-Death Experiences."

9. van Lommel, *Consciousness Beyond Life*, 46.

10. van Lommel, *Consciousness Beyond Life*, 41.

11. By out-of-body experiences I understand experiences in which the experiencers have the impression that the center of perception and action lies outside of their own physical body but not necessarily outside any kind of body; see similar definitions in Alvarado, "Out-of-Body Experiences," 183; Kelly et al.: "Unusual Experiences near Death," 394; Nahm, "Außerkörperliche Erfahrungen," 151; for criticism of equating out-of-body experiences with so-called autoscopic experiences, that is, perceptions of one's own physical body from a point outside it, see Nahm, "Außerkörperliche Erfahrungen," 160–61; see also Kelly et al., "Unusual Experiences near Death," 403–4.

12. Buhlman, *Beyond the Body*, 6.

4   THE CONFUSION OF WORLDS

Encounters with persons from other worlds[13] can have life-changing effects[14] and also significantly shape the experiencer's worldview. When encounters with the deceased are at issue, it is the understanding of death that is most affected.

> [B]ased on my experience more than thirty years ago, I believe that, in fact, we do survive after death in a way I can only describe as blissful.[15]

> After that [experience], I began to feel that life is a continuum, and that this life is but one step. Death is just going through a door.[16]

> This [experience] confirmed life after death for me. There is no death—there is only life.[17]

The neglect of transcendent experiences in the history of ideas

Judging by existing accounts, many prominent figures from religious history had intensive transcendent experiences. It is therefore likely that we might better understand their ideas in light of these experiences, as was already emphasized over a hundred years ago by William James.[18] It is thus astonishing that to date many religious studies scholars and theologians assign little importance to transcendent experiences for understanding religious ideas.[19] One can only guess why this is the case. Insufficient knowledge,

---

13. For the definition of such "transcendent encounters" see Schwenke, *Transzendente Begegnungen*, 20–26.

14. See, e.g., Arcangel, *Afterlife Encounters*, 276–300, and the overview in Schwenke, *Transzendente Begegnungen*, 160–67.

15. LaGrand, *Messages and Miracles*, 148.

16. Guggenheim and Guggenheim, *Hello from Heaven*, 133.

17. Guggenheim and Guggenheim, *Hello from Heaven*, 145.

18. William James believed that the investigation of religion must start with religious experiences which are "immediate personal experiences" (*Varieties of Religious Experience*, 64). They "spontaneously and inevitably engender myths, superstitions, dogmas, creeds, and metaphysical theologies [. . .]. But all these intellectual operations [. . .] presuppose immediate experiences as their subject-matter. They are interpretative and inductive operations, operations after the fact, consequent upon religious feeling" (*Varieties of Religious Experience*, 433, see also 456–57).

19. Recent exceptions are, e.g., Dale Allison, who links the Easter apparitions with the widespread phenomenon of encounters with the deceased (see *Resurrecting Jesus*,

the underestimation of the frequency of transcendent experiences, and the pathologization of the experiencers could all be important reasons.[20]

The hypothesis of this book and the course of the investigation

The leading hypothesis of this book is that the idea of a physical resurrection and a subsequent eternal, blissful life on earth is based on a projection of certain elements from otherworld experiences onto an earthly reality. Firstly, I will concern myself with otherworld journeys and some related otherworld experiences. I will address two issues: the experience of paradisiacal and similar-to-earth landscapes and encounters with deceased persons with luminous bodies. I will then discuss how these components came to be projected onto the earthly sphere. Finally, I will analyze the accounts of an earthly kingdom of God and the resurrected in Zoroastrianism, Judaism, and Christianity and examine their similarities to descriptions of the beyond and its inhabitants in reports of otherworld journeys. I pay particular attention to Jesus of Nazareth, by far the most important, historically tangible representative of the doctrine of physical resurrection and a kingdom of God on earth. In the case of the historically well-documented Ghost Dance movement of the Lakota, I then show that otherworld journeys in fact have an influence on belief in an afterlife on a paradisiacal earth. I will then return to Jesus of Nazareth. In his case, it does not seem to have been otherworld journeys but miracles that strengthened his belief in the resurrection and kingdom of God, as handed down to him from early Jewish apocalypticism. I understand the cry Jesus made on the cross that God had forsaken him as the epitome of the disappointment that necessarily accompanies the hope for a paradisiacal kingdom of God on earth. In the epilogue, I will reflect on the consequences that the results of my study may have on the understanding of Christianity and its founder. The appendix contains a discussion on the relationship between miracles and science.

269–99), and Carl Becker, who draws on near-death experiences to throw light upon Pure Land Buddhism (see "Centrality of Near-Death Experiences"). For parallels between accounts of near-death experiences and afterlife doctrines in various religions and cultures, see Shushan, *Conceptions of the Afterlife*, and Musamian, "World Religions and Near-Death Experiences."

20. For the pathologization of encounters with people from the beyond, see Schwenke, *Transzendente Begegnungen*, 192–226.

1

Otherworld Experiences

*The Key to Belief in Resurrection
and the Kingdom of God?*

Otherworld journeys

OTHERWORLD JOURNEYS ARE OF special interest as an experiential basis for the concept of an eternal, paradisiacal life on earth. I understand otherworld journeys to be experiences in which those experiencing them have the impression of being and operating in a real world beyond this cosmos. For my argument it makes no difference whether or not the otherworld *is* real, only whether or not the experiencers *consider* it to be real, not only during the experience but also afterwards. There can be no scientific proof for the existence of another world, in the same way that there can be no such proof for the existence of this one.[1] Otherworld journeys are a frequent element of near-death experiences, they are, however, albeit often less vividly and coherently, also experienced by people who are not close to death. By near-death experiences in the narrower sense I understand experiences in physiological proximity to death, for example, during cardiac arrest.[2] They are often accompanied by an "enhanced mentation," that is, an increased capacity for thinking and perception.[3] This may be related to the fact that

---

1. See Schwenke, *Transzendente Begegnungen*, 186.

2. I think it makes sense to reserve the term "near-death experience"—as the word implies—to those experiences where the experiencer is actually physiologically close to death, as otherwise it would cover a very heterogeneous set of experiences, as became clear through a German study (Knoblauch and Schmied, "Berichte aus dem Jenseits"). See also Owens et al., "Features of 'Near-Death Experiences,'" 1175: "patients who were really close to death were more likely [. . .] to report an enhanced perception of light and enhanced cognitive powers." See also the strict definition of "temporary death experience" in Fenwick and Fenwick, *Art of Dying*, 206–10. For near-death experiences in general, see Fenwick and Fenwick, *Truth in the Light*; Greyson, "Approaches to Near-Death Experiences"; Holden et al., *Near-Death Experiences*; Kelly et al., "Unusual Experiences Near Death"; Moody and Perry, *Glimpses of Eternity*; van Lommel, *Consciousness Beyond Life*; Sabom, *Recollections of Death*.

3. See Kelly et al., "Unusual Experiences Near Death," 384, 386–87.

memories of experiences and perceptions during near-death experiences tend to be more detailed than memories of normal earthly experiences, and all the more so than memories of imaginations or dreams.[4] Near-death experiences are often described as being more real than real. Even many years after the experience, the experiencer's belief in the reality of the experience appears to remain unchanged.

Paradisiacal, earth-like landscapes

Particularly for those otherworld journeys in the context of near-death experiences, experiencers often move in heavenly landscapes that appear paradisiacal but that are very similar to earthly ones. Pim van Lommel writes: "People often find themselves in a dazzling landscape with gorgeous colors, remarkable flowers, and sometimes also incredibly beautiful music. Some see cities and splendid buildings."[5] Peter and Elizabeth Fenwick gained a similar impression from their analysis of accounts of near-death experiences: "surprisingly uniform vision of Paradise emerges. It is a picture of a heavenly countryside where there may be brilliantly coloured birds and flowers, wonderful scents, heavenly music, friends or relatives who have died."[6]

In neurosurgeon Eben Alexander's account of his own near-death experience in 2008, similarities between the otherworld and earthly sceneries and their realistic character are explicitly addressed:

> [I] found myself in a completely new world. The strangest, most beautiful world I'd ever seen. Brilliant, vibrant, ecstatic, stunning [. . .]. Below me was a countryside. It was green, lush, and earthlike. It *was* earth . . . but at the same time it wasn't. [. . .] I was flying, passing over trees and fields, streams and waterfalls,

---

4. See Thonnard et al., "Near-Death Experiences Memories"; Moore and Greyson, "Memories for Near Death Experiences."

5. van Lommel, *Consciousness Beyond Life*, 32. According to van Lommel's prospective study, 29 percent of those people who had had near-death experiences perceived a "celestial landscape" (see van Lommel et al., "Near-Death Experience," 2041).

6. Fenwick and Fenwick, *Truth in the Light*, 111. According to the Fenwicks' research, almost a quarter of people who thought of themselves as having had near-death experiences experienced paradisiacal landscapes (*Truth in the Light*, 111); for relevant excerpts from accounts, see *Truth in the Light*, 109, 111–13. Similar descriptions are contained in accounts of medieval otherworld journeys such as the Vision of Dryhthelm in 700 CE (see Bede, *Hist. eccl.* 5.12), and the otherworld journey of a soldier in the *Dialogi* of Pope Gregory I from the sixth century (*Dial.* 4.37.8). For otherworld flowers and gardens, see also the accounts of near-death experiences of children in Moody, *Light Beyond*, 62, 75–76.

and here and there, people. There were children, too, laughing and playing. [. . .] A beautiful, incredible dream world. . . . Except it wasn't a dream. Though I didn't know where I was [. . .], I was absolutely sure of one thing: this place I'd suddenly found myself in was completely real. The word *real* expresses something abstract, and it's frustrating ineffective at conveying what I'm trying to describe.[7]

Alexander's report is of particular interest for our discussion because—due to similarities between otherworldly and earthly landscapes—he expresses his uncertainty about the nature and localization of the landscape he experienced. In the account that Dr A. S. Wiltse from Skiddy, Kansas gave of his near-death experience in the year 1889, the similarity becomes even clearer:

Underneath me lay a forest-clad valley, through which ran a beautiful river full of shoals, which caused the water to ripple in white sprays. I thought the river looked much like the Emerald River [in Arkansas], and the mountains, I thought, as strongly resembled Waldron's Ridge [in Arkansas]. On the left of the road was a high bluff of black stone and it reminded me of Lookout Mountain [in Georgia], where the railroad passes between it and the Tennessee River.[8]

William Buhlman, who claims to have regularly induced out-of-body experiences at will without being close to death, writes that the first nonphysical dimension or world that he crosses in these journeys is "so physical in appearance that most people believe they are observing the physical world."[9]

---

7. Alexander, *Proof of Heaven*, 38–39. See also the accounts of the otherworld journey in an earth-like environment of a terminally ill four-year-old girl, Ann from Glendale, California: "And then I saw . . . there was this astonishing beautiful world before me. It was like nothing else I have since seen on earth. Somehow I knew, inside of me, that the earth had been left behind. I had no idea where I was, and I didn't care. I felt a 'deep, profound peace . . . no, it was more than that. It was a world of peace and love. The new world looked sort of like the world I had left behind, but it was also very different. Everything glowed from the inside with its own light. The colors were beyond anything on earth—they were more vibrant, brilliant, and intense. And there were colors I had never seen before—don't ask me what they were. There were shrubs, trees and flowers, some of which I had seem on earth, like evergreens, and others which I hadn't seen before, and I haven't seen since. They were beautiful, beautiful" (Gibson, *Glimpses of Eternity*, 53–54). See further, Sabom, *Recollections of Death*, 67; Eadie, *Embraced by the Light*, 78–81.

8. A. S. Wiltse, *Case of Typhoid Fever*, 359.

9. Buhlman, *Beyond the Body*, 93.

Sometimes also experiences had while sleeping are interpreted as otherworld journeys. I quote extensively from this account of a woman who lost a child while pregnant and then gave birth to a stillborn son, in order to make clear the realistic nature of these experiences and because of her description of the luminescence of the otherworldly deceased, which we will come to shortly:

> For about six months after I lost my son, I was in very deep, deep sorrow. I didn't understand why—why me? I was just miserable and very close to wanting to end it all. On night in a dream, I was where I envisioned heaven to be. *I was in a beautiful pasture that was filled with beautiful flowers.* An angel came to me and said he had something very special to show me. The angel was holding a six-month-old baby boy in his right arm and was holding the left hand of a little girl, who was walking like a toddler. The girl was tiny, but she could talk. She said, "Mommy, I am Serena, and this is my little brother, Carlos. We are fine. We are very happy. We love you very much, and we don't want you to be sad anymore. We will all be together someday." They were both dressed in white robes. Serena had tiny little sandals on her feet, and Carlos was barefoot. *They had this beautiful glow, this perfect light around them that came from their heart center.* I asked the angel, "Can I get close to them?" and the angel nodded "Yes." It was like the angel was their babysitter for the time being. I remember sitting on the grass and putting Carlos on my lap, as Serena came close. I was crying and loving them both. I just wanted the children to know that I loved them and that their daddy loved them too. I wanted to be there and watch the children as long as I could. I was able to hug them and kiss them one more time. Then they walked away with the angel, and I had this inner peace as I woke up. What is so wonderful is that I learned the children have features of both me and my husband. Serena looks a lot like her father, and Carlos seems to look like me.[10]

Paradisiacal otherworld landscapes can also be experienced in visions that occur outside of the context of otherworld journeys. The experiencer's perspective of perception does not change. It is like looking into another world. Two examples of this: As a hospice chaplain stood at the coffin of her fourteen-year-old stepson Michael, in a sudden vision she saw "a pretty green rolling field with flowers, birds, and butterflies. It was very brightly lit, and the colors were clear and vivid. I saw Michael skipping and running along! He stopped and looked at me and had a beautiful

---

10. Guggenheim and Guggenheim, *Hello from Heaven*, 359–60 (emphasis added).

smile."[11] A terminally ill ten-year-old girl, Daisy Irene Dryden, had extensive deathbed visions during which she was clearly conscious and was able to talk to those present in the room. She said that during these visions "the walls seem to go away" and she could then see "ever so far."[12] As she looked into the otherworld—in her own words—she not only perceived and communicated with otherworld persons but also saw "heavenly flowers and trees [...], more beautiful than anything you could imagine."[13] The reality of the experience was beyond doubt for them both. Nevertheless, I believe that experiencers are more likely to consider their otherworld journeys an objective reality if they not only see the landscape but also move through it, in an out-of-body state.

Shining otherworldly persons

During near-death experiences otherworldly people are often encountered.[14] They appear corporeal, but they often emanate light. This light also emerges, as we will see, in religious texts on the resurrected.[15] This contradicts the idea that belief in resurrection and in the kingdom of God is merely based on an idealization of earthly circumstances, as in life on earth there are no shining persons.[16] Furthermore, the old and the sick are never encountered in otherworld journeys, also coinciding with religious concepts of the risen in the kingdom of God.[17] As an example of these experiences, I quote Pamela Reynolds's description of her encounter with numerous familiar and unfamiliar otherworldly persons in the context of a near-death experience, including her deceased grandmother: "[T]hey were all covered with light, they *were* light, and had light permeating all around them [...]. Everyone I saw [...] fit perfectly into my understanding what that person looked like at their best

---

11. Guggenheim and Guggenheim, *Hello from Heaven*, 116–17.

12. See Barrett, *Deathbed Visions*, 53.

13. Barrett, *Deathbed Visions*, 51.

14. According to van Lommel, "Near-Death Experience," 2041, 32 percent of those asked had met deceased persons in the context of their near-death experience; according to Schwaninger et al., "Prospective Analysis of Near-Death Experiences," 223, 27 percent of those asked admitted they had experienced the presence of deceased relatives, 36 percent reported the presence of angels.

15. See below, pp. 24–25, 33–35, 38, 41, 75.

16. For the very rare exceptions, see the cases in Treece, *Sanctified Body*, 29–85; Schamoni, *Wunder*, 235–45; Thurston, *Phenomena of Mysticism*, 162–70; Zander, *Seraphim von Sarow*, 139; Sekanek, *Mutter Silbert*, 186; Kasturi, "Bala Sai"; Haraldsson, "Miracles," 251–56; see also the discussion in Allison, *Historical Christ*, 72–75.

17. See below, pp. 23–24, 37–38, 121.

times during their lives."[18] The light that emanates from transcendent people can be overwhelming. During his near-death experience in 1985, Howard Storm perceived how a light approached him from far away:

> [T]he light was more intense and more beautiful than anything I had ever see. It was brighter than the sun, brighter than a flash of lightning. Soon the light was upon me. I knew that while it was indescribably brilliant, it wasn't just light. This was a living being, a luminous being approximately eight feet tall and surrounded by an oval of radiance. The brilliant intensity of the light penetrated my body. Ecstasy swept away the agony. Tangible hands and arms gently embraced me and lifted me up.[19]

The light of heavenly bodies is not limited to human or superhuman beings. This is shown by the following extract from a thirteen-year-old girl's account of her near-death experience:

> At the end of the tunnel was a bright light. From the light came two dogs of mine [who had died a few years earlier]. The dogs came running and jumped on me and kissed my face with their tongues. Their tongues weren't wet, and I felt no weight when they jumped on me. *The dogs seemed to glow from a light that was inside them.* [. . .] I hugged my dogs as tight as I could. [. . . T]ogether we started walking toward the light. [. . . T]here were people as far as the eye could see, and *they were glowing with an inner light—just as my dogs.*[20]

Deceased children are sometimes perceived as being grown up and in the prime of their life. Vicki Noratuk, blind since birth, experienced an otherworld journey in 1973, after a serious accident at the age of twenty-two. She recounts *seeing* her lifeless body in the hospital while two people attempted to resuscitate her. Then she had the sensation of being sucked into a dark tunnel. As she came out of the other side she found herself in a "balmy, bright summerland scene":[21] "There were trees and there were birds and quite a few people, but they were all, like, made out of light."[22] Noratuk became aware that she also had a nonphysical body that appeared to be

---

18. Sabom, *Light and Death*, 44. For general information about shining otherworldly persons, see Moody, *Light Beyond*, 12–13.

19. Storm, *Descent into Death*, 25. Before his near-death experience, Storm was an atheist but subsequently became a pastor.

20. Atwater, *New Children*, 73 (emphasis added).

21. Noratuk, *Blind Woman's Near-Death Experience*.

22. van Lommel, *Consciousness Beyond Life*, 25.

made up of light.²³ She met two former school friends who had died many years previously at the ages of six and eleven. During their earthly existence they had both been severely retarded and blind. In the other world, they appeared to Vicki to be "bright and beautiful, healthy and vitally alive. They were no longer children, but [. . .] 'in their prime.'"²⁴

Luminous otherworldly persons can also be perceived in this-worldly contexts. They then appear as if visiting the earthly sphere. A man's account of the out-of-body experience he had in 1975 at age twenty-four, supplies an example. He was lying in a dark windowless recovery room following wisdom-tooth surgery for which he had been administered a very large dose of the anesthetic sodium pentothal:

> I awakened from the surgery, blinded by a river of white light. I thought it was an aftereffect of the general anesthesia. I thought it was odd that it pushed beyond my optic nerve and went through my entire body. I immediately rose to my feet and looked at the nurse who had helped me up. She wasn't a nurse. *She was clothed in light, extraordinarily beautiful and loving.* She was the most beautiful woman I had ever seen, and I almost cry when I think about it. *She wore a loose-fitting white gown, and it gave off light of its own. . . . The light around her was flooding into me, and seemed to pour into everything. . . . The light that shone from the center of her was gloriously beautiful.* [. . .] The facial features were overpowered by this inner radiation. I could literally feel her love and care [. . .]. I looked back and down at my body, still lying on the recovery couch under a blanket. Here I was, standing beside a being of light, looking at my body. Something seemed wrong. Before I reasoned it through, she intercepted my thoughts, and said "Don't worry, you're not dead. You're quite alive. Your heart is still beating. Look!" I looked, I could see it. I could see the chambers emptying and filling with blood. I could see the vascular system and the life-sustaining materials working their way through the entire body. I turned away, contented that things were all right. Just as I started to wonder why she was there, and what was wrong with my body, she intercepted my thought again, and said, "You're not breathing regularly. There is some concern that your respiration might stop. I'm here to stabilize it and make sure the problem doesn't go any further."²⁵

---

23. See Ring and Cooper, "Experiences in the Blind," 110–11.
24. Ring and Cooper, "Experiences in the Blind," 111.
25. Ring and Elsaesser Valarino, *Lessons from the Light*, 37 (emphasis added).

Shining otherworldly persons are not only perceived during out-of-body experiences but sometimes also in a normal or only slightly altered state of consciousness and with the physical eyes, in the familiar, earthly environment. Here is an example:

> At 9½ years old I lost my father. I was always heartbroken and cried for him for many years. . . . Then one Christmas evening it happened. I was already in bed but wanted then to go to Christmas mass. It was time for me to get up again, then I got bad stomach pains and had to stay lying down. Shortly after they went away, but by then it was already too late for mass. So, I stayed in bed and then I heard the door and faint footsteps accompanied by a peculiar knocking. I was alone in the apartment and was quite scared. Then something wonderful happened, my blessed father came towards me, *so beautiful, so shining like gold*, as see-through as mist; he looked like he always had, I could recognize his silhouette, then he came to the end of my bed and looked at me with affection and smiled. I was filled with a profound peace and was happier than I had ever been. Then he went away again . . . .[26]

As a rule, such luminescent apparitions experienced while awake are brief. The otherworldly persons often appear to be, as in the previous example, transparent and hardly corporeal.[27] Such apparitions cannot be the model for physically resurrected, living persons in paradisiacal realms. The apparitions' brevity does not support the idea of a stable, lasting existence; their lack of corporeality contradicts the idea of a physical resurrection, and a paradisiacal environment is missing here. Presumably such experiences would tend to strengthen belief in a bodiless soul or ghosts rather than belief in a physical resurrection. It is rather the deceased who are encountered in otherworld journeys (as opposed to apparitions encountered while awake) who seem to form the paradigm of a luminous, and at the same time, physical existence in the afterlife.

---

26. Jaffé, *Geistererscheinungen*, 67–68 (trans. S. Kühne).

27. The more physical those apparitions perceived while awake seem to be, the less light appears to emanate from them (see Schwenke, *Transzendente Begegnungen*, 104). This does not seem to apply to apparitions of otherworldly persons that are perceived in out-of-body states.

Otherworld landscapes as earthly paradise

According to my hypothesis, the idea of a physical resurrection and an eternal afterlife on a paradisiacal earth is based on the projection of elements from otherworld journeys onto the earthly sphere. Otherworld paradisiacal landscapes and luminous otherworldly persons were erroneously located on earth. How could this have happened? In early history and antiquity, people were only familiar with a relatively small part of our planet. *They could easily have come to the conclusion that when journeying through earth-like landscapes of the other world, they were travelling in remote and unknown parts of this earth.* Well-known examples for sites of an afterlife situated on earth are the Elysian fields of Homer[28] and Hesiod's Isles of the Blessed, both lying at the ends of the earth.[29] Before the modern era, the whereabouts of the deceased, ghosts, and gods was generally thought of as this-worldly, facilitating a projection of otherworld landscapes (where the deceased lived) onto earth. Anyone who walked, drove, or flew for long enough, and was not stopped by guards, could go there. Gods and ghosts could come up to the earth's surface from the underworld[30] or descend from heaven to intervene and abide here on earth. This meant that the places and persons that we would describe as otherworldly were situated within this cosmos.

From existing paradise to utopia

We have not yet explained how the contents of otherworld experiences can be transformed into a model for a future resurrection and for a future kingdom of God. Those who themselves have an otherworld experience with the luminous deceased that is situated in a paradisiacal landscape will normally place this paradise in the present and not in the future. Neither

---

28. See Homer, *Od.* 4.563–68: "[B]ut to the Elysian plain and the ends of the earth will the immortals convey you [. . .] where life is easiest for men. No snow is there, nor heavy storm, nor ever rain, but always Ocean sends up blasts of the shrill-blowing West Wind that they may give cooling to men" (trans. Homer, *The Odyssey*, 159, 161).

29. See Hesiod, *Op.* 167–72: "[T]o some Zeus, the father, [. . .] granted a life and home apart from men, and settled them at the ends of the earth. These dwell with carefree heart in the Isles of the Blessed Ones, beside deep-swirling Oceanus: fortunate Heroes, for whom the grain-giving soils bears its honey-sweet fruits thrice a year" (trans. Hesiod, *Works and Days*, 41–42). In Celtic tradition there is likewise the idea of a western island paradise (see Ó hÓgain, *Sacred Isle*, 104). For further examples of the situation of an afterlife paradise in remote places on earth, see Braun, *Jenseits*, 33–35, 39–40; Eliade, *From Primitves to Zen*, 366–69.

30. See Epic of Gilgamesh 12.85–87 (Thompson, *Epic of Gilgamish*, 59); 1 Sam 28:13.

will they locate paradise in the land they currently live in. In order for this otherworldly experience to grow into a vision of the future for one's own land they would, for example, have to believe, as probably some members of the Lakota Ghost Dance Movement did, that this mysterious paradise will somehow come floating through the air like a cloud and lower itself down to the surface of the earth.[31] It is possible that this transformation of the contents of otherworldly experiences into an earthly utopia is rather something carried out by those who later receive the reports of pertinent experiences. Recipients of such accounts, who have not themselves experienced the otherworldly paradise, more readily tend to separate its description from its presence, and project that paradise into the future. The projection of paradisiacal ideas onto the future of *one's own land* could be stimulated by the fact that in certain aspects otherworld landscapes sometimes resemble home landscapes. This was the case in the experience of A. S. Wiltse or in the experiences of the Lakota during their Ghost Dance.[32] Presumably, contents from otherworld experiences are not only projected onto the future but also onto the past. The common idea of a primordial state of man without disease, suffering, or death in a literally paradisiacal environment is encountered in the biblical story of the garden of Eden.[33] The first human couple could have lived there forever if only they hadn't eaten from the tree of the knowledge of good and evil. Here we find the idea of a potentially eternal, earthly-physical life. A common belief about this primordial paradise was that it never ceased to exist. It was merely lost to humanity. For a long time, people searched for it and even marked it on maps.[34] It may also have been otherworld experiences that motivated this search for the primordial paradise. Mircea Eliade suggested that the long expeditions to the lost paradise,[35] which the central South American Guarani tribes conducted over centuries, were stimulated by the paradisiacal images of the dreams and ecstasies of their shamans.[36]

Resurrection

Experiencing otherworldly persons possessing a body that appears human might be especially likely to lead to the idea of a physical resurrection if

31. See below, p. 121n20.
32. See above, p. 8, and below, pp. 120–21.
33. See Gen 2:4—3:24, and generally Partin, *Paradise*.
34. See comprehensively Scafi, *Mapping Paradise*.
35. See Eliade, *Quest*, 101–11.
36. See Eliade, *Quest*, 103.

an otherworldly person is recognized as someone who is deceased, and whose body seems substantial and not transparent or shadowy in nature. For such an apparition to be interpreted as representing a physical resurrection, in addition, the experiencer should either not know where the corpse of the deceased person in question is, or this corpse must have already completely dissolved. If the corporeal apparition is experienced at a person's deathbed, the experiencer would be unlikely to imagine that the apparition could be the resurrected body of that particular person. Rather they would develop the idea that the person in question lives on with another body. Similarly, the perception of one's own physical body from an outside perspective, as often described in reports of out-of-body experiences, can hardly support belief in physical resurrection. Rather, this experience suggests the idea of an existence independent of the physical body, as shown by the already cited reflection of William Buhlman after his first out-of-body experience, where he saw his physical body from outside: "Suddenly, everything I had ever learned about my existence and the world around me had to be reappraised. [. . .] Most important, I now knew that my physical body was just a temporary vehicle for the real me inside, and that with practice I could separate from it at will."[37]

Similar considerations apply to the concept of a future resurrection on earth as to a future earthly paradise. Those who encounter deceased persons with bodies that appear substantial would not conclude from this that they were dead and buried and that they will only rise again some time later in the distant future. Maybe in the course of the reception of such accounts, the description of the otherworldly persons became detached from these experiences and was made into a model for a future life that the deceased, imagined as sleeping in the dust of the earth, still have ahead of them.

Belief in a soul vs. belief in resurrection

If belief in resurrection is based on projections from otherworld experiences onto the earthly sphere, what could the experiential basis for the Greek belief in a soul be, a belief that is often placed in opposition to belief in resurrection? It seems that the Greek concept of a soul does not have its roots in otherworld experiences but rather in earthly perceptions of deceased persons that happen during a normal state of consciousness and apparently using the physical senses, as with ghost experiences. In those experiences, the deceased often appear to be shadowy and unsubstantial. They tend not to walk but glide or float. Generally, you can put your hand right through

---

37. Buhlman, *Beyond the Body*, 6.

them, and they move through walls and furniture and disappear into thin air.[38] Such experiences appear to be reflected in Greek descriptions of the souls of the deceased. Odysseus grasps three times into thin air as he tries to put his arms around his deceased mother.[39] In Plato's *Phaedo,* the widespread concept of the soul as a subtle entity that floats away from the body after death, comparable to breath or smoke, is mentioned repeatedly.[40] The etymology of the Greek word for soul, ψυχή, also speaks for the origin of the Greek soul concept being based in this-worldly experiences. The word ψυχή is apparently not, as is often assumed, derived from "breath." It comes, rather, from "to blow, to cool" and originally meant "cool breeze."[41] In accounts of apparitions of the deceased that are perceived with the normal senses, a cool draught is often reported.[42]

If we follow this thought, it leads us to the hypothesis that the Greek belief in a soul, the leading paradigm of an otherworldly afterlife, has its origins in a this-worldly perception of the deceased. The apparition of the deceased is subtle and feeble to the physical senses. This feebleness and subtlety is considered characteristic of their existence in the otherworld, their normal residing place. Therefore, belief in a soul originates from earthly perceptions of the deceased being projected onto the otherworld. According to my assumption, belief in a physical resurrection and in a this-worldly afterlife functions the other way around: it is based on otherworldly experiences with corporeal, very present, shining deceased, which are projected into this world.

---

38. See, for example, the case reports No. 5, 8, 11, 15, 21, 58, 60–62, 64, 67–69, 77–78, 92–93, 97–98, 100, 104 in Evans, *Seeing Ghosts.*

39. See Homer, *Od.* 11.204–8.

40. See Plato, *Phaed.* 70a5, 77d8, 80d10.

41. See Mumm and Richter, *Etymologie von griechisch ψυχή.*

42. See Evans, *Seeing Ghosts,* 92–93, cf. 78; Mattiesen, *Überleben des Todes,* 1:122; Kemmerich, *Brücke zum Jenseits,* 489, 530–32.

2

Resurrection and the Kingdom of God in Zoroastrianism

The eschatology of Zoroastrianism

BELIEF IN AN EARTHLY resurrection and an earthly kingdom of God appears to have developed in Zoroastrianism, from where it may have gone on to inspire Judaism, Christianity, and Islam.[1] This doctrine is central to traditional Zoroastrianism.[2] It is embedded in an eschatology[3] that—in a somewhat simplified representation—comprises the following elements: the separation of body and soul at death; an individual judgment of the soul following death by crossing over the Cinwad bridge, from which the wicked are thrown down to hell and by which the righteous are admitted into paradise; the future resurrection of the bodies and their reunion with the souls; a universal final judgment, when the wicked will be punished but also purified of their sins; and finally an eternal paradisiacal life on earth where the powers of evil have been driven away.[4] We are dealing here with the resurrection of the physical bodies and an afterlife on earth.

---

1. See Boyce and Grenet, *History of Zoroastrianism*, 3:361–490; Boyce, *Zoroastrians*, 1, 29, 76–77, 150–52; Silverman, *Persepolis and Jerusalem*; Winston, *Iranian Component in the Bible*; see also the single case-study Hintze, "Treasure in Heaven." On Islam, see above, p. 1n2.

2. In modern Zoroastrianism, deviating eschatological concepts, such as a purely otherworldly afterlife or reincarnation, are also represented (see Modi, *Catechism of the Zoroastrian Religion*, 11–12 [§ 9]; Stausberg, *Religion Zarathustras*, 2:139, 146). Theological doctrine often meets little interest (see Kreyenbroek and Munshi, *Living Zoroastrianism*, 293–98, and the example 190; see also Stausberg, *Religion Zarathustras*, 2:150–51).

3. By eschatology I understand a religious doctrine about the last things, in other words, the final destiny of human beings and the world.

4. See Shaked, "Eschatology"; Skjærvø, "Afterlife in Zoroastrianism," 317–46.

History and tradition

It is believed that Zoroastrianism originated in the second millennium BCE. It potentially comes from a branch of the Andronovo culture from the Bronze Age period, from a region of present-day Kazakhstan. Those references to the Zoroastrian culture contained in the oldest texts suggest a sedentary, non-stratified pastoralist society without cities or temples and with almost no farming.[5] Zarathustra, the legendary founder of Zoroastrianism, appears most probably to have come from the Afghani province of Badakhshan, on the border of Tajikistan and Pakistan.[6] The sacred texts of Zoroastrianism were passed down for a long time orally and it seems were only first written down in late antiquity.[7] Avestan, the language they were written in, was at that point no longer spoken outside of religious worship.[8] Linguistic analyses have shown that old Avestan, the language of the *Gathas*, originates from the second millennium BCE. It is similar to Vedic, the language of the oldest scripts from Hinduism.[9]

Gathas: an eternal earthly life?

In the *Gathas*—seventeen difficult to interpret hymns, traditionally attributed to Zarathustra, probably dating to the second millennium BCE—an eternal earthly life in the kingdom of the creator god, Ahura Mazdā, is possibly promised in poetic form. If we follow the rendering of Herman Lommel,[10] then the righteous are promised wholeness and immortality[11] in a life made glorious[12] in the good kingdom[13] of the Lord of Wisdom, Ahura Mazdā, as a reward.[14] This life has a physical, earthly character. It is

---

5. See Boyce, *Zoroastrianism*, 27–52; Grenet, "Zarathustra's Time and Homeland," 21–22.

6. See Grenet, "Zarathustra's Time and Homeland," 22–24.

7. See Hintze, "Zarathustra's Time and Homeland," 36.

8. See Boyce, *Zoroastrianism*, 28; Hintze, "Older Avesta," 31; Skjærvø, "Afterlife in Zoroastrianism," 311.

9. See Boyce, *Zoroastrianism*, 29–31; Hintze, "Zarathustra's Time and Homeland," 33–34.

10. See Lommel, *Gathas*.

11. See Y. 31.6,21; 33.8; 34.1,11; 44.17–18; 45.5,10; 47.1; 51.7.

12. See Y. 30.9; 34.15; 50.11.

13. See Y. 34.1; 48.8; 49.8; 51.1.

14. See, e.g., Y. 34.1,13–14.

a bodily life,[15] a good dwelling[16] on fertile land[17] with milk and butter.[18] The idea of resurrection is not to be found explicitly in the *Gathas* but could, however, be hinted at there.[19] For the earthly-physical kingdom of salvation appears to be promised to anyone who follows the path of "good thinking."[20] One might conclude from this that those good people who die before his arrival will also share in this kingdom. That would though require that the deceased physically exist following death.

Zamyād Yasht: resurrection and Frashokereti

In the Younger Avesta, the doctrine of the resurrection is clearly articulated. The *Zamyād Yasht* (Hymn to the Earth), which according to Almut Hintze can be dated to the sixth century BCE,[21] prophesied the resurrection of the dead and following the defeat of the powers of evil, the Frashokereti,[22] such that the earth would be renewed and made immortal. This transfiguration will be brought about by the savior sent by Ahura Mazdā, the Saoshyant Astvat-ereta.[23]

> [The mighty Glory created by Mazdā,[24]]
> Which will accompany the Victorious one among the Saviours[25]
> and also his other companions,
> so that he will make life excellent,
> ageless, without decay,
> not rotting, not putrefying,
> living forever, thriving forever, ruling as it wishes.
> When the dead will rise,
> (then) will come the one without decay

15. See Y. 34.14; 43.16.
16. See Y. 29.10; 30.10; 48.11.
17. See Y. 48.11.
18. See Y. 49.5.
19. See Shaked, "Eschatology"; affirmative Lommel, *Religion Zarathustras*, 232–33; Boyce, *Zoroastrianism*, 77; Boyce, *Zoroastrians*, 27–29.
20. See Y. 49.5, and the explanation in Lommel, *Gathas*, 166.
21. See Hintze, *Der Zamyād-Yašt*, 43.
22. On this concept of the eschatological renewal of the earth, see Hintze, "Frašō. kərəti,"; Hultgård, "Persian Apocalypticism," 56–60.
23. On this figure, see Hintze, *Der Zamyād-Yašt*, 21, 41, 371–72; on the sending by Ahura Mazdā, see Yt. 19.92.
24. On glory (*khvarenah*), see Hintze, *Der Zamyād-Yašt*, 15–33.
25. *Khvarenah* is an attribute of Saoshyant Astvat-ereta, see Hintze, *Der Zamyād-Yašt*, 366.

reviving (the dead) (and) life will create excellent things according to its own wish.²⁶

The immortalization of the physical world happens through the eyes of the Saoshyant:

> At all corporeal life he will
> gaze with eyes that render strength,
> and his gaze will render the whole
> corporeal world indestructible.²⁷

Greek sources

In ancient Greek texts there are some references to Zoroastrian doctrine on resurrection, presumably before it was written down in Zoroastrianism itself. In the histories of Herodotus, originating in the fifth century BCE, the Persian Prexaspes alludes to the possibility of a dead man rising from the grave. Therefore, we might assume that the concept of resurrection already existed.²⁸ According to Diogenes Laertius, in the fourth century BCE the Greek historian Theopompus claimed, "in the eighth book of his *Philippica* [. . .] that according to the Magi, men shall come back to life and be immortal."²⁹ A similar statement was also accredited to Theopompus by Aeneas of Gaza in his dialogue *Theophrastus,* which was written shortly after 485 CE: "And Zoroaster prophesies that some day there will be a resurrection of all the dead. Theopompus knows of this and is himself the source of information concerning it for other writers."³⁰

---

26. Yt. 19.89 (trans. Hintze, *Zamyād Yašt*, 38). See also Yt. 19.11,19.

27. Yt. 19.94 (trans. Hintze, *Zamyād Yašt*, 39–40). For eschatological statements in other younger Avestan scriptures, see *EZIQ*, 36–41.

28. See Herodotus, *Hist.* 3.62.4. It is about Smerdis (Bardiya), the son of Cyrus the Great (Cyrus II), who founded the Persian Empire and reigned from circa 559 to 530 BCE. According to Herodotus, Smerdis was killed by Prexaspes on the orders of his elder brother, King Cambyses II. A herald came to Cambyses and announced that Smerdis should be recognized as king. Cambyses asked Prexaspes about it, who said that it would only be possible if the dead could rise again.

29. Diogenes Laertius, *Vit.* 1.8–9 (trans. de Jong, *Traditions of the Magi*, 213).

30. Enea di Gaza, *Teofrasto*, 64.8–10 (trans. Fox and Pemberton, *Passages in Greek*, 109).

Resurrection in middle Persian Zoroastrian scriptures

In middle Persian Zoroastrian scriptures dating from the early Middle Ages, resurrection, the Frashokereti, and the afterlife are dealt with extensively. Resurrection fundamentally concerns all deceased people.[31] The righteous will live on earth for eternity in the prime of their life "without age or weakness and without death."[32]

Recovery of the physical body from its components

The process of resurrection has been described and discussed in numerous scriptures. The requirement for resurrection is the collection and uniting of the elements of the body: "For at that time I [Ahura Mazdā] will demand the bony frame from the spirit of the earth, the blood from the water, the hair from the plants, and the life from the wind."[33] In this context the feasibility of resurrection is discussed. Even posing the question makes it indubitably clear that it concerns the recovery of a deceased physical body. In the *Greater Bundahishn*, Zarathustra asked Ahura Mazdā: "Whence shall they re-form the body which the wind has blown away, and the water has dragged down, and how shall resurrection occur?"[34] And in the *Wizīdagīhā ī Zādspram* he asked: "The one who is dead, separated by the dogs and the birds and carried away by the wolves and the vultures, how will one put him together again?"[35] The answer is, however, that a creation from nothing, something that had already been achieved by Ahura Mazdā, is much more difficult than raising the dead. "What has been can be again. Behold, if I [Ahura Mazdā] made that which was not, how can I not re-form that which was?"[36] In *Wizīdagīhā ī Zādspram*, Ahura Mazdā makes this very clear with the example of a wooden box: "If you who are Zardûst [middle Persian for: Zarathustra] want to build a wooden box, how would it be easier to make it, if you had no wood to cut and put together or if there was a box whose boards have been separated from one another and you had to reassemble

---

31. See GBd. 34.7; according to Pahl. Riv. 48.67, however, people who have killed another person will not be raised from the dead.
32. Ayādgār ī Jāmāspīg (Pers.) 6 (trans. *EZIQ*, 195; retrans. S. Kühne).
33. GBd. 34.5 (trans. Anklesaria, *Zand-Akasih*, 285). See also, very similar, Pahl. Riv. 48.55, and in more detail, WZ 34.7–19.
34. GBd. 34.4 (trans. Anklesaria, *Zand-Akasih*, 285).
35. WZ 34.3 (trans. *EZIQ*, 199; retrans. S. Kühne).
36. GBd. 34.5 (trans. Anklesaria, *Zand-Akasih*, 285).

them anew?"³⁷ As would be expected Zarathustra answered: "If there had been wood in one piece, it would have been easier than if there were no wood, and if there had been boards of a box, it would have been easier than if there had been no box."³⁸ The resurrection of the dead, according to the texts, will be carried out by either Ahura Mazdā himself or by the Saoshyant.³⁹

The eternal afterlife

The afterlife will be eternal. The *Greater Bundahishn* promises: "All men will become immortal up to eternity and eternal progress."⁴⁰ In the *Pahlawī Riwāyat* one reads that people "will all be immortal and deathless."⁴¹ This not only applies to people. The whole world "will become immortal unto all eternity."⁴²

The risen are in the prime of life

The description of the risen corresponds to the descriptions of the deceased that are experienced in the context of otherworld experiences. People no longer appear old, but in the prime of life. This is emphasized again and again, for example in the *Ayādgār ī Jāmāspīg*: "The exalted God grants his grace and he lets people be resurrected and the people will be without age and without weakness."⁴³ This afterlife state of the prime of life is repeatedly compared to the age of forty: "[M]ankind, in the likeness of a body of 40 years of age, will all be [. . .] ageless, and without [. . .] decay."⁴⁴ In the *Greater Bundahishn,* two different afterlife age groups are named: "They [the Saoshyant and his companions] will restore to the age of forty years those

---

37. WZ 34.4 (trans. *EZIQ*, 199; retrans. author).
38. WZ 34.5 (trans. *EZIQ*, 199; retrans. author).
39. See *EZIQ*, 174.
40. GBd. 34.23 (trans. Anklesaria, *Zand-Akasih*, 291).
41. Pahl. Riv. 48.101 (trans. Williams, *Pahlavi Rivāyat*, 87); see also Pahl. Riv. 48.53; Ayādgār ī Jāmāspīg (Pers.) 6; Ayādgār ī Jāmāspīg (Pāz.) 6.
42. GBd. 34.32 (trans. *EZIQ*, 191; retrans. S. Kühne).
43. Ayādgār ī Jāmāspīg (Pers.) 6 (trans. *EZIQ*, 195; retrans. S. Kühne).
44. Pahl. Riv. 48.101 (trans. Williams, *Pahlavi Rivāyat*, 87); cf. WZ 35.51: "In height and countenance they [the resurrected] will resemble forty-year-olds" (trans. *EZIQ*, 223; retrans. S. Kühne). In *Ayādgār ī Jāmāspīg (Pāz.)* 6, in contrast, the age of fifteen is given for all the risen ones: "People will be forever without death and be immortal, not aging and stay fifteen years old" (trans. *EZIQ*; retrans. S. Kühne).

who had attained adulthood. And they will restore to the age of fifteen years those who were minors and had not attained adulthood."[45] This doctrine of two age groups in the afterlife seems to be the standard position of Zoroastrian eschatology.[46] This corresponds better with modern accounts of encounters with deceased children in the beyond—according to which they appear there to be grown up to varying degrees[47]—than with the doctrine that all otherworldly deceased are of a completely consistent age.

Luminous resurrection bodies

A particular parallel with accounts of otherworld experiences consists of the fact that according to the Zoroastrian scriptures, the resurrected body emanates light.[48] The body of the righteous will be made out of "luminous clay," it says, and "their bones will be in light like crystal."[49] After

45. GBd. 34.24 (trans. Anklesaria, *Zand-Akasih*, 291, modified).
46. See Shaked, "Eschatology," 568.
47. See above, pp. 9, 12.
48. In the preserved Avestan texts, as far as I know, the luminosity of the risen is not referred to. The motif of the absence of shadows could, however, be an earlier reference to the shining. In Plutarch, it was already stated by the historian Theopompus in the fourth century BCE that, according to Zoroastrian doctrine, people in a blissful end state would no longer cast a shadow (see Plutarch, *Is. Os.* 47 [370 C]). If we follow Raei's translation, the shadowlessness emerges in the discussion of the characteristics of the resurrected body in the middle Persian scripture *Wizīdagīhā ī Zādspram* in a question from Zarathustra to Ahura Mazdā: "'Will the bodies that die on earth at the moment of the renewal become corporeal again or will they be as those who have no shadows?' Ohrmazd [middle Persian for: Ahura Mazdā] answered: 'They will become corporeal again and be risen.'" (WZ 34.1–2; trans. *EZIQ*, 199; retrans. S. Kühne). It is revelatory that Ahura Mazdā did not answer that the resurrected body would have a shadow, but rather asserted the corporeality of the risen. A body does not have to be without substance and translucent in order to cast no shadow. It could also be shadowless if it itself emanated light. A reference to this can be found further above in the same scripture where the enlightenment of Zarathustra is described. He approached seven godly beings, the Amesha Spentas (Avestan) or Ahmahraspands (middle Persian), and when he came to be only seven meters away "he no longer saw his own shadow on the ground, because of the great light of the Amahraspands" (WZ 21.11; trans. Boyce, *Textual Sources*, 75). The godly beings would certainly have cast no shadow because of the light shining out of them, if even Zarathustra, who was standing in their light, cast no shadow either. Shadowlessness is presumably also a characteristic of shining otherworldly persons as told of by persons having had near-death experiences. It is, however, seldom explicitly mentioned. Moody, *Light Beyond*, 94 cites a literary clothed near-death experience in a novella by Katherine Anne Porter (1890–1980), in which the shadowlessness of otherworldly persons is spoken of (see Porter, "Pale Horse, Pale Rider," 254); on Porter's own near-death experience in 1918, see Moody, *Light Beyond*, 28.
49. WZ 35.50–51 (trans. *EZIQ*, 222; retrans. S. Kühne).

their resurrection, people will wear "shining garments."[50] The light that was once given to the sun will beam out of those raised from the dead.[51] In other places, the light of some of the risen is compared to "the sun, the moon and the large or the small stars."[52] It is also possible that it is the eschatological ordeal and purification of the risen ones in the river of molten metal that gives their body its shining appearance: "Throughout the whole world all people will be resurrected and will pass through the molten metal so as to become clean, light and clear, as the sun with its light."[53] The extensively described light of the risen is a very strong indication that otherworldly experiences were involved in the expression of eschatology in Zoroastrianism. Luminous, corporeal human bodies are virtually unknown on earth.[54] Yet for those people who have had otherworldly experiences they appear to be normal.

Renewed paradisiacal earth, eternal spring

The afterlife will take place on earth, renewed in the Frashokereti, in an eternal, earthly paradise. In the *Pahlavi Rivāyat* there is this: "[E]very place (will be) like the spring, resembling a garden in which (there are) all (kinds of) plants and flowers."[55] The "principal kinds of plants will be restored, and there will be no diminution of them";[56] also, "All the beneficent animals will exist once again."[57] The afterlife environment is similar to descriptions of heavenly landscapes, like those experienced during otherworld journeys.[58]

---

50. WZ 35.60 (trans. *EZIQ*, 225; retrans. S. Kühne).

51. See GBd. 34.8: "[T]hen, when they [the Saoshyant and his companions] have restored the physical and astral bodies of all material lives, they will give [...] one half of the light accompanying the sun unto Gayomard [the first human being], and the other half to the other human beings" (trans. Anklesaria, *Zand-Akasih*, 287, modified); very similar WZ 35.59.

52. WZ 35.56 (trans. *EZIQ*, 224; retrans. S. Kühne); cf. WZ 35.54.

53. Ayādgār ī Jāmāspīg (Pāz.) 6 (trans. *EZIQ*, 193; retrans. S. Kühne).

54. For exceptions, see the references p. 10n16 above.

55. Pahl. Riv. 48.107 (trans. Williams, *Pahlavi Rivāyat*, 88).

56. Pahl. Riv. 48.107 (trans. Williams, *Pahlavi Rivāyat*, 88).

57. Pahl. Riv. 48.103 (trans. Williams, *Pahlavi Rivāyat*, 88). This does not necessarily mean that wild animals will no longer exist; the whole diversity of species from creation will seemingly remain (see Boyce, *History of Zoroastrianism*, 1:246 with fn. 74).

58. See above, pp. 7–10.

Further otherworldly characteristics of the post-mortem earthly life

Despite its earthly situation, the afterlife of Zoroastrianism exhibits further otherworldly features. A first example is the *living together of the risen with all divine beings* on the earth: "Then Ohrmazd [middle Persian for Ahura Mazdā], the amahraspands [the Holy Immortals] and all the yazads [beings worthy of worship] and mankind will be in one place, and the star[s] too and the moon and the sun [. . .] will all be in the form of a man, and they will come to the earth."[59] The doctrine that in the afterlife humans no longer require food seems likewise unearthly. This already resonates in the *Zamyād Yasht*: "Wholeness and Immortality will overcome evil Hunger and Thirst."[60] In the fourth century BCE, Theopompus is supposed to have stated that in the Zoroastrian doctrine, people in a blissful end state will no longer need food.[61] This does not mean that, according to the middle Persian scriptures of Zoroastrianism, they will no longer eat. Those who want to eat can do so and anyone who does not wish to, will not have to.[62] The variety of dishes and tastes will, in any case, be a thousand times greater than now.[63] Sometimes, one could be satisfied from just a taste.[64] Finally, it seems that sleeping with one another without having children is a rather unearthly element of the afterlife: "And man and woman will have desire for one another, and they will enjoy it and consummate it but there will be no birth from them."[65]

---

59. Pahl. Riv. 48.99 (trans. Williams, *Pahlavi Rivāyat*, 87).
60. Yt. 19.96 (trans. Hintze, *Zamyād Yašt*, 40).
61. See Plutarch, *Is. Os.* 47 (370 C).
62. See Pahl. Riv. 48.60.
63. See Pahl. Riv. 48.59.
64. See Pahl. Riv. 48.105: "If, after that, meat eating is not necessary, it is because the pleasure of the taste of all meats will remain in the mouth at all times" (trans. Williams, *The Pahlavi Rivāyat*, 88); WZ 35.60: "The sweet taste and the fat of the Hadayōš cow [a mythical ancient cow] will be given [to the people] as food" (trans. *EZIQ*, 225; retrans. S. Kühne).
65. Pahl. Riv. 48.106 (trans. Williams, *Pahlavi Rivāyat*, 88); similarly, GBd. 34.24: "And they will give everyone his wife and children, and they will have sexual intercourse with their wives, just as now in material life, but there will be no begetting of children" (trans. Anklesaria, *Zand-Akasih*, 291, modified on the basis of *EZIQ*, 190).

Conclusion

The parallels in Zoroastrian eschatology with accounts from otherworld experiences are very clear. Particularly obvious and significant is the luminescence of the bodies of the risen in Zoroastrian texts, often mentioned as being characteristic of deceased persons in descriptions of otherworld travelers. In addition, the Zoroastrian doctrine that the resurrected will be as in the prime of life and live in a spring-like, lush landscape, corresponds with descriptions of deceased persons and otherworldly landscapes in accounts of otherworld journeys.

3

Resurrection and the Kingdom of God in Judaism

Fading in Sheol

FOR THE JEWISH RELIGION, whose written sources go back to the eighth century BCE,[1] the concept of a physical afterlife on earth is not quite as fundamental as it is for Zoroastrianism. Originally, there was little interest in life after death. The deceased descended irrevocably into the underworld of Sheol. In their darkness, they led a shadowy and joyless existence.

> The standard biblical view of death took it as man's final state (cf. II Sam. 14:14). Aside from such anomalies as Enoch and Elijah who were "taken" by God (Gen. 5:24; II Kings 2:1), the common lot of all men, as it was then conceived, is aptly described in Job 7:7–9: "Remember that my life is a breath; My eye will not again see good . . . A cloud dissolves and it is gone; So is one who descends to Sheol; He will not ascend."[2]

Presumably, in earlier biblical times the dead of Sheol were respected and consulted. The development of a Yahweh-focused monotheism seems to have resulted in the dead being reduced to powerless and unconscious beings,[3] and existence in Sheol became some kind of non-being.[4]

Minor importance of the resurrection idea in the Tanakh

In the Tanakh, the Hebrew Bible, which essentially contains the same scriptures as the Christian Old Testament, the idea of a physical resurrection

---

1. See Gertz, "Tora und vordere Propheten," 216.
2. Greenberg, "Resurrection," 240.
3. See Lang and McDannell, *Heaven*, 7–11; Wan, "Ghosts"; Kühn, "Totenkult."
4. See, for example, the *Encyclopaedia of Judaism*, that identifies the belief in Sheol with the concept of the finality of death and does not count it among afterlife doctrines (see Gillman, "Death and Afterlife," 594–95).

plays only a minor role. It did not emerge until the Babylonian exile and in total is present in only three passages: in Ezekiel, Isaiah, and Daniel. The first two passages, according to prevailing opinion, seem to be concerned with the resurrection of the people of Israel rather than individual resurrection. But the two are connected, as we will see.

No clear distinction of body and soul

Unlike in Zoroastrian and Greek anthropology, the Tanakh does not consider people to be made up of two distinct, separable principles.

> A soul independent of the body does not exist. [...] After death the whole human being continues to exist in the kingdom of shadows, in the shape in which they were buried; and when a return from the dead is considered in the Old Testament, this is accordingly a return to full life and corporeality [...] back to earth. [...] Thus, neither is the resurrection a reuniting of body and soul, rather simply a revival of the whole human being and their return to the community of the living on an earth that has been purified of sin and freed from the consequences of sin, but not completely spiritualized.[5]

However, for our question it is not critical whether the resurrection consists of the bringing back to life of the physical body through the unification with the soul, or whether a shadowy spirit of the dead acquires full, physical corporeality once more, but only whether the post-mortem life has an earthly, physical nature.

Ezekiel's resurrection vision

The origins of the book of Ezekiel are dated to the first half of the sixth century BCE. The exact date of the resurrection vision in Chapter 37 is, however, unclear, as the text has clearly been subjected to various revisions. It reads as follows:

---

5. Stemberger, *Leib der Auferstehung*, 115 (trans. S. Kühne). See also Stemberger, "Auferstehung," 444: "Resurrection is not imagined as a reunification of body and soul, but as a revival of the 'shadow': for death does not break the psychosomatic unity of man, the dead also 'live' in the underworld in a kind of 'diluted' corporeality, they return with the strengthening of life again into full corporeality. The place of resurrected life is the renewed, earthly world" (trans. S. Kühne).

> The hand of the LORD was upon me, and he brought me out in the Spirit of the LORD and set me down in the middle of the plain; it was full of bones. And he led me around among them, and behold, there were very many on the surface of the plain, and behold, they were very dry. And he said to me, "Son of man, can these bones live?" And I answered, "O LORD God, you know." Then he said to me, "Prophesy over these bones, and say to them, O dry bones, hear the word of the LORD. Thus says the LORD God to these bones: Behold, I will cause spirit to enter you, and you shall live. And I will lay sinews upon you, and will cause flesh to come upon you, and cover you with skin, and put spirit in you, and you shall live, and you shall know that I am the LORD." So I prophesied as I was commanded. And as I prophesied, there was a sound, and behold, a rattling, and the bones came together, bone to its bone. And I looked, and behold, there were sinews on them, and flesh had come upon them, and skin had covered them. But there was no spirit in them. Then he said to me, "Prophesy to the spirit; prophesy, son of man, and say to the spirit, Thus says the LORD God: Come from the four winds, O spirit, and breathe on these slain, that they may live." So I prophesied as he commanded me, and the spirit came into them, and they lived and stood on their feet, an exceedingly great army. Then he said to me, "Son of man, these bones are the whole house of Israel. Behold, they say, 'Our bones are dried up, and our hope is lost; we are indeed cut off.' Therefore prophesy, and say to them, Thus says the LORD God: Behold, I will open your graves and raise you from your graves, O my people. And I will bring you into the land of Israel.[6]

The text appears incoherent. On the one hand there are bones lying openly on a plane; on the other hand, graves are being opened. On the one hand it is said that the bones are "the whole house of Israel," on the other hand the text speaks of "these slain." The latter cannot be identified with the whole house of Israel because not all of its members died a violent death. Neither can those who, far from their homeland, climb out of their graves and are brought back to the land of Israel represent the whole house of Israel, as not all Israelites were forced into exile. The interpretation and redactional history of the text are very controversial.[7] In ancient times, the text was often interpreted literally as a description of a future resurrection of the dead. Today it is often assumed that the vision metaphorically express-

---

6. Ezek 37:1–12 (ESV, modified).

7. See the overviews in Schöpflin, "Revivification," 76–80; Hiebel, *Ezekiel's Vision Accounts*, 139–55.

es—in connection with the emancipation of the exiled from Babylonian captivity—the restoration of the nation of Israel.[8] Some argue that the expression "these slain" betrays a late redactional addition, introducing the idea of an individual resurrection to take into consideration the martyrs from the Maccabean period.[9] Thus, the text could address both the restoration of Israel and a resurrection in the literal sense. National restoration and individual resurrection from the dead are in no way mutually exclusive. A people is nothing without its individuals. If extinguished, it can only be brought back to life through the resurrection of those individuals. Even if a large proportion of a nation's members is still alive, the resurrection of the deceased could significantly contribute to a renewed greatness and power of a people. This is perhaps the meaning of the talk of "an exceedingly great army" that the resurrected will form. This contradicts the idea that the text is only concerned with the homecoming of the living exiled, as this would have been no great number.[10] Though the focus of this text is on the restoration of Israel, it is possible that the resurrection of individuals was functionally associated with it.[11] Should one wish to discern the idea of an individual resurrection in the text, for our question it would be relevant to ask where it is that the life after resurrection will take place. The answer is clear: on earth. The people that rise from the grave do not ascend to heaven, they return home to Israel. There is no doubt about its earthly location.[12] The text, however, gives no indication about the quality and duration of the afterlife.

8. See Greenberg, *Ezechiel 21–37*, 453, 462–64; Sedlmeier, *Das Buch Ezechiel*, 207; Charlesworth, "Concept of Resurrection," 2–3; by contrast, Russell, *Jewish Apocalyptic*, 368, holds that this passage represents the doctrine of resurrection.

9. See Mosis, "Ezechiel 37:1–14," 169: The Maccabean period was confronted with the "problem of the post-mortem fate of the individual" because of its many battles; see further Bartelmus, "Ez 37:1–14," 387; Sedlmeier, *Das Buch Ezechiel*, 210–13; Schöpflin, "Revivification," 77; Schmid, "Hintere Propheten," 368–69; see also Hiebel, *Ezekiel's Vision Accounts*, 147–51 with fn. 53. The Maccabees led a Jewish rebellion against Seleucid rule and the resulting Hellenization (167–160 BCE) and founded the royal Hasmonean dynasty, which ruled Judea from 164 to 63 BCE.

10. According to Jer 52:28–30, a total of 4,600 people was deported, probably predominantly members of the upper class. Rudolf Mosis also points to the astounding size of the legion of resurrected in the Ezekiel vision (see Mosis, "Ezechiel 37:1–14," 170).

11. The Ezekiel text shows striking similarities with details from Zoroastrian doctrine on the resurrection. This includes the concept that bones are revived first, the noise during resurrection that might indicate a life-giving wind, and the awakening of an army (see Silverman, *Persepolis and Jerusalem*, 133–35 and the literature cited therein). As resurrection in Zoroastrianism is understood as being individual it is possible that the concept of an individual resurrection also entered into the Ezekiel text with the adoption of Zoroastrian resurrection motifs.

12. See also Ezek 36:24,28: "I [the Lord God] will take you [the house of Israel]

Apocalypse of Isaiah

The second passage in the Tanakh where the thought of physical resurrection can be discerned is in the book of Isaiah, in the so-called Apocalypse of Isaiah (Isaiah 24–27). It was probably written after the death of Alexander the Great.[13] The topic of resurrection emerges in Isaiah 26:19. The Hebrew original text is very dark and controversial. In the New King James Version, it reads: "Your dead shall live. *Together with* my dead body they shall arise. Awake and sing, you who dwell in dust; for your dew *is like* the dew of herbs, and the earth shall cast out the dead."[14] The phrase "my dead body" hardly seems to fit in the context at all,[15] which is why the translator added "together with." The last clause of Isaiah 26:19 is also translated very differently: "[B]ut the underworld will make the Rephaim fall."[16] Rephaim is understood here as the powerful shades of deceased tyrants,[17] who would now *not* rise again.[18] In the Septuagint, the oldest Greek translation of the Tanakh, Isaiah 26:19 is less dark: "The dead shall rise, and those who are in the tombs shall be raised, and those who are in the earth shall rejoice; for the dew from you is healing to them, but the land of the impious shall fall." As in Ezekiel's aforementioned vision, it is unclear whether the resurrection of the dead in the Isaiah Apocalypse is merely a metaphor for the restoration of Israel or whether it concerns the resurrection of individuals from the dead.[19] The passage is embedded in an eschatological scenario concerned with the worldwide assertion of the rule of Yahweh and, ultimately, the restoration of Israel. If one assumes that Isaiah 26:19 concerns an individual resurrection, then in the context of this passage the afterlife would, without a doubt, take place on earth, in the restored Israel, where the scattered "children of Israel" would be brought together.[20] Jerusalem would be the center of this future life, with Yahweh as king, ruling the earth

---

from the nations and gather you from all the countries and bring you into your own land. [. . .] You shall dwell in the land that I gave to your fathers, and you shall be my people, and I will be your God" (ESV).

13. See Schmid, "Hintere Propheten," 334. According to Gillman, "Death and Afterlife," 596, the date of the Isaiah Apocalypse has not yet been ascertained; it is probably a little earlier than the book of Daniel (165 BCE).

14. The words printed in italics were added by the translator of the NKJV.

15. For discussion on this passage, see McAffee, "Rephaim," 92–93.

16. McAffee, "Rephaim," 93.

17. See McAffee, "Rephaim," 78, 84–87, 93–94.

18. See McAffee, "Rephaim," 93. See also similar, Beuken, *Jesaja 13–27*, 384.

19. See Greenberg, "Resurrection," 241; Doyle, *Apocalypse of Isaiah*, 315.

20. See Isa 27:12–13.

from Mount Zion.[21] If one combines this with Isaiah 25:8, according to which God "will swallow up death"[22] and "wipe away tears from all faces,"[23] and if we understand this literally, which is also controversial,[24] the result would be the image of an eternal life in physical form, free from suffering.[25] Overall, however, our findings fail to confirm with certainty the presence in the Apocalypse of Isaiah of the concept of an individual, physical resurrection and an eternal, earthly afterlife.

Individual resurrection in Daniel

The first and only passage in the Tanakh which, according to prevailing opinion, expresses the doctrine of an individual resurrection and an eternal afterlife is to be found in the book of Daniel.[26] Its final version probably originated from the years between 167 and 165 BCE.[27] In the twelfth chapter it is foretold: "And many of those who sleep in the dust of the earth shall awake, some to everlasting life, and some to shame and everlasting contempt. And those who are wise shall shine like the brightness of the sky above; and those who turn many to righteousness, like the stars forever and ever."[28] The sleeping in the dust of the earth seems to refer to the corpses and not to the shadows of the dead in Sheol.[29] Their reawakening will mean thus a physical resurrection, although this is not explicitly stated. The life of the risen

---

21. See Isa 24:23; 27:13.

22. Blenkinsopp, *Isaiah 1–39*, 359, sees here an allusion to Mot, a Canaanite underworld deity of death personified, devouring the god Baal at the beginning of the dry period.

23. ESV.

24. For the view that Isa 25:8 does not express a general elimination of death or an individual resurrection, see Watts, *Isaiah 1–33*, 333; Doyle, *Apocalypse of Isaiah*, 257. Interestingly, the Septuagint does not at all mention that death will be devoured: "Death, having prevailed, swallowed them up, and God has taken every tear from every face" (LXX Isa 25:8 NETS).

25. Cf., however, Isa 65:17–25, which speaks only of a long life on the new earth under God's rule; according to Isa 66:22 the "offspring" and "name" of the chosen will remain, from which it could be concluded, *ex silentio*, that this does not apply to the individual.

26. See Charlesworth, "Concept of Resurrection," 12; Collins, *Daniel*, 394; Greenberg, "Resurrection," 241; Witte, "Schriften (Ketubim)," 504–5.

27. See Witte, "Schriften (Ketubim)," 503.

28. Dan 12:2–3.

29. Particularly in Theodotion, a Greek translation of the Tanakh from the second century CE, it becomes clear that it concerns corpses in the grave: "And many of those who sleep in a mound of earth will be awakened" (TH Dan 12:2 NETS).

seems to be eternal. There is a division between a good and a bad afterlife destiny.[30] Where the afterlife will be is not expressly given here. However, the context implies that it will be on earth. Firstly, nowhere does it speak of a celestial or heavenly place of the resurrected. Secondly, the book of Daniel is concerned with the emancipation of Israel from the yoke of foreign rule. The text emerged against the background of the battle against the King of the Seleucid Empire, Antiochus IV Epiphanes, who had attempted to Hellenize the Yahweh cult.[31] His rule should be ended, and the temple purified of the foreign culture.[32] Israel and Jerusalem should be freed and not abandoned in favor of a celestial life.[33] The prophesied and in the near-future expected[34] kingdom of God is thus situated on earth.[35] It will spread over the whole earth[36] and be everlasting and indestructible.[37] This kingdom will be ruled by the people of Israel.[38] Where, if not there, will the risen live?

Some of the risen are attributed a luminescence, such as we have already learned of in Zoroastrianism. Sometimes, a heavenly existence after death is concluded from this.[39] Without any further indication about the place of

30. For a contrasting view, Fischer, *Tod und Jenseits*, 247–48.

31. See also the reference to the abolition of sacrifice and the setting up of an "abomination of desolation," by which probably a Hellenistic cult object is meant that was erected in the temple (see Dan 9:27; 11:31; 12:11).

32. See Dan 8:13–14; 12:11–13.

33. See Horsley, *Revolt of the Scribes*, 81–104, 193–207.

34. According to Dan 8:14, the end of the desecration of the temple from a foreign cult and with that also the beginning of God's kingdom, was expected in 1,150 days, in Dan 12:11 the delay is extended to 1,290 days; in the next possibly later added verse it is seemingly 1,335 days (see Collins, "From Prophecy to Apocalypticism," 145).

35. See, e.g., Russell, *Jewish Apocalyptic*, 376.

36. See Dan 2:44; 7:14,18,27.

37. See Dan 2:34–35.

38. See Dan 7:27.

39. According to Collins, "From Prophecy to Apocalypticism," 144 "the wise" will "be like the stars": "They can afford to lose their lives in this world, because they are promised a greater glory in the next." But the text speaks only of how they *shine* like stars, not that they *are* like stars, i.e., that they will possess all the characteristics of stars. Moreover, nowhere is there mention of an end to this world or talk of a next one. The forecast in the book of Daniel is not aimed at an end of the world, but rather an end to Seleucid rule (see also Horsley, *Revolt of the Scribes*, 207). Assumptions about a loan from the Hellenistic concept of an astral existence after death (see, e.g., Collins, *Daniel*, 394) seem unconvincing to me because it is generally accepted that the editors of the book of Daniel counted among those who according to Dan 12:3, were wise and would lead many to righteousness, and thus were also among those who would shine after death (see Collins, "From Prophecy to Apocalypticism," 144; Collins, *Daniel*, 385; Witte, "Schriften (Ketubim)," 503; Horsley, *Revolt of the Scribes*, 97). But it would be astonishing if exactly those who stood most decidedly against the yoke of the Seleucid

the afterlife this conclusion is, however, premature, as similar descriptions in Zoroastrianism show. There, one is able to shine like the sun, moon, and stars, and yet still live on earth. The point of my theory of the confusion of the worlds is precisely that elements from otherworldly experiences, such as luminous, otherworld bodies, are projected onto the earth.

Book of the Watchers

The Book of Enoch (also called First Enoch or Ethiopic Enoch), which does not count as part of the Tanakh, is made up of several books. In two books, the foretelling of a physical afterlife on earth is clearly recognizable, in the Book of the Watchers[40] and the Book of Parables.[41] The Book of the Watchers is the older of the two. Its current form probably dates from the third century BCE.[42] It does foretell a physical afterlife on earth, though it is located in places normally hidden from human beings.[43] On a visionary journey Enoch comes to a large and high mountain in the west of the earth.[44] Inside the mountain there are four chamber places.[45] Therein the souls or spirits—the terminology used varies—of the dead, are gathered and kept until the day of the great judgment.[46] These souls or spirits are the dead. They are not completely inactive, as Enoch hears Abel's spirit complain.[47] Although it is

---

empire and the Hellenization of the Jewish religion, foresaw an astral existence for themselves (as Kaiser and Lohse, *Tod und Leben*, 75 presume). Firstly, they would then be separated from the people of Israel whose earthly whereabouts can hardly be doubtable. Secondly, with this they would be adopting a Hellenistic concept, a fact they could hardly have missed, and which would completely contradict their fight against the Hellenization of the Jewish religion at that time. Thirdly, there is *no* resurrection associated with the Greek concept of an afterlife existence in the ether. The physical body rests in the earth, only the soul floats upwards (see Peres, *Griechische Grabinschriften*, 81–89).

40. 1 En. 1–36.

41. 1 En. 37–71. Further possible allusions to a physical resurrection in 1 Enoch can be found, for example, in the Epistle of Enoch (see 1 En. 92:3–5) and in the Book of Dream Visions (see 1 En. 90:20–38).

42. See Nickelsburg and VanderKam, *1 Enoch*, 3; in more detail Nickelsburg, *1 Enoch 1*, 169–71, 230, 279, 293. Uhlig, "Das äthiopische Henochbuch," 494, 506, assumes a composition between the end of the third and the middle of the second century BCE.

43. See Collins, "From Prophecy to Apocalypticism," 139.

44. See 1 En. 22:1.

45. See 1 En. 22:1–4,8–13. On these chambers see Stuckenbruck, "The 'Otherworld' and the *Epistle of Enoch*," 84–85.

46. See 1 En. 22:3–4.

47. See 1 En. 22:5–7.

said only that the souls or spirits are brought back to life, the afterlife of the righteous is very probably earthly and physical. This can be concluded from a further vision of Enoch. In another place on earth[48] he sees a mountain, surrounded by fragrant trees.[49] Among them is the Tree of Life, whose leaves and blossoms will not wither for all eternity.[50] After the judgment, the chosen will be allowed to eat from its fruit[51] and "its fragrances" will be "in their bones."[52] Thus they are no longer only spirits or souls. "Eating" and "bones" indicate a physical existence.[53] The statement, that no "flesh" is allowed to touch the Tree of Life *before* the final judgment,[54] shows a similar direction. After the judgment, one can conclude, this tree can be touched by the flesh of the chosen. We are in the dark as to how this post-mortem physical existence comes to be.[55] A resurrection of the body is never spoken of. The afterlife of the chosen will be long, but not eternal.[56] Suffering is banished from it: "[T]orments and plagues and suffering will not touch them."[57]

Book of Parables

In the Book of Parables, that is today often dated to the turn of the era,[58] and whose thoughts possibly influenced Jesus of Nazareth,[59] an eternal, physical afterlife on earth is prophesied. But it is not made clear how the in-

48. See 1 En. 24:1; 25:3.
49. See 1 En. 24:3.
50. See 1 En. 24:4.
51. See 1 En. 25:4–5.
52. 1 En. 25:6 (trans. Nickelsburg and VanderKam, *1 Enoch*, 45).
53. According to Nickelsburg, "bones" could also mean the location of sensation or the self (see *1 Enoch 1*, 315).
54. 1 En. 25:4 (trans. Nickelsburg and VanderKam, *1 Enoch*, 45).
55. See also Stemberger, *Leib der Auferstehung*, 38: "If the righteous return to the earth, they will of course regain their full corporeality. But this would not be a radical change of their condition, only a gradual one, since the whole otherworld is also corporeal" (trans. S. Kühne).
56. See 1 En. 25:6; see also 1 En. 10:17.
57. 1 En. 25:6 (trans. Nickelsburg and VanderKam, *1 Enoch*, 45).
58. See Charlesworth, "Date and Provenience," 56; Bock, "Dating the *Parables*," 112. Nickelsburg dates the Book of Parables ranging from the late period of the rule of Herod the Great (37–4 BCE) to the first decades of the first century CE, with preference for the earlier part of this time frame (see Nickelsburg and VanderKam, *1 Enoch 2*, 62–63); for early dating of the essential parts of 1 Enoch, see already Uhlig, "Das äthiopische Henochbuch," 494, 574–75.
59. See Charlesworth, "Did Jesus Know?" and more comprehensively below, pp. 144–45; see also below, pp. 61, 130, 143n91

dividual resurrection will take place: "In those days, the earth will give back what has been entrusted to it, and Sheol will give back what has been entrusted to it, and destruction will restore what it owes."[60] Is there a monistic concept according to which the subtle, corporeal shadows of the dead are restored to full, physical reality and vitality through resurrection?[61] Or is the scheme of resurrection dualistic: Does the earth return the bodies and Sheol return the souls or spirits and both are then reunified?[62] Regardless of the answer to these questions: the subsequent post-mortal life will be earthly and physical. The resurrected righteous will live on the earth that will be transformed into a paradisiacal place: "And I [the Lord of Spirits] shall transform the earth and make it a blessing. And my chosen ones I shall make to dwell on it."[63] Later the text says: "And the earth will rejoice, and the righteous will dwell on it, and the chosen will go upon it."[64] The manner of movement, the "going," indicates a physical life. If the bodies were not physical, the resurrected would rather float or fly. A third strong indication is the eating. The resurrected righteous and chosen will live together with the Son of Man, sent from heaven by the Lord of Spirits: "[W]ith that Son of Man they will eat, and they will lie down and rise up forever and ever."[65] Thus the afterlife on earth will proceed with a seemingly earthly, daily rhythm of rest, getting up, and eating.[66] In the last quote also the *eternity* of the afterlife is expressed. In other passages it is said that the living days of the resurrected, righteous, and holy will have "no end" and be "innumerable."[67] The eternity of the afterlife can also be inferred from the description of the garments of the chosen. They will be clothed in "the garment of glory" that "will not wear out."[68] The garment of glory is

---

60. 1 En. 51:1 (trans. Nickelsburg and VanderKam, *1 Enoch*, 65).

61. See Stemberger, *Leib der Auferstehung*, 47; Nickelsburg and VanderKam, *1 Enoch 2*, 184.

62. See Nickelsburg and VanderKam, *1 Enoch 2*, 184.

63. 1 En. 45:5 (trans. Nickelsburg and VanderKam, *1 Enoch*, 59). For the earthly localization of the post-mortem life in the Book of Parables, see also Nickelsburg, "Four Worlds that are 'Other,'" 55, 70–75.

64. 1 En. 51:5 (trans. Nickelsburg and VanderKam, *1 Enoch*, 65). From 1 En. 38:4 it is also possible to conclude *ex negativo* that the chosen will *possess* the earth: "And thereafter, it will not be the mighty and exalted who possess the land" (trans. Nickelsburg and VanderKam, *1 Enoch*, 51; for the interpretation, see Nickelsburg, "Four Worlds that are 'Other,'" 72–73).

65. 1 En. 62:14 (trans. Nickelsburg and VanderKam, *1 Enoch*, 81).

66. See Nickelsburg and VanderKam, *1 Enoch 2*, 267.

67. 1 En. 58:3 (trans. Nickelsburg and VanderKam, *1 Enoch*, 71).

68. 1 En. 62:15–16 (trans. Nickelsburg and VanderKam, *1 Enoch*, 81).

possibly a metaphor for the body of the risen.[69] "Glory" is first an attribute of the garment, then in the next verse it is attributed to the resurrected themselves: "And your glory will not fade."[70] The attribute of "glory" likely includes a shining glow that the resurrected emanate.[71] The luminescence of the resurrected is also explicitly mentioned: "[T]he light of the Lord of Spirits will have appeared on the face of the holy, righteous, and chosen," so that the sinners and the wicked would be unable to look at them.[72] Life on the transformed earth will take place in eternal light: "The righteous will be in the light of the sun, and the chosen, in the light of everlasting life. [...] There will be light that does not cease, [...] for darkness will first have been destroyed [...] and light will endure before the Lord of Spirits."[73]

Second Book of Maccabees

In the Second Book of Maccabees, which probably dates from the last third of the second century BCE,[74] the idea of a physical resurrection is clearly expressed. Like the First Enoch, it does not belong to the Tanakh, but is contained in the Septuagint and in the Old Testament for the Catholic and Orthodox churches. The theme of resurrection appears in connection with the description of the martyrdom of a mother and her seven sons and with the suicide of a certain Razis. The second brother says of his tongue and his hands before they were cut off: "I got these from Heaven [...] and from him I hope to get them back again."[75] Razis, who falls on his sword and throws his own entrails to his attackers, calls "upon the Lord of life and spirit to give them back to him again."[76] The resurrected body in these cases is obviously a physical one. Judging from the wording of these passages it seems to be exactly the same body as the one that dies.[77] "Resurrection" and "being raised"

---

69. See also Nickelsburg and VanderKam, *1 Enoch 2*, 267–68.

70. 1 En. 62:16 (trans. Nickelsburg and VanderKam, *1 Enoch*, 81).

71. See also Nickelsburg and VanderKam, *1 Enoch 2*, 267–68.

72. 1 En. 38:4 (trans. Nickelsburg and VanderKam, *1 Enoch*, 51).

73. 1 En. 58:3,6 (trans. Nickelsburg and VanderKam, *1 Enoch*, 71–72); cf. 1 En. 38:2; 50:1.

74. See Berlejung, "Makkabäerbücher," 581.

75. LXX 2 Macc 7:11 (NETS).

76. LXX 2 Macc 14:46 (NETS). See also Stemberger, *Leib der Auferstehung*, 23.

77. Stemberger does not share this "common view": "The resurrection is physical, but not necessarily in the sense of a resurrection of the materially same body. Otherwise, the brothers would also have to speak of a reunification of body and soul, which they, however, do not" (*Leib der Auferstehung*, 17; trans. S. Kühne). Stemberger sees here rather the "old Israeli view of the dead" who descend into Sheol, just as they died;

are expressly mentioned in the text.[78] Of the life following resurrection it is said only that it is eternal.[79] The possibility of resurrection is justified with an indication of God's creative powers. The God, who formed single people in the mother's body and created humanity as such,[80] will give back "life and breath" to those killed.[81]

Further deuterocanonical and apocryphal texts from pre-Christian times

Resurrection and the afterlife on earth are hinted at in additional non-biblical Jewish texts. In the *Psalms of Solomon*, which probably date from sometime between 70 and 40 before the turn of the era, there is this: "[T]hose who fear the Lord shall rise to everlasting life, and their life is in the light of the Lord and shall never end."[82] There is no explicit mention of the *death* of the god-fearing, so it cannot be said with any certainty whether a resurrection of the dead is meant.[83] Moreover, it remains unclear whether the eternal life of the god-fearing in the light will be earthly or heavenly.[84] The *Testaments of the Twelve Patriarchs*, which apart from Christian revisions appear to date from the Maccabean period,[85] teach in several passages, with more or less clarity, a physical afterlife on the earth, that is, in Israel.[86] The *Testament of Judah*, for example, says: "And after this

---

that is in the case of the seven brothers: without tongues and limbs. On their return to life their limbs would be returned to them. The resurrected body that is revived and completed emerges from the shadow body in Sheol. It is "in a sense [...] identical to the deceased [body], as it cannot be differentiated from it. Nevertheless, it is not necessarily the same; it can also be a new body, that corresponds exactly with the old one" (*Leib der Auferstehung*, 20; trans. S. Kühne).

78. See LXX 2 Macc 7:9 slightly awkward: "[B]ut the King of the universe will raise (ἀναστήσει) us to an everlasting renewal of life" (NETS); LXX 2 Macc 7:14: "It is desirable that those who die at the hands of human beings should cherish the hope God gives of being raised again by him. But for you [Antiochus IV] there will be no resurrection (ἀνάστασις) to life!" (NETS).

79. See LXX 2 Macc 7:9,36.

80. See LXX 2 Macc 7:22,28.

81. LXX 2 Macc 7:23 (NETS).

82. LXX Pss. Sol. 3:12 (NETS).

83. See Stemberger, *Leib der Auferstehung*, 57.

84. Stemberger believes a life for the resurrected, on earth, is probable (see *Leib der Auferstehung*, 60).

85. See Kee, "Testaments of the Twelve Patriarchs," 777–78.

86. See Stemberger, *Leib der Auferstehung*, 71 (trans. S. Kühne): "The TestXII [teach] resurrection in the form of the return of (of course physical) man to earth. His

Abraham, Isaac, and Jacob will be resurrected to life and I and my brothers will be chiefs (wielding) our scepter in Israel [. . .]. And those who died in sorrow shall be raised in joy; [. . .] those who died on account of the Lord shall be wakened to life."[87]

Fourth Book of Ezra

The Fourth Book of Ezra which—apart from the Christian additions—must date to the turn of the first century CE,[88] also seems to foretell an afterlife on earth. However, after a period of seven days of primeval chaos, the corruptible will perish.[89] The dead will rise again: "The earth shall give up those who are asleep in it; and the dust those who rest there in silence; and the chambers shall give up the souls which have been committed to them."[90] The process of resurrection remains a mystery. Some passages tell of the body separating from the soul in death.[91] One might thus think that the dead bodies will be surrendered from the earth and dust and the souls are released from their chambers and that both are reunified. But that is not stated here. The relative pronoun "who" points not to dead things lying in the earth but to dead persons.[92] For us the important question is whether the afterlife is physical and where it takes place. It's safe to say that with resurrection, material substance comes from the interior of the earth to the surface as also souls are not thought to be completely incorporeal. When the resurrected are shown "the pit of torment" and "the furnace of hell"

---

body will be the same one he had during his earthly life, as body and spirit completely correspond to one another—but it will not be the restored, deceased body of flesh."

87. T. Jud. 25:1,4 (trans. *OTP* 1:801–2). See also T. Sim. 6:7; T. Zeb. 10:1–2; T. Ben. 10:6–10.

88. See Schreiner, "Das 4. Buch Esra," 301; Metzger, "The Fourth Book of Ezra," 520.

89. See 4 Ezra 7:31; see also 4 Ezra 7:113 and thereto Stemberger, *Leib der Auferstehung*, 83.

90. 4 Ezra 7:32 (trans. *OTP* 1:538).

91. See 4 Ezra 7:78,100.

92. See for this passage also Stemberger: "In the resurrection the souls are released from their chambers. [. . .] Even in the chambers, the souls were not understood as nonphysical, but only now do they regain their full corporeality. It is not expressly stated whether this means a reunification with the same body that the soul had in its earthly life. This thought is evidently not far away, but not yet fully developed. What dust and earth represent, in light of the wording, are the dead; in the context, it is most likely the body, the matter (without necessarily thinking about the identity of the body)" (*Leib der Auferstehung*, 82; trans. S. Kühne).

"opposite" "the place of rest" and "the Paradise of delight,"[93] then one must assume that these are earthly places,[94] as nowhere is a transfer to another region mentioned. True, the motif of the luminescence of the good resurrected does appear. The light of those "who have kept the ways of the Most high" will be "like the light of the stars," and their faces will "shine like the sun," and "the faces of those who practised self-control" even shall "shine more than the stars."[95] But this in itself does not imply heavenly existence, as we saw in the discussion of the topic in Zoroastrianism, in the book of Daniel and in the First Enoch.[96]

Second Book of Baruch (Syriac Apocalypse of Baruch)

The Second Book of Baruch, also known as the Syriac Apocalypse Baruch,[97] probably dates from the first third of the second century CE.[98] It knows not only physical resurrection but also the idea that the dead are resurrected with the same appearance they die with, so that they are recognizable:

> For the earth will surely give back the dead at that time; it receives them now in order to keep them, not changing anything in their form. But as it has received them so it will give them back. And as I have delivered them to it so it will raise them. For then it will be necessary to show those who live that the dead are living again, and that those who went away have come back. And it will be that when they have recognized each other[.][99]

But after the judgment, the risen are transformed, the righteous "into the splendor of angels," the sinners however into "horrible shapes."[100] The latter then go to a place of punishment, torment, and fire.[101] Its location is

---

93. 4 Ezra 7:36 (trans. *OTP* 1:538).

94. See also Stemberger, *Leib der Auferstehung*, 83.

95. 4 Ezra 7:88,97,125 (trans. *OTP* 1:539-41).

96. See above, pp. 24-25, 34-35, 37-38.

97. The full text is only available in the Syriac language. The Syriac version is based on a Greek version, which is possibly based on a Hebrew original text; see Klijn, "2 Baruch," 616; Oegema, "Apokalypsen," 59.

98. According to Oegema, "Apokalypsen," 60, a time frame between the Diaspora Uprising of 115-117 CE and the Bar Kochba Uprising 132-135 CE, is most likely.

99. 2 Bar. 50:2-4 (trans. *OTP* 1:638).

100. 2 Bar. 51:5 (trans. *OTP* 1:638).

101. See 2 Bar. 30:4-5; 44:12,15; 51:6.

not specified. The righteous will live in the heights of a now invisible world, thus apparently not on this earth.¹⁰²

> And it will happen after this day [the day of the final judgment] which he [God] appointed that both the shape of those who are found to be guilty as also the glory of those who have proved to be righteous will be changed. [. . . T]he glory of those who proved to be righteous on account of my law, [. . .]—their splendor will then be glorified by transformations, and the shape of their face will be changed into the light of their beauty, so that they may acquire and receive the undying world which is promised to them. [. . .] For they shall see that world which is now invisible to them, and they will see a time which is now hidden to them. And time will no longer make them older. For they will live in the heights of that world and they will be like angels and be equal to the stars. And they will be changed into any shape which they wished, from beauty to loveliness, and from light to the splendor of glory. For the extents of Paradise will be spread out for them, and to them will be shown the beauty of the majesty of the living beings under the throne as well as all the hosts of angels[.]¹⁰³

An existence in heaven is prophesied to the nation of Israel, but without reference to the resurrection of the nation of Israel, in the Assumption of Moses (also called Testament of Moses),¹⁰⁴ which originated a hundred years earlier: "And God will raise you to the heights. Yea, he will fix you firmly in the heaven of the stars, in the place of their habitations. And you will behold from on high. Yea, you will see your enemies on the earth. And recognizing them, you will rejoice."¹⁰⁵

---

102. According to Henze, *Jewish Apocalypticism*, 316, this still invisible world is identical to paradise, which had been hidden since Adam's fall (see 2 Bar. 4:3–4).

103. 2 Bar. 51:1,3,8–11 (trans. *OTP* 1:638).

104. For a composition shortly after the turn of the era, see Brandenburger, "Himmelfahrt Moses," 60; Oegema, "Apokalypsen," 35; Priest, "Testament of Moses," 921–22. The text is only available in Latin. It was probably translated from the Greek; a Hebrew original form is suspected (see Brandenburger, "Himmelfahrt Moses," 59; Priest, "Testament of Moses," 920).

105. As. Mos. 10:9–10 (trans. *OTP* 1:932). The *Liber antiquitatum biblicarum*, in contrast, speaks of reviving the dead and raising the sleeping ones from the earth, but the place of the afterlife remains somewhat unclear, because the location of the prophesied other earth is not specified (see LAB 3:10).

Fourth Book of Baruch (Paralipomena of Jeremiah)

This scripture, also attributed to the scribe of the prophet Jeremiah, Baruch,[106] originated, apart from the Christian additions, probably around the year 130 CE.[107] In it, Abimelech, mentioned in the book of Jeremiah,[108] walks with a basket of figs and falls asleep under the shade of a tree in the midday heat. He sleeps for sixty-six years. When he awakes the figs in his basket are still just as fresh as when they had been picked. When Baruch hears the story and sees the figs in the basket, he interprets the event as a parable of physical resurrection:

> Prepare yourself, my heart, and be glad and rejoice in your tent, I mean, in your fleshly house, because your sorrow has been transformed into joy. [. . .] Revive, my virginal faith, and believe that you will live. Look at this basket of figs! For behold, they are sixty-six years old, yet they did not shrivel up or begin to stink, but they are still dripping milky sap. The same thing is going to happen with you, my flesh, if you do what has been commanded you by the angel of righteousness. He who preserved the basket of figs, he it is who will again preserve you by his power.[109]

Fourth Book of the Sibylline Oracles

The resurrection is also taught in the Fourth Book of the Sibylline Oracles. It is generally held that this text is of Jewish origin and probably dates to the end of the first century:[110]

> But when everything is already dusty ashes, and God puts to sleep the unspeakable fire, even as he kindled it, God himself will again fashion the bones and ashes of men and he will raise up mortals again as they were before. And then there will be a judgment over which God himself will preside, judging the world again. As many as sinned by impiety, these will a mound of earth cover, and broad Tartarus and the repulsive recesses of Gehenna. But as many are pious, they will live on earth again when God gives spirit and life and favor to these pious ones. Then they will all see themselves beholding the delightful and

---

106. See, e.g., Jer 36:4–32.
107. See Herzer, *4 Baruch*, xxxiv.
108. See, e.g., Jer 38:7–13.
109. 4 Bar. 6:3–7 (trans. Herzer, *4 Baruch*, 21).
110. See Gauger, "Einführung," 451–54; Merkel, "Sibyllinen," 1064.

pleasant light of the sun. Oh most blessed, whatever man will live at that time.[111]

The afterlife of the pious will take place on the earth. It is, however, neither expressly stated that it will be for eternity, nor is the life on earth or the mode of existence of the risen described further.

Later developments

In rabbinic Judaism, after the destruction of the second temple[112] in the year 70 CE, resurrection and an afterlife on earth were seen as one of the central doctrines of Judaism.[113] A pictorial representation of the resurrection can be found in wall paintings that probably originate from the third century, in the Dura-Europos synagogue on the river Euphrates in Syria. There, the resurrection of the dead is depicted according to the thirty-seventh chapter of the book of Ezekiel.[114] The hope of resurrection was so concrete that there was speculation about how it would be possible to resurrect those Jews who had been exiled, at the right place—the Mount of Olives, near Jerusalem.[115] It was presumed that their mortal remains would roll there via underground tunnels.[116] The belief in an earthly-physical resurrection is still shared by many Jews today, and in the last decades the number seems

---

111. Sib. Or. 4.179–92 (*OTP* 1:389).

112. The so-called second temple was built in Jerusalem after the Babylonian exile, following the destruction of the first Jerusalem temple by Nebuchadnezzar II in 586 BCE.

113. See m. Sanh. 10:1 and Boyarin and Siegel, "Resurrection," 241; Avery-Peck, "Resurrection of the Body," 265; more comprehensively, Morgenstern, "Künftige Welt." Even if in rabbinic Judaism body and soul are distinguished, their relation is not to be thought of as in Greek philosophy where the soul contains the whole character and the body is only its vessel. Rather for rabbinic Judaism, the body and the soul together make up the person (see Boyarin and Siegel, "Resurrection," 241–42, with reference to the rabbinic parable of the body as a blind man and the soul as a lame man, in b. Sanh. 91a–b).

114. It is striking that the representation of the resurrection in the wall paintings in the Dura-Europos synagogue deviates from the Ezekiel text. In the text there are bones lying on the earth, while in the painting flesh and body parts can be seen. Bernhard Lang suggests that this alteration was a conscious decision in order to conceal the similarities between Ezek 37 and the Zoroastrian resurrection doctrine. In Zoroastrianism, only the dry bones of the dead were stored for the resurrection (see "Zoroastrian Prophecy of Resurrection," 84–89; see also Silverman, *Persepolis and Jerusalem*, 130–33).

115. The idea that the Mount of Olives would be the place of resurrection appears to be based on Zech 14:4–5, although it mentions there only the arrival of Yahweh at the Mount of Olives and the splitting of this mountain.

116. See Allison, *Resurrecting Jesus*, 220 with fn. 85; Allison, *Constructing Jesus*, 51 with fn. 89; Vetter, "Leben nach dem Tod," 96.

to be increasing.[117] The understanding of resurrection as a revival of the physical body has not changed. Even today the *Encyclopaedia Judaica* defines resurrection as: "the dead will be revived in their bodies and live again on earth."[118] Alongside belief in resurrection goes—through contact with Greek culture—the concept of an *immortal soul* and the belief in a postmortem existence without a physical body in another world.[119] According to the Book of Jubilees, which seems to date from the mid-second century BCE,[120] the mortal remains of the righteous will rest in the earth, while their spirits rejoice for eternity.[121] The Wisdom of Solomon, which probably dates to the turn of the era,[122] promises: "But the souls of the righteous are in the hand of God, and no torment will ever touch them. In the eyes of the foolish they seemed to have died, and their departure was considered to be suffering, and their going from us to be destruction, but they are at peace."[123] The belief in an immortal soul would, in the course of time, go on to become "one of the cornerstones" of the Jewish faith.[124] Since the Middle Ages the reincarnation of the soul has also been a part of the Jewish faith.[125]

Conclusion

The doctrine of resurrection and an eternal afterlife on earth probably developed in Judaism from the third century BCE onwards. The concept was linked to the restoration of Israel. In the book of Daniel, the luminescence of the resurrected is emphasized. This important parallel with descriptions of the deceased in accounts of otherworld experiences also appear in the Book of Parables, which mentions some details of an afterlife on earth: the Lord of Spirits will make the earth into a paradisiacal place, and the chosen will live together for eternity, eating and resting with the Son of Man, who descended from heaven. In later texts, the idea of an earthly, paradisiacal

---

117. See Gillman, "Death and Afterlife," 607–9.

118. Greenberg, "Resurrection," 240.

119. See Gillman, "Death and Afterlife," 597–98; Segal, *Life after Death*, 367–68; Pines, "Soul".

120. See Berger, "Buch der Jubiläen," 300.

121. See Jub. 23:30–31; for an opposing view see Berger, "Buch der Jubiläen," 446 fn. 30e.

122. See Witte, "Weisheit Solomos," 547.

123. LXX Wis 3:1–3 (NETS). See also T. Ab. 20.

124. Grintz, "Soul," 35; for the medieval discussion about the immortality of the soul and its inseparability from the body, see Pines, "Soul."

125. See Gillman, "Death and Afterlife," 603–4; Scholem, "Soul."

afterlife is not developed further. In the Second Book of Baruch, the life of the transformed resurrected is relocated to heavenly regions. In the Book of Jubilees, in pre-Christian times, the Hellenistic thought of an afterlife of the soul without the revival of the physical body can already be found.

4

Resurrection and the Kingdom of God in Jesus of Nazareth

THE CHARISMATIC JEWISH PREACHER and miracle worker, Jesus of Nazareth was probable by far the most influential, historically concrete proponent of the doctrine of an earthly resurrection and an eternal afterlife on earth.[1] For this reason I will examine him in detail, particularly as I believe that his case paradigmatically showed the tragic consequences of this doctrine.[2]

> 1. It is possible that Zarathustra exerted an even greater influence on the history of religion through the infiltration of his ideas into Judaism, Christianity, and Islam. According to Mary Boyce, Zarathustra was the first to have taught an individual postmortal judgment, heaven and hell, the resurrection of the body, a universal last judgment, and an eternal life of the reunified soul and body. These thoughts then became the articles of faith for a significant part of humanity (see *Zoroastrians*, 1, 29). However, the sources on Zarathustra's existence and doctrine are extremely sparse.
>
> 2. In the following, I consciously avoid the terms "apocalyptic" and "millenaristic," which have often been used in connection with Jesus. On the one hand, they have implications that possibly do not apply to the worldview of Jesus, such as the idea of an end of the world, a periodization of history or a thousand-year reign. On the other side, they do not necessarily include an element that, in my eyes, was essential to Jesus, the eternal afterlife on earth. See, for example, Hellholm's definition of apocalypticism (from the Greek αποκάλυψις: uncovering, revelation) as a revelation-based doctrine of the last days and the end of the world, in which the following elements are typical: "(1) the periodization of history in four or seven eras and their decline (cyclically or linearly); (2) the eschatological end-times with the destruction and renewal of the world by an eschatological deliverer and with resurrection of the dead; (3) the final military struggle between good and evil on both the cosmic and earthly planes; (4) natural occurrences along with cosmic disruptions such as a worldwide conflagration, floods, earthquakes; (5) social disorder in the ruling class impacting society, family, and religious community" (Hellholm, "Apocalypse"). The term "millenarianism," like its Greek-derived counterpart, "chiliasm," actually refers to "the notion of a 1,000-year period immediately preceding the Last Judgment and the end of the world" (Pezzoli-Olgiati, "Millenarianism / Chiliasm"), but is used very similarly to "apocalypticism." See further the comprehensive inter-cultural representation of the characteristics of millenarianism in Allison, *Jesus of Nazareth*, 78–94, and the definition of "millennialism" in Duling, "Millennialism," 183, as a "social movement of people whose central belief is that the present oppressive world is in crisis and will soon end [...] and that this world will be replaced by a new, perfect, blissful and trouble free world."

Methodological questions

In order to clarify the question whether Jesus really taught a physical resurrection and an earthly afterlife, we must not only analyze the ideas in the teachings of Jesus as preserved in the extant sources, but also try to move beyond those sources to learn what the historical Jesus really said and did. This is a methodologically controversial and ambitious undertaking. I largely subscribe to the methodology of Dale Allison.[3] In terms of human long-term memory, which tends to retain general impressions rather than exact details, he considers it very unlikely that the sayings and acts of Jesus in the long years before their being written down, could have been precisely fixed in memories.[4] Moreover, it is almost impossible to prove individual words and acts of Jesus as historical with the help of the so-called criteria of authenticity.[5] But because long-term memory does reliably retain general impressions, one can conclude from recurring themes and motifs from tradition that Jesus did say and do *this kind* of thing.[6] One can also gain historical insight from traditions about events, even if they, in all likelihood, did not occur or did not occur as reported.[7] To ascertain the *beliefs of Jesus* concerning resurrection and the kingdom of God, I will above all draw on the *sayings of Jesus* that are recorded in writing, probably in the first century CE. These are primarily the words of Jesus in the canonical Gospels. The dating to the first century of the Gospels of Luke and John, however, is uncertain.[8] The apocryphal Gospel

---

3. In the attempt to reconstruct the eschatology of Jesus I will, in particular, reference Dale Allison's work, not only methodologically but also in terms of content. A fundamental problem in an interdisciplinary study like this one is that the author cannot take into account the whole body of research literature in the various disciplines, especially when it comes to the boundless literature and diversity of opinion on Jesus of Nazareth, which is why he must make a selection. Dale Allison is, in my opinion, not only a leading authority in the field of the eschatology of Jesus, in addition, his way of working is very self-conscious, he processes a plethora of sources and literature, and discusses with great neutrality numerous views on each issue. See his exemplary book, *Constructing Jesus: Memory, Imagination, and History*, where these advantages are explicitly clear.

4. See Allison, *Constructing Jesus*, 1–20.

5. See Allison, "Traditional Criteria of Authenticity."

6. See Allison, "Traditional Criteria of Authenticity," 26.

7. See, e.g., Allison, "It Don't Come Easy," 191, on the probable truths about Jesus in the temptation narratives in Matt 4:1–11 and Luke 4:1–13.

8. For the Gospel of Luke, Martin Meiser sees a time range of 90–120 CE (see "Standort des lukanischen Doppelwerks," 101–11 and the literature referenced there); as many others, Mathias Rein dates the Gospel of John to between 90 and 110 CE (see "Johannesevangelium," 155). In contrast, most scholars assume that the Gospel of Mark was completed around 70 CE, and the Gospel of Matthew between 80 and 90 CE (see Schröter, "Gospel of Mark," 277–78; Duling, "Gospel of Matthew," 298).

of Thomas seems to have originated much later.[9] The other scriptures of the New Testament contain only a few of Jesus' logia.[10] I also include accounts of the *miracles of Jesus*. They are found almost exclusively in the canonical Gospels, apart from the eleven miracles in the Infancy Gospel of Thomas from the end of the second century.[11]

Physical resurrection

Linguistic indications of the doctrine of a physical resurrection

The pertinent sources do not contain a theoretical discourse of Jesus on his worldview. Therefore, one has no choice but to infer it from his sayings. Linguistic indices play an important role here. The core idea of a physical resurrection is that the same body that dies and was buried, rises again. There is thus an identity and continuity of the physical body. This identity and continuity appears in the Gospels as in other New Testament writings in the two verbs used to describe the process of the revivification of the dead.[12]

The most commonly used verb is ἐγείρω. Jesus employs this word to describe the general resurrection of the dead[13] and his own resurrection, or that of the Son of Man[14] as well as miraculous revivifications.[15] With this word he commands apparently dead people to arise, that is, to come back to life,[16] as well as sick people to get up and be well.[17] Jesus uses ἐγείρω further for standing up and getting up from sitting,[18] from eating,[19] from lying

---

9. See the discussion in Gathercole, *Gospel of Thomas*, 112–27. Gathercole himself dates the Gospel of Thomas to between 135 and 200 CE (see *Gospel of Thomas*, 124); for a dating to the second half of the second century CE, see Evans, "Jesus and the Extracanonical Works," 635–47; Popkes, *Menschenbild des Thomasevangeliums*, 356–62.

10. See, e.g., 1 Cor 7:10; 9:14; 11:24–25; Acts 1:7–8; 11:16; 20:35.

11. See Inf. Gos. Thom. 2; 9–18.

12 An exception could be Paul's doctrine on resurrection, as he develops in 1 Cor 15, see below, pp. 96–98.

13. See Matt 12:42; Mark 12:26; Luke 11:31; 20:37; John 5:21.

14. See Matt 16:21; 17:9,23; 20:19; 26:32; 27:63; Mark 14:28; Luke 9:22; John 2:19.

15. See Matt 10:8; 11:5; Luke 7:22.

16. See Mark 5:41; Luke 7:14; 8:54.

17. See Matt 9:5–6; Mark 2:9,11; Luke 5:23–24; John 5:8.

18. See Matt 26:46; Mark 3:3.

19. See Mark 14:42; John 14:31.

on the ground,[20] from sleeping,[21] and also in parables for the nocturnal rising of the virgins at the arrival of the bridegroom,[22] for the standing up of a house master to lock his door,[23] for getting out of bed,[24] for the lifting of a sheep that had fallen in a pit,[25] as well as in a metaphorical sense for standing up in court or in war against someone[26] and for the appearance of prophets.[27] Particularly significant is the fact that Jesus calls his miraculous revivifications of apparently dead individuals, "ἐγείρω," as well as his own resurrection from the dead and the general resurrection of the dead. In the cases of miraculous revivifications, it is undeniable that the very same physical body that had (apparently) died, comes alive again and gets up. Apart from the metaphorical meanings of ἐγείρω, this verb always refers to actions or changes of a specific body whose continuity in this process is beyond question. The use of ἐγείρω in the New Testament scriptures,[28] outside of the sayings of Jesus, is the same. Also here, miraculous revivifications are expressed using ἐγείρω.[29]

The other verb used in the New Testament to describe the process of revival from the dead is ἀνίστημι. In the traditional sayings of Jesus it is

20. See Matt 17:7.
21. See Mark 4:27.
22. See Matt 25:7.
23. See Luke 13:25.
24. See Luke 11:8.
25. See Matt 12:11.
26. See Matt 24:7; Mark 13:8; Luke 21:10.
27. See Matt 24:11,24; Mark 13:22.
28. Ἐγείρω describes, outside of the words of Jesus, the revivification or coming alive of deceased persons; beside the resurrection of Jesus (Matt 27:63-64; 28:6-7; Mark 16:6; Luke 24:6,34; John 2:22; 21:14; Acts 3:15; 4:10; 5:30; 10:40; 13:30,37) the resurrection of John the Baptist (as Jesus) (Matt 14:2; Mark 6:14,16; Luke 9:7), in which case the reawakening would, however, not mean the revivification of the same body; the resurrection of the bodies of many saints fallen into (death) sleep at Jesus' death (Matt 27:52); the resurrection of the dead by God (Acts 26:8); miraculous revivifications (Matt 9:25; John 12:9,17); the standing up of a healed person (Matt 8:15; 9:7; Mark 2:12; Acts 3:6); the getting up of a sick person (Mark 1:31; 9:27; Acts 3:7); the standing up of a healthy person (Acts 10:26); waking from sleep (Matt 1:24; 8:25; Mark 4:38; Acts 12:7); getting up from sleeping, from rest, from sitting or from the ground (Matt 2:13-14,20-21; 8:26; 9:19; 25:7; Mark 10:49, John 13:4; Acts 9:8); embarking on something (John 11:29; Rev 11:1). The primary doctrinal and instructive epistles of the New Testament contain almost no sayings or deeds of Jesus. In them, ἐγείρω seldom appears in any other sense than the becoming alive or making alive of the deceased (see Rom 13:11, Eph 5:14: "to awake spiritually"; Phil 1:17: "to cause"). In one passage Paul employs ἐγείρω to refer to the revivification of *bodies* (1 Cor 15:44).
29. See Matt 9:25; John 12:1,9,17.

used very similarly to ἐγείρω. Jesus not only describes with it his own or the Son of Man's resurrection from the dead,[30] the resurrection of others from death[31] and the eschatological rising of the dead,[32] but also his revivification of apparently dead persons,[33] the rising of sick people,[34] getting up from sleep,[35] or out of bed,[36] embarking on something,[37] stepping out of a crowd,[38] the producing of offspring,[39] as well as, in a metaphorical sense, the rising against someone to fight.[40] Apart from the metaphorical use of the word, ἀνίστημι implies, like ἐγείρω, the continuity of the body that stands up, rises up, or is re-erected.[41] Especially meaningful for the evaluation of Jesus' concept of resurrection are the uses of ἀνίστημι for the arising of miraculously revived persons.[42] Beyond the words of Jesus, ἀνίστημι is used in New Testament sources very similarly, among other things for the arising of people miraculously returned to life,[43] or for the raising (transitive) of an apparently dead person,[44] for the resurrection of Jesus,[45] for the resurrection of earlier prophets,[46] for the general resurrection from the dead,[47] for the standing up of a person healed of sickness,[48] for the getting up from sitting or lying down, from sleep or to depart[49] as well as for standing up in court or in a dispute against someone.[50]

30. See Mark 8:31; 9:9,31; 10:34; Luke 18:33; 24:46.
31. See Luke 16:31.
32. See Matt 12:41–42; Mark 12:25; Luke 11:31–32; John 6:39–40,44,54.
33. See John 11:23.
34. See Luke 17:19.
35. See Luke 22:46.
36. See Luke 11:7–8.
37. See Luke 15:18,20; John 11:31.
38. See Luke 6:8.
39. See Matt 22:24.
40. See Mark 3:26.
41. The awakening of offspring from stones preserves a physical continuity, but not the continuity of a particular body.
42. See Mark 5:42; Luke 8:55.
43. See Mark 5:42; Luke 8:55; Acts 9:40.
44. See Mark 9:27; Acts 9:41.
45. See Mark 16:9; John 20:9.
46. See Luke 9:8,19.
47. See Matt 12:41; Mark 12:23; Luke 11:32; John 11:24.
48. See Luke 4:39; 5:25.
49. See Matt 9:9; 26:62; Mark 1:35; 2:14; 7:42; 10:1; Luke 1:39; 4:16,29,38; 5:25,28; 22:45; 23:1; 24:12,33.
50. See Mark 14:57,60; Luke 10:25.

The described usage of ἐγείρω and ἀνίστημι that consistently shapes the sayings of Jesus is, in my eyes, one of the strongest proofs that Jesus held the doctrine of a physical resurrection.[51] Further indications, which I will present in the following pages, are more selective. In their entirety, however, they also provide considerable evidence for my theory that Jesus advocated a physical resurrection and an earthly afterlife.

Physical resurrection implies physical afterlife

If the physical body arises from death, and if no fundamental transformation of the resurrected body occurs, then existence after death is likewise physical. Jesus never explicitly talks of a post-mortal transformation of the human body. The fact that, in the case of Jesus, resurrection from the dead does not necessarily mean transformation is shown by his miraculous revivifications. He describes them using the same verbs as he uses for the eschatological resurrection of the dead.[52] However, in the descriptions of those called back to life by Jesus, there is no indication of a transformation.

Physical movement after resurrection

Jesus' sayings contain a clue that the resurrected body moves like a normal physical body. According to the Gospel of Mark, Jesus prophesies: "But after I am raised up, I will walk ahead of you to Galilee."[53] Albert Schweitzer pointed out that here Mark uses the same word (προάγω) as for the migration to Jerusalem of Jesus and his followers before his death: "And they were on the road, going up to Jerusalem, and Jesus was walking ahead of them."[54] The parallel between the two passages is obvious and it is clear that προάγω, in this context, normally describes a mode of continual physical movement[55] and not some sort of supernatural transport from one place to another.

---

51. See also Cook, "Use of ἐγείρω and ἀνίστημι."
52. See above, pp. 49–51.
53. Mark 14:28.
54. Mark 10:32 (ESV); see Schweitzer, *Quest*, 525 n. 26; Schweitzer, *Kingdom of God*, 133.
55. See also Matt 2:9; 21:9; Mark 6:45; 11:9; Luke 18:39.

Eating, drinking, and satiety in the kingdom of God

The physical character of the post-mortal life promised by Jesus is reinforced by his words on eating and drinking in the kingdom of God:[56] "Blessed is everyone who will eat bread in the kingdom of God!"[57] In another prophesy, drinking is added: "[Y]ou may eat and drink at my table in my kingdom."[58] That this eschatological banquet in the kingdom of God will happen after resurrection is clearly shown by the participation of the deceased patriarchs and prophets. As Jesus prophesies in the Gospel of Luke: "In that place there will be weeping and gnashing of teeth, when you see Abraham and Isaac and Jacob and all the prophets in the kingdom of God but you yourselves cast out. And people will come from east and west, and from north and south, and recline at table in the kingdom of God."[59] All three Synoptic Gospels[60] contain Jesus' prophesy that he will drink wine in God's kingdom after his resurrection. In the Gospel of Mark it reads: "Truly, I say to you, I will not drink again of the fruit of the vine until that day when I drink it new in the kingdom of God."[61] In the Beatitudes of the Sermon on the Plain, the kingdom of God is also explicitly referred to.[62] There, Jesus promises the hungry that they will be satisfied in the kingdom, while those who were now full will be hungry,[63] probably because they will not be admitted to the kingdom of God. Feeling full and being hungry are states that, according to normal understanding, are linked to physical bodily functions.

---

56. See below, pp. 55–61, 67–70.

57. Luke 14:15 (ESV).

58. Luke 22:30.

59. Luke 13:28–29 (ESV). Cf. similarly Matt 8:11: "I tell you, many will come from east and west and recline at table with Abraham, Isaac, and Jacob in the kingdom of heaven" (ESV).

60. That is, Matthew, Mark, and Luke.

61. Mark 14:25 (ESV); almost word for word Matt 26:29; very similar Luke 22:18.

62. See Luke 6:20. On the fundamental eschatological character of the Beatitudes of Jesus, see Davies and Allison, *Matthew*, 1:439–40; Frenschkowski, "Beatitudes"; for the Beatitudes of Sermon on the Plain, see also Allison, *Constructing Jesus*, 123–25. The promise of the kingdom of God in Luke 6:20 in no way implies that the kingdom of God is already here. This is also supported by the fact that, after the fourth and last beatitude, Jesus says: "Rejoice in that day, and leap for joy" (Luke 6:23 ESV). The expression, "that day" (), means, when it is used as here without a reference word, the eschatological day of the coming of the Son of Man and the judgment (see, e.g., Matt 7:22; 24:36; Luke 10:12; 17:31; 21:34). In the Old Testament, "that day" stands similarly for the "day of Yahweh," where his coming and judgment of his enemies will occur (see, e.g., Isa 2:11,17,20; Hos 2:18; Amos 8:3,9).

63. See Luke 6:21,25.

The risen and the not yet deceased together in the kingdom of God

From words attributed to Jesus we can also conclude that those not yet deceased will be gathered for judgment and will enter either into the kingdom of God or the eternal fire.[64] Neither in these words nor in other eschatological statements does Jesus say that one must first die in order to reach the judgment and eternal life. He does not teach a fundamental transformation before entry into eternal life. Thus, entry into the kingdom of God for the living speaks for its physical nature and its earthly localization.

Entering the kingdom of God mutilated

A physical afterlife in the kingdom of God can also be deduced from some very radical advice given by Jesus in the Gospel of Mark:

> And if your hand causes you to sin, cut it off. It is better for you to enter life crippled than with two hands to go to hell, to the unquenchable fire. And if your foot causes you to sin, cut it off. It is better for you to enter life lame than with two feet to be thrown into hell. And if your eye causes you to sin, tear it out. It is better for you to enter the kingdom of God with one eye than with two eyes to be thrown into hell, where "their worm does not die and the fire is not quenched."[65]

Jesus seems to presuppose here that it is possible to enter the kingdom of God with one's current physical body. The text leaves open whether he has in mind those still living at the time of judgment or the already deceased and resurrected persons with their previous physical bodies.[66] In any case,

---

64. See, e.g., Matt 13:41-43; 16:27-28; 24:29-31,34,37-41; 25:31-46; Mark 13:26-27.

65. Mark 9:43-48 (ESV).

66. Cf. Allison, "Eschatology of Jesus," 284: this passage points to proof of a physical resurrection. It implies that the body is resurrected exactly as it was buried. He refers also to 2 Bar. 50:2: "For the earth will surely give back the dead at that time; it receives them now in order to keep them, not changing anything in their form. But as it has received them so it will give them back. And as I have delivered them to it so it will raise them" (trans. *OTP* 1:638). Because Jesus does, however, not talk here of death and resurrection (as Allison, *Jesus of Nazareth*, 140 notes), I believe it possible that Jesus, at least for a time, expected the coming of the kingdom so soon that the majority of his listeners would have been affected by it in their lifetime. On the imminence of Jesus' expectation, see below, pp. 141-45.

entry into the kingdom of God with a physical body points to the afterlife being physical in nature, as there is no talk of a transformation.

Earthly kingdom of God

The kingdom of God and its synonyms

The kingdom of God has already often been mentioned. It is the most commonly used term for the kingdom proclaimed by Jesus, where the righteous will live for eternity.[67] The Gospel of Matthew, as a rule, uses "kingdom of the heavens" instead of the "kingdom of God."[68] "Heaven" here expresses the origin of the kingdom, and not its location. It is a kingdom that comes from heaven. Its heavenly constitution and government are probably placed in opposition to the earthly origin of the Roman Empire.[69] Jesus also calls this kingdom, "my father's kingdom,"[70] "his [God's] kingdom,"[71] "my kingdom,"[72] "the kingdom of their [the resurrected righteous] Father"[73] or simply "kingdom."[74]

Physical afterlife points to an earthly localization of the kingdom of God

The fact that the deceased are physically resurrected and continue to live on physically strongly indicates that the kingdom of God, into which the righteous will enter, will be situated on earth.

---

67. See, e.g., Matt 19:24; 21:31,43; Mark 1:14–15; 9:1,47; 10:14–15,23–25; 12:34; 14:25; 15:43; Luke 4:43; 6:20,7:28; 8:10; 9:2,11,27,60,62; 10:9,11; 13:28–29; 14:15; 17:20; 18:16–17,24–25; 19:11; 21:31; 22:16,18; 23:51.

68. See Matt 3:2; 4:17; 5:3,10,19–20; 7:21; 8:11; 10:7; 11:11–12; 13:11,24,31,33,44–45,47,52; 16:19; 18:1,3–4,23; 19:12,14,23; 20:1; 22:2; 23:13; 25:1. On the expression "kingdom of the heavens" (βασιλεία τῶν οὐρανῶν), see Allison, *Constructing Jesus*, 181–83, and comprehensively Pennington, *Heaven and Earth*.

69. See Pennington, *Heaven and Earth*, 296, 330, 336–37, 343. Pennington refutes the traditional theory of Gustaf Dalman, that with the expression "kingdom of the heavens," Matthew wanted to allude to the name of God reverently (see *Heaven and Earth*, 13–37).

70. Matt 26:29.

71. Luke 12:31.

72. Luke 22:30; John 18:36.

73. Matt 13:43.

74. Luke 22:29.

56 THE CONFUSION OF WORLDS

Judgment on earth

A further indicator for an earthly afterlife is the place of the Last Judgment that the Jesus of the Synoptics proclaims. It will occur on earth. The judge is, in so far as he is named, the Son of Man. He will *come* down from heaven[75] to earth for the judgment.[76] The people on earth will see him coming.[77] The best-known judgment scene can be found in the Gospel of Matthew:

> When the Son of Man comes in his glory, and all the angels with him, then he will sit on his throne of glory. Before him will be gathered all the nations, and he will separate people one from another as a shepherd separates the sheep from the goats. And he will place the sheep on his right, but the goats on the left. Then the King [the Son of Man] will say to those on his right, "Come, you who are blessed by my Father, inherit the kingdom prepared for you from the foundation of the world [. . .]." Then he will say to those on his left, "Depart from me, you cursed, into the eternal fire prepared for the devil and his angels [. . .]." And these will go away into eternal punishment, but the righteous into eternal life.[78]

---

75. See Matt 24:30; 26:64; Mark 13:26; 14:62; Luke 21:27; 22:69.

76. See, e.g., Matt 10:23; 16:27–28; 24:30,44; 25:31; 26:64; Mark 8:38; 13:26; 14:62; Luke 9:26; 12:40; 18:8; 21:27. See also Luke 12:49, where Jesus says, probably alluding to the fire of the last judgment: "I came to cast fire on the earth, and would that it were already kindled!" (ESV).

77. See Matt 16:28: "Truly, I say to you, there are some standing here who will not taste death until they see the Son of Man coming in his kingdom" (ESV); Matt 24:30: "All the tribes of the earth [. . .] will see the Son of Man coming on the clouds of heaven with power and great" (ESV; very similar Mark 13:26 und Luke 21:27); Mark 14:62: "And you will see the Son of Man seated at the right hand of Power, and coming with the clouds of heaven" (ESV; very similar Matt 26:64).

78. Matt 25:31–34,41,46 (ESV, modified). See also Matt 16:27: "For the Son of Man is about to come with his angels in the glory of his Father, and then he will repay each person according to what he has done" (ESV, modified); Matt 13:41–42: "The Son of Man will send his angels, and they will gather out of his kingdom all causes of sin and all law-breakers, and throw them into the fiery furnace. In that place there will be weeping and gnashing of teeth" (ESV). Also the threat of punishment of cities and countries speaks for an earthly judgment, see Matt 10:15: "Truly, I say to you, it will be more bearable on the day of judgment for the land of Sodom and Gomorrah than for that town"; Matt 11:22 (ESV; similar Luke 10:14): "But I tell you, it will be more bearable on the day of judgment for Tyre and Sidon than for you"; Matt 11:24 (ESV; similar Luke 10:12): "But I tell you that it will be more tolerable on the day of judgment for the land of Sodom than for you." For further passages on judgment, see the comprehensive list of relevant sayings of Jesus in Allison, *Resurrecting Jesus*, 63–67, which, however, does not distinguish between individual and general judgment.

As neither here nor in Jesus' other sayings is there any mention of people being carried from the place of judgment to an unearthly place—rather they *go* to their destination—, an earthly judgment also speaks for an earthly afterlife.

"On earth as it is in heaven"

In the Our Father, according to the tradition the only prayer that Jesus taught his disciples, the earth is the place where the eschatological kingdom of God is situated. There it says: "Your kingdom come, your will be done, on earth as it is in heaven."[79] The coming of the kingdom of God and God's will being done on earth, express the same thing in two different ways: the kingdom of God shall be established on earth.[80]

"To inherit the land"

In the Beatitudes of the Sermon on the Mount, whose promises have an eschatological character,[81] Jesus promises the meek that they will inherit τὴν γῆν.[82] This is clear evidence of an earthly postmortal life as ἡ γῆ means "earth," "land," "soil," or "region" but definitely not "heaven."[83] In the context of the beatitude concerned, γῆ probably has a territorial meaning. The expression used here, "to inherit the land," also occurs in the Old Testament, where the territorial meaning of the expression is, to my knowledge, undisputed. The Psalms prophesy: "But the meek shall inherit the land"[84]—"[T]hose blessed by the Lord shall inherit the land"[85]—"[H]e [Yahweh] will exalt you to inherit the land."[86]

Restoration of Israel with Zion as its center

The passages already quoted make clear that Jesus did not have the earth generally in view as the place of the kingdom of God—he is very specific

---

79. Matt 6:10 (ESV).
80. See on this passage, Davies and Allison, *Matthew*, 1:603–5.
81. For the eschatological character of the Beatitudes of Jesus see above, p. 53n62.
82. Matt 5:5.
83. See BDAG, 196.
84. Ps 37:11 (ESV).
85. Ps 37:22 (ESV).
86. Ps 37:34 (ESV). See also Isa 57:13; 65:9.

about the land of Israel and Jerusalem with Mount Zion at its center. Jesus promises his disciples, for example, that they will sit on twelve thrones (with him)[87] and will rule the twelve tribes of Israel.[88] This points to Jesus striving for the restoration of Israel,[89] further confirming the earthly localization of the kingdom of God in Jesus' view. This is also implied in Jesus' already cited prophecy of the eschatological pilgrimage to the kingdom of God: "[M]any will come from east and west and recline at table with Abraham, Isaac, and Jacob in the kingdom of heaven."[90] And: "[P]eople will come from east and west, and from north and south, and recline at table in the kingdom of God."[91] The saying about the ingathering of the chosen in the Gospel of Mark also belongs in this context: "[H]e will send out the angels and gather his elect from the four winds, from the ends of the earth to the ends of heaven."[92] An antecedent for this eschatological ingathering appears in Deuteronomy: "If your dispersion be from an end of the sky to an end of the sky, from there the LORD your God will gather you, and from there he will take you. And the LORD your God will bring you into the land that your fathers inherited, and you will inherit it."[93] The goal of the

---

87. According to all four Gospels, there was a label fixed on the cross of Jesus that said Jesus is "the King of the Jews" (see Matt 27:37; Mark 15:26; Luke 23:38; John 19:19). According to Allison, *Constructing Jesus*, 240, this is probably linked to the fact that Jesus did not distance himself from this title. See also Allison, *Constructing Jesus*, 303: "[W]hen he [Jesus] looked into the future, he saw thrones, including one for himself."

88. See Luke 22:28-30: "[Jesus said to his disciples:] You are those who have stayed with me in my trials, and I assign to you, as my Father assigned to me, a kingdom, that you may eat and drink at my table in my kingdom and sit on thrones ruling (κρίνοντες) the twelve tribes of Israel" (ESV, modified). Similarly, Matt 19:27-28. On the translation of κρίνοντες with "ruling" instead of the more common "judging," see Davies and Allison, *Matthew*, 3:55-56; Allison, "Eschatology of Jesus," 285; BDAG, 569.

89. See Sanders, *Jesus and Judaism*, 61-156; Allison: "Eschatology of Jesus," 285-86; Horsley, "Jesus and the Politics," 359-60. The Christian tradition tried to separate the kingdom-of-God proclamation of Jesus from the territorial expectations of the Jewish tradition (see Allison, *Constructing Jesus*, 175-76, and below, pp. 69n174, 101).

90. Matt 8:11 (ESV).

91. Luke 13:29 (ESV).

92. Mark 13:27 (ESV).

93. LXX Deut 30:4-5 (NETS); see Allison, "Eschatology of Jesus," 300, En. 9. There Allison also points out, that the phrase "from east and west and north and south" appears in various Jewish texts in connection with the return of the Jews to the promised land of Abraham, e.g., in Ps 107:2-3: "[T]he redeemed of the LORD [...], whom he [...] gathered in from the lands, from the east and from the west, from the north and from the south" (ESV) and in Isa 43:5-6: "I will bring your offspring from the east, and from the west I will gather you. I will say to the north, Give up, and to the south, Do not withhold; bring my sons from afar and my daughters from the end of the earth" (ESV).

eschatological pilgrimage will be Jerusalem with Mount Zion at its center.[94] In the Old Testament, it is explicitly given as the destination of the returning Jewish diaspora. The book of Zechariah promises: "This is what the Lord Almighty says: 'I will save my people from the countries of the east and the west. I will bring them back to live in Jerusalem; they will be my people, and I will be faithful and righteous to them as their God.'"[95] And according to the book of Isaiah "the ransomed of the Lord shall return and come to Zion with singing; everlasting joy shall be upon their heads; they shall obtain gladness and joy, and sorrow and sighing shall flee away."[96] Finally, his talk of a new temple also indicates Jerusalem as the center of the kingdom of God in Jesus' worldview.[97]

General resurrection

In Judaism, the restoration of Israel is connected with the resurrection of, if not all, at least a significant number of the dead.[98] According to the tradition, Jesus also advocated this doctrine, even if in the Synoptics it is rather incidental. Jesus' prophecies, for example, that the "queen of the South"—the legendary queen of Sheba, who was a contemporary of Solomon[99]—and the inhabitants of the long-lost city of Nineveh "will rise with this generation" at the Last Judgment.[100] He further prophesies that "many will [. . .] recline at table with Abraham, Isaac, and Jacob" in the kingdom of the Heavens, and further that "all the prophets"[101] will arrive there. This presupposes the res-

---

94. See Allison, *Constructing Jesus*, 42–43 fn. 56; Davies and Allison, *Matthew*, 2:26–29. Exegetes who do not understand the pilgrimage to the eschatological banquet not (only) as the return of the Jewish exiles but (also) as a gathering of the redeemed gentiles do not contest that the place of the eschatological gathering is earthly and situated in Jerusalem, or rather Zion (see, e.g., Bird, "Who Comes from East and West?").

95. Zech 8:7–8 (ESV).

96. Isa 35:10; 51:11 (ESV). According to the Old Testament prophecies Yahweh will one day live (again) in Zion and rule, see below, p. 103.

97. See Matt 26:61; Mark 14:58.

98. See above, pp. 30–35.

99. See 1 Kgs 10:1–13.

100. Matt 12:41–42; Luke 11:31–32. According to some translations, the queen of the South and the inhabitants of Nineveh will stand up at the Last Judgment *against* the current Jewish generation, to condemn them. That would also presuppose their resurrection. The preposition μετά with the genitive (ἀναστήσονται / ἐγερθήσεται [. . .] μετά [τῶν ἀνδρῶν] τῆς γενεᾶς ταύτης) means, however, "(together) with." On this passage, see Davies and Allison, *Matthew*, 2:357–59; Allison, "Eschatology of Jesus," 284; Allison, *Constructing Jesus*, 39–40 fn. 40.

101. Matt 8:11; Luke 13:28.

urrection of the patriarchs and the prophets. The Gospel of Luke has Jesus speak of a "resurrection of the just."[102] Also well-known is his discussion, described by all the Synoptics, with the Sadducees who deny the resurrection of the dead and seek to reduce it to absurdity.[103] They ask Jesus about a woman who was married to seven men: to whom will she be married after the resurrection? In his answer, Jesus initially simply presupposes the fact of the resurrection: "[W]hen they rise from the dead, they neither marry nor are given in marriage, but are like the angels which are in heaven."[104] But then he goes on to justify the doctrine *that* the dead will be resurrected with reference to scripture. In Mark, it is somewhat awkwardly expressed: "Concerning the dead, that they rise: Have you not read in the book of Moses [. . .]?"[105] The Gospel of Luke is more adeptly formulated: "That the dead are raised, also Moses made known."[106] The fact that Jesus speaks of "the dead" without qualification indicates a resurrection for all. In the Gospel of John, he speaks several times about the eschatological resurrection of the dead.[107] It remains slightly unclear whether "all those in the tombs"[108] will rise, or only those who believe in Jesus.[109] According to the New Testament, the doctrine of a universal resurrection seems to have been a central tenet of faith among the followers of Jesus,[110] and it has remained so in Christian churches to this day.[111] In my eyes, this strengthens the assumption that Jesus too taught a general resurrection.

---

102. Luke 14:14.
103. See Matt 22:23–33; Mark 12:18–27; Luke 20:27–40.
104. Mark 12:25 (ESV, modified).
105. Mark 12:26.
106. Luke 20:37.
107. See John 5:28–29; 6:39–40,44,54; see also 11:24–26.
108. See John 5:28–29: "[F]or an hour is coming when all who are in the tombs will hear his voice and come out, those who have done good to the resurrection of life, and those who have done evil to the resurrection of judgment" (ESV).
109. See, e.g., John 6:40: "For this is the will of my Father, that everyone who looks on the Son and believes in him should have eternal life, and I will raise him up on the last day" (ESV); John 6:54: "Whoever feeds on my flesh and drinks my blood has eternal life, and I will raise him up on the last day" (ESV).
110. See Acts 4:2; 17:18,32; 23:6; 24:15,21; Rom 4:17; 6:4–5,8; 8:11; 1 Cor 15:12–57; Phil 3:11; 1 Thess 4:13–14; Heb 6:2; Rev 20:4–6,12–13. See also the conclusion from Hoffmann, "Auferstehung," 451: "In accordance with statements of contemporary apocalypticism, the Jesus tradition thus shares the expectation of the resurrection of the righteous and the sinners."
111. See below, pp. 87–89.

Contextual indications

Jesus of Nazareth knew the biblical story of the garden of Eden and was thus familiar with the idea of an eternal, paradisiacal life on earth.[112] That idea, however, did not concern a *post-mortal* life.[113] Furthermore, he seems to have been part of a tradition which believed in resurrection and an eternal afterlife in a kingdom of God on earth. One can find echoes from Daniel and from the First Enoch in the words of Jesus, especially from the Book of Parables, in which these things are taught.[114] Tradition says little of John the Baptist, who baptized Jesus, except that he proclaimed an imminent eschatological judgment, a redeemer coming to earth, and a kingdom of God.[115] Finally, Jesus' followers proclaimed a physical resurrection after the death of Jesus, as evidenced by the narratives of the empty tomb.[116] The expectation of an eternal, earthly kingdom of God, however, soon faded in Christianity. Concepts of a post-mortal transformation and a non-earthly afterlife gained in significance.[117]

Objections to the preceding reconstruction of the teachings of Jesus

Afterlife of the person without the physical body?

In the Gospel of Matthew, Jesus says: "And do not fear those who kill the body but cannot kill the soul. Rather fear him who can destroy both soul

---

112. See Gen 2:4—3:24, and the words of Jesus referring to Gen 2:24 in Mark 10:7–8; Matt 19:5.

113. See above, p. 15.

114. See the references in McDonald, "Scriptures of Jesus," 837–39, 859, 861–61, and in particular the parallels between Dan 12:3 and Matt 13:43 with regard to the luminescence of the resurrected righteous, and between 1 En. 45:3; 51:3; 55:4; 61:8; 62:2–3,5; 69:27,29 and Matt 19:28; 25:31 with regard to the "Son of Man" and the "chosen one," who will sit on the "throne of glory" at the eschatological judgment. For the potential influence of the thoughts of the Book of Parables on Jesus and on the image of the Jesus of the Gospels, see below, pp. 144–45.

115. See Matt 3:1–12; Mark 1:3–8; Luke 3:2–18. According to Erich Gräßer, it is "historically hardly doubtable that Jesus took his point of departure from the Baptist's proclamation of an imminent eschaton" (*Problem der Parusieverzögerung*, xvii; trans. S. Kühne). Allison also underlines the continuity between John the Baptist and Jesus (see Allison, *Constructing Jesus*, 204–20).

116. See below, pp. 83–85.

117. See below, pp. 93–108.

and body in hell."¹¹⁸ One might be tempted to deduce from this passage an afterlife of the person independent from the body. Nothing, however, is said of the consciousness of the soul or of its ability to act, when separated from the body. Moreover, soul and person need not be identical. If the *soul* can live on independent of the physical body, this does not necessarily mean that the *person* survives without the physical body. It thus remains doubtful whether Jesus implies here an afterlife of the person, independent of a physical body.

Nor do the two sayings with which Jesus soothes the disciples' fear of ghosts or spirits unambiguously attribute him the belief in the existence of a human *person* independent of a physical body. The first of the two of Jesus' sayings is found in connection with his "walking on water": "But when the disciples saw him walking on the sea, they were terrified, and said, 'It is a ghost!' (φάντασμα) and they cried out in fear."¹¹⁹ Jesus reassures them with the words, "it is I myself."¹²⁰ If the disciples had believed that the person Jesus could also have been a ghost (φάντασμά), he wouldn't have been able to convince them by simply saying "it's me" that he was not one. It would not have been the fact that they were seeing *him* that would have needed clarification but that he was *not a ghost*. This is similarly the case for the other saying. At the sight of his post-mortem apparition his disciples "were terrified and frightened and thought they saw a spirit (πνεῦμα)."¹²¹ Jesus does not reassure them by saying that he is *not a spirit*, but he says instead: "See my hands and my feet, that it is I myself."¹²² From this I conclude that neither Jesus nor the disciples assumed that Jesus "himself," the person Jesus, could be a pure spirit without physical hands and feet. Allison is right when he states that here the concept of a bodiless spirit—or rather: a ghost without a physical body, as Jesus must have had a body of some kind for him to be visible—is suggested.¹²³ But the crucial question is whether the concept of a *person* without a physical body is articulated. I am not convinced here by the theory that "it is myself" does not serve as a self-identification of Jesus but is rather a revelatory wording by which Jesus expresses his godliness or messiahship.¹²⁴

---

118. Matt 10:28 (ESV).
119. Matt 14:26; similar Mark 6:49.
120. Matt 14:27; Mark 6:50.
121. Luke 24:37 (ESV, modified).
122. Luke 24:39 (ESV).
123. See Allison, *Night Comes*, 33; Allison, "Scriptural Background," 180.
124. Cf. Davies and Allison, *Matthew*, 2:506; Förster, "Selbstoffenbarung und Identität," 83; Roose, "Ich-bin-Worte."

Afterlife without a physical body in the otherworld

In the Gospel of Luke, there are two passages in which Jesus speaks of an already *existing otherworld parallel to the earthly world*, where the deceased live. The first is the parable of the rich man and Lazarus, who directly following their deaths come respectively into Hades and Abraham's bosom.[125] Though Luke seems to be more concerned with their eschatological destiny than with an intermediary state,[126] a later resurrection is not ruled out.[127] In Jewish scriptures from Hellenistic Roman times, intermediary afterlife states were definitely taught.[128] The other passage is Jesus' word to a repentant man crucified with him: "Truly, I say to you, today you will be with me in paradise."[129] This would mean that, as in the parable of the rich man and Lazarus, there is an afterlife immediately after death without a physical body, in another world.[130] As discussed, this would not, however, necessarily contradict the belief in resurrection if one understands this afterlife in paradise to be an intermediary state. Moreover, this saying may not go back to Jesus. According to Luke's own representation, the followers of Jesus were standing too far away from the cross to have been able to understand the words

---

125. See Luke 16:19–31: "There was a rich man who was clothed in purple and fine linen and who feasted sumptuously every day. And at his gate was laid a poor man named Lazarus, covered with sores, who desired to be fed with what fell from the rich man's table. Moreover, even the dogs came and licked his sores. The poor man died and was carried by the angels to Abraham's side. The rich man also died and was buried, and in Hades, being in torment, he lifted up his eyes and saw Abraham far off and Lazarus at his side. And he called out, 'Father Abraham, have mercy on me, and send Lazarus to dip the end of his finger in water and cool my tongue, for I am in anguish in this flame.' But Abraham said, 'Child, remember that you in your lifetime received your good things, and Lazarus in like manner bad things; but now he is comforted here, and you are in anguish. And besides all this, between us and you a great chasm has been fixed, in order that those who would pass from here to you may not be able, and none may cross from there to us.' And he said, 'Then I beg you, father, to send him to my father's house—for I have five brothers—so that he may warn them, lest they also come into this place of torment.' But Abraham said, 'They have Moses and the Prophets; let them hear them.' And he said, 'No, father Abraham, but if someone goes to them from the dead, they will repent.' He said to him, 'If they do not hear Moses and the Prophets, neither will they be convinced if someone should rise from the dead'" (ESV).

126. So Lehtipuu, *Afterlife Imagery*, 275, 302–3; *CCC* 1021.

127. According to most manuscripts, Jesus speaks of resurrection in the last verse of this parable (Luke 16:31). In the context of the parable this means that a deceased person returns from an otherworld place to earth.

128. See, e.g., 1 En. 22; 4 Ezra 7:78–99; 2 Bar. 30:2–5. See above, pp. 35, 40.

129. Luke 23:43 (ESV).

130. See for contemporary Jewish concepts of paradise, Lehtipuu, *Afterlife Imagery*, 277–284.

of Jesus if spoken at a normal volume.[131] In addition, this saying of Jesus is only handed down by Luke and his version of the scene contradicts those of both Matthew and Mark. According to them, those being crucified with Jesus mocked him, and neither of them showed repentance.[132]

If Jesus really believed, as the Zoroastrians or the Greeks, that the soul separates from the body at death and goes to the otherworld, he would most likely have referred to retrieving the soul from the otherworld when speaking of his miraculous revivifications. But nothing of the sort has been handed down. Instead, when referring to revivifications, he talks mostly about "waking up" (ἐγείρω), which would imply mental inactivity or at least a reduced state of consciousness.[133] If Jesus imagined his deceased friend Lazarus to be in paradise or in the bosom of Abraham, it would not fit with his talking of "waking him from sleep" (ἐξυπνίζω).[134] In this context it would also appear difficult to understand, and appear really selfish, that Jesus becomes almost angry,[135] and tries with all his force to bring Lazarus back from paradise to this comparably bleak, earthly life. Jesus' behavior better fits with him assuming that in death Lazarus sank into an unconscious and lifeless state, from where he had to be saved.

Physical resurrection to an eternal life vs. an eternal life that believers already possess

In the sayings of Jesus in the Gospel of John, at first glance there seems to be a conflict between the resurrection on the judgment day and an eternal life that believers already now possess through their faith in Jesus.[136] On the one hand, Jesus says: "An hour is coming when all who are in the tombs will hear his voice and come out, those who have done good to the resurrection of life, and those who have done evil to the resurrection of judgment."[137] On

---

131. See Luke 23:49, and below, p. 138.

132. See Matt 27:44; Mark 15:32; see also Lehtipuu, *Afterlife Imagery*, 255, whereupon the saying of Jesus in Luke 12:43 is an invention of the Gospel of Luke.

133. See above, p. 49. ἐγείρω also has the meaning of raising up (see above, p. 49–50), but the meaning of waking up is probably the primary one and has been preserved in numerous translations. But see van der Horst, *Ancient Jewish Epitaphs*, 117: "sleep" can also stand for a blissful state in paradise.

134. See John 11:11; ἐξυπνίζω comes from ὕπνος (sleep).

135. Twice (John 11:33,38) the verb ἐμβριμάομαι is used, possibly with the meaning "to be angry" (cf. BDAG, 322), used to describe Jesus' state of mind when faced with Lazarus's death.

136. See John 3:36; 5:24.

137. John 5:28–29 (ESV); see also John 5:21,25; 11:23–25,27.

the other hand, he promises: "Whoever believes in the Son *has* eternal life."[138] He also says: "[W]hoever hears my word and believes him who sent me *has* eternal life."[139] But there is a saying of Jesus in John that combines the resurrection of the dead on the last day with the present possession of eternal life: "The one who eats my flesh and drinks my blood has eternal life, and I will raise him upon the last day."[140] I therefore cannot see any contradiction between the doctrine of an eternal life already possessed by his believers and the doctrine of a future physical resurrection.[141] I understand these sayings of Jesus more in the sense that the future resurrection to eternal life is assured by a connection with Jesus already existing now through faith and mystically eating his flesh and drinking his blood.[142] It is understandable then when Jesus says the one who believes in him will live "even if he dies."[143] That the Jesus of the Gospel of John believes in a physical resurrection is also proved by the word about the dead coming out of the grave.[144] The evangelist, moreover, does not appear to believe in an otherworldly, intermediary state, or else he would not say that the dead will hear his voice *in the grave*.[145] The personal self appears to be located in the grave and not in the otherworld. The author of the Gospel of John undoubtedly affirms, outside the words of Jesus, the possibility of a physical resurrection, both by his classification of the revival of Lazarus as a resurrection from the dead,[146] and by his strong emphasis on the emptiness of the tomb of Jesus.[147]

---

138. John 3:36 (ESV, emphasis added).

139. John 5:24 (ESV, emphasis added); see also John 3:16,18; 6:47. The eschatological judgment appears on the one hand to have been fulfilled through the incarnation of Jesus (see John 3:18–19), although on the other hand there is talk of an eschatological "resurrection of judgment" (John 5:29 ESV).

140. John 6:54.

141. See also John 11:25: "Whoever believes in me will live, even if they should die."

142. See John 6:56: "Whoever feeds on my flesh and drinks my blood abides in me, and I in him" (ESV); see on "Jesuphagy" in the Gospel of John, Kobel, *Dining with John*, 236–37, 247. In addition, Jesus mentions being reborn of water and the Spirit (see John 3:5), an allusion to baptism as a requirement for acquiring eternal life (see Rein, "Johannesevangelium," 167 with fn. 46).

143. John 11:25.

144. See John 5:29.

145. See John 5:28.

146. See John 12:1,9,17.

147. John 20:1–9.

Return of the soul into the light

The apocryphal Gospel of Thomas teaches the return of the soul into the light. It mentions neither the resurrection of Jesus, nor the resurrection of other persons, nor an eternal life, but tells only how not to die. It is not faith that is decisive for whether one "will not taste death,"[148] but awareness.[149] "To not taste death" does not mean, as in the Synoptics, that the physical body does not die and that the person lives on in it forever.[150] On the contrary, the earthly-physical is radically rejected.[151] The aim is the freeing of the soul from the body in death and its return[152] to the eternal, supramundane light of God. The Jesus of the Gospel of Thomas even gives the disciples advice as to what they should say to the Archons, the seven malevolent rulers of the planets, should they stand in their way when they make their journey through the planetary spheres towards the light.

> Jesus said, "Blessed are the solitary and elect, for you will find the kingdom. For you are from it, and you will return there again."
> Jesus said, "If they [the Archons] say to you, 'From where have you come?', say to them, 'We have come from the light, where the light came into being all of its own accord.' [. . .] If they say to you, 'Is it you?', say, 'We are its children and we are the elect of the living Father.'"[153]

---

148. Gos. Thom. 1, 18, 19, 85. This turn of phrase plays on the eschatological teaching of Jesus in Mark 9:1: "Truly, I say to you, there are some standing here who will not taste death until they see the kingdom of God after it has come with power" (ESV; similar Matt 16:28; Luke 9:27; see also John 8:52); see Allison, *Constructing Jesus*, 126.

149. See Gos. Thom, Prologue and Logion 1: "These are the secret sayings which the living Jesus spoke, and Didymus Judas Thomas wrote them down. And he said, 'Whoever finds the interpretation of these sayings will not taste death'" (trans. Gathercole, *Gospel of Thomas*, 189, 195).

150. See Gathercole, *Gospel of Thomas*, 196–97.

151. See Popkes, *Menschenbild des Thomasevangeliums*, 354: According to the Gospel of Thomas "the corporeal constitution of human existence was created by the inferior powers of the lower cosmos." To be able to return to the light from which originated the "spirit-soul component of their existence," the disciples must "radically differentiate [it] from its earthly-corporeal constitution (EvThom 56; 80; 87; 112)." For this purpose, they must "refrain from reproduction, as in this way they perpetuate their physical existence (EvThom 79,3). They must overcome the difference between masculinity and femininity to be able to return to the androgynous unity from which they originate (EvThom 22,4f; 114 etc.). They must learn 'to pass by the world' (EvThom 42), to find their way back home" (trans. S. Kühne).

152. On the pre-existence of the disciples in the eternal light, see Popkes, *Menschenbild des Thomasevangeliums*, 234–38.

153. Gos. Thom. 49:1–50:2 (trans. Gathercole, *Gospel of Thomas*, 404, 406). On this passage, see Tornau, "Die neuplatonische Kritik," 344–45: "The New Testament

The kingdom of God of the canonical Gospels is identified in the Gospel of Thomas with this otherworldly kingdom of light.[154] The present cosmos of heaven and earth is ultimately destroyed, a fact which, however, can no longer affect the souls that have returned to the transcendental light.[155] These ideas are a far cry from what seems compatible with the bulk of Jesus' words in the Synoptic Gospels and with the contemporary context of Jesus.

No earthly-spatial conception of the kingdom of God

A further objection to my reconstruction of the doctrine of Jesus of the Gospels is that he did not teach an earthly-spatial conception of the kingdom of God. Some theologians maintain that the expression, βασιλεία τοῦ θεοῦ, that I have translated as "kingdom of God," in fact means rather God's power and activity as ruler.[156] Dale Allison has, however, comprehensively established the spatial aspect of βασιλεία τοῦ θεοῦ.[157] In addition to the indications of an earthly, spatial kingdom of God I presented above—for example, the fact that the kingdom of God is called "the land," or the prophecy of the eschatological pilgrimage to Zion, the center of the kingdom of God—I would like to invoke just three more points from Allison's abundance of arguments. Firstly, Jesus talks about "entering the kingdom of God."[158] This can also occur in negative form, when it is said that due to moral transgressions someone will not be allowed to enter the promised kingdom or land.[159] Here the kingdom of God is obviously something spatial. What could it mean to be able to "enter into" the power of God or into

---

'kingdom' becomes here the realm of light that the Gnostics originally belong to and that they will return to. The condition for this return, in addition to being chosen, is [. . .] the 'taking off' of the bodily 'clothes' and the liberation of the soul from foreign, contaminating accessories that keep them in the world. Logion 50 then describes the modalities of the ascent. Jesus envisages the situation familiar to Gnosticism that the disciples, on their way through the [higher] worlds [back to the light], are stopped by the Archons and questioned about their origin and their destination" (trans. S. Kühne). See also comprehensively Gathercole, *Gospel of Thomas*, 404–10.

154. See Gathercole, *Gospel of Thomas*, 145–46: Thomas imagined the kingdom of God as a pre-existing, paradisiacal kingdom of light. It was certainly not a geographical place in this cosmos.

155. See Gos. Thom. 11:1–2; 111, and also Gathercole, *Gospel of Thomas*, 247; 598–601; Gathercole, "'Heavens,'" 296–99, 302.

156. See Allison, *Constructing Jesus*, 168–69 with fn. 597.

157. See Allison, *Constructing Jesus*, 164–204.

158. See Allison, *Constructing Jesus*, 179, and Matt 5:20; 7:21; 23:13; Mark 9:47; 10:15,23–25.

159. See Allison, *Constructing Jesus*, 180–1, and Matt 5:20; 7:21; 23:13; Mark 10:15.

his rule? Allison suspects that this turn of phrase is based on the expression "enter the land (of Canaan)" in Old Testament and extra-canonical Jewish scriptures.[160] This would further strengthen the interpretation of a spatial, territorial kingdom of God.[161] Secondly, Jesus prophesies that angels will remove the wicked from the kingdom of God and throw them into the furnace of fire. This image is obviously spatial. Semantically it seems hardly possible to remove someone from a non-spatial rule of God.[162] Thirdly, according to the sayings of Jesus, a particular group will possess or inherit the kingdom of God.[163] A country can be owned or inherited, but can people own or inherit God's power or rule?[164] Furthermore, the spatial nature of the kingdom of God is not undone by the fact that "kingdom of God" and "eternal life" are almost synonymous in the Synoptics.[165] On the contrary, an "eternal life" is also a designation for a place. In the phrase "to enter eternal life," the same verb is used (εἰσέρχομαι) as for the entering the kingdom of God.[166] This speaks against a metaphorical sense for εἰσέρχομαι with regard to eternal life.[167] Another issue regarding (eternal) life and the kingdom of God concerns the verb "inherit" (κληρονομέω). One can *inherit* the promised life,[168] just as one can *inherit* the promised land or the kingdom of God after the Last Judgment.[169] The understanding of eternal life

---

160. See Allison, *Constructing Jesus*, 180–1, and LXX Exod 12:25 ; Lev 19:23, Num 15:2; Deut 1:8; 4:1; 6:18; 16:20; 27:3; Judg 18:9; As. Mos. 2:1; T. Levi 12:5; cf. Num 20:24; Deut 4:21; Ezek 13:9; 20:38. See also Allison, *Constructing Jesus*, 191–92, 195–96, for parallels in the rabbinic literature.

161. See Allison, *Constructing Jesus*, 179–81.

162. See Matt 13:41–42, and thereto Allison, *Constructing Jesus*, 178–79.

163. See Matt 5:3,5,10; 25:34; Mark 10:14; Luke 6:20; cf. Num 33:54; Deut 1:8; 6:18; 16:20; Josh 1:6; Ps 37:9,11,22,29,34; Tob 4:12; Allison, *Constructing Jesus*, 179, 181–83, 196.

164. See Allison, *Constructing Jesus*, 179. See also his discussion of the wording of Jesus in Matt 25:34 that the kingdom that the righteous will inherit will be "prepared [for them] from the foundation of the world": one can prepare a place or a country for someone, but in what sense could this be said of God's rule? (*Constructing Jesus*, 179).

165. See Allison, *Constructing Jesus*, 186–89.

166. See Matt 18:8–9; 19:17; on entering (eternal) life, Mark 9:43,45; on entering the kingdom of God, or heaven: Matt 5:20; 7:21; 18:3; 19:23; Mark 9:47; 10:23–24; Luke 18:24–25. (Eternal) life and the kingdom of God are directly interchangeable in Mark 9:43,45; Matt 18:9 (to enter life) and Mark 9:47 (to enter the kingdom of God). In the Gospel of John, the expression "kingdom of God" is replaced by "(eternal) life" (see Allison, *Constructing Jesus*, 188).

167. See also Allison, *Constructing Jesus*, 189 for the equation of the "life of the coming world" and "coming world" in Jewish sources.

168. See Matt 19:29; Luke 10:25; 18:18.

169. See Matt 5:5; 25:34.

as a spatial, localized area of existence is present in Jesus' announcement that, after the Last Judgment, the cursed will *go away* (ἀπέρχομαι) from the place of court to their place of punishment, the eternal fire, while the chosen will *go* to eternal life.[170] One can be thrown into the eternal fire.[171] This place of punishment is also referred to as Gehenna[172] or as the furnace of fire.[173] Allison comes to the conclusion that the expression βασιλεία τοῦ Θεοῦ in the Synoptics refers to "a realm as well as a reign; it is a place and a time yet to come in which God will reign supreme."[174]

Presence of the kingdom of God

Against the interpretation of the kingdom of God as the place of future eternal life, some also put forward that Jesus proclaimed the kingdom of God to be *present*.[175] However, essential elements of the eschatology of the Synoptic Jesus, such as the resurrection of the dead, the Last Judgment, victory over evil, the regathering of the peoples of Israel to Zion, the eschatological banquet in the kingdom of God, and the life without suffering and death of the righteous, still without a doubt lie in the future. There is, however, a saying of Jesus in the Gospel of Luke that, according to predominant opinion, unequivocally expresses the presence of the kingdom of God:[176] ἡ βασιλεία τοῦ Θεοῦ ἐντὸς ὑμῶν ἐστιν.[177] These days it is often translated as: "the kingdom of God is in the midst of you." But a purely presentist understanding of the kingdom of God cannot be grounded on this passage, for immediately afterwards Jesus speaks in detail about the future coming of the Son of Man that will precede the eschatological judgment and, with that, also the king-

---

170. See Matt 25:46; Mark 9:43.

171. See Matt 5:29; 13:42,50; 18:8–9; Mark 9:45,47; Luke 12:5.

172. See Matt 5:22,29–30; 10:28; 18:9; 23:15,33; Mark 9:43,45,47; Luke 12:5.

173. See Matt 13:42,50.

174. Allison, *Constructing Jesus*, 201. The ambiguity of βασιλεία, among other things, could be linked with the fact that prior to the emergence of modern territorial states with exact borders, rule was defined not exclusively through territory but also through *personal* characteristics such as tribal affiliation. For this reason, it is probably appropriate not to reduce βασιλεία to "ruled territory." A βασιλεία totally without "ruled territory" would however be something like a king without a country. The refusal of Christian theologians to allocate a spatial dimension to the kingdom of God probably rests not simply of philological reasons, but is also linked to the fact that an earthly-territorial kingdom of God has not come and, moreover, is hardly imaginable, so that it would be embarrassing to attribute an expectation of this kind to Jesus.

175. See Lindemann, "Herrschaft Gottes / Reich Gottes," 202.

176. See Strobel, "Passa-Erwartung," 158.

177. Luke 17:21.

dom of God.[178] One might perhaps entertain the idea that Jesus regarded his miracles as flashes of the reality of the kingdom of God without it having already unfolded fully.[179] Even more problematic than the time aspect of the kingdom of God is its localization in this saying. "ἐντὸς ὑμῶν ἐστιν" was traditionally translated with "within you," which perhaps better complies with the Greek original than "in the midst of you."[180] Situating the kingdom of God within people does not rule out that it simultaneously also possesses an inter-subjective, earthly-spatial dimension. Even in the Gospel of Thomas, where it is likewise said that the kingdom of God is in the disciples, an external, spatial aspect to the kingdom is also suggested.[181]

Afterlife in heaven

From one of the few suggestions of the Gospel of John about the place of the afterlife, one can conclude that at least Jesus' disciples will live with him in heaven. He says to them that he will (after his death) go to his Father,[182] so to heaven. They cannot follow him there now.[183] But he will return[184] and take them with him so that they may also be where he is.[185] This life with

---

178. See Luke 17:22–37.

179. See also below, p. 125 and Matt 12:28; Luke 11:20. See on this passage and on the presence of the kingdom of God generally, Allison, *Constructing Jesus*, 98–116; see also Sanders, *Jesus and Judaism*, 123–56.

180. See the translations of the Vulgate (*regnum Dei intra vos est*), Luther, *Biblia*, 290a ("Das reich Gottes ist inwendig in euch"), and the King James Version ("the kingdom of God is within you"). The translation common today, "in the midst of you" probably goes back to Johannes Weiß' criticism of the traditional translation, "within you" (so Holmén, "Alternatives of the Kingdom," 206; see Weiss, *Predigt Jesu*, 85). On the translation problem comprehensively, see Holmén, "Alternatives of the Kingdom." According to Holmén, a philologically correct alternative to "within you" would be "within the circle of the specific group of people," which here would address the Pharisees. But such an interpretation seems very implausible. Weiß admits the philological difficulties with the translation of ἐντὸς ὑμῶν as "in the midst of you" and writes that ἐν μέσῳ would be more accurate (see *Predigt Jesu*, 86). Weder, *Gegenwart und Gottesherrschaft*, 39 translates ἐντὸς ὑμῶν by "within your realm of experience," Lindemann, "Herrschaft Gottes / Reich Gottes," 205 with "at your disposal"; similar Scriba, *Echtheitskriterien der Jesus-Forschung*, 78.

181. See Gos. Thom. 3:3: "But the Kingdom is inside you and outside of you"; 113:4: "[T]he Kingdom of the Father is spread out upon the earth" (trans. Gathercole, *Gospel of Thomas*, 207, 603).

182. See John 7:33; 14:12,28; 16:5,10,28.

183. See John 7:34; 13:33,36.

184. See John 14:3,18,28.

185. See John 14:3.

Jesus has an obvious spatial character because Jesus says that in his father's house are many rooms, and he will go there and prepare a place for the disciples.[186] Jesus' words in the Gospel of John on the future resurrection of all dead on the last day[187] and the judgment,[188] seem to stand in tension with a post-mortal existence in heaven.

"Heaven and earth will pass away"

The Gospels contain two of Jesus' sayings on the passing away of heaven and earth. "But it is easier for heaven and earth to pass away than for one dot of the Law to become void."[189] And: "Heaven and earth will pass away, but my words will not pass away."[190] At first glance, one could conclude from this that the afterlife according to Jesus would no longer be earthly because the earth will no longer exist. But then also the land promised to the meek by Jesus in the Sermon on the Mount would no longer exist, let alone Jerusalem and Mount Zion, which were to form the center of the kingdom of God for Jesus.[191] Jesus uses the wording of the passing away of heaven and earth, however, apparently not primarily to indicate eschatological events, but to emphasize the permanence of the law or his own words.[192] His concrete eschatological prophecies also refer to persecutions, wars and famines on earth and astronomical phenomena like solar and lunar eclipses, as well

---

186. See John 14:2–3: "In my Father's house are many rooms. [. . .] I go to prepare a place for you. And if I go and prepare a place for you, I will come again and will take you to myself, that where I am you may be also" (ESV, modified).

187. See John 6:39–40,44,54; see also 11:24–26.

188. See, in particular, John 5:24,27; 12:48. In the Gospel of John there are also clear traces of a criticism and reinterpretation of the apocalyptic teachings of Jesus, see Allison, *Constructing Jesus*, 131–32 with reference to John 2:19–22; 21:20–23. The expression, "kingdom of God," is used by Jesus in the Gospel of John only twice (3:3,5). The kingdom of God in John also has no purely spiritual character as one can see and enter it. Otherwise it is transformed into "eternal life" (ζωή αἰώνιος), which, however, shares many features with the kingdom of God in the Synoptics (see Allison, *Constructing Jesus*, 188), see also above, p. 68n166. When Jesus says to Pilate in John 18:36: "ἡ βασιλεία ἡ ἐμὴ οὐκ ἔστιν ἐκ τοῦ κόσμου τούτου," βασιλεία seems primarily to mean "rule" or "kingly power," and οὐκ ἔστιν ἐκ τοῦ κόσμου τούτου something like "not have an origin in this world." It does not follow from this, however, that βασιλεία has no spatial dimension.

189. Luke 16:17 (ESV); similar Matt 5:18.

190. Mark 13:31 (ESV); similar Matt 24:35; Luke 21:33.

191. See above, pp. 57–59.

192. See Davies and Allison, *Matthew*, 1:490.

as meteorite showers,[193] but not to the annihilation of heaven and earth.[194] Never does he speak of a new earth. Only once does the word παλιγγενεσία, which means "regeneration" or "renewal," come up in his promises. The context suggests that it probably refers to the restoration of Israel.[195]

In Judaism, the idea of the transience of heaven and earth was a common conviction.[196] It seems to refer to the destruction of things on earth rather than to the complete disappearance of the earth itself. When a new world is spoken about, this does not apparently mean the creation of a whole new cosmic entity, but rather the *restoration* of something already existent.[197] Through this restoration, life, especially that of the people of Israel, seems to continue in a better but quite earthly form.[198] The topog-

---

193. See Mark 13:24–25: "But in those days, after that tribulation, the sun will be darkened, and the moon will not give its light, and the stars will be falling from heaven" (ESV); very similar Matt 24:29; in a somewhat toned-down version it appears in the parallel passage Luke 21:25: "And there will be signs in sun and moon and stars, and on the earth distress of nations in perplexity because of the roaring of the sea and the waves" (ESV); see also Isa 13:10; 34:4; Ezek 32:7–8; Joel 2:10; 3:4; 4:15; Acts 2:20; Rev 6:12–13. That this concerns stars and meteorite showers is suggested by Rev 6:13: "And the stars of the sky fell to the earth as the fig tree sheds its winter fruit when shaken by a gale" (ESV). The imagery suggests that the falling stars are innumerable, rather small, and light objects; see Drößler, *Weltuntergang*, 127; see also Isa 34:4. Incidentally, the fact that a lunar eclipse always takes place when the moon is full and the moon turns reddish is quite accurately reproduced in Rev 6:12. "[T]he full moon (σελήνη ὅλη) became like blood" (ESV); see also similarly Joel 2:31: "The sun shall be turned to darkness, and the moon to blood, before the great and awesome day of the Lord comes" (ESV) and the Joel quotation in Acts 2:20.

194. Allison shares the opinion that Jesus did not expect the end of the world but rather the restoration of a decaying one (see *Constructing Jesus*, 32 fn. 7).

195. See Matt 19:28: "Truly, I say to you, at the renewal (ἐν τῇ παλιγγενεσίᾳ), when the Son of Man will sit on his throne of glory, you who have followed me will also sit on twelve thrones, ruling the twelve tribes of Israel" (ESV, modified). For the translation of this passage, see also above, p. 58n88. In the parallel passage in Luke 22:30, Jesus does not say "at the renewal," but "in my kingdom."

196. See Davies and Allison, *Matthew*, 3:368 with fn. 283, where they refer to, among other texts, Gen 8:22: "While the earth remains, seedtime and harvest, cold and heat, summer and winter, day and night, shall not cease" (ESV); Ps 102:25–27: "Of old you [God] laid the foundation of the earth, and the heavens are the work of your hands. They will perish, but you will remain; they will all wear out like a garment. You will change them like a robe, and they will pass away, but you are the same, and your years have no end" (ESV); Isa 51:6: "[F]or the heavens vanish like smoke, the earth will wear out like a garment, and they who dwell in it will die in like manner; but my [God's] salvation will be forever, and my righteousness will never be dismayed" (ESV); Isa 65:17: "For behold, I [God] create new heavens and a new earth, and the former things shall not be remembered or come into mind."

197. See Isa 65:17–25.

198. In the vision of the new earth in Isaiah 65:17–25, there will be no more weeping

raphy of Israel with Jerusalem and its holy mount seems to remain: "[I]n Mount Zion and in Jerusalem there shall be deliverance" in the midst of eschatological destruction, promises the book of Joel.[199] In this tradition, Jesus too seems to have hoped for a restored Israel.[200] According to Richard Horsley, just as the Jewish apocalyptics of the Hellenistic-Roman times in general, he sought, not "the end of the world, [. . . but] the end of the empire."[201] "Empire" refers primarily to the occupying powers that oppressed and exploited Israel, firstly the Seleucid Empire, and later, at the time of Jesus, the Roman Empire and its vassals.

Conclusion

From the discussion of the objections to my view of Jesus' conception of the afterlife it can be concluded that the tradition of Jesus' teachings that actually contradict a physical resurrection and an earthly kingdom of God are minimal and tend to be of a later date. Therefore, the reconstruction of the relevant doctrines of Jesus is not seriously called into question.[202]

Otherworldly elements of the afterlife

As in Zoroastrianism, in the book of Daniel, and in the Book of Parables from the First Enoch, the afterlife in the teachings of Jesus is situated on earth but possesses, as well as physical and this-worldly characteristics, also otherworldly attributes.

Eternal life

An unequivocal otherworldly element is the eternity of life in the kingdom of God. As already mentioned, according to our cosmological and biological knowledge, an eternal life on earth can be ruled out.[203] It could

---

or cries of distress. Furthermore, the animals will live in peace. But although the people will grow significantly older than up to now, they will continue to die. They will bear children, build houses and cultivate wine.

199. Joel 2:32 (NKJV).

200. See above, pp. 57–59.

201. Horsley, *Revolt of the Scribes*, 207.

202. See also, generally, the comprehensive discussion of the eschatology of Jesus in Allison, *Constructing Jesus*, 31–220; Allison, *Jesus of Nazareth*, 95–171.

203. See above, pp. 1–2.

only be realized in another world. Although the eternal life in Jesus' teachings of the Synoptic Gospels is only rarely expressed, it is undisputed that the Synoptic Jesus proclaimed an eternal life. The resurrected will not only no longer die, but "they *cannot* die anymore," says Jesus in the Gospel of Luke.[204] In the Gospel of Matthew, he says, that after the final judgment, the condemned "will go away into eternal punishment, but the righteous into eternal life."[205] In the Gospels of Mark and Luke, Jesus promises those who follow him "in the age to come eternal life"[206] or—in the wording in the Gospel of Matthew—that they will "inherit eternal life."[207] Sometimes Jesus speaks simply of "life" (ζωή), when he means "eternal life" (ζωή αἰώνιος).[208] Replying to a person's question: "Teacher, what good deed must I do to have *eternal life*?" Jesus answers: "If you would enter *life*, keep the commandments."[209] Those condemned at the Last Judgment will also apparently exist for eternity as they will receive an "eternal punishment."[210] It is not a contradiction that they do not share in eternal life. "Eternal life" has an emphatic meaning that goes beyond an infinite continuation of existence and includes the fullness of life.[211]

A life without poverty, hunger, or tears

In the beatitudes of the Sermon on the Plain in the Gospel of Luke, Jesus promises the chosen a life in the kingdom of God without poverty, hunger, or tears: "Blissfully happy (μακάριοι) are you who are poor, for yours is the kingdom of God.[212] Blissfully happy are you who are hungry now, for you shall be satisfied. Blissfully happy are you who weep now, for you shall

---

204. Luke 20:36 (ESV, emphasis added).
205. Matt 25:46 (ESV).
206. Mark 10:30; Luke 18:30 (ESV).
207. Matt 19:29.
208. See Allison, *Constructing Jesus*, 186.
209. Matt 19:16–17 (ESV, emphasis added). See similarly, Luke 10:25–28, and further Matt 7:14; 18:8–9; Mark 9:43,45.
210. Matt 25:46; see also Matt 18:8; 25:41; Mark 9:48.
211. See BDAG, 430.
212. According to Davies and Allison, *Matthew*, 1:442–45, in the relevant beatitude in the Sermon on the Mount (Matt 5:3: "Blissfully happy are the poor in spirit") the addition "in spirit" is secondary.

laugh.²¹³ [. . .] Rejoice in that day, and leap for joy."²¹⁴ It is obvious here that Jesus is describing features of a non-earthly reality. As already mentioned, disease and death are significant characteristics of biological life. They will always be present on earth and therefore so too will suffering and tears. Drought and flooding and other natural catastrophes mean that hunger and poverty can never be completely banished. Just like disease and death, they belong to the earthly *conditio humana*. A life in which they no longer feature is not of this world.

Shining bodies

One further and very characteristic otherworldly element is the luminescence of the righteous in the kingdom of God. Jesus prophesies in the Gospel of Matthew, "Then [after the Last Judgment] the righteous will shine like the sun in the kingdom of their father,"²¹⁵ in accordance with the book of Daniel.²¹⁶ Here on earth we do not know people or other living creatures who shine like the sun. Luminescence is very rarely reported of earthly people.²¹⁷ According to the word of Jesus, however, all the righteous will emanate light, and it seems as if they will be constantly shining just like the sun or the stars shine incessantly. A constant shining is, however, typical of otherworldly persons as they are perceived in otherworldly experiences.²¹⁸

Seeing God

In the Gospel of Matthew, Jesus promises "the pure in heart" that they "shall see God."²¹⁹ Also in the Revelation the resurrected are promised that they will see God in the kingdom of God:

213. See also Matt 5:4: "Blissfully happy are those who mourn, for they will be comforted!" (ESV, modified). However, according to Davies and Allison, *Matthew*, 1:449 Matthew does not mean any mourning, but only mourning about the situation of the chosen people of Israel.

214. Luke 6:20–21,23 (ESV, modified).

215. Matt 13:43 (ESV).

216. See Dan 12:3. For the parallel passages in the rabbinic literature, see Allison, *Constructing Jesus*, 197.

217. See the story of the transfiguration of Jesus (Matt 17:1–9; Mark 9:2–9; Luke 9:28–36) and the literature mentioned above, p. 10n16.

218. See above, pp. 10–13.

219. Matt 5:8 (ESV). A similar promise is given in Psalm 11:7: "For the LORD is righteous; he loves righteous deeds; the upright shall behold his face" (ESV). In Psalm 17:15, David hopes: "As for me, I shall behold your face in righteousness; when I awake,

> [T]he throne of God and of the Lamb will be in it [the city of Jerusalem], and his servants will worship him. They will see his face, and his name will be on their foreheads. And night will be no more. They will need no light of lamp or sun, for the Lord God will shine upon them, and they will reign forever and ever.[220]

Here it is not about seeing another world. Rather, as described in Zoroastrian eschatology, God will be in the same world or sphere as humans.[221] Some verses from the previous chapter leave no doubt about that:

> And I saw the holy city, new Jerusalem, coming down out of heaven from God, prepared as a bride adorned for her husband. And I heard a loud voice from the throne saying, "Behold, the dwelling place of God is with man. He will dwell with them, and they will be his people and God himself will be with them as their God."[222]

Similarly, it seems to me, the Jesus of the Gospel of Matthew does not mean that people with a pure heart in the earthly kingdom of God will now and then have a mystical vision of God. Rather he means that God will be seen naturally and potentially permanently in normal consciousness and in the earthly sphere,[223] just as the servants of God in the Revelation of John will see him and the risen in Zoroastrianism will see Ahura Mazdā on earth.[224] Such a seeing of God does not fit well with normal consciousness and the ordinary senses, and to my knowledge there are no serious accounts of such a thing from our earthly sphere. It might only exist beyond this world. In the Latin Middle Ages, the otherworldly vision of God was the epitome of the highest bliss.[225]

I shall be satisfied with your likeness" (ESV).

220. Rev 22:3–5 (ESV, modified); see also Isa 60:19–20 on the shining of God.

221. See above, p. 26.

222. Rev 21:2–3 (ESV).

223. On this interpretation see also Allison, "Seeing God," 45–48.

224. See above, p. 26.

225. See Dante Alighieri, *La Divina Commedia, Paradiso*, canto 33; Oberdorfer, "Visio Dei"; Frenschkowski, "Vision," 141–42; according to Karl Rahner, seeing God is "the totality of perfect salvation" (Rahner, "Anschauung Gottes," 159).

Conclusion

The investigation of the doctrine of Jesus of Nazareth as handed down in the sources gives us the image of an afterlife with resurrected, physical bodies in a kingdom of God on earth. As this image runs throughout the Synoptic Gospels, I believe it probable that it was a significant component of the doctrine of the historical Jesus. In the earthly kingdom of God proclaimed by Jesus, also the living, who at the time of the final judgment will not yet have died, can be admitted. Life in the kingdom of God combines earthly elements such as eating, drinking, and physical movement with otherworldly features such as immortality, freedom from suffering and death, luminous bodies, and beatific vision. In that sense, one can say that Jesus was expecting an "otherworldly-earthly kingdom."[226]

---

226. Sanders, *Jesus and Judaism*, 237; see also Schweitzer, *Kingdom of God*, 92–96.

5

Resurrection and the Kingdom of God in Christianity after Jesus

Overview

THE CHRISTIAN DOCTRINES ON the afterlife form a complex and confusing assortment of ideas. I am able to present only a few essential features here. Jesus' proclamation of a physical resurrection and an eternal life on earth after death faced two challenges in early Christianity, challenges which supported belief in an *otherworldly,* eternal life. One of them was the *Hellenistic world view* that Christianity encountered as it spread. In Hellenism, the concepts of a death-enduring soul and of heaven as the abode of the blessed were widespread. The soul was mostly thought of as subtly corporeal. It was identical to the person or at least its carrier. In death, the soul could separate from the body and float away to heaven. The other challenge consisted of the fact that it is *effectively impossible* to lead an eternal life on earth with a physical resurrected body, free from suffering.

Although large parts of Christianity adopted Hellenistic conceptions of the soul, at the same time, the New Testament tradition brought about a lasting dogmatic attachment to a resurrection of the deceased, physical body and an eternal life on earth. The combination of these doctrines led to resurrection being understood, not as a return to life of the person, but rather as a reunification of the soul with the reconstructed physical body. The obvious impossibility of an immortal, earthly, and physical life led to speculation about a transformation of the resurrected body and to a tacit transferal of eternal life to the otherworld under the label of a "new earth," which had barely any earthly features.

The physical resurrection of Jesus as a paradigm

*The apparitions of Jesus after his death
in the New Testament*

According to the descriptions in the New Testament Gospels, Acts, and the Letters of Paul, quite a few of his followers had experiences of a deceased Jesus.[1] It is fair to say that, without the post-mortem apparitions of Jesus, Christianity would probably never have existed. They were the most important experiential basis of Christian faith in a resurrection of the physical body. Admittedly, according to the New Testament descriptions, Jesus' risen body was in no way always unequivocally physical. It can sometimes be seen and heard by more than one person, or even many people at the same time.[2] One account says that he was touched,[3] another that he ate.[4] And yet, he appears suddenly from nowhere or seems to be able to pass through walls, disappearing again just as suddenly.[5] Physical bodies do not normally behave this way. Furthermore, if the physical body of Jesus was really resurrected, then it would be astonishing that in some apparitions the disciples did not recognize him.[6] The so-called Emmaus disciples discussed at length with the risen Jesus without realizing that it was him.[7] The appendix to Mark seems to reference this episode in the Gospel of Luke with the notice that Jesus appeared "in another form."[8] In the Gospel of John, Mary Magdalene[9] mistakes

---

1. See Mark 16:9,12,14–19; Matt 28:9–10,16–20; Luke 24:15–31,36–51; John 20:11–22,26–29; 21:4–22; Acts 1:1–11; 9:3–8; 13:31; 22:6–11; 26:12–18; 1 Cor 15:5–8, and the comprehensive presentation and discussion in Allison, *Resurrecting Jesus*, 228–99.

2. See Matt 28:16–20; Mark 16:12,14; Luke 24:15–31,36–51; John 20:19–23,26–29; 21:4–22; Acts 1:4–9; 1 Cor 15:5–7.

3. See Matt 28:9: "And they came up and took hold of his [Jesus'] feet and worshiped him" (ESV). According to Allison, *Resurrecting Jesus*, 278 with fn. 317, the account of grasping the feet might show that Jesus was not a ghost, because according to popular folklore ghosts often have no feet. In the Gospel of John, the appearing Jesus in fact says to Thomas that he should touch him, but it is not explicitly said that Thomas does so (see John 20:27–28; see similarly also Luke 24:39–40). In the first post-mortem apparitions of Jesus in the Gospel of John, Jesus says to Mary Magdalene, on the contrary, that she should not touch him (see John 20:17).

4. See Luke 24:41–43; Acts 10:41; see also John 21:15.

5. See Luke 24:31; John 20:19,26.

6. See also Allison, *Resurrecting Jesus*, 227–28.

7. See Luke 24:15–29.

8. Mark 16:12 (ESV).

9. In the list of witnesses of the first post-mortem apparition of Jesus, Mary Magdalene is named first in all of the Gospels (see Allison, *Resurrecting Jesus*, 249 and Matt 28:1; Mark 16:1; Luke 24:10; John 20:1; see also Gos. Pet. 12:50–51).

Jesus for the gardener and first recognizes him when he speaks to her.[10] In the apparition of Jesus by the Sea of Galilee, his disciples do not initially recognize him, despite him speaking with them.[11]

It is noticeable that the physical character of the post-mortem apparitions of Jesus is presented in greater detail in both the later Gospels—Luke and John—and more strongly emphasized than in Mark and Matthew and in the Letters of Paul. This points to a theologically motivated composition in the later apparition accounts. Before its probably later-added second, longer ending,[12] the Gospel of Mark did not contain any explicit apparitions of Jesus at all, only the apparition of an anonymous young man in a white robe in the tomb who talks about the resurrection of Jesus. However, it is possible that here an apparition of Jesus was transformed into an angel apparition.[13]

Physical resurrection or physical post-mortem manifestation?

Apparitions of the deceased are a very common experience.[14] Sometimes they take on the character of a physical manifestation of the deceased which—it would seem—can not only be seen with physical eyes but which can also be touched.[15] Occasionally, during these apparitions, physiological processes such as breathing, heartbeat, and bowel sounds are observed.[16] Eating and drinking are also reported.[17]

---

10. See John 20:14–16. Goforth refers to this passage in the Gospel of John when he describes two of his own afterlife encounters in which the otherworldly person looked different (namely much younger) than at the time of his death and, therefore, he did not immediately recognize them (see Goforth and Gray, *The Risen*, 130–32, 140).

11. See John 21:4–7. Cf. further Matt 28:17: "And when they [the disciples] saw him [Jesus] they worshiped him, but some doubted" (ESV).

12. Mark 16:9–20.

13. See Allison, *Resurrecting Jesus*, 249–53, 335–37.

14. See Schwenke, *Transzendente Begegnungen*, 26–27, and the literature cited therein.

15. See Schwenke, *Transzendente Begegnungen*, 101–3, 108–11, on spontaneous multi-sensory apparitions with haptic experiences, and 138–40 on such apparitions in connection with seances.

16. See Mikulasch, "Medium Mirabelli," 75–77. The apparition of the late Bishop José de Camargo Barros (1848–1906) is described there as very complete and witnessed by many witnesses. The teeth and palate were touched, among other things, and heart and respiratory rhythms, and noises in the intestines were detected. The apparition gave the impression that it could also consume food.

17. In Evans, *Seeing Ghosts*, 85, the apparition of a woman (Hester Marshall) is described, who unbeknown to the witness (Marie Benoist), was already deceased. She appeared to be completely life-like, only much younger. Unusually for her, she wore no

The description of the Pentecostal events,[18] fifty days after the death of Jesus, provides an indication that lifelike and apparently material post-mortem manifestations of Jesus were not merely invented to underpin the doctrine of his physical resurrection. According to the representations in Acts, Jesus' disciples were in a house together when "suddenly there came from heaven a sound like a mighty rushing wind." "And divided tongues as of fire appeared to them and rested on each one of them." The "tongues as of fire" when touched, apparently invoked an altered state of consciousness: "And they were all filled with the Holy Spirit and began to speak in other tongues as the Spirit gave them utterance."[19] On another occasion, when the followers of Jesus "were all filled with the Holy Spirit," "the place in which they were gathered together was shaken."[20] Similarly, in modern times, wind and light phenomena and trance speaking are often observed during seances, in which materializations occur that are recognized by the witnesses as deceased people.[21] They are sometimes described as a prelude to stronger physical phenomena.[22] From time to time also earthquake-like tremors are observed during such seances.[23] In modern accounts, similarly

---

jewelry and said, on being questioned, that where she was now she had no need of it. She drank coffee, ate a sandwich, and went with the witness to the tram, but did not want to come home with her. Harold Sharp reported that his dog Hector materialized in a seance and slurped from a water bowl on the floor until it was empty (see Sharp, *Animals in the Spirit World*, 21–22).

18. Pentecost was originally the Jewish holiday of Shavuot that was celebrated fifty days after Passover (see Lev 23:15–21).

19. Acts 2:2–4 (ESV).

20. Acts 4:31 (ESV).

21. George Henslow cited a seance attendee: "With regard to 'lights', 'rushing wind', 'tongues of fire' we get them nearly every Sunday, in fact they are always the prelude to a successful physical seance" (Henslow, *Spirit World*, 202); see Haraldsson and Gissurarson, *Indridi Indridason*, 10–11, 23–24, 134, 147, 202 for (sometimes tongue-shaped) lights, accompanied by gusts of wind in seances with the Icelandic medium Indridi Indridason (1883–1912); see also Crookes, *Phenomena of Spiritualism*, 86 (wind before materialization phenomena), 91 (lights moving around the room that in part landed on the heads of the people); Ballou, *Exposition of Views*, 86–87; P., "Evidences of Spiritualism," 90. Contemporary reports of seance phenomena also report on lights and breezes indoors, see Keen et al., *Scole Report*, 54–65 (lights), 230, 241 (breezes); Solomon and Solomon, *Scole Experiment*, 21, 28, 30, 187–88, 224–28 (lights), 6 (breezes).

22. See Crookes, *Phenomena of Spiritualism*, 92; Henslow, *Spirit World*, 203; Wills-Brandon, *Heavenly Hugs*, 183; Guggenheim and Guggenheim, *Hello from Heaven*, 86, 110–1.

23. A witness personally known to me reported similar phenomena in the run-up to particularly impressive materialization phenomena at a seance in May 2016, in Basel: "The floor and the walls [of the room] shake, I am almost worried that there is an earthquake or something else concerning. [. . .] The whole room quakes violently" (account

to what is written in Acts, touching the lights that appear during seances is described as having an unusual effect.[24] Among other things, the contact with such a light is reported to have regularly triggered a trance in which the entranced person spoke in another voice and maybe sometimes in languages unknown to them.[25] Parallels between the Pentecostal phenomena and seance phenomena were already drawn in the nineteenth century.[26] The Easter narratives of Jesus appearing in physical form are under suspicion of being exaggerated reports of hallucinations due to bereavement, feelings of guilt, or wishful thinking for kerygmatic purposes. This does not apply to the Pentecost phenomena. It seems improbable that the disciples longed for or expected tongues as of fire, wind, speaking in tongues, and earthquake-like tremors. Neither do these phenomena make much kerygmatic sense. Moreover, it seems it would have been difficult to invent such a combination of unlikely, but related phenomena without an experiential basis. Hence it seems reasonable to believe that the Pentecost narrative does contain traces of real events. The Pentecost phenomena are reported to have been observed by the same group of people that also witnessed the Easter phenomena, during the same period of time and partly under similar conditions. It appears quite possible that at some gatherings these people might have witnessed strong materializations, on other occasions lights, wind, earthquake-like tremors, and trance speaking. The author of Acts is obviously ignorant of a connection between the Pentecostal phenomena and the physical apparitions of Jesus. He evidently does not recount the Pentecostal happenings to substantiate the veracity of reports of physical apparitions of Jesus. Based on these considerations I think that the Pentecost story increases the credibility

---

available to the author); see also Henslow, *Religion of the Spirit World*, 204.

24. See Wills-Brandon, *Heavenly Hugs*, 183–84: "These balls of light started to get bigger, and it looked like they were trying to take form. One began to take the shape of a head, and I thought to myself, *I wonder if that is my grandmother*. . . . The next part of the experience is still hard to talk about. I get very emotional. One of these bluish-white orbs, not very large in size, hit me on my left side, near my heart area. Though it felt like a light push, it literally took my breath away. It was as if the light had gone through me. With this, I suddenly felt very peaceful, joyous, calm, and intensely loved."

25. Arthur Findlay reports such a thing from the spiritualist medium John Campbell Sloan (1869–1951). A bluish light visible to everyone floated through the room to Sloan before the beginning of the speaking in a trance, and as it reached him, his mouth began to speak but not with his own voice. Another personality, who announced to have control of the medium, spoke out of him. Similar instances have also been observed in seances with other mediums. Findlay compares the phenomena with the Pentecostal events (see *Way of Life*, 78–79). For cases of xenoglossy, see Mattiesen, *Überleben des Todes*, 1:247, 257–63.

26. See, e.g., Ballou, *Exposition of Views*, 87; Crowell, *Modern Spiritualism*, 489; Jones, *Natural and Supernatural*, 403; P., "Evidences of Spiritualism," 89–90.

of the Easter stories, according to which a certain figure, recognized as the deceased Jesus, physically appeared to his followers.

A reasonably adequate discussion of the post-mortem apparitions of Jesus and the Pentecostal phenomena would require a separate discourse. For my purposes it suffices to hold on to the fact that the post-mortem apparitions of Jesus partially conveyed the impression of a physical presence of the deceased Jesus. That is probably why, I suspect, they are interpreted by his disciples as appearances of his resurrected, physical body, in light of the doctrine of resurrection that he proclaimed during his life on earth. This interpretation of the post-mortem apparitions of Jesus has shaped Christianity's belief in resurrection to the present day. But the phenomenology of the reported apparitions—altered form, sudden appearance, and disappearance even in closed rooms—on closer consideration rather contradicts the doctrine that it was Jesus' revived physical body. I do not, by the way, believe that the concept of resurrection with a luminescent body in the prime of life has its origin in the very material-appearing apparitions of the deceased that are perceived in normal consciousness and with the physical senses. These kinds of apparition are not only relatively rare, but as a rule they do not shine.[27] In the Gospels, Jesus' resurrected body is not attributed luminescence. According to my hypothesis, the idea of the luminous risen in the prime of their lives is based rather on those perceptions of visions of deceased persons without the participation of the physical senses, namely, those that occur in the context of otherworldly experiences.[28]

The physical resurrection of Jesus and the empty tomb

Despite their enigmatic nature, the post-mortem apparitions of Jesus are unequivocally understood by the canonical Gospels as being a sign and proof of his physical resurrection. He has a body with "flesh and bones,"[29] namely the same body that was laid in the tomb following his crucifixion.[30] A neces-

---

27. See Schwenke, *Transzendente Begegnungen*, 104. Also in tangible apparitions during seances (see the example in Schwenke, *Transzendente Begegnungen*, 139–40), in the cases known to me, no luminescence is reported.

28. See above, pp. 10–12.

29. Luke 24:39 (ESV).

30. There are only a few weak indications that the Gospels wanted to proclaim a non-physical afterlife for Jesus following death. Some interpreters believe that according to the somewhat cryptic Easter story of the Gospel of Matthew, Jesus had already escaped from the tomb before the stone was rolled away from the entrance: "Now after the Sabbath [. . .] Mary Magdalene and the other Mary went to see the tomb. And behold, there was a great earthquake, for an angel of the Lord descended from

sary requirement of this doctrine is that, after the resurrection, the corpse of Jesus was no longer to be found in the tomb.[31] Therefore the Gospels had to put great significance on the emptiness of the tomb. All four Gospels report that, following the crucifixion, Jesus' corpse was laid in a tomb and that this tomb was closed with a stone—in Matthew and Mark, described as being "large" or "extremely large"—and that after the resurrection the corpse was no longer to be found inside.[32] The Gospels do not leave it there, but explicitly bring the empty tomb into a logical context with the resurrection. There is a reciprocal explanatory relationship to be found between resurrection and the empty tomb: On the one hand, to the women who come to the tomb and find the corpse of Jesus to no longer be there, the missing corpse is *explained* by the resurrection of Jesus.[33] On the other hand, the empty

---

heaven and came and rolled back the stone and sat on it. [...] And for fear of him the guards trembled and became like dead men. But the angel said to the women, "Do not be afraid, for I know that you seek Jesus who was crucified. He is not here, for he has risen, as he said. Come, see the place where he lay" (Matt 28:1–6 ESV). Although it is not explicitly stated, it seems as if the tomb was only opened once the two Marys reached it, so that they would have had to have seen Jesus if he had only just come out after the opening of the tomb (see von Campenhausen, "Ablauf der Ostereignisse," 27; Allison, "Scriptural Background," 178). But von Campenhausen believes that "the strange consequence" that Jesus had to go through solid rock at his resurrection was "probably totally unintended" ("Ablauf der Ostereignisse," 27). Even assuming that Matthew wanted to assert Jesus' escape from the closed tomb, it does not mean that he had a non-physical post-mortem existence of Jesus in mind. The empty tomb is explained in the Gospel of Matthew with the resurrection of Jesus: "He [Jesus] is not here, for he has risen, as he said. Come, see the place where he lay" (Matt 28:6 ESV). A non-physical post-mortal mode of existence would—in contrast to a resurrection of the deceased physical body—not require the disappearance of the physical body and thus, in no way explain the empty tomb. The scene immediately afterwards, in which the women embrace the feet of Jesus meeting them before the tomb (Matt. 28:9), clearly argues against the Gospel author attributing a non-physical mode of being to the risen Jesus. Moreover, a physical continuity of Jesus in other Gospels was evidently not in contradiction to passing through walls and locked doors (see Luke 24:31–36, 51; John 20:19,26).

31. See Oberlinner, "Auferweckung Jesu," 165; Hoping, *Christologie*, 71–72.

32. See Matt 27:57—28:8; Mark 15:42–16:8; Luke 23:50–24:12; John 19:38—20:15. The empty tomb is, however, only directly mentioned in Mark and Matthew: "He [Jesus] has risen; he is not here. See the place where they laid him" (Mark 16:6; similar Matt 28:6). Empty tombs after resurrection are also implied in the story of the resurrection of the saints after Jesus' death in the Gospel of Matthew: "And the earth shook, and the rocks were split. The tombs also were opened, and many bodies of the saints who had fallen asleep were raised and, coming out of the tombs after his resurrection, they went into the holy city and appeared to many" (Matt 27:51–53 ESV). On the exegetical discussion of Jesus' empty tomb, see comprehensively, Allison, *Resurrecting Jesus*, 299–337.

33. See Matt 28:6, and above, n. 30; very similar Mark 16:6; more detailed Luke

tomb also becomes proof of the resurrection. The large stone at the opening of the tomb and, in addition, in Matthew, the seals and guards,[34] are there to make it plausible that an emptying of the tomb through the removal of the corpse—and with it the pretense of a resurrection—was barely or not at all possible.[35] Since other than such a grave robbery and Jesus' physical resurrection, no other possibility is mentioned in the Gospels as to how the corpse of Jesus could have disappeared from a well-closed, guarded, yet nonetheless empty tomb, an argument for resurrection emerges.

The physical resurrected body of Jesus in early Christian scriptures

The *Epistula Apostolorum*, the Letter of the Apostles, an apocryphal work that probably dates to the first half of the second century,[36] emphasizes that the apostles were able to touch the resurrected Jesus.[37] Moreover, Jesus does not walk through closed doors as in the Gospel of John,[38] but rather calls the disciples to walk outside from the house they are in, which better serves the physical character of his appearance.

> Then the Lord [Jesus] said to Mary and also to her sisters, "Let us go to them." And he came and found us inside, veiled. He called us out. But we thought it was a ghost, and we did not believe it was the Lord. Then he said to us, "Come, do not be afraid [. . .]" But we went to him, doubting in our heats whether it was possibly he. Then he said to us "Why do you still doubt and are you not believing? I am he who spoke to you concerning my flesh, my death, and my resurrection. That you may know that it is I, put your finger, Peter, in the nailprints of my hands; and you, Thomas, put your finger in the spear-wounds of my side; but you,

---

24:3–7; cf. John 20:8–9.

34. See Matt 27:65–66.

35. The Gospel of Matthew has the opponents of Jesus tell Pilate to give the order to guard Jesus' grave "lest his disciples go and steal him away and tell the people, 'He has risen from the dead'" (Matt 27:64 ESV). Mary Magdalene supposed, according to the Gospel of John, that Jesus' corpse had been taken away (see John 20:2,13,15). The indication that Jesus' linen wrappings remained in the tomb (see John 20:5–7) is understood as an argument against his corpse having been stolen from the tomb (see Hoping, *Christologie*, 71).

36. See Hornschuh, *Epistula Apostolorum*, 116.

37. See Ep. Apos. 2:3; 12:1 (verse division according to Berger and Nord, *Testament*).

38. See John 20:19,26.

Andrew, look at my feet and see if they do not touch the ground. For it is written in the prophet, 'The foot of a ghost or demon does not join the ground.'" But we touched him that we might truly know whether he had risen in the flesh, and we fell on our faces confessing our sin, that we had been unbelieving.[39]

The Letter of the Apostles represents the entry of Jesus into heaven as a physical process, perceivable by the normal senses:

> And as he [Jesus] spoke there was thunder and lightning and an earthquake, and the heavens divided and a bright cloud came and took him away. And we heard the voice of many angels as they rejoiced and praised and said, "Assemble us, O priest, in the light of glory." And when he had come near to the firmament of heaven, we heard him say, "Go in peace."[40]

The Letter of Ignatius of Antioch[41] to the Smyrnaeans, which may have been written after the death of Ignatius in the second half of the second century,[42] clearly defends the fact that after the resurrection, Jesus had a body of flesh. The author argues against the docetists, who claim that Jesus' body was a phantasm.

> For I know and believe that he [Jesus] was in the flesh even after the resurrection; and when he came to Peter and those with him, he said to them: "Take hold of me; handle me and see that am not a disembodied demon."[43] And immediately they touched him and believed, being closely united with his flesh and blood. [. . .] And after his resurrection he ate and drank with them like one who is composed of flesh, although spiritually he was united with the Father.[44]

Some faith documents explicitly state that Jesus not only ascended to heaven with his physical body but that he will also return with the same body from heaven for the Last Judgment. The *Ancoratus* of Epiphanius of Salamis from the year 374 says: "[B]ut the same one [Jesus] suffered in the flesh and arose again and ascended into heaven *with the same body;*

---

39. Ep. Apos. 11:1—12:2 (Coptic version) (trans. *NTApoc*, 1:255–56).

40. Ep. Apos. 51:3,5 (Ethiopic version) (trans. *NTApoc*, 1:278).

41. Ignatius was Bishop of Antioch in Syria. According to the Church History of Eusebius, he was supposed to have died under Trajan in Rome before the year 117. Some historians put his death in the late second century.

42. See Schmithals, "Ignatius von Antiochien."

43. Cf. Luke 24:39.

44. Ign. *Symrn.* 3:1–3 (trans. Holmes, *Apostolic Fathers*, 251).

he sits in glory at the right hand of the Father, he will some in glory *in the same body* to judge the living and the dead."[45] The same thing is taught in the Great Creed of the Armenian Church that possibly dates to the fourth century as well.[46]

Physical resurrection as Christian dogma

Resurrection of the physical body in Christian creeds and doctrinal documents

The resurrection of the physical body, modeled on the resurrection of Jesus, has until today remained an important element of official church doctrine.[47] It is explicitly formulated in the Apostle's Creed, the most popular creed of Western Christian churches.[48] Its numerous early forms reach back into the second century.[49] It teaches the "resurrection of the flesh" (*carnis resurrectionem*, σαρκὸς ἀνάστασιν),[50] though in the English versions today, as a rule, this extreme wording is softened to "resurrection of the body."[51]

Christian creeds and doctrinal documents emphasize that at the resurrection of the flesh a person will not arise with a similar physical body but *with exactly the same one that was buried*. "We believe that we who have been cleansed in his [Jesus'] death and in his blood shall be raised up by him

---

45. Trans. Denzinger, *Compendium*, 30 (D 44) (emphasis added).

46. See Denzinger, *Compendium*, 32 (D 48). That Jesus will come from heaven to the judgment in the same body he had lived in on earth is also taught in Augustine, *Civ.* 20.6.

47. On the resurrection doctrine up to the late Middle Ages, see Bynum, *Resurrection of the Body*.

48. See Denzinger, *Compendium*, 27 (D 30). The Niceno-Constantinopolitan Creed, that supposedly goes back to the Council of Constantinople in the year 381 and is widely used in the Eastern churches, uses the wording "resurrection of the *dead*" (*resurrectio mortuorum*, ἀνάστασις νεκρῶν) (see Denzinger, *Compendium*, 66 [D 150]).

49. See Denzinger, *Compendium*, 19.

50. This wording is apparently first found in the Epistle of Clement (1 Clem. 26:3), see Lona, *Auferstehung des Fleisches*, 23. From 170 CE, this formula increasingly supplanted talk of the resurrection of the body or the dead (see Lona, *Auferstehung des Fleisches*, 265).

51. When the wording was weakened from "resurrection of the flesh" to "resurrection of the dead" in German-speaking Catholicism in 1970, the Papal Congregation for Divine Worship and the Discipline of the Sacraments argued that giving up the wording "resurrection of the flesh" posed the danger of supporting teachings that relocated the resurrection to the moment of death and with that, ruled out the resurrection of the body, in particular, of this flesh (see Kongregation für die Sakramente und den Gottesdienst, "De Symbolo Apostolico," 35 [marginal no. 4785g]).

on the last day *in this flesh in which we now live*," is the formulation in the formula, *Fides Damasi*, at the end of the fifth century.[52] The current version of the Catechism of the Catholic Church repeats the statement of the Fourth Lateran Council, that "all [. . .] will rise again with their own bodies which they now bear."[53] Evidently, this had not always been obvious. On several occasions, the view that the resurrection will take place in a different flesh is explicitly disputed.[54] This topic was, for example, part of a test of faith for episcopate candidates in the fifth century: "Let the person who is to be ordained bishop first be examined [. . .]. It must also be asked whether he believes <in> the re*surrection of this flesh that we bear and not of some other*."[55] At the end of the seventh century, the Sixteenth Synod of Toledo specified the disputed idea of another flesh: "Just as he [Jesus] gave us an example by his own Resurrection [. . .], we believe at all times that at the close of this age we too will be resurrected, *not as thin air or some shadowy phantasm*, as the condemnable opinion of some affirms, but in the substance of the real flesh in which we now are and live."[56]

A literal understanding of the physical resurrection has decreased among Christians,[57] to the regret of conservative theologians.[58] Yet it is still

---

52. Trans. Denzinger, *Compendium*, 38 (D 72) (emphasis added). Almost word for word, the Fourth Synod of Toledo, that began on December 5, 633, confesses: "Cleansed by his [Jesus'] death and blood, we have attained remission of sins in order to be resurrected by him in the last days in that flesh in which we now live" (trans. Denzinger, *Compendium*, 167 [D 485]). Pope Leo IX writes in his letter *Congratamulur vehementer* of April 13, 1053, to Peter III, Patriarch of Antioch: "I believe also in the true resurrection of the same flesh that I now bear and in life eternal" (trans. Denzinger, *Compendium*, 232 [D 684]). In the Profession of Faith of the Byzantine Emperor Michael VIII Paleologos (1259–1282), read at the Second Council of Lyon on July 6, 1274, it equally says: "We also believe <in> the true resurrection of this body [*huius carnis*] that we now bear and in the life eternal" (trans. Denzinger, *Compendium*, 283 [D 854]). See also Irenaeus, *Haer.* 5.15.1.

53. *CCC* 999; Denzinger, *Compendium*, 266 (D 801).

54. Already Tertullian, *Res.* 55, fights against the meaning, "that it is a different flesh which is to rise again" (trans. *ANF* 3:588).

55. *Statuta Ecclesiae Antiqua*, written in Gallia Narbonensis (Roman province in the area of today's Provence in France) (trans. Denzinger, *Compendium*, 117 [D 325]; emphasis added).

56. Profession of Faith of the Sixteenth Synod of Toledo (693) (trans. Denzinger, *Compendium*, 201 [D 574]; emphasis added). See similarly the Profession of Faith of the Eleventh Synod of Toledo (675) (see Denzinger, *Compendium*, 187 [D 540]).

57. See Allison, *Night Comes*, 25–30; see also Bynum, *Resurrection of the Body*, 14–15. According to Harpprecht, "Auferstehung," 40 percent of German Catholics and half of German Protestants affirm the resurrection. Figures for US Christians are similar (see Regnerus, "Resurrecting the Dead").

58. See, e.g., Wright, *Surprised by Hope*, 3–27. According to Albert Mohler,

officially taught, for example, as we have already seen in the Catechism of the Catholic Church, although the catechism also postulates the immortality of a soul separable from the body:

> The Christian Creed [. . .] culminates in the proclamation of the resurrection of the dead on the last day and in life everlasting. [. . . J]ust as Christ is truly risen from the dead and lives for ever, so after death the righteous will live for ever with the risen Christ and he will raise them up on the last day. [. . .] The "resurrection of the flesh" (the literal formulation of the Apostles' Creed) means not only that the immortal soul will live on after death, but that even our "mortal body" [Rom 8:11] will come to life again.[59]

Orthodox churches likewise hold on to the dogma of the resurrection of the physical body. Philaret's authoritative *Longer Catechism of the Orthodox, Catholic, Eastern Church,* defines resurrection as "an act of the almighty power of God, by which all bodies of dead men, being reunited to their souls, shall return to life." To the question, "How shall the body rise again after it has rotted and perished in the ground?" the Catechism answers: "Since God formed the body from the ground originally, he can equally restore it after it has perished in the ground."[60] In the twentieth century, Protestant theologians frequently rejected the immortality of the soul and thus placed particular importance on bodily resurrection.[61] With exactly what kind of corporeality the resurrected will be seen, remains, however, often unclear.

Miraculous revivifications as proof of the possibility of a physical resurrection

As in the teachings of Jesus of the New Testament, also in early Christian literature, miraculous revivifications are seen as proof of the possibility of

---

President of the Southern Baptist Theological Seminary in Louisville, the comparably weak support for the doctrine of bodily resurrection "reflects the very low state of doctrinal preaching in our churches" ("Resurrection of the Body").

59. *CCC* 988–90.

60. Philaret, "Longer Catechism," 502–3, §§ 366–67.

61. See Schwöbel, "Resurrection": "For Protestant theology of the past century, affirmation of the *resurrection* of the dead has largely stood 'in exclusive opposition' (P. Althaus, *RGG* 3 I, 1957, 697 [= Althaus, 'Auferstehung']) to the notion of the immortality of the soul. This view chimes with the understanding of death as death of the whole person rather than as separation of the soul from the body, so that *resurrection* must be understood as new creation rather than recombination of the soul with a new corporeality."

the resurrection of a dead, physical body. This, on the one hand, supports the theory that Jesus himself understood his miraculous revivifications as resurrection in this sense, and on the other hand underlines the faith in the resurrection of a physical body in early Christianity. In the *Church History* of Eusebius of Caesarea, there is an extract from a lost scripture of Quadratus of Athens, that probably dates from just after the turn of the first to the second century. It mentions resurrected persons, who were known by Quadratus's contemporaries:

> But the works of our Saviour were always present, for they were genuine:—those that were healed, and those that were raised from the dead, who were seen not only when they were healed and when they were raised, but were also always present; and not merely while the Saviour was on earth, but also after his death, they were alive for quite a while, so that some of them lived even to our day.[62]

Some decades later, Irenaeus of Lyons cites Jesus' miraculous revivifications as examples of physical resurrection:

> Let our opponents—that is, they who speak against their own salvation—inform us [as to this point]: The deceased daughter of the high priest;[63] the widow's dead son, who was being carried out [to burial] near the gate [of the city];[64] and Lazarus, who had lain four days in the tomb,[65]—in what bodies did they rise again? In those same, no doubt, in which they had also died. For if it were not in the very same, then certainly those same individuals who had died did not rise again. For [the Scripture] says, "The Lord took the hand of the dead man,[66] and said to him, Young man, I say unto thee, Arise. And the dead man sat up,[67] and He commanded that something should be given him to eat;[68] and He delivered him to his mother."[69] Again, He called Lazarus "with a loud voice, saying, Lazarus, come forth;

---

62. Eusebius, *Hist. eccl.* 4.3.1–2 (trans. *NPNF2* 1:175). Quadratus was probably Bishop of Athens in the twenties of the second century and counts as the oldest Christian apologist.

63. See Mark 5:22. The girl was the daughter of Jairus, one of the leaders of the synagogue (see Mark 5:22).

64. See Luke 7:12.

65. See John 11:17,39.

66. This is said of the resurrection of the daughter of Jairus in Mark 5:41.

67. See Luke 7:14–15.

68. This is said of the resurrection of the daughter of Jairus in Mark 5:43.

69. See Luke 7:15.

RESURRECTION AND THE KINGDOM OF GOD IN CHRISTIANITY AFTER JESUS 91

and he that was dead came forth bound with bandages, feet and hands."[70, 71]

In the fourth century, Cyril of Jerusalem also cites raisings from the dead by Old Testament prophets and by apostles as examples of resurrection:

> And many Scriptures there are which testify of the Resurrection of the dead. [. . .] I speak but in passing of Elias, and the widow's son whom he raised;[72] of Elisseus also, who raised the dead twice; once in his lifetime, and once after his death.[73] [. . .] But be it remembered, that the Apostles also raised the dead; Peter raised Tabitha in Joppa,[74] and Paul raised Eutychus in Troas;[75] and thus did all the other Apostles, even though the wonders wrought by each have not all been written.[76]

The unsolvable problem of the reassembly of body parts

In the first half of the third century, Origen of Alexandria argued convincingly that the collection of particles of a corpse cannot be decisive to the identity of the person, because during earthly life, elements of the body are constantly being replaced.[77] Even so, for hundreds of years the predominant Christian doctrine on the resurrection remained rooted in the paradigm of the collection and reassembly of the scattered elements of the dead body.[78] This confirms once again that it was thought to be the very same physical body that will be resurrected. A much-discussed question was how it would be possible to recollect the particles scattered across the whole world. Cyril of Jerusalem describes the objections the doctrine was confronted with:

> Now Greeks and Samaritans together argue against us thus. The dead man has fallen, and mouldered away, and is all turned into worms; and the worms have died also; such is the decay and

---

70. See John 11:43–44.
71. Irenaeus, *Haer.* 5.13.1 (trans. *ANF* 1:539).
72. See 1 Kgs 17:22.
73. See 2 Kgs 4:34; 13:21.
74. See Acts 9:40.
75. See Acts 20:10.
76. Cyril of Jerusalem, *Catech. illum.* 18.16–17 (trans. *NPNF2* 7:138).
77. See Origen, *Fr. Ps.* 1.5, in Methodius of Olympus, *Res.* 1.22–23; Bynum, *Resurrection of the Body*, 64–66.
78. See Bynum, "Death and Resurrection," 594; Bynum, *Resurrection of the Body*, 30, 32, 35, 38, 72, 75–76, 89, 103–4, 118–19, 158, 162–63, 213, 220, 263–64.

destruction which has overtaken the body; how then is it to be raised? The shipwrecked have been devoured by fishes, which are themselves devoured. Of them who fight with wild beasts the very bones are ground to powder, and consumed by bears and lions. Vultures and ravens feed on the flesh of the unburied dead, and then fly away over all the world; whence then is the body to be collected? For of the fowls who have devoured it some may chance to die in India, some in Persia, some in the land of the Goths. Other men again are consumed by fire, and their very ashes scattered by rain or wind; whence is the body to be brought together again?[79]

Such questions were already posed early on. In the Letter of the Apostles, the apostles ask Jesus himself about his resurrection: "[I]s it then possible that what is dissolved and destroyed should be whole?"[80] They, however, received no answer.[81] In his *Treatise on the Resurrection* around the year 180,[82] Athenagoras of Athens assumed that God both knows "whither each of the particles has passed," and also possesses the power to "reunite what is dissolved."[83] He discusses the oft-treated problem that the human body directly or indirectly (via the eating of animals that have eaten humans) is eaten by humans. This could not, he argues, hinder the reassembly of the body from its original elements as "the bodies of men [can] never combine with bodies like themselves,"[84] namely, incorporate elements of the bodies of other humans into their own body. Likewise, around the year 180, Irenaeus of Lyons wrote that it would be much easier for God to bring the

---

79. Cyril of Jerusalem, *Catech. illum.* 18.2 (trans. NPNF2 7:134).

80. Ep. Apos. 24:2 (trans. NTApoc 1:263).

81. See Ep. Apos. 24:3: "And he was angry with us, saying to us, 'O you of little faith, until what day do you ask?'" (trans. NTApoc 1:263).

82. Kiel, *Ps-Athenagoras*, recently argued that the *Treatise* is pseudonymous and dates from the first half of the third century.

83. Athenagoras, *Res.* 2–3 (trans. ANF 2:150). See also Cyril of Jerusalem, *Catech. illum.* 18.3 following the passage quoted above, pp. 91–92: "To you, poor little feeble man, India is far from the land of the Goths, and Spain from Persia; but to God, who holds the whole earth in the hollow of His hand, all things are near at hand. [...] Imagine a mixture of seeds of different plants (for as you are weak concerning the faith, the examples which I allege are weak also), and that these different seeds are contained in your single hand; is it then to you, who art a man, a difficult or an easy matter to separate what is in your hand, and to collect each seed according to its nature, and restore it to its own kind? Can you then separate the things in your hand, and cannot God separate the things contained in His hand, and restore them to their proper place? Consider what I say, whether it is not impious to deny it [the resurrection]?" (trans. NPNF2 7:134).

84. Athenagoras, *Res.* 8 (trans. ANF 2:153); see also *Res.* 7.

corpse, dissolved into the earth, back to existence than to re-create man.[85] Tertullian argued similarly a few decades later.[86]

Contrary to Athenagoras's answer, it is undeniable that particles of a human organism are constantly being incorporated into other human beings. If a corpse is not completely hermetically sealed off from the environment, it is only a matter of time before other people ingest its atoms, molecules, and ions through their food. If resurrection is based on the recomposition of the particles of the corpse, this multiple use of body particles necessarily leads to incomplete resurrected bodies, because at the resurrection the particles cannot be assigned to two persons at the same time.[87] The problem of a restoration of the resurrected body from the same particles cannot really be solved. However, a restoration from similar particles would be logically possible and would probably serve the same purpose.

The transformation of the resurrection body for the eternal life

The necessity of transformation

It is unimaginable that a biological organism could live forever. For this reason, a transformation must be added to the restoration of the physical body to render it indestructible. If earth is not the place where the afterlife will

---

85. See Irenaeus, *Haer.* 5.3.2: "But that He is powerful in all these respects, we ought to perceive from our origin, inasmuch as God, taking dust from the earth, formed man. And surely it is much more difficult and incredible, from non-existent bones, and nerves, and veins, and the rest of man's organization, to bring it about that all this should be, and to make man an animated and rational creature, than to reintegrate again that which had been created and then afterwards decomposed into earth (for the reasons already mentioned), having thus passed into those [elements] from which man, who had no previous existence, was formed. For He who in the beginning caused him to have being who as yet was not, just when He pleased, shall much more reinstate again those who had a former existence, when it is His will [that they should inherit] the life granted by Him" (trans. *ANF* 1:528).

86. See Tertullian, *Res.* 11: "For if God produced all things whatever out of nothing, He will be able to draw forth from nothing even the flesh which had fallen into nothing; or if He moulded other things out of matter, He will be able to call forth the flesh too from somewhere else, into whatever *abyss* it may have been engulphed. And surely He is most competent to re-create who created, inasmuch as it is a far greater work to have produced than to have reproduced, to have imparted a beginning, than to have maintained a continuance. On this principle, you may be quite sure that the restoration of the flesh is easier than its first formation" (trans. *ANF* 4:553). *De resurrectione carnis* has been dated to the year 211 (see Butterweck, "Tertullian," 101). See also Minucius Felix, *Oct.* 34.9–10.

87. See Allison, *Night Comes*, 19–21.

be situated, but rather heaven or eternal hell fire, there is an additional need for transformation for the purpose of adapting the body to a completely different environment.

No clear time distinction in Christianity between resurrection and transformation

In Zoroastrianism, resurrection and transformation were two processes occurring at separate times.[88] This also applies to the Jewish Second Book of Baruch.[89] In Christianity, on the other hand, resurrection and transformation are often not clearly distinguished. Paul contributed significantly to this. He allowed resurrection and transformation to merge. Despite this, Christianity often, at least logically, differentiates between resurrection and transformation. Irenaeus of Lyons writes, for example: "God, when He resuscitates our mortal bodies which preserved righteousness, will render them incorruptible and immortal."[90] More tangible is the separation of resurrection and transformation in the case of miraculous revivifications. Here, it is indisputable that the bodies of the raised were still normal and mortal. Among authors who postulate a millennial kingdom before the Last Judgment, there is a considerable period of time between resurrection and transformation. Those raised at the beginning of this kingdom will be transformed only at its end.[91]

Transformation of the resurrected body in Cyril of Jerusalem

Cyril of Jerusalem, for example, talks about the transformation of the resurrected body. He writes in his *Catechetical Lectures* that the resurrected, physical bodies of the righteous will be transformed "as iron in fire becomes fire"; they will then be imperishable, no longer need food and be able to float and shine. The body of the righteous will be a "heavenly body, that [they] may be able worthily to hold converse with Angels." Sinners, on the other hand, will get "an eternal body, fitted to endure the penalties of sins, that they may burn eternally in fire, yet never ever be consumed."[92]

88. See above, pp. 20–21.
89. See 2 Bar. 50:2; 51:1–3,5,9–10.
90. Irenaeus, *Haer.* 2.29.2 (trans. *ANF* 1:403).
91. See, e.g., Irenaeus, *Haer.* 5.36.1; Lactantius, *Inst.* 7.26.5; Lactantius, *Epit.* 72.
92. Cyril of Jerusalem, *Catech. illum.* 18.18–19 (trans. *NPNF2* 7:139).

Here it becomes clear that the transformation of the resurrected body not only enables its eternal durability but also its adaptability to different afterlife environments.

Adapting to afterlife environments: Can flesh burn forever?

The problem of the adaptation to a non-earthly afterlife environment shows itself also indirectly in late Augustine. He insists on the resurrected body still being one of flesh, in other words, on its physical character. In order to prove that a body of flesh is capable of floating up to heaven and abiding there,[93] or burning for all eternity in the fires of hell without being reduced to nothing, he presents extravagant examples in his *City of God*. Augustine goes to great lengths to prove, above all, that a body made out of flesh can endure the fires of hell.[94] He cites transient creatures who live in fire, namely, salamanders,[95] the non-decaying flesh of the peacock, incombustible diamonds,[96] and even Cappadocian mares that are impregnated by the wind.[97] Ultimately, Augustine resorts to the knockout argument of the almighty power of God, perhaps because he feels that he is unable to factually render his doctrine of the eternity of a resurrected body of flesh plausible.[98]

How will the resurrected survive world conflagration?

An even more specific problem is the survival of the resurrected during the cosmic transformation. In Lactantius, the resurrected ensconce themselves in subterranean caves,[99] in Augustine they survive high above the conflagration: "[T]hey shall be in the upper regions into which the flame of that conflagration shall not ascend, as neither did the water of the flood."

---

93. See Augustine, *Civ.* 13.18; 22.11; see also 22.4.
94. See Augustine, *Civ.* 21.2–9.
95. See Augustine, *Civ.* 21.2,4.
96. See Augustine, *Civ.* 21.2,4.
97. See Augustine, *Civ.* 21.5.
98. See Augustine, *Civ.* 21.6–8. In a similar vein, Lactantius wrote that in hell the flesh of the wicked will be "indestructible, and abiding for ever, that it may be able to hold out against tortures and everlasting fire" (*Inst.* 7.21.3; trans. *ANF* 7:217).
99. According to Lactantius, the righteous of the millennial kingdom survive the final battle of God against the heathen nations for three days in caves under the earth, while God on the surface wipes out the impious people with excessive heat, fire, and showers of stones (see *Inst.* 7.26. 2–3).

This seems, however, to be a purely precautionary measure. As "they have become immortal and incorruptible, they shall not greatly dread the blaze of that conflagration."[100]

Transformation into a non-physical body according to Thomas Aquinas

According to Thomas Aquinas the body that rises is the same as the one that died.[101] This body will be so transformed as to no longer have any bodily functions of animal life such as eating, drinking, sleeping and reproducing.[102] It will be extremely subtle but not like the air or wind,[103] move without resistance at will,[104] and "be lightsome" with the saints.[105] Especially the fact that the transformed resurrected body follows the will without resistance, shows that we are no longer dealing with a physical body. For general experience demonstrates that matter from this cosmos cannot be influenced by the will of humans without resistance. Since Descartes, philosophers often doubt that will can have any influence on matter at all.

Paul's seed metaphor: resurrection as transformation

Paul did not understand resurrection as the revivification of a corpse. The physical body remains dead.[106] From it, in the resurrection, arises a different type of body, a "pneumatic body (σῶμα πνευματικόν)."[107] The Pauline idea of a pneumatic body is apparently rooted in the stoic concept of a bodily, pneumatic soul, as was, for example, propagated by Cicero.[108] In order to illustrate how the pneumatic body arises out of the dead physical body, Paul makes use of the seed metaphor. Just as new plants grow out of the seed that germinates in the earth so arises the pneumatic body from the physical

---

100. Augustine, *Civ.* 20.18 (trans. *NPNF1* 2:437).

101. See Thomas Aquinas, *S. Th.*, Suppl., q. 79, a. 1, co.

102. See Thomas Aquinas, *S. Th.*, Suppl., q. 81, a. 4, co.

103. See Thomas Aquinas, *S. Th.*, Suppl., q. 83, a. 1, co.

104. See Thomas Aquinas, *S. Th.*, Suppl., q. 84, a. 1, co.

105. See Thomas Aquinas, *S. Th.*, Suppl., q. 85, a. 1, co.

106. Paul calls it the "psychic body" (σῶμα ψυχικόν) (1 Cor 15:44), but it is clear from the context that he more or less means what we call here an earthly-physical body (see Litwa, *We are Being Transformed*, 137).

107. 1 Cor 15:44.

108. See Engberg-Pedersen, *Cosmology and Self*, especially 19–37; Litwa, *We are Being Transformed*, 127–51.

one, albeit in an instant, at the moment of resurrection. The central passage can be found in First Corinthians: "But someone will ask, 'How are the dead raised? With what kind of body do they come?' You foolish person! What you sow does not come to life unless it dies. [. . .] So is it with the resurrection of the dead. What is sown is [. . .] a natural body; it is raised a pneumatic body."[109] According to the logic of the seed metaphor, the "perishable" physical body[110] is not first revived[111] and then transformed. Rather the resurrected body is immediately an imperishable pneumatic body, that by its very nature can live eternally. The seed metaphor makes a completely empty tomb at the resurrection not directly obvious, because during the germination process a seed only gradually transforms and dissolves. The image fits better with a decomposing corpse in the grave.[112] Thus, it is unsurprising that Paul does not mention the empty tomb. Theology, nevertheless, still predominantly assumes that according to Paul the graves will be emptied at the resurrection.[113] Those who are still alive at the return of Christ will, however, be transformed without first having to die: "Behold! I tell you a mystery. We shall not all sleep, but we shall all be changed, in a moment, in the twinkling of an eye, at the last trumpet. For the trumpet will sound, and the dead will be raised imperishable, and we shall be changed."[114] The physical body of the still living will also be transformed into a pneumatic body *in vivo*. In the cited passage, in which it also very clearly speaks of the expectation of the eschatological return of Christ within the lifetimes

---

109. 1 Cor 15:35–36,42,44 (ESV, modified).

110. See 1 Cor 15:42: "What is sown is perishable; what is raised is imperishable" (ESV).

111. But see Rom 8:11: "[H]e who raised Christ Jesus from the dead will also give life to your mortal bodies" (ESV).

112. There are further indications still that Paul's doctrine did not necessarily require an empty tomb. Paul does not exclude the possibility of an existence of the person outside of the physical body. One example is 2 Cor 5:6,8: "We know that while we are at home in the body we are away from the Lord [. . .]. Yes, we are of good courage, and we would rather be away from the body and at home with the Lord" (ESV). The other example is his otherworld journey: "I know a man in Christ who fourteen years ago was caught up to the third heaven—whether in the body or out of the body I do not know, God knows. And I know that this man was caught up into paradise—whether in the body or out of the body I do not know, God knows—and he heard things that cannot be told, which man may not utter" (2 Cor 12:2–4 ESV).

113. See Allison, *Resurrecting Jesus*, 305–7; Schnelle, *Paulus*, 459–60. Novakovic, "Jesus' Resurrection," 927 warns that the fact that early Christian tradition in 1 Cor 15:3–7 does not mention the empty tomb should not be ignored lightly. The assumption that the wording "that he was buried" assumes a knowledge of the empty tomb, reads something into the text.

114. 1 Cor 15:51–52 (ESV).

of some readers, Paul designates his transformation theory a secret. This speaks for it representing something unknown in Christian doctrine. Also in Philippians, we meet with the transformation theory: "Jesus Christ [. . .] will transform our lowly body to be like his glorious body, by the power that enables him even to subject all things to himself."[115] According to First Thessalonians, the resurrected can defy gravity and fly in the air or float, which would be possible with a pneumatic body in contrast to a physical one: "And the dead in Christ will rise first. Then we who are alive, who are left, will be caught up together with them in the clouds to meet the Lord in the air, and so we will always be with the Lord."[116]

The early church, especially Origen, picked up on the seed metaphor of First Corinthians and took Paul's words, "flesh and blood shall not inherit the kingdom of God," literally.[117] From the seed of the earthly body decomposed into dust, God will allow a body to arise, "as it pleases Him."[118] Those destined for heaven arise from it a "spiritual" body, "capable of inhabiting the heavens," those who stand on a lower level, a less glorious and less worthy body, and "those who are to be destined to everlasting fire or to severe punishment"[119] an incorruptible body, that can also stand hell's punishments.[120]

A combination of a physical resurrection and the seed metaphor

In catechisms of the Catholic and Russian Orthodox churches, the theory of the recovery of the physical body is combined with the seed metaphor. As we have already seen, the Catechism of the Catholic Church teaches that "all [. . .] will rise again with their own bodies which they now bear."[121] In the same breath, citing Paul, it says that the earthly body which is only a "bare kernel" will be transformed into a "spiritual body."[122] Here, it seems at least logically to distinguish between the resurrection and transformation.

---

115. Phil 3:20–21 (ESV). Cf. Col 3:1: "[S]eek the things that are above [in heaven], where Christ is, seated at the right hand of God" (ESV).

116. 1 Thess 4:16–17 (ESV).

117. See Origen, *Princ.*2.10.3 with reference to 1 Cor 15:50.

118. Origen, *Princ.* 2.10.3 (trans. *ANF* 4:294). Origen refers here to 1 Cor 15:38.

119. As is well known, elsewhere in his work Origen envisages an eschatological reconciliation including the devil, see Markschies, "Origenes und sein Erbe," 11.

120. Origen, *Princ.* 2.10.3 (trans. *ANF* 4:294).

121. *CCC* 999.

122. *CCC* 999, with reference to 1 Cor 15:35–37,42,44,52–53.

The Orthodox Catechism of Philaret Drozdov taught, however, the restoring back to life of the decaying body and its transformation according to the seed metaphor.[123]

Resurrection with another body without transformation

According to Paul, the earthly-physical body and the pneumatic resurrected body exist one after the other. His seed metaphor does not illuminate this consecutiveness very convincingly, because, as just mentioned, during germination the existence of the seed and the new plant overlap. It is thus no wonder that, subsequent to Paul, a resurrection concept appears in which, it would seem, a simultaneous existence of an earthly body and a resurrected body is postulated. This can be found in *The Treatise on the Resurrection*, sometimes called *Epistle to Rheginus*. It dates to the year 150.[124] It reads: "Surely the visible parts of the body are dead and will not be saved. Only the living parts that are within will arise."[125] "Living parts" probably means parts of an invisible body within the physical body.[126] From a phenomenological view; the doctrine of two bodies corresponds with many out-of-body experiences during which the experiencers have the sensation of leaving their physical body in a separate, second body. They perceive the physical body from the outside and simultaneously have the sensation of being in another body.[127] In official Christian doctrine such a two-body doctrine has, however, to my knowledge never been presented.[128]

Superfluousness of the physical resurrection

Alongside the problem of the *possibility* of a resurrection of the physical body in an eternal afterlife, comes the problem of the *superfluousness* of the physical resurrection. I see two aspects here. Firstly, it is superfluous that exactly the same body rises again. The metabolic organs, heart, lungs,

---

123. See Philaret, "Longer Catechism," 502–3 (§§ 366–67).

124. See Berger and Nord, *Testament*, 1043. Berger and Nord believe the text to be one of the few further developments of the Paul doctrine (see *Testament*, 1043).

125. Treat. Res. 9:2–3 (Meyer, *Nag Hammadi Scriptures*, 54).

126. See the translation of Treat. Res. 7:3 and 9:2–3 in Berger and Nord, *Testament*, 1047–48.

127. See above, p. 3.

128. It is disputed whether the *Treatise on the Resurrection* belongs to Christian literature. Berger and Nord, *Testament*, 1043, count this letter as part of early Christian literature and believe the position of the author not to be gnostic.

stomach, intestine, kidneys, bladder, and blood with their many functions will no longer be needed as the body is now immortal and no longer requires oxygen and food to live. The resurrected body could just as well be hollow.[129] Secondly, through the doctrine of an immortal soul the question is raised whether a physical resurrected body is at all necessary. Pope Benedict XII explained in 1336 that the souls of the saints already enjoyed seeing God face to face, the highest aim of the afterlife, before the resurrection of the body. The resurrection of the body would not contribute anything further to eternal bliss.[130] Shortly before, on his deathbed, Pope John XXII had largely revoked his opposing opinion.[131]

The transferal of eternal life to the otherworld

Fundamentals

In contrast to physical resurrection, the earth as the place of the afterlife soon receded into the background. This happened for several reasons. The expectation of an earthly kingdom of God faded. In addition, a subtle-corporeal soul that leaves the physical body at death required a suitable place to abide. This requirement met with the Greco-Roman concept of heaven as the place of the blessed, which was quickly adapted by Christianity.[132] Heaven was also the place of God, so that after death the good souls could

---

129. See Allison, *Night Comes*, 23–24.

130. See the papal Constitution *Benedictus Deus* from January 29, 1336: "By this Constitution which is to remain in force for ever, We, with apostolic authority, define the following: according to the general disposition of God, the souls of all the saints [. . .] and other faithful who died after receiving the holy baptism of Christ—provided they were not in need of any purification when they died, or will not be in need of any when they die in the future, or else, if they then needed or will need some purification, after they have been purified after death—already before they take up their bodies again and before the general judgment, [. . .] these souls have seen and see the divine essence with an intuitive vision and even face to face, without the mediation of any creature by way of object of vision [. . .]. Moreover, by this vision and enjoyment the souls of those who have already died are truly blessed and have eternal life and rest. Also the souls of those who will die in the future will see the same divine essence and will enjoy it before the general judgment. [. . .] And after such intuitive and face-to-face vision and enjoyment have or will have begun for these souls, the same vision and enjoyment have continued and will continue without any interruption and without end until the last Judgment and from then on forever" (trans. Denzinger, *Compendium* 302–3 [D 1000–1001]). This text is also cited in *CCC* 1023; see also Rahner, "Eschatologie," 1185.

131. See his bull *Ne super his* from December 3, 1334 (Denzinger, *Compendium*, 301–2 [D 990–91]) and on this controversy, Bynum, *Resurrection of the Body*, 283–91.

132. See also, e.g., Lang, *Himmel und Hölle*, 43–49.

immediately go to God. The souls of those who die in mortal sin, on the other hand, descended to hell directly after death.

Jesus' expectation of a kingdom not communicable in the Hellenistic arena

The fading of the kingdom expectation was partly due to the failure of the desired second coming of Jesus of Nazareth to occur. Beyond that, an earthly kingdom of God with Jerusalem at its center was hardly imaginable in the Hellenistic world in which Christianity was spreading, as Benedict Viviano writes:

> The reason the kingdom hope was lost so early in the history of the Church is that this hope presupposes a late Jewish apocalyptic worldview such as we find in the book of Daniel. Once Christianity moved out of the sphere of Palestinian and diaspora Judaism into the Greco-Roman world the cultural presuppositions which could have made such a hope intelligible were no longer present.[133]

Heaven as the abode of the blessed in Hellenism

Contact with the Greco-Roman world also directly encouraged the transferal of the afterlife to the otherworld. According to early Greek concepts, the deceased lived as shadows in Hades or in the Elysian fields on the other side of the ocean at the end of the earth.[134] Plato, on the contrary, advocated the concept of an immortal soul, the home of which would be heaven.[135] In popular Greek beliefs, the fate of the deceased increasingly lay on high, in the air, in the ether, in the stars, in heaven or in Olympus, thought to be in heaven as well.[136] The doctrine of heaven as the place of the blessed had an overwhelming influence on Christianity. This was possibly due to the fact that, from many perspectives, it was much more plausible and attractive than the doctrine of an earthly afterlife.

---

133. Viviano, *Kingdom of God*, 32.
134. See above, p. 14.
135. See, in particular, Plato, *Phaedr.* 245a5–49d2.
136. See, in general, Peres, *Griechische Grabinschriften*, 106, and in particular, 81–89, 110–21.

The instability of the sub-lunar world

With the Greco-Roman doctrine of the sub-lunar world as a backdrop, an eternal life on earth seemed implausible. In the world under the moon everything is subject to constant coming and going. Permanence and eternity can only exist in the trans-lunar world of heaven, above the moon.[137] Aristotle wrote that heaven was eternal and had neither an end nor a beginning. The ancients have rightly assigned heaven to the gods because "it alone is immortal" and "suffers from none of the ills of a mortal body."[138] The doctrine of an eternal heaven and a transient sub-lunar world can be found in Cicero's influential story, *Dream of Scipio*. Already in ancient times, it was one of the most well-known prose writings.[139] It states that below the moon "is [. . .] nothing that is not mortal and frail except the souls given to the human race by the god's gift; above the Moon everything is eternal."[140] Accordingly, one should not focus his pursuit on the transient earth, inevitably plagued by catastrophes such as floods and conflagrations,[141] but rather on heaven. "That life [of justice and piety] is a way to heaven,"[142] Cicero has the deceased biological father of Scipio Africanus the younger, Lucius Aemilius Paullus, say: the "seat and eternal home"[143] of man are the shining stars of the Milky Way.[144]

The great heaven and the small earth

In addition, in the *Dream of Scipio* the earth appears to be extremely small and insignificant and a place not worthy of eternity. Scipio Africanus the

---

137. See Hoppe, "Sublunar."
138. Aristotle, *Cael.* 2.1 (283b26—84a14) (trans. Aristotle, *Heavens*, 133, modified).
139. See Büchner, "Einleitung," 333.
140. Cicero, *Rep.* 6.21(17) (trans. Cicero, *Republic*, 120). In *De natura deorum* 2.43,56, Cicero refers to the "order and eternal regularity of the constellations" of the stars. In heaven there is "nothing of chance or hazard, no error, no frustration, but absolute order, accuracy, calculation and regularity. Whatever lacks these qualities, whatever is false and spurious and full of error, belongs to the region between the earth and the moon (the last of all the heavenly bodies), and to the surface of the earth" (trans. Cicero, *Nature of the Gods*, 165, 177).
141. See Cicero, *Rep.* 6.27(23).
142. Cicero, *Rep.* 6.20(16) (trans. Cicero, *Republic*, 120).
143. Cicero, *Rep.* 6.29(25) (trans. Cicero, *Republic*, 123).
144. See Cicero, *Rep.* 6.20(16).

younger regarded this space from a "lofty place and one full of stars, illustrious and shining":[145]

> As I contemplated everything, the other things seemed splendid and marvelous. There were actually stars that we have never seen from this place, the size of all of which we have never suspected. The smallest one was the farthest from heaven and closest to Earth and shone with borrowed light. And the globes of the stars easily surpassed the size of Earth. Earth itself now seemed so small to me that I was discontented with our empire, through which we touch a point of Earth, so to speak.[146]

He is admonished by the deceased Scipio Africanus the Elder, not to focus on earth: "I sense [he said] that you are even now contemplating the seat and home of human beings. If it seems as small to you as it is, look always at these heavenly things, scorn those human things."[147]

Heaven as the space for development and the ascent to God

The constant dwelling place or throne of the Old Testament God was apparently first located in heaven after the Babylonians destroyed the Jerusalem temple in the year 586 BCE.[148] According to eschatological prophecies in the books of the Old Testament and also the Revelation of John, God shall return to the earth: "Thus says the LORD: 'I will return to Zion, And dwell in the midst of Jerusalem. Jerusalem shall be called the City of Truth, The Mountain of the LORD of hosts, The Holy Mountain.'"[149] In Greco-Roman philosophy, heaven, on the contrary, is the natural place of the divine. According to Aristotle, the deity lives in the very highest heaven.[150] If man's highest goal is to be with God, then after death he must leave earth to reach God by ascend-

---

145. Cicero, *Rep.* 6.15(11) (trans. Cicero, *Republic*, 118).

146. Cicero, *Rep.* 6.21(17) (trans. Cicero, *Republic*, 120).

147. Cicero, *Rep.* 6.24(20) (trans. Cicero, *Republic*, 121).

148. See Schmid, "Himmelsgott," 115.

149. Zech 8:3 (NKJV); cf. Zech 2:10: "Sing and rejoice, O daughter of Zion [Jerusalem], for behold, I come and I will dwell in your midst, declares the LORD" (ESV). According to Ezek 43:7,9 God will live in a new temple forever among the Israelites; according to Isa 24:23 God will be on Mount Zion and rule in Jerusalem; according to Joel 4:16–17,21 God promises, he will live on Zion his holy mountain, and Jerusalem will be sacred; according to Mic 4:7 God will be on Mount Zion and rule as king for eternity; in Isa 40:3–4 a road should be built through the desert for God, all mortals will see his rule (when he comes); and according to Isa 52:8 the guardians of Zion "will see the return of the LORD to Zion" (ESV). See similarly, Ps 132:13–14; Zech 1:17.

150. See Aristotle, *Cael.* 1.9 (278b14–15).

ing through the heavenly spheres. This process is often understood as one of spiritual development. An early example for this view is Origen. According to him a holy person continues to develop after death:

> I think, therefore, that all the saints who depart from this life will remain in some place situated on the earth, which holy Scripture calls paradise, as in some place of instruction, and, so to speak, class-room or school of souls, in which they are to be instructed regarding all the things which they had seen on earth, and are to receive also some information respecting things that are to follow in the future. [. . .] If any one indeed be pure in heart, and holy in mind, and more practised in perception, he will, by making more rapid progress, quickly ascend to a place in the air, and reach the kingdom of heaven, through those mansions, so to speak, in the various places which the Greeks have termed spheres, i.e., globes, but which holy Scripture has called heavens; in each of which he will first see clearly what is done there, and in the second place, will discover the reason why things are so done: and thus he will in order pass through all gradations, following Him who has passed into the heavens, Jesus the Son of God [. . .]. When, then, the saints shall have reached the celestial abodes, they will clearly see the nature of the stars one by one, and will understand whether they are endued with life, or their condition, whatever it is. And they will comprehend also the other reasons for the works of God, which He Himself will reveal to them. [. . .] And so, when they have finished all those matters which are connected with the stars, and with the heavenly revolutions, they will come to those which are not seen, or to those whose names only we have heard, and to things which are invisible [. . .]. And thus the rational nature, growing by each individual step, not as it grew in this life in flesh, and body, and soul, but enlarged in understanding and in power of perception, is raised as a mind already perfect to perfect knowledge, no longer at all impeded by those carnal senses, but increased in intellectual growth; and ever gazing purely, and, so to speak, face to face, on the causes of things[.][151]

---

151. Origen, *Princ.* 2.11.6–7 (trans. *ANF* 4:299–300). The ascent through the spheres and the afterlife education and development go hand in hand for Origen, see on this also Recheis, *Engel, Tod und Seelenreise*, 192.

Where shall the immortal soul go?

An essential factor in the transferal of the afterlife to another world was the already mentioned, not limited to Platonism, Hellenistic idea that in death the person is released from their physical body and lives apart from it. "[I]t is not you that is mortal but this body," we read in Cicero's *Dream of Scipio*.[152] Such a belief is often labeled as a belief in a soul, yet this term is somewhat misleading when used in connection with ancient philosophy, because it is shaped by the strict Cartesian opposition of body and soul. In ancient times, that which survives death was, in fact, often called soul (ψυχή). It had, however, as a rule, a subtle-corporeal nature. This is also the case for Plato, the main representative of the doctrine of an immortal soul in ancient philosophy. The famous otherworld story of a soldier named Er in Plato's *Republic* depicts the souls in the beyond as physical in all facets: They can speak, wail and lament, and also go, jump, settle down or line up, take up things from the ground, beat their breast, carry and drink. Others can see them, touch, tie up hands and feet, fling then down, flay them, card them on thorns, and hurl them into Tartarus.[153]

Also in Christianity the soul is often, or even mostly, conceived in some kind of corporeal form. Tertullian writes, for example, that the soul possesses all normal and necessary features of a body, such as shape and three-dimensionality.[154] The soul has the form of the body it lived in.[155] Tertullian draws from visions of a fellow Christian: "Amongst other things, says she, there has been shown to me a soul in bodily shape, and a spirit has been in the habit of appearing to me; not, however, a void and empty illusion, but such as would offer itself to be even grasped by the hand, youthfully, shining, and of an etherial colour, and in a form resembling that of a human being in every respect."[156] According to popular ideas in the Middle Ages, the soul is "not an invisible ghost, a non-body, but rather a second body, that the first body carries with it, that is especially important at the end."[157] Also in Dante's *Divine Comedy*, souls have the characteristics of corporeality. They not only look like physical people, they also act like them apart from the fact that some souls float through the air.[158]

---

152. Cicero, *Rep.* 6.30(26) (trans. Cicero, *Republic*, 123).

153. See Plato, *Resp.* 10.13–16 (613e6–621d2). Also in Plato's *Phaedo* numerous physical activities are attributed to the soul (see 80b8–81e2; 112d4–114c6).

154. See Tertullian, *An.* 9.1.

155. See Tertullian, *An.* 9.7.

156. Tertullian, *An.* 9.4 (trans. ANF 3:188, modified).

157. Sprandel, "Seele der Analphabeten," 98 (trans. S. Kühne).

158. See, e.g., Dante Alighieri, *Divina Commedia*, *Inferno*, canto 5, line 84.

These subtle corporeal souls, that do not remain in the grave, must be somewhere after death. Cicero, for example, does not specify what substance they are made up of but says it is in any case finer than the air here on earth.[159] Thus after death, these corporeal souls will rise up high above the earth to an environment that corresponds to their nature.[160] There above they will feed on the same things the stars feed on.[161] Heaven is their proper home.[162] That Cicero thinks the deceased to be corporeal is also apparent in *Dreams of Scipio* where the deceased Paullus embraces and kisses his son.[163] As far as I see, also in Christianity, the conception that souls do not rest in the grave but abide in otherworldly places spread very quickly.[164] However, it took a while before this was reflected in doctrinal documents. The Second Council of Lyon in 1274 declared:

> As for the souls of those who, after having received holy baptism, have incurred no stain of sin whatever and those souls who, after having contracted the stain of sin, have been cleansed, either while remaining still in their bodies or after having been divested of them [. . .], they are received immediately into heaven. As for the souls of those who die in mortal sin or with original sin only, they go down immediately to hell[.][165]

---

159. See Cicero, *Tusc.* 1.42,65. Litwa, *We are Being Transformed*, 137, states that according to the doctrine of Stoicism souls were made up of pneuma.

160. See Cicero, *Tusc.* 1.43.

161. See Cicero, *Tusc.* 1.43; see also Litwa: *We are Being Transformed*, 135–36.

162. See Cicero, *Tusc.* 1.51: "For my own part, when I reflect on the nature of the soul, it appears to me a far more perplexing and obscure question to determine what is its character while it is in the body—a place which, as it were, does not belong to it—than to imagine what it is when it leaves it, and has arrived at the unrestricted heaven, which is, if I may so say, its proper, its own home" (trans. Cicero, *Cicero's Tusculan Disputations*, 31).

163. See Cicero, *Rep.* 6.18(14).

164. In the early Syrian Church, some theologians advocated, as later also the Nestorians, the doctrine of soul sleep between death and resurrection. In this state the soul remained in the grave or would be stored in another place (see Gavin, "Sleep of the Soul"). Irenaeus of Lyons taught that until resurrection the souls stayed in the underworld (see Irenaeus, *Haer.* 5.31.2). For Augustine, the awake and active soul lives in a place separate from the earth (see Augustine, *Cur.* 16).

165. Profession of Faith of Emperor Michael VIII Paleologos (trans. Denzinger, *Compendium*, 283 ([D 857–58]). The belief in the final reunification of the soul with the body is, however, retained (see Denzinger, *Compendium*, 283 [D 859]).

Contempt for the earthly

The transferal of the afterlife to the beyond was advanced by a contempt for earthly life on the part of spiritually-orientated Christian theologians. An example of this is Origen. He condemns expectations of an earthly-physical life after the resurrection. The relevant statements in the Bible should be understood metaphorically:

> Certain persons, then, refusing the labour of thinking, and adopting a superficial view of the letter of the law, and yielding rather in some measure to the indulgence of their own desires and lusts, being disciples of the letter alone, are of opinion that the fulfilment of the promises of the future are to be looked for in bodily pleasure and luxury; and therefore they especially desire to have again, after the resurrection, such bodily structures as may never be without the power of eating, and drinking, and performing all the functions of flesh and blood, not following the opinion of the Apostle Paul regarding the resurrection of a spiritual body. And consequently they say, that after the resurrection there will be marriages, and the begetting of children,[166] imagining to themselves that the earthly city of Jerusalem is to be rebuilt, its foundations laid in precious stones, [. . .].[167] Moreover, they think that the natives of other countries are to be given them as the ministers of their pleasures, whom they are to employ either as tillers of the field,[168] or builders of walls, and by whom their ruined and fallen city is again to be raised up;[169] and they think that they are to receive the wealth of the nations to live on, and that they will have control over their riches; [. . .].[170] Then, again, agreeably to the form of things in this life, and according to the gradations of the dignities or ranks in this world, or the greatness of their powers, they think they are to be kings and princes, like those earthly monarchs who now exist; chiefly, as it appears, on account of that expression in the Gospel: "Have thou power over five cities."[171] And to speak shortly, according to the manner of things in this life in all similar matters, do they desire the fulfilment of all things looked for in the promises, viz., that what now is should exist again. Such are the views of those

---

166. Cf. Irenaeus, *Haer.* 5.34.2; 5.35.1.
167. Cf. Rev 21:18–20; Irenaeus, *Haer.* 5.34.4.
168. Cf. Isa 61:5.
169. Cf. Isa 60:10.
170. Cf. Isa 60:5–6.11,17; 61:7.
171. See Luke 19:17,19.

who, while believing in Christ, understand the divine Scriptures in a sort of Jewish sense, drawing from them nothing worthy of the divine promises.[172]

Problems with a physical heaven

Right up to modern times, according to Christian ideas, the afterlife was situated, at least in part, in the known cosmos, although the Empyrean heaven, the paradise of the blessed, was repeatedly placed in a genuinely transcendental, spiritual space.[173] Through the observation that, in the sublunar space, the same natural rules apply as in the trans-lunar world—by proving that the celestial bodies are made up of the same elements as the earth and by the discovery of the origin and decay of stars, solar systems and galaxies, and a development of the universe as a whole—the cosmic sky was ultimately ruled out as the place of eternal life after death.[174] This is also the case for the inside of the earth as the place of an eternal hell.

Afterlife on earth: resurrection, judgment and an intermediate kingdom

Resurrection and the Last Judgment take place on earth

If resurrection is understood as the restoration of a known physical body through the gathering and reassembling of its particles, then it is almost obligatory that this will happen on earth, because it is here that the components of the body are to be found. But also, the subsequent Last Judgment was expected to take place on earth, at least until the Middle Ages. The resurrected will not be brought to Jesus, the eschatological judge, to heaven, but he will come to earth for the judgment. This idea connects with Jesus' statements about the Son of Man coming to the judgment from heaven.[175] In the *Epistle of the Apostles,* Jesus says explicitly: "I will come down to earth to judge the living and the dead."[176] Even Thomas Aquinas still believed it to be very likely that Jesus would come down to the judgment near Jerusalem

---

172. Origen, *Princ.* 2.11.2 (trans. *ANF* 4:297).
173. See Kurdzialek and Maurach, "Empyreum."
174. Cf. Evers, "Chaos im Himmel."
175. See above, pp. 56–57, and below, p. 130.
176. Ep. Apos. 16:4 (Coptic version) (trans. *NTApoc*, 258).

at the Mount of Olives, from where he ascended to heaven.[177] The judgment itself will then possibly take place in or near the Valley of Josaphat, the Kidron Valley between the Temple Mount and the Mount of Olives, as it is written in the book of Joel.[178]

The millennial kingdom in the book of Revelation

As we have seen, for Hellenistic thought, the earth was not suitable as the place of eternal life.[179] It is thus not surprising that the Christian tradition devised an unequivocally earthly post-mortal life to last only a limited time, in an intermediate kingdom. The doctrine of this kind of intermediate kingdom was established by the book of Revelation in the New Testament canon.[180] It probably originated around 100 to 110 CE,[181] and it is the most influential apocalyptic text of all.[182] According to Revelation, Jesus will come down from heaven with his heavenly legion and fight against and destroy the kings of the earth and their armies. Then Satan will be imprisoned for thousand years. During this period of time, Jesus will reign over the nations of the earth together with the resurrected martyrs:

> Then I saw heaven opened, and behold, a white horse! The one sitting on it is called Faithful and True, and in righteousness he judges and makes war. [. . .] And the armies of heaven, arrayed in fine linen, white and pure, were following him on white horses. From his mouth comes a sharp sword with which to strike down the nations, and he will rule them with a rod of iron. He will tread the winepress of the fury of the wrath of God the Almighty. [. . .] And I saw the beast[183] and the kings of the earth with their armies gathered to make war against him who was sitting on the horse and against his army. And the beast was captured, and with it the false prophet who in its presence had done the signs by which he deceived those who had received the mark of the beast and those who worshiped

---

177. See Thomas Aquinas, *S. Th.*, Suppl., q. 88, a. 4, co.
178. See Thomas Aquinas, *S. Th.*, Suppl., q. 88, a. 4, ad 1 with arg. 1 and s.c.; cf. Joel 4:2.
179. See above, pp. 101–3.
180. On parallels with 2 Baruch and 4 Ezra, see Böcher, "Chiliasmus," 725.
181. See Witetschek, "Ein weit geöffnetes Zeitfenster?" 147.
182. See Collins, "Book of Revelation," 384.
183. This animal is probably identical to the beast out of the sea in Rev 13:1–4 and represents an anti-Christian, world-controlling power, probably the Roman Empire, perhaps personified in a specific emperor.

its image. These two were thrown alive into the lake of fire that burns with sulfur. And the rest were slain by the sword that came from the mouth of him who was sitting on the horse, and all the birds were gorged with their flesh. Then I saw an angel coming down from heaven, holding in his hand the key to the bottomless pit and a great chain. And he seized the dragon, that ancient serpent, who is the devil and Satan, and bound him for a thousand years, and threw him into the pit, and shut it and sealed it over him, so that he might not deceive the nations any longer, until the thousand years were ended. After that he must be released for a little while. Then I saw thrones, and seated on them were those to whom the authority to judge was committed. Also I saw the souls of those who had been beheaded for the testimony of Jesus and for the word of God, and those who had not worshiped the beast or its image and had not received its mark on their foreheads or their hands. They came to life and reigned with Christ for a thousand years. The rest of the dead did not come to life until the thousand years were ended. This is the first resurrection. Blessed and holy is the one who shares in the first resurrection! Over such the second death has no power, but they will be priests of God and of Christ, and they will reign with him for a thousand years.[184]

Not everyone will be resurrected in the millennial kingdom but only particular Christian martyrs. From then onwards, they will be immortal. Normal people, it would seem, will continue to be mortal. Death, as well as disease, hunger, poverty, and sadness are not explicitly banned from the millennial kingdom. It is not primarily about an afterlife, but an earthly life and an earthly dominion. This becomes even more clear if we look at two later versions of the millennial kingdom.

Irenaeus and Lactantius: a very earthly intermediate kingdom

Irenaeus of Lyons offers a rich embellishment of the millennial kingdom.[185] To this end he employs Old Testament prophecies and also some of Jesus' promises of a physical afterlife, such as the prophecies of the drinking of wine in the kingdom of God.[186] Jesus will, writes Irenaeus, descend from heaven and cast the Antichrist and his followers into the lake of fire.[187] Then

---

184. Rev 19:11,14–15,19—20:6.
185. See Lang and McDannell, *Heaven*, 48–53, 67.
186. See Irenaeus, *Haer.* 5.33.1; cf. Matt 26:29; Mark 14:25.
187. See Irenaeus, *Haer.* 5.30.4.

the righteous shall arise and reign over the remaining people[188] for a thousand years.[189] The earth will be unbelievably fertile[190] and the remaining people there will multiply[191]—a strong indication for the earthliness of this kingdom. Peace will extend to the animal kingdom, according to the vision of Isaiah.[192] People, it seems, will remain fundamentally mortal. Only the resurrected righteous will no longer die, not because they have been transformed, but because they "shall then forget to die."[193]

Lactantius also presented a detailed version of the millennial kingdom. In his *Divine Institutes*, finished at the latest in 311,[194] he first portrays Jesus' deliverance of the righteous from the great danger of the armies of the Antichrist.[195] The hostile armies will be destroyed, the blood of the enemies "shall flow like a torrent,"[196] and the Antichrist and the other lords and tyrants will be consigned "to deserved tortures."[197] Then the millennial kingdom will be established as an earthly empire with a capital city, with officials, and with a ruling and a subservient class.[198] The righteous from times past will be raised[199] and those righteous still alive at the coming of Jesus will no longer die but will multiply. As in Irenaeus, nature will be abundantly fertile, and peace will rule among the animals:

---

188. See Irenaeus, *Haer.* 5.32.1: "[I]t behoves the righteous first to receive the promise of the inheritance which God promised to the fathers, and to reign in it, when they rise again to behold God in this creation which is renovated, and that the judgment should take place afterwards. For it is just that in that very creation in which they toiled or were afflicted, being proved in every way by suffering, they should receive the reward of their suffering; and that in the creation in which they were slain because of their love to God, in that they should be revived again; and that in the creation in which they endured servitude, in that they should reign. For God is rich in all things, and all things are His. It is fitting, therefore, that the creation itself, being restored to its primeval condition, should without restraint be under the dominion of the righteous" (transl. *ANF* 1:561).

189. See Irenaeus, *Haer.*, 5.23.2 and 5.28.2, in connection with 5.30.4: At his second coming Jesus will bring about the seventh day of the completion of creation. This seventh day, the day of rest for God, is the time of the kingdom of God on earth and according to 2 Pet 3:8, is equivalent to thousand human years.

190. See Irenaeus, *Haer.* 5.34.2; 5.35.1.

191. See Irenaeus, *Haer.* 5.34.2; 5.35.1.

192. See Irenaeus, *Haer.* 5.33.4, and Isa 11:6–8; 65:25.

193. Irenaeus, *Haer.* 5.36.2 (trans. *ANF* 1:567).

194. See Freund, "Einleitung," 4–5.

195. See Lactantius, *Inst.* 7.17.10–11.

196. Lactantius, *Inst.* 7.19.5 (trans. *ANF* 7:215).

197. Lactantius, *Inst.* 7.19.7 (trans. *ANF* 7:215).

198. See Freund, "Kommentar," 545.

199. See Lactantius, *Inst.* 7.24.2.

> But He [Christ], when He shall have destroyed unrighteousness, and executed His great judgment, and shall have recalled to life the righteous, who have lived from the beginning, will be engaged among men a thousand years, and will rule them with most just command. [. . .] Then they who shall be alive in their bodies[200] shall not die, but during those thousand years shall produce an infinite multitude, and their offspring shall be holy, and beloved by God; but they who shall be raised from the dead shall preside over the living as judges.[201] But the nations shall not be entirely extinguished, but some shall be left as a victory for God, that they may be the occasion of triumph to the righteous, and may be subjected to perpetual slavery. [. . .] After its coming [the coming of the people of God] the righteous shall be collected from all the earth, and the judgment being completed, a sacred city shall be planted in the middle of the earth, in which God Himself the builder may dwell together with the ruling righteous. And [. . .] the earth will open its fruitfulness, and bring forth most abundant fruits of its own accord; the rocky mountains shall drop with honey; streams of wine shall run down, and rivers flow with milk [. . .]. Throughout this time beasts shall not be nourished by blood, nor birds by prey; but all things shall be peaceful and tranquil. Lions and calves shall stand together at the manger, the wolf shall not carry off the sheep, the hound shall not hunt for prey; hawks and eagles shall not injure; the infant shall play with serpents.[202]

The doctrine of an earthly intermediate kingdom was never universally recognized in Christianity, and from the fourth century onwards it was largely rejected. Against the chiliastic expectation, the Niceno-Constantipolitan Creed states that the kingdom of the returned Christ will have no end. Augustine identifies the thousand-year reign of Christ with the existing church.[203] With the reform movements of the modern era from the seventeenth century onwards, the idea of a millennial kingdom recovered[204] and is now, among conservative Christians, perhaps more widespread than ever.[205]

200. These are the righteous that are still alive at the coming of Jesus.

201. This preference for the resurrected righteous over the still living ones appears to be somewhat lacking in motivation (see Freund, "Kommentar," 548).

202. Lactantius, *Inst.* 7.24.2–4,6–8 (trans. *ANF* 7:219, modified).

203. See Blum, "Chiliasmus," 731–32; Schaff, *Creeds of Christendom*, 2:59; Augustine, *Civ.* 20.9.

204. See Bauckham, "Chiliasmus," 739–43.

205. See Bauckham, "Chiliasmus," 743.

An eternal life on an unearthly earth after the end of time

For an eternal, blissful life on earth, not only must the physical body of the resurrected be transformed, but also the earth itself, and with it, the entire cosmos.[206] It is thus logical that Christian theologians postulate an eternal, earthly life only for a transformed, new earth. They mostly describe this new earth quite vaguely or admit that it will have few earthly characteristics.

Jesus' silence on the transformation of the cosmos

Judging by the available sources, it is probable that Jesus remained silent on the transformation of the cosmos.[207] It appears that his eschatology had a rather regional focus. His expectation of the restoration of Israel with Jerusalem at its center stands in tension with the later Christian ideas of a world's end and a complete new creation of the earth. Following Old Testament prophecies, Jesus himself predicted astronomical phenomena such as a solar eclipse, a lunar eclipse and meteor showers,[208] yet none of this would mean that the earth would be transformed or that its existence would be fundamentally endangered. On other occasions Jesus spoke—also picking up on Old Testament ideas—of the passing of heaven and earth, but this, above all, to symbolize the eternal validity of his own words, not to make a concrete apocalyptic statement.[209]

New earth without the end of the world: book of Revelation

The book of Revelation is the first New Testament text to speak of a new earth (and a new heaven) at the end of time. However, it does not appear to foresee an annihilation of the old earth.[210] Alongside earthquakes, Revelation can only muster the astronomical phenomena already named by Jesus: "When he opened the sixth seal, I looked, and behold, there was a great earthquake, and the sun became black as sackcloth, the full moon became like blood, and the stars of the sky fell to the earth as the fig tree sheds its

---

206. See above, pp. 1–2.

207. See above, p. 72n195 on his single use of the word παλιγγενεσία in Matt 19:28, which probably meant the renewal of Israel there.

208. See above, pp. 71–72.

209. See above, p. 71.

210. See Rev 21:1.

New earth after the end of the world: Second Epistle of Peter

The Second Epistle of Peter, probably the latest of all the New Testament scriptures,[213] is the only book in the New Testament that prophesies a complete destruction of the known earth (and the heavens). In its end-of-the-world scenario through fire, the Second Epistle of Peter seems to pick up on the widespread Stoic concept of *ekpyrosis*, or universal conflagration.[214] Subsequently, as in the book of Revelation, new heavens and a new earth will be created. The Second Epistle of Peter says nothing of resurrection:[215]

> But the day of the Lord will come like a thief, and then the heavens will pass away with a roar, and the elements will be burned up and dissolved, and the earth and the works that are done on it will be burn up. Since all these things are thus to be dissolved, what sort of people ought you to be in lives of holiness and godliness, waiting for and hastening the coming of the day of God, because of which the heavens will be set on fire and dissolved, and the heavenly bodies will melt as they burn! But according to his promise we are waiting for new heavens and a new earth in which righteousness dwells.[216]

Later on, above all in the Latin West of Christianity, it has been repeatedly taught that before a new one emerges, the old world will be destroyed by universal conflagration, with the exception of people and angels.[217]

---

211. Rev 6:12–13 (ESV); cf. Joel 2:10; 3:4; Isa 34:4; Matt 24:29; Acts 2:20.

212. Rev 22:6–7,10,20 (ESV).

213. Possibly around 125–130 CE (see Feldmeier, "Der zweite Petrusbrief," 335 with fn. 27).

214. See Harrill, "Stoic Physics," 118–19, 127, 131. Ekpyrosis was, however, not thought of as an apocalyptic event but as a periodic, natural event that would purify the world and would always allow the same thing to arise again (see Stückelberger, "Ekpyrosis," 433). This does not, however, speak against an influence of the stoic *ekpyrosis* concept on the Epistle of Peter.

215. Harrill attempts to show that the Epistle of Peter preaches steadfastness (στηριγμός, see 2 Pet 3:17) against the backdrop of the Stoic doctrine of a unity of the ethical and physical, or of soul and body and of the ideal of a stable, holistic psychophysical self. Through this steadfastness it is possible to avoid the eschatological dissolution (see "Stoic Physics," 119–32).

216. 2 Pet 3:10–13 (ESV, modified).

217. See, in general, Seils, "Weltende," 465, and in particular, e.g., Justin, *1*

Theological perplexity with regard to the new earth

In contrast to the description of the intermediate kingdom, Christian theologians are mostly reticent when it comes to what life on the new earth will be like. A well-known example is Irenaeus of Lyons. As comprehensively as he expresses himself on the intermediate kingdom of thousand years in *Against Haereses*, he says little about the circumstances on the new earth and in the new heaven.[218] He mentions only the three locations of the afterlife of the righteous: heaven, the city—the new Jerusalem of the Revelation that came down from heaven—and paradise, but nothing further.[219]

Also, in Lactantius the new earth is only briefly outlined. There are only a few lines in the *Divine Institutes* on the world after the millennial kingdom:

> But when the thousand years shall be completed, the world shall be renewed by God, and the heavens shall be folded together, and the earth shall be changed, and God shall transform men into the similitude of angels, and they shall be white as snow;[220] and they shall always be employed in the sight of the Almighty, and shall make offerings to their Lord, and serve Him for ever.[221]

Nothing is said about the kind of world the righteous live in, so there is no clue as to the earthly features of this world.

Modern theologians also struggle to say something about the eternal new earth (and the new heaven). Paul Althaus emphasizes "the utter otherness of the new world," as well as its identity with the current one. He treats

---

Apol. 20; Minucius Felix, *Oct.* 34,1–5; Tertullian, *Spect.* 30; see later Augustine, *Civ.* 20.16,18,24,30; Thomas Aquinas, *S. Th.*, Suppl., q. 74, a. 2–9.

218. See Lang and McDannell, *Heaven*, 53.

219. See Irenaeus, *Haer.* 5.36.1.

220. According to Freund, "Kommentar," 585–86, this points to the immortalization of the resurrected. Freund also refers to the wording "garment of immortality" in Lactantius, *Epit.* 72 ("Kommentar," 585–86). The righteous of the millennial kingdom must hide under the earth during the final battle between God against the wicked nations (see Lactantius, *Inst.* 7.26.2–3). From this it can be concluded that the righteous are not immortal at this point in time. According to Augustine, during world conflagration the risen ones stay in the higher regions, where the flames do not reach, although he himself says that they do not actually have to fear the fire of world conflagration (see above, p. 96).

221. Lactantius, *Inst.* 7.26.5 (trans. ANF 7:221). Cf. Lactantius, *Epit.* 72: "After these things God will renew the world, and transform the righteous into the forms of angels, that, being presented with the garment of immortality, they may serve God for ever; and this will be the kingdom of God, which shall have no end" (trans. ANF 7:255).

this obvious contradiction as a "mystery."[222] N. T. Wright ventures somewhat further. For him, life in the new world is physical.[223] Perhaps the immortal resurrected bodies will consist of molecules.[224] Immortality is not an intrinsic quality of the resurrected body and the whole new world. Rather it is a gift from God, as God alone is immortal in nature.[225] Wright ultimately avoids giving a factual answer to the question of how a physical body can be indestructible and live for eternity and just refers to the power of God.[226] John Polkinghorne believes in the possibility that this universe can be transformed by God to "a temporal world whose character is everlasting."[227] The new creation must exhibit a "totally different 'physical fabric' from that of the old creation."[228] How this physical tissue would have to be such that a material life—with bacteria, dinosaurs, lions, and pets[229]—could be possible and be free of suffering and death in all eternity, Polkinghorne does not say, despite his being a theoretical physicist as well as a theologian. He sees the only grounds for hope in a material, eternal life in the "steadfast love and faithfulness of God."[230] Polkinghorne's abstention from giving rational arguments for his eschatology resembles the approach of Jehovah's witnesses, who preach an eternal, earthly life based solely on biblical references.[231] On the Catholic side there is even greater reluctance to speculate about an eternal, new earth. According to Karl Rahner, matter is "only the seedbed of spirit and of subjectivity and of freedom." He expects that "the material cosmos as a whole, whose meaning and goal is the fulfillment of freedom" will transcend and abolish itself one day.[232]

---

222. Althaus, *Die letzten Dinge*, 361, 363.

223. Jesus, after his resurrection, received a "new *kind* of physical body," writes Wright (*Surprised by Hope*, 63). Also, Paul did not abolish the physical nature of the resurrection body (see *Surprised by Hope*, 156); it will have "a new mode of physicality" and be even "more bodily" than our present body (*Surprised by Hope*, 154).

224. Wright writes that it doesn't matter whether the identical molecules return, but some continuity is quite possible (see *Surprised by Hope*, 157).

225. See Wright, *Surprised by Hope*, 161.

226. See Wright, *Surprised by Hope*, 158–59, 161, 164.

227. Polkinghorne, *God of Hope*, 117.

228. Polkinghorne, *God of Hope*, 143.

229. See Polkinghorne, *God of Hope*, 122–23.

230. Polkinghorne, *God of Hope*, 149.

231. See Watchtower Bible and Tract Society, *Bible*, 27–28, 33–37, 54, 65, 80–81, 84, 110, 153.

232. Rahner, *Foundations*, 445–46. See also his criticism of the level of reflection of Christian eschatology in Rahner, "Eschatologie," 1186; Rahner, "Letzte Dinge," 222.

Descriptions of an unearthly, new earth

When, on the other hand, the new earth is described in more detail, it mostly seems barely earthly.[233] This begins already in the Revelation of John. It is the only text in the New Testament that describes the circumstances on the renewed earth. Above all, the splendor of the wall and the twelve gates of the new Jerusalem are described. It is an unearthly cubic city that is 1,400 miles long, wide and high(!). In this city, God lives together with Jesus (as lamb) without a temple. They light up the city in such a way that it needs neither a sun nor a moon. The river of the water of life flows out of God's throne. The only sign of non-human life in the city is the tree of life. Its leaves have healing powers. From the area outside the city it is said only that there are nations and kings. Only the chosen can come to the city, although its gates are always open.[234]

Thomas Aquinas attempted to define more closely the conditions of eternity on the renewed earth according to contemporary thought categories. Everything transient will be eradicated in a final conflagration. The bodies of all people will be completely burned to ash. The good will not suffer any pain.[235] The movement of the celestial bodies will stop.[236] There will be no animals, plants, minerals, and no other bodies made up of different elements.[237] Animals and plants do not have immortal souls able to survive the conflagration. Inorganic bodies made up of different elements already carry the cause of decay within them, because their elements can be separated.[238] Only the heavenly bodies, the elements, and human beings will persist.[239]

For the Mormons, the new earth is also barely earthly. All that is perishable will—as in Thomas Aquinas—be melted in glowing fire. The renewed

---

233. The little-known Syriac Apocalypse of Daniel from the fourth or fifth century presents an exception with regard to this. It knows no thousand-year intermediate kingdom, instead the eternal kingdom on earth is unmistakably earthly. Jesus comes as a warrior from the heavens back to earth, destroys his enemies with fire, cuts off death's power, and brings peace to the world. After the general resurrection, all Israelites return to the new Jerusalem, and all peoples undertake a pilgrimage there. They go on foot and do not obviously float or fly. The earth still has mountains, hills, rivers, seas, beaches, and islands. The text mentions palm trees, cedars, olive trees, myrtles and cypresses, beautiful flowers, delicious herbs, and fragrant reeds (see Syr. Apoc. Dan. 30–40).

234. See Rev 21:1—22:5.

235. See Thomas Aquinas, *S. Th.* Suppl., q. 74, a. 8, co.

236. See Thomas Aquinas, *S. Th.* Suppl., q. 77, a. 1, co.

237. See Thomas Aquinas, *S. Th.* Suppl., q. 91, a. 5, co.

238. See Thomas Aquinas, *S. Th.* Suppl., q. 74, a. 1, ad 3.

239. See Thomas Aquinas, *S. Th.* Suppl., q. 91, a. 5, co.

earth will then "be like a sea of glass and fire."²⁴⁰ A new earth similar to the present one is, to my knowledge, not taught by academic theologians, but by Christian denominations such as the Jehovah's Witnesses or the Seven-day Adventists, who support their belief with a literalist interpretation of the Bible.²⁴¹ The factual possibility of an eternal, physical life without suffering is not discussed.

Conclusion

The history of the Christian doctrine of the afterlife is characterized by the problem of the effective impossibility of an eternal, earthly-physical life. On the one hand, right up to the present day, Christian dogma holds on to the physical resurrection of Jesus and all other people. On the other hand, a transformation of the resurrected body that frees it from the transience of physicality is speculated. The same applies to the earth, which according to predominant tradition should be the final place of the eternal life. It should, along with the whole cosmos, be fundamentally transformed to provide a suitable site for a life of eternal bliss. In the microcosm of the resurrected body and in the macrocosm of the transformed earth, we have a very similar situation. Both should be in this world but, at the same time, exhibit otherworldly characteristics.

---

240. The Church of Jesus Christ of Latter-Day Saints, *Doctrine and Covenants*, 264 (Section 130:7); see also Lang and McDannell, *Heaven*, 317: "The renewed earth—a sea of glass mingled with fire—will be [. . .] the highest heaven, the [realm of] celestial glory"; Riskas, "New Heaven." There will be procreation on this heavenly new earth (see Lang and McDannell, *Heaven*, 318–19).

241. For the pertinent doctrine of the Jehovah's Witnesses, see above the references p. 116n231; on the doctrine of the Seventh-day Adventists, see General Conference of Seventh-Day Adventists, *28 Fundamental Beliefs*, 11 (No. 28), and also in more detail, McKenzie, "New Earth"; Pierce, "World Made New."

6

The Lakota Ghost-Dance Movement

Otherworld Experiences Stimulate a Belief in a Future Kingdom of God

IF ONE WISHES TO increase the plausibility of otherworldly experiences as a source for religious ideas about resurrection and an earthly kingdom of God, then it would be beneficial not only to point out the parallels between accounts of otherworldly experiences and religious descriptions of the resurrected and the kingdom of God, but also to provide historical reference points for a corresponding causal relationship. In the case of the origin of belief in resurrection and in a kingdom of God this is impossible because it lies hidden in the fog of ancient history. But there is a concise, modern case example of the adoption of the belief in a future paradisiacal kingdom of God on earth on the basis of otherworld journeys: the well-documented Ghost Dance movement of the Lakota, a group of the Sioux people.

Otherworld journeys during the ghost dance

In 1889, tidings of an imminent kingdom of God came to the Lakota people, who were living in South Dakota.[1] They originated from the Paiute Indian prophet, Wovoka.[2] Wovoka was influenced by Christian ideas.[3] In the kingdom that he prophesied, all Indians, alive and deceased, would live on a paradisiacal, renewed earth.[4] The Lakota did not easily accept this prophecy, but sent a delegation to Wovoka, who lived some 1,400 miles away in Nevada, to find out more about this prophet and his message.[5] Above all else they were convinced by otherworld journeys. Wovoka taught them a dance

---

1. See Andersson, *Lakota Ghost Dance*, 31.
2. See Andersson, *Lakota Ghost Dance*, 31.
3. See Andersson, *Lakota Ghost Dance*, 25, 27, 29.
4. See Andersson, *Lakota Ghost Dance*, 25, 27, 29.
5. See Andersson, *Lakota Ghost Dance*, 31–40.

that the white people called the "ghost dance."[6] The Lakota believed that this dance would ensure their participation in the new world and would hasten its coming.[7] The ghost dance was trance-inducing. While partaking in the dance many participants fell to the floor as if dead and had visionary experiences.[8] According to multiple accounts, some of those who made otherworld journeys met with deceased relatives and friends in the other world and spoke with them.[9] Little Wound of the Lakota, for example, saw "broad and fertile lands [that] stretched in every direction" in his otherworld experience, and they "were most pleasing" to his eyes. The deceased had come to the call of a divine figure:

> They appeared, riding the finest horses I ever saw, dressed in superb and most brilliant garments, and seeming very happy. As they approached, I recognized the playmates of my childhood, and I ran forward to embrace them while tears of joy ran down my cheeks. [. . .] Then we [. . .] looked into a great valley where there were thousands of buffalo, deer, and elk feeding.[10]

The landscapes, the otherworldly persons, and the strong impression of reality during these experiences resemble the otherworldly landscapes and persons in accounts of near-death experiences. The description of the "most brilliant garments" of the deceased Indians suggests that Little Wound also experienced the luminescence of otherworldly persons.

Black Elk

For one of the chief ghost dancers—the young medicine man and later holy man of the Oglala Lakota, Black Elk[11]—a connection between an otherworldly experience and belief in Wovoka's prophecy is particularly clear. Black Elk was an extraordinarily religious individual.[12] He was regarded as a healer and mystic. He was even credited with nature miracles.[13] In the be-

---

6. See Andersson, *Lakota Ghost Dance*, 29, 306–8.
7. See Andersson, *Lakota Ghost Dance*, 75, 310.
8. See Andersson, *Lakota Ghost Dance*, 34, 45, 57, 61–62, 299.
9. See Andersson, *Lakota Ghost Dance*, 35, 45, 62.
10. Andersson, *Lakota Ghost Dance*, 63 (emphasis added).
11. Born 1865, died 1950. On his designation as a medicine man and holy-man, see Steltenkamp, *Nicolas Black Elk*, 45. For his role in the ghost dance, see DeMallie, *Sixth Grandfather*, 266.
12. Michael Steltenkamp describes him as a "religious giant" (*Nicolas Black Elk*, 233).
13. See Steltenkamp, *Nicolas Black Elk*, 23–32, 63–64 for visions; 48, 155–56 for

ginning, Black Elk did not seem to think much of the new movement. This can be concluded from the stenographic records of his discussions with John Neihardt.[14] According to Neihardt's representation, Black Elk explicitly commented on this: "[W]hen I first heard of it, I thought it was only foolish talk that somebody had started somewhere. [. . .] I did not yet believe. I thought maybe it was only the despair that made people believe, just as a man who is starving may dream of plenty of everything good to eat."[15] However, Black Elk could not escape the similarities between Wovoka's message and his own earlier vision of the rebirth of his people.[16] He joined the Ghost Dance movement and obviously became convinced by otherworld experiences during the dance. In the beyond, he saw not only wonderful landscapes full of wild animals,[17] but also deceased Indians. His description resembles accounts of near-death experiences: "The men that I saw were all beautiful und it seemed there were no old men there. They were all young."[18] In his speeches, Black Elk proclaimed that he had seen the "Promised Land,"[19] and was convinced that this land was in reach and would come to them very soon.[20] In the same year, on December 29, 1890, the Ghost Dance movement of the Lakota died in the US army massacre at Wounded Knee.

---

healings; 156, 160, for the containing of a fire through a sun dance and on the aversion of storms and wind.

14. See DeMallie, *Sixth Grandfather*, 256–58.
15. Neihardt, *Black Elk Speaks*, 186–87.
16. See DeMallie, *Sixth Grandfather*, 257–58.
17. See DeMallie, *Sixth Grandfather*, 261, 263–64.
18. DeMallie, *Sixth Grandfather*, 263–64.
19. DeMallie, *Sixth Grandfather*, 266, 268.

20. In the Ghost Dance movement there were very different but mostly vague descriptions of how the new world would come. Black Elk said it would come like a cloud and crush out all the whites (see DeMallie, *Sixth Grandfather*, 257). According to James Mooney, the Sioux had expected that after the eschatological earthquake the white people would be swallowed up in a deep landslide, perhaps in connection with a flood or a whirlwind, during which time the Indians would be carried up to reach the surface of the promised land (see *Ghost Dance Religion*, 786–89). Wovoka himself seems to have spoken of an earthquake (see *Ghost Dance Religion*, 781–82). In other tribes they expected a flood of mud and water would destroy the white people while the Indians survived in the mountains. When the floods receded then the new world would appear (see *Ghost Dance Religion*, 784); others believed that the world would arrive following a deep sleep for the Indians (*Ghost Dance Religion*, 786); others again that the new world would arrive from the west and would slide over the old world. A wall of fire would lead the way and force the white people over the water back to their land while the Indians would surmount the fire with sacred feathers, enabling them thus to reach the promised land (see *Ghost Dance Religion*, 786). Others awaited a hurricane with thunder and lightning and that would destroy the white people only (see *Ghost Dance Religion*, 786).

7

Did Jesus Have Transcendent Experiences That Might Explain His Eschatological Belief?

The search for a specific explanation

IN MY ANALYSIS OF the traditional doctrine of Jesus of Nazareth, I came to the conclusion that the belief in an earthly-physical resurrection and the establishment of an eternal, earthly kingdom of God, were not merely attributed to him by the sources, but they probably really did form an integral part of the historical Jesus' message. This raises the question why precisely Jesus believed so intensively in this eschatological idea that he proclaimed it publicly. The answer should, if possible, specifically address Jesus as we know him from the early transmissions, and not his contemporaries. For this reason, merely referring to the reading of known eschatological writings, such as the book of Daniel, would be insufficient. I believe the search for specific psychological and cognitive deficits of Jesus that might explain his eschatological belief hold little promise.[1] If we keep in mind the case of the Ghost Dance movement of the Lakota, the more important question is whether Jesus of Nazareth's eschatological belief was inspired and strengthened by transcendent experiences.

---

1. At the beginning of the twentieth century there was a tendency to classify Jesus as mentally ill, in part due to his eschatological beliefs (see Schweitzer, *Quest*, 292–95; Schweitzer, *Psychiatrische Beurteilung Jesu*; Capps, "Schweitzer and the Psychiatrists," 402–3). As a consequence, Albert Schweitzer wrote that "it is those who oppose, completely or in part, the eschatological interpretation of Jesus who believe that they are saving him from the madhouse" (Schweitzer, *Quest*, 295). In his medical dissertation, *Die psychiatrische Beurteilung Jesu*, from 1913, Schweitzer discredited attempts at a remote psychiatric diagnosis of Jesus as unsustainable. But he had no explanation for the fact that Jesus (amongst others) could seriously believe in a general resurrection of the dead and a subsequent kingdom of God that "comes to earth from heaven" and in which all possess "eternal life" (*Kingdom of God*, 92–93). Therefore, his only remaining option was to emphasize the alien, enigmatic and offensive of Jesus' world view (see *Quest*, 478, 480, 482–85).

Otherworld journeys or encounters with the deceased?

In the case of the Lakota Ghost Dance movement, otherworld journeys were able to move people to believe in an earthly, paradisiacal kingdom, in which all deceased live in the prime of life, and where hunger and danger will be forgotten. Participants in the ghost dance saw and experienced a kingdom of this sort with wondrously vibrant and luminous deceased individuals. Through the experience of the mystical proximity of this new world, their conviction that its arrival was imminent was strengthened. For the Lakota, it was not, however, about resurrection in the biblical sense but the coming of an already existing paradisiacal world in which the deceased were already living.

In the case of Jesus of Nazareth, analysis of the sources gives a different picture. If, as the Lakota, he had experienced an otherworld journey in a paradisiacal world with luminous deceased, he would have inferred that this kingdom already existed, of course not in Israel, but rather in another place, hard to locate. Also, if he had encountered the already deceased in this kingdom, the general resurrection of the dead could not have been thought of as a purely future event.[2] This observation matches the scarcity of evidence for the otherworld journeys of Jesus. There are only a few vague hints in the Gospel of John.[3] Descriptions of otherworldly landscapes and encounters with deceased are nowhere to be found. In the transfiguration narrative, Jesus encounters two otherworldly persons, Moses and Elijah, who according to the Gospel of Luke are shining.[4] However, according to understanding at the time, they were not deceased. According to the Old Testament, Elijah did not die but went up into heaven in a whirlwind.[5] Moses, according to Deuteronomy, was buried by God himself in an unknown place.[6] According

---

2. Bernhard Lang suggested that otherworld journeys of Jesus were the key to understanding him (see *Jahwe*, 241–43). In a previous contribution, I was more sympathetic to his hypothesis than I am now (see "Synoptic Jesus," 209).

3. For evidence of otherworld journeys of Jesus, the following Bible passages come into question, John 3:13: "No one has ascended into heaven except he who descended from heaven, the Son of Man" (ESV), John 1:18: "No one has ever seen God; the only-begotten God, who is in the bosom of the Father, he has made him known" (ESV, modified); and John 6:46: "[N]ot that anyone has seen the Father except he who is from God; he has seen the Father" (ESV). These passages, however, can be understood in light of John's doctrine of the pre-existence of Jesus. They do not necessarily imply that Jesus had otherworld journeys during his life on earth.

4. Luke 9:31 says that they appeared ἐν δόξῃ, which here means "splendor" or "brightness" (see BDAG, 257; see a similar use of δόξα, e.g., in Luke 2:9; 9:32; Acts 22:11; 1 Cor 15:40–41; 2 Cor 3:7; Rev 18:1).

5. See 2 Kgs 2:9–12.

6. See Deut 34:5–7.

to later legend he was, however, also taken into heaven.[7] The transfiguration experience—if historical—could have strengthened Jesus' idea of luminous otherworldly persons already found in the book of Daniel,[8] but probably not his belief in the resurrection of the dead.

Do miracle experiences hold the key?

A key to the eschatology of Jesus could, however, lie in other kinds of transcendent experiences, namely, those commonly called miracles. Once again it makes no difference here whether these happenings really transcend the boundaries of normal categories of explanation.[9] It is more decisive that they did so for Jesus and for those around him. There is an overwhelming consensus in the sources that Jesus was a miracle worker.[10] The number of miracles attributed to him seems to have been, in ancient times, without parallel.[11]

Miraculous revivifications as experiential basis for Jesus' belief in resurrection?

Miraculous revivifications may have been of particular importance for Jesus' belief in a physical resurrection. He not only preached a physical resurrection, but according to his understanding, he also produced resurrections.[12]

---

7. See Davies and Allison, *Matthew*, 1:698 fn. 69 with references. The title of the apocryphal, incomplete text *Assumptio Mosis*, which originates from the time of Jesus (see Brandenburger, "Himmelfahrt Moses," 59–60), also points to the idea of Moses being carried away to heaven at the end of his earthly life. According to Brandenburger, the transfiguration narrative presupposes the assumption of Moses (see "Himmelfahrt Moses," 62).

8. See Dan 10:5–6: "I lifted up my eyes and looked, and behold, a man clothed in linen, with a belt of fine gold from Uphaz around his waist. His body was like beryl, his face like the appearance of lightning, his eyes like flaming torches, his arms and legs like the gleam of burnished bronze" (ESV).

9. For the further question of whether they contradict current scientific knowledge, see below, pp. 157–62.

10. See Allison, Historical Christ, 66–68; Twelftree, "Miracle Story"; Theissen and Merz, *Historical Jesus*, 281–313; Theißen, "Wunder Jesu," 68–74.

11. See Twelftree, "Miracle Story," 416; see also Blackburn, "Miracles of Jesus," 124, as well as John 21:25: "Now there are also many other things that Jesus did. Were every one of them to be written, I suppose that the world itself could not contain the books that would be written" (ESV). Most of the miracles of Jesus by far were healings.

12. See, e.g., Matt 11:5; Luke 7:22; John 11:14–44. The first time Jesus sends out his disciples, he also asks them to: "Heal the sick, raise the dead, cleanse lepers, cast out

Here lies the most tangible experiential basis in the sources for his belief in resurrection. We have seen that, according to the gospels, he described miraculous revivifications with the same vocabulary as the eschatological resurrection from the dead, which suggests he did not fundamentally differentiate between the two.[13] That not only the population, but also Jesus himself was impressed by his miraculous revivifications, is shown in his answer to the request of the disciples of John the Baptist as to whether he is the one (Savior), who shall come. He lists the revivifications alongside other healings as proof of his mission:

> Now when John heard in prison about the deeds of the Christ,[14] he sent word by his disciples and said to him, "Are you the one who is to come, or shall we look for another?" And Jesus answered them, "Go and tell John what you hear and see: the blind receive their sight and the lame walk, lepers are cleansed and the deaf hear, and *the dead are raised up*, and the poor have good news preached to them."[15]

Miracles as flashes of the reality of God's kingdom?

Jesus' belief in the possibility of a post-mortal eternal life in a paradisiacal, earthly kingdom of God, without hunger and disease, and in peace with nature, could also have been inspired by miracles, or at least strengthened by them. The reality of the kingdom of God "flashed"—so it would appear—into the miracles of Jesus.[16] This interpretation would help to explain passages in which Jesus seems to speak of the direct proximity or presence of the kingdom of God, although the decisive eschatological events still lie in the future.[17] Followers of the modern Hindu guru Sathya Sai Baba believed, in the face of his abundant miracles, that "the Golden Age" had dawned.[18] I think it is very likely that Jesus and those around him had similar thoughts. In view of Jesus' miracles, there could be little doubt that a paradisiacal life on earth was possible. If Jesus could already raise the dead, heal all kinds

---

demons" (Matt 10:8 ESV).

13. See above, pp. 49–52.
14. The Greek word "Christos" is a translation from the Hebrew "Messiah": the Anointed.
15. Matt 11:2–6 (ESV, emphasis added), very similar Luke 7:18–23.
16. Cf. Weder, *Gegenwart und Gottesherrschaft*, 30, 32–33.
17. See Mark 1:15; Luke 11:20; 17:20–21, and above, pp. 69–70.
18. Kasturi, "Rain Cloud"; Kasturi, "You and Me."

of disease,[19] provide food for the hungry from almost nothing,[20] and even appease the threats of the natural world,[21] then the thought that it would be easy for God to realize these things in his kingdom on a large scale would not have been far away.

Miracles and Jesus' self-conception

Such an accumulation of miracles associated with one's own person was probably not without a profound effect on Jesus' self-conception. One might assume that he asked himself what it meant that *he* had brought about these unusual things. In this context, whether Jesus understood himself to be a magician, as has been claimed in recent times by Morton Smith, is a relevant question.[22] If Jesus attributed his miracles to the application of learned magical techniques, they would have impressed him less than if he himself found them mysterious. I see, however, no great evidence for the magician hypothesis. His miracles are marked by their great effortlessness. In the miracle accounts, there is no talk of complicated rituals or incantations.[23]

---

19. See, e.g., Matt 4:23–25; 8:1–17; 9:1–8,27–34; 12:9–13; 15:29–31; 20:29–30; Mark 1:29–34,39–44; 2:1–12; 3:1–6,7–12; 6:54–56; 7:31–37; 8:22–26; 10:46–52; Luke 4:33–41; 5:12–14,17–26; 6:6–11,17–19; 7:1–15; 8:40–56; 9:11; 13:10–17; 14:1–4; 17:11–19; 18:35–43; 22:49–51; John 4:46–53; 5:1–9; 9:1–12; 11:14–44.

20. See the multiplication of the loaves and the fish, Matt 14:15–21; 15:32–39; 16:9-10; Mark 6:30–44; 8:1–9; 8:18–20; Luke 9:11–17; John 6:1–13,26; see also the changing water into wine, John 2:1–10.

21. See the calming of a storm, Matt 8:23–27; Mark 4:35–41; Luke 8:22–25.

22. See Smith, *Jesus the Magician*; on this question, see generally, Yamauchi, "Magic,"; Kollmann, "Jesus and Magic"; Twelftree, "Message of Jesus," and the literature cited therein.

23. On the meaning of rituals and incantations for magic, see Wiggermann, "Magic": "Every ceremonial act of *magic* comprises a manipulation of and with objects (Ritual) and an incantation often arranged in rhythmical speech." These features are missing from the descriptions of Jesus' miracles. At healings, he simply commanded the lame and dead to get up (see, e.g., Matt 9:6; Mark 2:11; 5:41; Luke 5:24; 7:14; 8:54; John 5:8; see also Acts 3:8; 9:34,40; 14:10) or to come out of the grave (see John 11:43), lepers, to be clean (see, e.g., Matt 8:3; Mark 1:41; Luke 5:13), the blind to see (see Luke 18:42; quite without healing words, Mark 10:52), a man with a "withered" (probably paralyzed) hand to stretch out his hand (see Matt 12:13; Mark 3:5; Luke 6:10). Sometimes he takes the hand of the sick without speaking and raises them up (see, e.g., Matt 9:25; Mark 1:31; 9:27) or simply touches them (see Matt 8:15; Luke 22:51), places his finger or hand on the affected place (see, e.g., Matt 9:29; 20:34; Mark 8:25) or on the hands of the sick (unspecific) (see, e.g., Mark 6:5; Luke 4:40; 13:13; further Mark 5:23; 7:23; 10:16; Matt 9:18; cf. Acts 9:12). Exceptions where Jesus heals not only with words or touch are Mark 8:23 (Jesus spits on a blind man's eyes), John 9:6 (Jesus makes a paste from saliva and earth and spreads it on the eyes of a blind man) and Mark 7:33

The tremendous sensation that the miracles of Jesus seem to have aroused among the general population,[24] and the hope of salvation projected onto him as a result,[25] will not have been without influence on Jesus himself. A comparison with the above-mentioned Sai Baba[26]—whose miracles, in number and type, seem to be very roughly comparable with those of Jesus[27]—speaks for his miracles leaving a decisive imprint on his self-image. Sai Baba's miracles led, not only to the almost limitless admiration of his followers but were also the main reason for his superhuman self-consciousness. "No one can comprehend My Glory,"[28] he wrote at twenty

(Jesus touches the tongue of a deaf man with saliva). It is also reported that he unintentionally healed a woman who touched his robe from behind, in a crowd (see Mark 5:24–34; Matt 9:20–22; Luke 8:43–48). The idea that one had only to touch Jesus to be healed was common (see Matt 12:36; Mark 6:56; Luke 6:19). The unclean spirits could sometimes be cast out "by a word" (Matt 8:16; cf. similar Matt 8:28; Mark 1:25; 5:8; 9:25; Luke 4:35), sometimes without a word (see Matt 15:28; Mark 7:25–30). Finally, there are accounts of healing without any healing words or touch (see, e.g., Mark 10:52; Luke 17:14), including a distant healing (Matt 8:5–10,13; Luke 7:1–10; John 4:46–53). With mass healings it seems there was no opportunity for more extensive rituals to take place (see Mark 1:32–34; 3:7–10; 6:53–56; Matt 4:23–25; 12:15; 14:34–36; Luke 6:17–19). The descriptions of other miracles contain no indication of specific rituals and incantations either. Before the so-called multiplications of the loaves and fishes he speaks only normal words of blessing (see Matt 14:19; 15:36; Mark 6:41; 8:6; Luke 9:16; John 6:11), at the changing water into wine he does and says nothing (see John 2:6–10), at the calming of the storm he rebukes the wind and waves with few words (see Mark 4:39; similar Matt 8:26; Luke 8:24) and he leaves a fig tree without fruit to wither with one sentence (see Mark 11:14; similar Matt 21:19).

24. See, e.g., Mark 3:7–10; Matt 4:23–25; Luke 6:17–19.

25. Cf. about Matt 8:27: "And the men marveled, saying, 'What sort of man is this, that even winds and sea obey him?'" (ESV; very similar Mark 4:41); John 6:14–15: "When the people saw the sign that he had done, they said, 'This is indeed the Prophet who is to come into the world!' Perceiving then that they were about to come and take him by force to make him king, Jesus withdrew again to the mountain by himself" (ESV); John 7:31: "Yet many of the people believed in him. They said, 'When the Christ appears, will he do more signs than this man has done?'" (ESV).

26. See above, p. 125.

27. As in the case of Jesus, the extraordinary phenomena attributed to Sai Baba are not predominantly of a mental nature (such as clairvoyance, precognition, or telepathy), but have a strong physical component, though the focus of Jesus' miracles was more on healing and Sai Baba was more focused on the materialization of objects. The parapsychologist Erlendur Haraldsson estimated 1987 that Sai Baba seemed to materialize an average of twenty to forty objects per day (see *"Miracles,"* 290). The extraordinary experiences of Black Elk (see above, pp. 120–21) seem, in comparison, to have lay more in the area of trance visions and otherworld journeys, although there are also accounts of healings and nature miracles from him. On the contrary, no accounts of Jesus' otherworld journeys exist, at least in the New Testament; neither do I know of any for Sai Baba.

28. Letter of May 25, 1947 ("Loving Legend").

years old to his older brother Seshama Raju, who was worried about the stir Sai Baba was causing.[29] According to the Synoptic Gospels, Jesus attributed himself a central role as the Son of Man and the Messiah in the eschatological events, which would involve tribulation,[30] resurrection, judgment, and the kingdom of God.[31] It seems to me that, without consideration of the miracles associated with Jesus, a convincing explanation of that kind of self-consciousness is hardly imaginable.

---

29. See "Loving Legend."

30. See, e.g., Mark 13:3–25, and the parallels in Matt 24:3–29; Luke 21:10–26, as well as further indications in Allison, "Eschatology of Jesus," 286–89.

31. See below, pp. 130–32. It is possible that also visionary experiences had an impact on the self-consciousness of Jesus. From the sources, however, it cannot be established whether Jesus had such experiences, which are quite common, in unusual intensity or frequency. Explicitly named are only his baptismal vision (see Mark 1:10–11; Matt 3:16–17; in the versions of Jesus' baptism in Luke 3:21–22 and John 1:29–34 a vision of Jesus is not spoken of) and his vision of the fall of Satan (Luke 10:18). Perhaps the already mentioned transfiguration experience also was of a visionary nature (see Matt 17:1–9; Mark 9:2–9; Luke 9:28–36). Contact with angels is also attributed to him (see Matt 4:11; Mark 1:13; Luke 22:43). An indication of visionary experiences could also be Jesus' unusually frequent talk of God as Father with the aura of a personal relationship (see, e.g., Matt 10:32–33; 11:27; 26:53; Luke 10:22; 22:29; John 1:18; 5:19; 6:46 as well as Wilk, "Vater . . ."; Poirier, "God," 228; on the rare addresses of God as father in the Old Testament and in the texts from Qumran, see Spieckermann, "'Father'"; Doering, "God as Father"). It speaks for a mystical life of Jesus that he sometimes retired to a quiet place in order to pray (see Matt 14:23; Mark 1:35; 6:46; Luke 5:16; 6:12; 9:28).

8

The Great Disappointment

The inevitability of disappointment

ACCORDING TO MY HYPOTHESIS, the fundamental flaw of belief in the resurrection and kingdom of God consists of projecting the contents of otherworld experiences onto an earthly reality. The non-physical bodies of luminous, otherworldly deceased become the model for the resurrected corpses, transformed for the eternal life. The resurrected will live in an eternal, earthly kingdom of God that resembles the otherworld places in which the deceased are often encountered during otherworldly experiences. This projection of otherworld landscapes and bodies onto earth leads to otherworldly conditions being expected in this world, literally heaven on earth. But this is something that by its very nature will never happen. Thus the story of the expectation of resurrection and the kingdom of God is necessarily one of disappointment.[1] One of these disappointments is actually known as "The Great Disappointment," namely, the failure of Christ to arrive on October 22, 1844, what should have been the date of the second coming according to William Miller's calculations.[2] To begin with it was a resurrection of the saints and then all people, and the righteous would live an eternal life on a renewed earth.[3] Miller had found a significant following in the state of New York and the surrounding areas of perhaps fifty thousand people.[4] Many fields had ceased to be harvested and livestock were slaughtered and distributed amongst the poor. Many sold their belongings to help others to pay their debts.[5] When the day that had been reckoned passed without the appearance of Jesus, the disappointment was colossal. One of Miller's followers, Henry Emmons, reported:

---

1. See Allison, *Jesus of Nazareth*, 94; Dawson, "Prophetic Failure," 150.
2. The Baptist pastor William Miller lived from 1782 to 1849; on Miller, see Judd, "William Miller."
3. See Miller, "Views," 33–35.
4. See Rowe, "Millerites," 7.
5. See Boutelle, *Sketch of the Life*, 63.

> I waited all Tuesday [22th October 1844] and dear Jesus did not come;—I waited all the forenoon of Wednesday, and was well in body as I ever was, but after 12 o'clock I began to feel faint, and before dark I needed some one to help me up to my chamber, as my natural strength was leaving me very fast, and I lay prostrate for 2 days without any pain—sick with disappointment[.][6]

This recalls the great disappointment of the Lakota Ghost Dance movement. In my eyes, at least as tragic was the fate of Jesus of Nazareth.

Jesus' role in the eschatological process

The Jesus of the Synoptic Gospels does not stop at the proclamation of the kingdom of God. He ascribes to himself, as already indicated, a decisive role in the eschatological drama of the coming kingdom of God. He understands it as his mission to bring the eschatological judgment.[7] According to the Synoptic Gospels, he sees himself as the yet-to-be-revealed Son of Man,[8] who on the clouds of heaven[9] with his angels[10] will come to the eschatological judgment[11] and then—like the Son of Man of the Enochic Book of Parables—will sit on the throne of glory.[12] In the kingdom of God, which he also calls "my kingdom,"[13] he will then gather his chosen.[14] His twelve disciples will sit on twelve thrones and—probably under his supremacy—

---

6. Emmons, "Letter," 6.

7. See Luke 12:49: "I came to cast fire on the earth" (ESV), and also Luz, "Warum zog Jesus nach Jerusalem?" 422.

8. See, e.g., Matt 16:13,27; 19:28–29; 24:24–27; 26:64; Mark 8:31–38; 14:62; Luke 9:26; 12:8–10; 17:22–25,30; 22:69; see also John 12:23,34; cf. Acts 7:55–56. On the question of whether the historical Jesus understood himself to be the Son of Man, see the discussion in Allison, *Constructing Jesus*, 293–303. For the hiddenness of the Enochic Son of Man, see 1 En. 48:6; 62:6–7.

9. See Matt 24:30; 26:64; Mark 13:26; 14:62; Luke 21:27.

10. See Matt 13:41–42; 16:13,27; 24:31; 25:31; Mark 8:38; 13:27; Luke 9:26; see also Matt 26:53.

11. See Matt 13:41–42; 16:27; 24:30–31,37–44; 25:31–46; Mark 8:38; 13:26–27; Luke 9:26; 12:8; 17:24,26–36; 21:36.

12. See also the references above, p. 61n114. According to Boyarin, *Jewish Gospels*, 101, in the christology of the Gospels the only new thing is the statement that the Son of Man of the Book of Parables is already here in Jesus of Nazareth.

13. Matt 24:31; Mark 13:27; cf. 1 En. 61:5.

14. Luke 22:30; see also Matt 13:41; 19:28; 20:21,23; Mark 10:37,40. Speaking of "my kingdom," it is fitting that Jesus saw himself as the Messiah according to the Gospels (see Matt 16:20; 24:5; 26:64; Mark 8:29–30; 14:61–62; Luke 4:41; 9:20–21; 22:67–70; John 10:24–25; 17:3); see also Allison, *Constructing Jesus*, 279–93.

will rule the twelve tribes of the restored Israel.[15] Correspondingly, at least some of his disciples hope that he will "liberate Israel."[16] In order to fulfill his mission, he goes with his disciples to Jerusalem.[17] This seems to make them afraid.[18] On the other hand, some expected Jesus' arrival in Jerusalem to result in the kingdom of God appearing on the spot.[19] However, it does not quite fit with this imminent earthly reign of Jesus that, according to the Synoptic Gospels, at one point Jesus foretells not only his suffering, but also his death.[20] In some passages, he makes very concrete statements about his death and his resurrection.[21] However, along with Theißen and Merz, I believe that, given the flight of the disciples at the arrest of Jesus and the collapse of their expectations due to his crucifixion, it is unlikely that Jesus made clear prophecies about his death.[22] As Hermann Samuel Reimarus already rightly noted, the behavior of Jesus' disciples following his death and the first reports of his resurrection do not point to them having been familiar with the idea of Jesus' resurrection.[23] For these reasons, I do not use Jesus' very specific prophecies of his own death and resurrection[24] in my argumentation. The unspecific prophecies of his passion, according to which he would be baptized with a special "baptism," drink from a special "cup,"[25] be handed over, treated with contempt, be rejected, and would suffer

15. See Allison, *Constructing Jesus*, 251, 303; see Matt 19:28; 25:31; Luke 22:30, and above, p. 58n88.

16. Luke 24:21.

17. See, e.g., Matt 16:21; 20:18; Mark 10:33; Luke 9:31,51; 13:33; 18:31.

18. See Mark 10:32: "Now they were on the road, going up to Jerusalem, and Jesus was going before them; and they were dumbfounded. And as they followed they were afraid" (NKJV, modified).

19. See Luke 19:11; see also below, p. 142n77.

20. See Matt 17:12; 26:2,21,45; Mark 9:12,31; 10:33; 14:21,41; Luke 9:44; 17:25; 18:32–33.

21. See Matt 16:21; 17:23; 20:18–19; 26:2; Mark 8:31; 9:31; 10:33–34; Luke 9:22; 18:32–33.

22. See Theissen and Merz, *Historical Jesus*, 430; on the flight of the disciples, see Matt 26:56; Mark 14:50; on the collapse of their expectations with reference to the liberation of Israel, see Luke 24:21; cf. on this expectation also Acts 1:6.

23. See [Reimarus], "Ueber die Auferstehungsgeschichte," 451–52; [Reimarus], *Von dem Zwecke Jesu*, 121–25.

24. See the references above, n. 21.

25. See Mark 10:38–40 (similar Matt 20:22–23): "Jesus said to them, 'You do not know what you are asking. Are you able to drink the cup that I drink, or to be baptized with the baptism with which I am baptized?' And they said to him, 'We are able.' And Jesus said to them, 'The cup that I drink you will drink, and with the baptism with which I am baptized, you will be baptized, but to sit at my right hand or at my left is not mine to grant, but it is for those for whom it has been prepared'" (ESV); Luke

many things,²⁶ are very difficult to evaluate. On the one hand, the flight of the disciples at Jesus' arrest indicates that they were not seriously expecting it. On the other hand, it is reported that Peter wanted to prevent Jesus from going to his suffering and death, which would mean that he would have had to have known about Jesus' plan and taken it seriously.²⁷ Yet even in this pericope there is a precise prophesy of the passion and resurrection which seems to be retrospectively framed. Thus I suggest, along with Theißen and Merz, that the conviction of the disciples concerning the necessity of Jesus' suffering came only later: "All the prophecies of the passion which already make the earthly Jesus state this necessity might be later insights which were subsequently put on the lips of the earthly Jesus."²⁸

But what did Jesus himself expect? His public conduct in Jerusalem was very careless and provocative. According to tradition, he entered Jerusalem as a messianic king of peace on a donkey.²⁹ He violently drove out money-changers and those selling animals for sacrifice in the temple complex, which amounted to an attack on the temple aristocracy that profited significantly economically from the temple market.³⁰ He prophesied

---

12:50: "I have a baptism to be baptized with, and how great is my distress until it is accomplished!" (ESV); Mark 14:36 (similar Matt 26:39,42; Luke 22:42): "And he said, 'Abba, Father, all things are possible for you. Remove this cup from me. Yet not what I will, but what you will'" (ESV); John 18:11: "So Jesus said to Peter, 'Put your sword into its sheath; shall I not drink the cup that the Father has given me?'" (ESV). The baptism and the drinking from the cup here means, according to Davies and Allison, *Matthew*, 3:89–90, the eschatological suffering of God's wrath or judgment, but not necessarily death. See also Bird, "Passion Predictions," 443–44.

26. See, e.g., Matt 17:12; Mark 9:12; Luke 9:44; 17:25, and the more general statements in the presumably *ex eventu* specified prophecies, Matt 16:21; 17:22; Mark 8:31; 9:31; Luke 9:22. See also the comprehensive list of passion predictions of Jesus in Bird, "Passion Predictions," 443–44.

27. See Matt 16:21–22: "From that time Jesus began to show his disciples that he must go to Jerusalem and suffer many things from the elders and chief priests and scribes, and be killed, and on the third day be raised. And Peter took him aside and began to rebuke him, saying, 'Far be it from you, Lord! This shall never happen to you'" (ESV); similar Mark 8:31–33.

28. Theissen and Merz, *Historical Jesus*, 429.

29. See Matt 21:1–11; Mark 11:1–11; Luke 19:28–40; John 12:12–19; cf. Zech 9:9: "Rejoice greatly, O daughter of Zion! Shout aloud, O daughter of Jerusalem! Behold, your king is coming to you; righteous and having salvation is he, humble and mounted on a donkey, on a colt, the foal of a donkey." See also Kittel et al., *Theological Dictionary*, 369: Riding on horses is associated with war, which is why the messianic king of peace rides on a donkey. See further Davies and Allison, *Matthew*, 3:116–17.

30. See Mark 11:15–17: "And he [Jesus] entered the temple and began to drive out those who sold and those who bought in the temple, and he overturned the tables of the money-changers and the seats of those who sold pigeons. And he would not allow anyone to carry anything through the temple. And he was teaching them and saying to

divine judgment against the priestly establishment[31] and announced the destruction of the temple.[32] Jesus thus did a lot to turn the Jerusalem authorities against him.[33] He must have known that this would put him in danger. He himself reportedly said that Jerusalem was a dangerous place for prophets,[34] and had "every reason to feel threatened."[35] But was Jesus really prepared for suffering and death, and did he go willingly and consciously into it? To a large extent this is the image that tradition portrays. Jesus knows that one of his disciples will give him up to the authorities but allows him to do so.[36] Shortly before his arrest, he almost recoils from the imminent suffering but surrenders himself to it as ordained by God.[37] He does not resist his arrest[38] and condemns those who seek to defend him with violence.[39] Ultimately, Jesus does not defend himself in the trial against him.[40] Moreover, he does not protest flagellation and abuse at the hands of his torturers.[41] According to the Gospels, it seems unequivocally

---

them, 'Is it not written, 'My house shall be called a house of prayer for all the nations'? But you have made it a den of robbers'" (ESV); similar Matt 21:12–16; Luke 19:45–46. See also Luz, "Warum zog Jesus nach Jerusalem?" 419–21; Stowasser, "Jesu Konfrontation." According to Stowasser, the temple market made substantial profits for the clans from which the Romans recruited the high priests and was probably an important pillar of the wealth of these families (see "Jesu Konfrontation," 42–43).

31. See, e.g., Matt 21:33–46; 23:1–36; Mark 12:1–12,35–40.

32. See Mark 14:58; 15:29; similar Matt 26:61; 27:40; see also Luz, "Warum zog Jesus nach Jerusalem?" 421.

33. Ulrich Luz resumes that Jesus had behaved very conspicuously and did not care about the obvious risk he was taking because of it. At the latest after his cleansing of the temple, it was high time for him to leave the city and to go into hiding, but Jesus did not do this (see "Warum zog Jesus nach Jerusalem?" 421; see also Goppelt, *Theology of the New Testament*, 1:226). According to Craig Evans, Jesus' death was "the result of his entry into Jerusalem, where he threatened the ruling priestly establishment" (Evans, "Death and Burial," 144).

34. See, e.g., Matt 23:37; Luke 13:33; see also Luz, "Warum zog Jesus nach Jerusalem?" 412–16.

35. Theissen and Merz, *Historical Jesus*, 431; see also Luz, "Warum zog Jesus nach Jerusalem?" 413–14, 419, 421.

36. See Matt 26:21–24; Mark 14:17–21; Luke 22:21–22; John 6:64; 13:2,11,21,26–27.

37. See Matt 26:36–46; Mark 14:32–42; Luke 22:39–46.

38. Matt 26:47–56; Mark 14:43–50; Luke 22:47–53; John 18:1–9.

39. See Matt 26:51–54; Luke 22:51; John 18:10–11.

40. See Matt 26:57–68; 27:11–14; Mark 14:53–65; 15:1–5; Luke 22:63–71; 23:3,6–11; John 18:19–23; 19:8–11; only in John 18:36–37 does Jesus seem to defend himself against an accusation, namely, that he has arisen politically against the occupational power of Rome.

41. See Matt 27:27–30; Mark 15:15–20; John 19:1–3; see also 1 Pet 2:23.

as if Jesus went into his passion of his own accord. They nonetheless contain indications that he did not go to his *death* willingly.[42]

The two cries of Jesus on the cross

In the traditional Christian view, Jesus, with his death, was fulfilling a divine plan for redemption.[43] But the Gospels of Mark and Matthew report that, very shortly before his death Jesus cried out: "My God, my God, why have you forsaken me?"[44] With one further inarticulate cry, Jesus died.[45] The first cry, in particular, is problematic for Christianity because its contents do not fit with the doctrine that Jesus' dying and death happened in accordance with a plan of salvation agreed upon between him and the "Father."[46] The second cry is also unusual.

42. Allison argues that the thesis that Jesus did not willingly go to his death presumes "either a widespread conscious cover-up or a catastrophic memory failure in the early Christian sources" (Allison, *Constructing Jesus*, 433). On the other hand, Werner Kelber is probably right when he says that at no other event in Christian origins is the transmission of the raw facts less likely than when it comes to the death of Jesus. This event certainly left Jesus' disciples massively traumatized (see "Works of Memory," 245–46). This was accompanied by difficult feelings of guilt, as they had deserted their master at the time of his arrest (see Allison, *Resurrecting Jesus*, 368). Both these factors could have encouraged an idealization of the story of the Passion of Jesus in early tradition.

43. See also, comprehensively, the sections "Christ's Redemptive Death in God's Plan of Salvation" and "Christ Offered Himself to His Father for Our Sins" in the Catechism of the Catholic Church (*CCC* 599–623) with numerous references to the New Testament; see also Philaret's orthodox catechism: "[H]e [Jesus], by his death on the cross, delivered us from *sin*, the *curse*, and *death*. [. . .] His voluntary suffering and death on the cross for us [. . .] is both a perfect satisfaction to the justice of God, which had condemned us for sin to death, and a fund of infinite merit, which has obtained him the right, without prejudice to justice, to give us sinners pardon of our sins, and grace to have victory over sin and death" (Philaret, "Longer Catechism," 475–76 [§§ 206, 208]); Martin Luther wrote in his Small Catechism: "I believe that Jesus Christ, true God, has redeemed me, a lost and condemned creature, secured and delivered me from all sins, from death, and from the power of the devil [. . .] with His holy and precious blood, and with His innocent sufferings and death" ([Luther], *Small Catechism*, 5). The classic concept of Jesus' redemptive death has been theologically questioned many times in the last decades, see, e.g., the discussion in Sattler, *Erlösung?* 128–66; Nitsche, *Christologie*, 117–29, and in particular the refusal to understand the execution of Jesus as an expiatory sacrifice in Jörns, *Notwendige Abschiede*, 286–341. However, a complete departure from the idea of salvation, seems to me, to be rare in Christianity (see also the survey results in Jörns, *Notwendige Abschiede*, 55).

44. Matt 27:46; Mark 15:34.

45. See Matt 27:50; Mark 15:37.

46. See on this the doctrines in Matt 26:39,42,44; Mark 14:36,39; Luke 22:42; John 4:34; 10:17; 12:27; 18:11; Phil 2:8; see also *CCC* 606–12 with further references to

Historicity of the cries of Jesus on the cross

If we follow Dale Allison, no historical certainty can be reached in relation to most of the individual words and actions of Jesus. However, regarding the cries of Jesus on the cross, it does not seem to me impossible to put forward some plausible arguments for their historicity, although certainty cannot be attained. A cry is easier to remember than a specific word. I also find it unlikely that the authors of the first two Gospels would report the cries of Jesus if they were not convinced that Jesus did cry out, since his words are not only scandalous but do not fit either a divine plan of salvation or the high dignity of Jesus. They must have been deeply embarrassing for early Christians.

When looking at the content of the first cry of Jesus, we should note the reactions to it:

> And about the ninth hour Jesus cried out with a loud voice, saying, "Eli, Eli, lema sabachthani?" that is, "My God, my God, why have you forsaken me?" And some of the bystanders, hearing it, said, "This man is calling Elijah." And one of them at once ran and took a sponge, filled it with sour wine, and put it on a reed and gave it to him to drink. But the others said, "Wait, let us see whether Elijah will come to save him." And Jesus cried out again with a loud voice and yielded up his spirit.[47]

These contextual details increase the likelihood that the content of the first cry is not fictitious. Even if, according to the Gospels, the bystanders misunderstand Jesus, they nonetheless took him to be calling out to an eminent, transcendent person.[48]

---

passages from the New Testament.

47. Matt 27:46–50 (ESV).

48. Although I consider the possibility Jesus was calling out to Elijah to be unlikely, I would like to point out that Elijah is associated with the coming of the kingdom of God. The Old Testament foretells that Elijah will return before the eschatological judgment, see Mal 4:5–6: "'Behold, I will send you Elijah the prophet before the great and awesome day of the Lord comes. And he will turn the hearts of fathers to their children and the hearts of children to their fathers, lest I come and strike the land with a decree of utter destruction'" (ESV); see also Sir 48:10–11. According to Öhler, *Elia*, 109, the Elijah prophecy played an important role in first-century Judaism. It was also alive among Jesus followers. Some believed him to be the returned Elijah (see Matt 16:14; Mark 8:28; Luke 9:19). Jesus spoke of John the Baptist as the returned Elijah (see Matt 11:14: "And if you are willing to accept it, he is Elijah who is to come."; Matt 17:12–13; Luke 7:27 as well as Mark 9:11–13, and also Öhler, *Elia*, 289–94). The Gospel of John, however, has the Baptist deny that he is Elijah (see John 1:21). The eschatological return of Elijah is not understood as a resurrection. Elijah is with Enoch and Ezra among those who did not die but were taken up to heaven alive (see 2 Kgs 2:9–12; Sir 48:9;

Weakness or disappointment?

A further characteristic of the first of Jesus' cries on the cross is that it is described as being *extraordinarily loud*.[49] This is astonishing in view of his physical condition. Jesus was close to his death and seemed to have been extremely weakened. The flagellation,[50] it seems, was so brutal,[51] that afterwards he was no longer able, as was customary, to carry the crossbeam of the cross by himself.[52] It agrees with this that he died abnormally quickly on the cross.[53] On top of this, hanging on a cross greatly restricts breathing. Suffocation is the main cause of death for a person being crucified.[54] In this situation, to cry out extremely loudly would probably have required an enormous effort. An involuntary cry from weakness or pain is less likely. Cries of pain from Jesus would have been more likely when he was being flagellated or nailed to the cross, but nothing is said of this. If we add to this the scandalous content of the scream, I am of the impression that Jesus summoned his last bit of strength to reach God in heaven with his cry, because events had not developed as he had hoped.[55] Also the last, inarticulate cry

---

49:14; 1 En. 70–71; 4 Ezra 14:9; for a possible rapture of Baruch, see 2 Bar. 46:7; 76:2) and should reappear, see 4 Ezra 6:26: "And they shall see the men who were taken up, who from their birth have not tasted death; and the heart of the earth's inhabitants shall be changed and converted to a different spirit" (trans. *OTP* 1:535). Apart from this, in Jewish folklore there is the idea that Elijah comes as a heavenly emissary on the eve of Passover to help the poor and punish the unjust. This coming of Elijah is, however, not connected with the eschatological redemption of Israel (see Noy, "Elijah," 335).

49. The verb used by Mark, βοάω, means "to use one's voice at high volume" (BDAG, 218). The loudness of the cry is once again reinforced through the addition "with a loud (great) voice" (φωνῇ μεγάλῃ) (see Mark 15:34: ἐβόησεν ὁ Ἰησοῦς φωνῇ μεγάλῃ; cf. on the second cry Mark 15:37: ἀφεὶς φωνὴν μεγάλην). Matthew intensifies βοάω through the use of the prefix ἀνά (ἀναβοάω), also in connection with "loud (great) voice" (see Matt 27:46: ἀνεβόησεν ὁ Ἰησοῦς φωνῇ μεγάλῃ; cf. the second cry, Matt 27:50: κράξας φωνῇ μεγάλῃ).

50. See Matt 27:26; Mark 15:15; John 19:1.

51. An indication of this in the Scriptures could be 1 Pet 2:24, where it possibly alludes to Jesus' wounds from flagellation.

52. Matt 27:32; Mark 15:21; Luke 23:26; see Retief and Cilliers, "Crucifixion."

53. See Edwards et al., "Physical Death."

54. See Retief and Cilliers, "Crucifixion." Death by crucifixion is induced by a number of factors "but the most important factor was progressive asphyxia caused by impairment of respiratory movement" (Retief and Cilliers, "Crucifixion," 938, see also 940–41).

55. If, from Jesus' perspective, everything had happened according to the plan of salvation agreed upon with the "Father," then this cry must not be understood as an expression of disappointment but an expression of weakness, which I consider less likely based on the stated reasons. My interpretation does not support the thesis of Albert

with which Jesus dies can be understood in this way. Davies and Allison write that it is unusual for someone to die with a cry, particularly if they have been tortured.[56] It is possible that Jesus had wanted to say something more but that he did not have sufficient strength left to articulate it.

Mitigation and omission of the cries of Jesus on the cross

Considering the big problem that Jesus' cry of reproach to God represents for the doctrine that he died according to the plan of salvation agreed upon between him and the heavenly Father,[57] it is not surprising that both of the Gospels presumed to be written later, only contain the cries of Jesus in mitigated form or do not contain them at all. Luke reports that Jesus spoke only once. And it is not a disappointed reproachful cry but rather a very dignified, loud calling or speaking.[58] "Father, into your hands I commit my spirit!"[59] In the Gospel of John, Jesus apparently speaks with a normal voice. His last words—"it is fulfilled!"[60]—express, in contrast to Mark and Matthew, his awareness of having completed a project that was planned.

Removal of other embarrassments of the crucifixion scene

In the third and fourth Gospels additional embarrassing aspects of the crucifixion scene partly or completely disappear. In Mark and Matthew,

---

Schweitzer that Jesus wanted to bring about the kingdom of God with his death (see *Kingdom of God*, 123–25). Then, there would have been no obvious reason for disappointment because in that case events had not departed from Jesus' plan of salvation, as Schweitzer put it. In Allison's view, the first cry is not consistent with Jesus' belief system. He believes the cry could *only* say something about the disoriented state of mind of Jesus *after* the torture and *nothing* about his convictions *before* the arrest (*Constructing Jesus*, 432). If the cry of Jesus on the contrary expressed not weakness but disappointment about the non-intervention of God, then it does not have to represent a sign of mental confusion but could indeed reflect Jesus' eschatological convictions *before* the arrest.

56. See Davies and Allison, *Matthew*, 3:627.

57. Davies and Allison consider that Jesus' cry could have an eschatological significance (*Matthew*, 3:625 fn.71).

58. Luke 23:46 uses the verb φωνέω, which can also mean "speak loudly" (BDAG, 1071).

59. Luke 23:46.

60. John 19:30. τετέλεσται is translated in most English Bibles as "it is finished." But τετέλεσται has a stronger connotation than simply "it is finished." It means that something is completed or fulfilled (see BDAG, 996). The Vulgate translates the relevant words with *consummatum est*. All common German versions have "es ist vollbracht," French Bibles "tout est accompli" or "c'est achevé."

of Jesus' followers only *women* witness the crucifixion and then only *from afar*.⁶¹ His male followers flee at the arrest of Jesus,⁶² and abandon him. This embarrassed the disciples and involved an unfavorable witness situation because a woman's testimony counted for little or nothing at all.⁶³ The reliability of the witnesses was further complicated by their distance from the crucifixion. The Gospel of Luke suggests, on the contrary, that those who witnessed the crucifixion were mainly men, albeit from a long way off.⁶⁴ In the Gospel of John, it is the anonymous beloved disciple of Jesus, by tradition equated with John the Evangelist, and three women who stand *beside* the cross and to whom Jesus speaks.⁶⁵ If the situation was as indicated in the three Synoptic Gospels, then the followers of Jesus would not have been able to hear him speak.⁶⁶

---

61. See Mark 15:40-41: "There were also women looking on from a distance (ἀπὸ μακρόθεν), among whom were Mary Magdalene, and Mary the mother of James the younger and of Joses, and Salome. When he was in Galilee, they followed him and ministered to him, and there were also many other women who came up with him to Jerusalem" (ESV); Matt 27:55-56: "There were also many women there, looking on from a distance, who had followed Jesus from Galilee, ministering to him, among whom were Mary Magdalene and Mary the mother of James and Joseph and the mother of the sons of Zebedee" (ESV).

62. See Mark 14:50: "Then they all forsook Him and fled"; Matt 26:56: "Then all the disciples forsook Him and fled" (NKJV).

63. See, e.g., Flavius Josephus, *A.J.* 4.219; Allison, *Resurrecting Jesus*, 328-29; Lapide, *Auferstehung*, 54-55.

64. See Luke 23:49: "But all those who knew him, also women who followed him from Galilee, stood far off (ἀπὸ μακρόθεν), seeing these things."

65. See John 19:25-27: "[B]ut standing by the cross of Jesus were his mother and his mother's sister, Mary the wife of Clopas, and Mary Magdalene. When Jesus saw his mother and the disciple whom he loved standing nearby, he said to his mother, 'Woman, behold, your son!' Then he said to the disciple, 'Behold, your mother!' And from that hour the disciple took her to his own home." On the omission of the flight of the disciples in Luke and John, see also Theissen and Merz, *Historical Jesus*, 454: "Throughout his Gospel Mark depicts the disciples as incomprehending followers of Jesus. They sleep in Gethsemane and flee when Jesus is arrested. Only the women observe the crucifixion 'from afar.' Matthew accentuates this failure [. . .]. By contrast, Luke emphasizes that the disciples have persisted with Jesus 'in his tribulations' (22.28) and consistently omits their flight (cf. 22.47-53). [. . .] The crucifixion is observed not only by the women but by all the 'acquaintances' of Jesus (i.e. also by his disciples, 23.49). The Gospel of John shows a comparable tendency. The disciples do not flee, but Jesus makes sure that they can depart (18.9). At least the Beloved Disciple stands—with the women—beneath (!) the cross (19.26f.)."

66. This, however, also includes the two sayings that Jesus *speaks* according to the Gospel of Luke (Luke 23:34: "Father, forgive them, for they know not what they do" (ESV); 23:43: "Truly, I say to you, today you will be with me in paradise" (ESV); see further also pp. 63-64).

On the whole, the information from Matthew and Mark, that Jesus called for God from the cross, seems more consistent and to be more reliable than the completely different versions in Luke and John. The fact that the traditional wording of the first cry of Jesus coincides with the beginning of the Twenty-Second Psalm in no way means it is not authentic.[67] I think it more probable that a similar-sounding cry was scripturalized, i.e., put in the form of a Bible quote.[68] A judgment on the historicity of the first cry of Jesus is far from certain, but I suspect that Jürgen Moltmann is right: "The idea that Jesus' last words to God whom he had called upon as Abba, dear Father, could have been 'You have abandoned me', could surely never have taken root in Christian belief unless these terrible words had really been uttered, or unless they had at least been heard in Jesus' death cry."[69]

Disappointed eschatological expectation as a motif for Jesus' cry to God

If one accepts that Jesus cried to God from the cross as is reported by the Gospels of Mark and Matthew, what is the most plausible explanation for this? Why would Jesus directly accuse God of abandoning him shortly before his death? What had his expectation been that such disappointment could result? I suspect that Jesus' expectation and disappointment were about the coming of the kingdom of God. On the cross, Jesus was expecting an eschatological intervention from God or his angels, ultimately, with the goal of establishing the kingdom of God. Yet there was no divine intervention. The doctrine on the kingdom of God had always assumed, as far as I see, that man alone could not bring about the kingdom of God. The righteous could neither defeat evil nor transform the earth into an eternal paradise. God or his angels would have to come and intervene. The expectation of the kingdom of God is thus inextricably linked to the cry to God.

---

67. Davies and Allison reject the common interpretation that Jesus was in reality reciting Psalm 22, namely, calling out its beginning loudly and praying more quietly this long Psalm that ends in praise of God (*Matthew*, 3:624–25). This does not fit the passion accounts of Mark and Matthew. The good ending of Psalm 22 is in tension with the last, immediately following, no longer understandable, loud cry of Jesus at the moment of his death (see Matt 27:50, Mark 15:37).

68. On scripturalization in general, see Goodacre, "Scripturalization."

69. Moltmann, *Way of Jesus Christ*, 166. See similar, Goppelt, *Theology of the New Testament*, 1:192: "He [Jesus] died crying out to God in prayer (Mk. 15:34). This cry was so offensive that it was reproduced only by Matthew (27:46), while the other evangelists could not use it. It was not invented by anyone."

Crying out to God and the eschatological divine intervention in Lactantius

This is represented very vividly by Lactantius. In his *Divine Institutions,* he writes about the salvation of the righteous that precedes the creation of God's kingdom on earth:

> Thus the earth shall be laid waste, as though by one common robbery. When these things shall so happen, then the righteous and the followers of truth shall separate themselves from the wicked, and flee into solitudes. And when he [the antichrist] hears of this, the impious king, inflamed with anger, will come with a great army, and bringing up all his forces, will surround all the mountain in which the righteous shall be situated, that he may seize them. But they, when they shall see themselves to be shut in on all sides and besieged, *will call upon God with a loud voice, and implore the aid of heaven;* and God shall hear them, and send from heaven a great king to rescue and free them, and destroy all the wicked with fire and sword.[70]

Did Jesus expect God's intervention in his lifetime?

To explain Jesus' cry from the cross requires something further. If Jesus had expected that he would have to die on the cross, so that subsequently the kingdom of God could be established, then his reproach of God that he had abandoned him, expressed shortly before his death, would not have been in accordance with this expectation. If, however, he expected the eschatological intervention of God or his angels to bring the kingdom of God to occur *during his earthly lifetime* and then realized as death approached that God was not going to come, then the contents of his first cry would be understandable.[71] Hermann Samuel Reimarus pleaded in this direction, but he overlooked the fact that the kingdom of God proclaimed by Jesus was not simply a "worldly kingdom," but rather possessed an earthly-otherworldly, hybrid nature:

---

70. Lactantius, *Inst.* 7.17.9–11 (trans. *ANF* 7:214–15, emphasis added). As evidence, Lactantius cites the very similar prophecy of Hystaspes "that the pious and faithful, being separated from the wicked, *will stretch forth their hands to heaven with weeping and mourning, and will implore the protection of Jupiter*: that Jupiter will look to the earth, and hear the voices of men, and will destroy the wicked. All which things are true, except one, that he attributed to Jupiter those things which God will do" (*Inst.* 7.18.2; trans. *ANF* 7:215; emphasis added).

71. See further also pp. 135–36n55.

> He [Jesus] ended his life with the word *"Eli, Eli, lama sabacthani?"* "My God, my God, why hast Thou forsaken me?"—a confession which can hardly be otherwise interpreted than that God had not helped him to carry out his intention and attain his object as he had hoped. It was then clearly not the intention or the object of Jesus to suffer and to die, but to build up a worldly kingdom, and to deliver the Israelites from bondage. It was in *this* that God had forsaken him, it was in *this* that his hopes had been frustrated.[72]

The imminent eschatological expectation of Jesus in the sources

If Jesus believed that the kingdom of God would come soon, then this means that he had a so-called *Naherwartung*, an imminent expectation of the Last Things.[73] From many of the traditional words of Jesus, an imminent eschatological expectation is obvious. According to Mark and Matthew, Jesus began his public appearance with the same message as John the Baptist: "The kingdom of God has come near."[74] His proclamation of the kingdom of God was accompanied by a calling for constant vigilance: "Be on guard, keep awake. For you do not know when the time will come. [. . .] Therefore stay awake [. . .] And what I say to you I say to all: Stay awake."[75] Tradition does not always seem to ascribe to Jesus exactly the same imminent eschatological expectation.[76] This could be due either to a wavering or a development of the convictions of Jesus, or it could reflect an attempt by the evangelists to soften the nonfulfillment of Jesus' prophecies. The Gospels were probably written forty to eighty years after Jesus' death, and the kingdom of God had yet to arrive. Some passages express that Jesus expected the Last Judgment preceding the kingdom of God in the very near future. He told his disciples,

---

72. [Reimarus], *Von dem Zwecke Jesu*, 153–54 (trans. Reimarus, *Fragments*, 27).

73. See Allison, *Jesus of Nazareth*, 147–51; Gräßer, *Naherwartung Jesu*; Richter, "Die 'konsequente Eschatologie.'"

74. Mark 1:15; similarly Matt 4:17; cf. on the similar message of John the Baptist in Matt 3:2. According to Allison, ἤγγικεν cannot here be translated with "has arrived" because otherwise the kingdom of God would have arrived with John the Baptist and not first with Jesus, which was certainly not what the Gospel writer intended to say (see *Constructing Jesus*, 124 with fn. 424).

75. Mark 13:33–37 (ESV); see similarly, Matt 24:36–51; 25:1–13; Luke 12:35–48; 21:36; see also 1 Thess 5:2; 2 Pet 3:10.

76. See also, e.g., Theißen and Merz, "Gerichtsverzögerung," 233–53; Allison, *Jesus of Nazareth*, 150.

whom he had sent to Israel on a missionary journey: "[T]ruly, I say to you, you will not have gone through all the towns of Israel before the Son of Man comes."[77] He prophesied to the high priest and the Council (Sanhedrin) that they would see the Son of Man coming on the clouds of heaven.[78] His call to be rid of bodily organs that cause one to sin, in order to be able to enter the kingdom of God without them,[79] is not about death and resurrection.[80] Jesus rather seems to reckon with the establishment of the kingdom of God during the lifetime of the majority of his listeners. In any case, he does not announce the kingdom of God for future generations but for those living at the time.[81] According to the description of the eschatological events in Mark 13—tribulation, cosmic phenomena, and the coming of the Son of Man with his angels—he predicts: "Truly, I say to you, this generation will not have passed away until all these things will have taken place."[82] All three Synoptics hand down the word of Jesus that some of the listeners "will not taste death" until the kingdom of heaven arrives.[83] In the Gospel of Luke, which avoids giving specific eschatological dates, Jesus says God will "give justice to his elect [. . .] speedily."[84] It is astonishing that this kind of prophesy was handed down in the Gospels considering that, with the exception of Mark, they were probably completed at a time when almost no one from Jesus' generation was still alive. Further indications of Jesus' imminent eschatological expectation are his statement that the eschatological return of Elijah had already happened in John the Baptist,[85] as well as the absence of

---

77. Matt 10:23 (ESV). According to Luke's Gospel, some unspecified listeners of Jesus, holding an extreme imminent eschatological expectation, believed that, with Jesus' arrival in Jerusalem, "the kingdom of God would appear on the spot (παραχρῆμα)" (Luke 19:11).

78. See Mark 14:62; Matt 26:64.

79. See Mark 9:43–48; Matt 18:8–9.

80. See above, pp. 54–55.

81. See Gräßer, *Naherwartung Jesu*, 127.

82. Mark 13:30 (= Matt 24:34).

83. Mark 9:1; Luke 9:27; see also Matt 16:27–28. Luke 11:50–51 probably also implies that the eschatological event will affect the generation of Jesus: "[T]he blood of all the prophets, shed from the foundation of the world, may be charged against this generation, from the blood of Abel to the blood of Zechariah, who perished between the altar and the sanctuary. Yes, I tell you, it will be required of this generation" (ESV); see similar Matt 23:34–35. According to Allison, this prophesy implies that this generation would be the last (see *Historical Christ*, 92; *Constructing Jesus*, 33–34).

84. Luke 18:7–8. On the other hand, there are words of Jesus in the Gospel of Luke that displace the coming of the kingdom of God to an unspecified future time, see Luke 21:9: "[B]ut the end will not come soon."

85. See above, pp. 135–36n48.

any instructions and rules of conduct for a more distant future. In the words of Jesus in the Gospels, there is neither a church order nor any guidance how his followers should live within society, politics and the economy.[86]

Jesus to be carried away on Passover night?

Although all these passages hint at a very urgent imminent eschatological expectation of Jesus in Jerusalem, they do not provide a positive indication of this. There is, however, one word of Jesus that does. According to Mark and Matthew, Jesus said to the high priest and to the members of the Council that they would see the Son of Man, i.e., him, Jesus, sitting at the right hand of God and coming on the clouds of heaven.[87] This word of Jesus also appears in Luke, only "coming on the clouds of heaven" is left out, perhaps to avoid a statement about the time of the final judgment.[88] In Matthew and Luke, however, there is a more precise time determination of when Jesus is to be carried away to heaven and revealed as the Son of Man, namely, *"from this moment on."*[89] Is there any indication that Jesus believed this event was that imminent? Many Jews expected the arrival of the Messiah on Passover night.[90] As according to the Gospels, Jesus also identified himself with the Messiah,[91] it is at least thinkable that he applied this calendrical expectation to the actual Passover and to himself.[92]

86. See Gräßer, *Naherwartung Jesu*, 127–28.
87. See Matt 26:64; Mark 14:62.
88. See Luke 22:69.
89. See Matt 26:64 (ἀπ' ἄρτι) and Luke 22:69 (ἀπὸ τοῦ νῦν). See also the comprehensive discussion in Davies and Allison, *Matthew*, 3:529–32.
90. See the references in Allison, *Constructing Jesus*, 146 fn. 518; see also Scriba, *Echtheitskriterien der Jesus-Forschung*, 203–8.
91. See the references p. 130n14; already in the Enochic Book of Parables the Son of Man and the Messiah are one and the same figure (see 1 En. 48:10; 52:4); there the Son of Man is also the Chosen One and the Righteous One; see Charlesworth, "Did Jesus Know?" 191–202, and Nickelsburg and VanderKam, *1 Enoch 2*, 44–45, 113–20, with numerous substantiations as well as, Boyarin, *Jewish Gospels*, 80, 86, 93–95.
92. Scriba, *Echtheitskriterien der Jesus-Forschung*, 218, argues that Jesus expected the advent of the kingdom of God in Jerusalem the night before his crucifixion, namely the Passover night of the fifteenth Nisan in the year 28 CE. See Scriba, *Echtheitskriterien der Jesus-Forschung*, 206–8, 218 with fn. 90 on traces of an eschatological expectation related to Passover in the New Testament, in particular in the Gospel of Luke. According to Scriba's calendar calculations the year of Jesus' death was a Sabbath year, which is important for his hypothesis because according to common belief the Messiah would come on a Sabbath year (see *Echtheitskriterien der Jesus-Forschung*, 217–18; Rooker, *Leviticus*, 303, and Lev 25:1–7); According to Strobel, "Ausrufung des Jobeljahres," it is possible that Jesus believed that he was living in a Jubilee year, one of particular

The Son of Man does not die but will be carried up to heaven

The hypothesis that Jesus knew of the Son of Man concept of the Enochic Book of Parables and applied it to himself could, however, help to explain, even without an extreme imminent eschatological expectation of Jesus, why he saw his hope crushed in the face of death.[93] For a long time, the Book of Parables was dated to a time after Jesus of Nazareth, so that its potential influence on his thinking was deemed impossible. Recently, its composition has been reassigned to a time before the appearance of Jesus.[94] Geographical and archaeological indications are that the text was written in Lower Galilee, perhaps in Migdal (Magdala).[95] Nazareth is not much more than twenty miles away. It would thus be quite possible that Jesus and those around him knew the doctrine of the Book of Parables and were influenced by it.[96] According to current research, the Enochic Son of Man is, besides the Son of Man in the book of Daniel, the only pre-Christian model of the Son of Man and is, in addition, much more detailed.[97] The parallels between the Son of Man in the Book of Parables and the Son of Man in the words of Jesus in the Synoptic Gospels are striking. Both will come—it would seem in physical form[98]—from heaven to earth, to sit on the throne of glory as the eschatological judge of good and evil, and thereafter reside and reign eternally on earth.[99] According to the representation in the Synoptic Gospels, Jesus was obviously convinced that he would be the heavenly Son of Man.[100] If

---

significance for messianic expectation, which was proclaimed every seven Sabbath years (see Luke 4:16–30; Lev 25:8–24).

93. On Jesus and the Son of Man in the Book of Parables, see Charlesworth, "Did Jesus Know?"; Macaskill, "Matthew and the *Parables*"; Walck, "Parables of Enoch"; Reynolds, "Enochic Son of Man"; Boyarin, *Jewish Gospels*, 74–95.

94. See above, p. 36n58.

95. See Aviam, "Book of Enoch"; Charlesworth, "Did Jesus Know?" 184–91.

96. See Charlesworth, "Did Jesus Know?" 205–17, and Charlesworth, "Date and Provenience," 56.

97. There are only two verses in the book of Daniel on the Son of Man: "I saw in the night visions, and behold, with the clouds of heaven there came one like a son of man, and he came to the Ancient of Days and was presented before him. And to him was given dominion and glory and a kingdom, that all peoples, nations, and languages should serve him; his dominion is an everlasting dominion, which shall not pass away, and his kingdom one that shall not be destroyed" (Dan 7:13–14 ESV).

98. This is evident, among other things, from the fact that the Enochic Son of Man will live eternally and *eat* with the righteous and chosen on earth (see 1 En. 62:14).

99. See the references above, p. 61n114.

100. See above, p. 130.

he was following the Enochic model he would thus have to assume *that he would not die*,[101] because the Enochic Son of Man, who lives unrecognized on earth at first, does not die,[102] but is carried away to heaven alive, in his physical body, and is revealed there as the heavenly Son of Man.[103] Jesus' word to the high priest and the members of the Council, that from this moment on, they would see him sitting at the right hand of God, suggests that he reckoned with his immediate rapture without premature death. But even if one does not accept that Jesus had an extreme imminent eschatological expectation, he would have realized, as death approached, that his kingdom-of-God mission was threatened with failure precisely because in the doctrine the Enochic Son of Man does *not* die. If he was this Son of Man, then God or his angels would have to come and carry him away before his death. But that is not what happened.

Jesus' death on the cross and the tragedy of the confusion of the worlds

All of these considerations remain very hypothetical. Despite this, on the whole they support the theory that Jesus' reproach of God on the cross is at its core historical and that it is best understood as an expression of disappointment about the absence of divine intervention, and not as an expression of Jesus' weakness. It seems, with this in mind, absolutely possible that Jesus died in the consciousness that he had been brutally tortured and delivered to a cruel death in vain. If we understand the crucifixion events in this way, then Jesus' cry to God can be understood as the epitome of the disappointment of hopes that occurred through the confusion of worlds: hopes for a physical coming and intervention of divine powers to create otherworldly conditions on earth.

---

101. See above, pp. 135–36n48 to men like Elijah, Enoch, and Ezra, who were taken to heaven without death, i.e., they did not "taste death," but will come down from heaven at the end of time.

102. On the initial hiddenness of the Enochic Son of Man, see 1 En. 48:6; 62:6-7.

103. See 1 En. 70-71.

Epilogue

THOSE WHO SHARE THE essential conclusions of this study may ask what the consequences and perspectives are for the religions in question. A thorough response would require its own book. I would, however, like to make some suggestions.

My examination demonstrates that the belief in a physical resurrection and an eternal, earthly afterlife in a paradisiacal kingdom of God belongs to the traditions of the three closely analyzed religions—Zoroastrianism, Judaism, and Christianity.[1] However, these three religions could, it would seem, largely abandon this belief without placing their identity under threat.[2] In the case of Christianity, however, my conclusions do touch on the central doctrine of the redemption of humanity through the death of Jesus of Nazareth on the cross[3] and the related image of a superhuman Jesus.[4] For this reason, the Epilogue will concentrate on Christianity.

According to my interpretation, the Jesus of Nazareth discernible in the sources was fundamentally mistaken in his kingdom-of-God mission.

---

1. See above, pp. 27, 45–46, 77, 118.

2. See above, pp. 18n2, 45, 88–89, 98, 116.

3. See above p. 134n43. According to Berner and Figl, "Christentum," 422, Christianity has the essential character of a religion of redemption.

4 According to the Nicene Creed Jesus is "true God" (see Denzinger, *Compendium*, 63 [D 150]; see identical Christian doctrines in Denzinger, *Compendium*, 28 [D 41], 29 [D 42, 44], 31 [D 46], 32 [D 48], 33 [D 50], 34 [D 51], 38 [D 72], 39 [D 74], 51 [D 125], 62 [D 144], 68 [D 168], 75 [D 189], 77 [D 209], 97 [D 252, 253, 256], 100 [D 272], 105 [D 293, 294], 109 [D 301], 114 [D 317, 318], 117 [D 325], 143 [D 402], 149 [D 427], 150 [D 432], 154 [D 442], 183 [D 534], 189 [D 545], 190 [D 547], 193 [D 554], 194 [D 558], 196 [D 564], 211 [D 617], 212 [D 619], 232 [D 681], 246 [D 750], 262 [D 791], 282 [D 852], 345 [D 1339], 511 [D 2529]). According to Martin Luther, "Jesus Christ [is] true God, begotten of the Father from eternity" ([Luther] *The Small Catechism*, 5); see also Philaret, "Longer Catechism," 466–68 (§§ 139, 144–47). Berner and Figl, "Christentum," 422, write on the relationship between the divinity of Jesus and his role as the redeemer: only if Jesus Christ was like God and consubstantial with him, could he truly redeem mankind.

I do not refer to Jesus' near expectation.⁵ The error in his near expectation is one of time: a specific event, the possibility of which is not disputed, is expected *too early*. The confusion that I am referring to, on the contrary, consists of the fact that Jesus was *expecting something impossible*: a physical, eternal life on earth for the resurrected deceased as well as those still living. He was expecting something which *by its very nature could never happen*. To be sure, the concept of an eternal, paradisiacal life in an earthly kingdom of God is comprehensible against the background of the cosmological, geographical, and biological knowledge of antiquity.⁶ However, the error that is expressed in the projection of otherworldly conditions onto the earth seems to reveal a greater lack of judgment than a near expectation, which is only mistaken in terms of the timing of a possible event.⁷ For this reason, exalting Jesus above all other people is simply not justifiable. But most importantly, this eschatological error undermines Jesus' traditional redeemer role: *if the kingdom of eternal life that Jesus proclaimed, could not possibly exist, then neither could his death on the cross nor anything else provide entry into this kingdom*.⁸ The traditional Christian view of Jesus' acts of redemption are also questionable because of another consideration: probably because of a metaphysical illusion, which is closely connected to what was just described, Jesus was led to behave carelessly, and without this behavior his execution in Jerusalem would never have resulted.⁹ The establishment of the kingdom of God, a kind of heaven on earth, would, according to the conviction of the Synoptic Jesus, be brought about by an immense, physical intervention of the heavenly powers. This emerges from many of Jesus' words.¹⁰ He thus believed in the possibility of removing the

---

5. See above, pp. 141–43.

6. See above, pp. 14–15.

7. Karl Rahner wrote on the presumed imminent expectation of Jesus that he, as true man, had "a genuine human consciousness that *must* have an unknown future ahead of it." Therefore "there is no reason to speak of an error of Jesus in his imminent expectation" (*Foundations*, 250). But see, for example, the constitution of Pope Vigilius *Inter innumeras sollicitudines* of 14 May 553: "If anyone says that the one Jesus Christ, the true Son of man and the true Son of God, was ignorant of future events or the day of the Last Judgement [. . .], let him be anathema" (trans. Denzinger, *Compendium*, 147 [D 419]).

8. According to Edvin Larsson, the kingdom of God was not only for the Synoptics but also Jesus himself, the "central concept of salvation" ("Heil und Erlösung," 617).

9. Here, above all, I think that according to the literature Jesus behaved provocatively in Jerusalem, did not escape the foreseeable prosecution, and did not defend himself at the trial (see above, pp. 132–33).

10. See above, pp. 56n78–79, 130n10, and in addition, Matt 13:39, 49–50; 24:40–41; Luke 17:34–36; see also Matt 26:53: "Do you think that I cannot appeal to my Father, and he will at once send me more than twelve legions of angels?" (ESV).

limits between the heavenly realm of God and the angels and this earthly world.[11] His cry on the cross shortly before his death that God had forsaken him is easiest to understand if he had expected an eschatological intervention from God that would save him from death.[12] One possible explanation for this expectation is that he believed himself to be the Son of Man according to the Enochian model, who would physically come from heaven as the eschatological judge, but who before doing so would have to be carried away to heaven, alive in his physical body, without dying.[13] Aside from this explanation, I get the overall impression that through his illusionary confusion of this world and the world beyond, Jesus went unwittingly to his downfall. This view would not, however, be compatible with the traditional doctrine that declares Jesus' path to his death to have been a conscious act of redemption in agreement with God.[14]

However, as I see him, Jesus of Nazareth could continue to be considered a model of humanity, despite his eschatological errors. He sought to improve human living conditions on this planet. This is an important and noble objective even today. He not only proclaimed a kingdom of God on earth without suffering, he also took action to lessen suffering. Jesus' work as a healer was possibly unparalleled in ancient times. Of no other person in his time are so many healing stories handed down.[15] His food and nature miracles could primarily be understood as healing acts in a broader sense, reducing the hardship and suffering of the people.[16] This is also the case for his caring for the socially marginalized, which according

---

11. For Jesus and his contemporaries, the heavenly location where God and the angels lived belonged to the same cosmos as the earth (see above, p. 14).

12. See above, pp. 136–37, 139–40, 145.

13. See above, pp. 144–45.

14. See above p. 134n43. Even modern interpretations of Jesus' execution as an act of redemption seem unable to escape the assumption that Jesus consented to his death and saw it as redemptive. Karl Rahner is, for example, convinced that Jesus' death can "be regarded as a cause of our salvation in a true sense" (*Foundations*, 282). A prerequisite for this is, however, that Jesus had accepted his death freely (see *Foundations*, 284). Elsewhere, he says even more clearly that "the pre-Easter Jesus himself interpreted his death as redemptive" (Rahner, "Erlösung," 1166).

15. See above, p. 124, and Henriksen and Sandnes, *Jesus as Healer*, 248; on Jesus as a healer, see also Niebuhr, "Jesus," 422–24.

16. Within the food miracles, the so-called multiplication of the loaves of bread can be seen in a broader sense as healing (see Matt 14:19; 15:36; Mark 6:41; 8:6; Luke 9:16; John 6:11), less so the changing of water into wine (see John 2:1–10); within the nature miracles, the calming of the storm on the lake can be understood similarly (see Matt 8:23–27; Mark 4:35–41; Luke 8:22–25), but of course not the withering of the fig tree without fruit (see Matt 21:19; Mark 11:14).

to the Synoptic Gospels, he also described as acts of healing.[17] The tragic end to his kingdom-of-God mission in Jerusalem does not detract from his image as a healer. Today, our attempts at improving living conditions on earth are more based on scientific and technical knowledge than on metaphysical concepts. Nonetheless, catastrophic errors and failures are a daily occurrence. For example, the building of wells funded by development aid accelerated the desertification of the Sahel region.[18] Production of biofuel from grains, which through CO_2 neutrality should slow global warming, has resulted in deforestation, land grabbing, famine, and even increased CO_2 release.[19]

Even if one understands Jesus of Nazareth not as the redeemer but rather "only" as an inspiring example, we are left with the problem that all scholarly reconstructions of his 2000-year-old acts, words, and convictions remain speculative. Who would want to steer their life based on something so uncertain? Already Gotthold Ephraim Lessing doubted that one "would risk anything of great, permanent worth [. . .]?"[20] based on historical findings. The gulf between us and the historical Jesus, the much-cited "ugly, broad ditch" of Lessing,[21] cannot be bridged by science. The scholarly images of Jesus are diverse and contradictory.[22] His very existence is questioned by some researchers.[23] Christianity, however, requires a real Jesus. From the very beginning on, it understood itself as the religion of a living, mystical communion with Jesus.[24] Without the disciples' experiences of

17. See Mark 2:16–17: "And the scribes of the Pharisees, when they saw that he was eating with sinners and tax collectors, said to his disciples, 'Why does he eat with tax collectors and sinners?' And when Jesus heard it, he said to them, 'Those who are well have no need of a physician, but those who are sick. I came not to call the righteous, but sinners'" (ESV). Very similarly, Matt 9:11–12; Luke 5:30–31. On Jesus' care for marginalized groups—besides accounts of his physically healing persons on the edge of society—see, e.g., Matt 9:9–13; 11:19; 21:31; Mark 2:15–17; Luke 5:27–32; 7:36–50; 14:13–23; 19:1–10; see also Matt 11:28.

18. See Blümel, *Wüsten*, 59; Heineberg, *Anthropogeographie*, 146.

19. See, e.g., Biesalski, *Der verborgene Hunger*, 147–219; Righelato and Spracklen, "Carbon Mitigation"; DeCicco et al., "Carbon Balance Effects of Biofuel."

20. Lessing, *Theological Writings*, 54.

21. Lessing, *Theological Writings*, 55; see on this also Theissen, Historical Scepticism."

22. See, e.g., Allison, "Traditional Criteria of Authenticity," 9.

23. See Theissen and Merz, *Historical Jesus*, 90–91, 122–24.

24. According to Matt 28:20, Jesus promised his disciples: "I am with you always, to the end of the age" (ESV); according to Matt 18:20 he said to them: "[W]here two or three are gathered in my name, there am I among them" (ESV) (see Allison, *Resurrecting Jesus*, 366). The Catechism of the Catholic Church, declares that it is possible for everyone "to enter into fellowship with Jesus [*cum Iesu communionem habere*] by the

their deceased master, the Jesus movement would probably have ended with his death, and Christianity would never have been established.[25] Experiences of the deceased Jesus have molded the history of Christianity until the present day.[26] If Paul of Tarsus had not met Jesus in his Damascus Road experience,[27] he would not have been instrumental in promoting the spread of Christianity in the Roman Empire. Without his mystical Jesus experience,[28] Francis of Assisi would probably not have developed into one of the most formidable Christian figures of the Middle Ages, whose influence reaches into our own time.[29] Experiences with other deceased persons also had enormous significance for Christian piety. First and foremost, the apparitions of Mary, mother of Jesus.[30]

The question is, however, how one can come into real contact and maintain a communion with people who are deceased. According to the prevailing worldview, inspired by science, this is impossible because deceased persons—and this includes Jesus of Nazareth—no longer exist.[31] Does this mean Christianity is based on illusions and that it continues to feed on them?

I can only hint at the answers here. For further details, I refer readers to my book *Transzendente Begegnungen*.[32] My argument runs basically as follows: If one understands a person to be a being that is or could be conscious, then the currently prevailing form of science is unable to state whether a person is bound to earthly-physical structures or not. This kind

---

most ordinary events of daily life" (*CCC* 533). Often the communion of Christians with Jesus is expressed through the metaphor of the body and the head, see *CCC* 787-95, the section "The Church—Body of Christ" with reference to Matt 28:20; John 6:56; 15:4-5; Col 1:18; on a real, mystical communion with Jesus, see also Biser, "Christentum," 43: "Christianity is a mystical religion, founded on communion with the founder"; Jentzsch, *Evangelischer Erwachsenenkatechismus*, 910: "Christians stand with Christ in a real communion"; Schweitzer, "Jesus und wir," 275: For the "whole of the old theology" the connection with Jesus was "neither knowledge, nor taking a stand, but a mystical communion" (trans. S. Kühne).

25. See above, pp. 79-80.
26. See, e.g., Wiebe, *Visions of Jesus*, 15-88.
27. See Acts 9:1-21; 22:3-16; 26:9-20.
28. See, in particular, his audition before the crucifix in San Damiano, in which Jesus said to him that he should rebuild his church (see Karrer, *Franz von Assisi*, 42-43).
29. For Dante, Francis of Assisi was "a sun upon the world" (*La Divina Commedia, Paradiso*, canto 11, line 50; trans. Dante Alighieri, *Divine Comedy*, 331), for others he was a second Christ (see Feld, *Franziskus von Assisi*, 63-64).
30. On modern day Marian apparitions, see Rogo, *Miracles*, 205-57, 284-86.
31. See Schwenke, *Transzendente Begegnungen*, 171, 211.
32. See Schwenke, *Transzendente Begegnungen*, 170-230.

of science is based on intersubjective methods, which can, in principle, be carried out by everybody. Consciousness is, however, not measurable using such methods.[33] Therefore, no scientific statement about the existence of consciousness, and consequently, no scientific statement about a necessary coupling of the physical body and consciousness is possible.[34] According to the understanding of many experiencers, certain forms of transcendent experiences, such as near-death experiences or experiences with deceased persons, speak in favor of an afterlife of persons after the death of the physical body. These assessments are not scientific knowledge, to be sure. This does not, however, mean that they cannot contain any kind of knowledge, or only provisional and inferior knowledge. We go about our daily lives predominantly on the basis of non-scientific knowledge.[35] Science, also, in the described sense, can only function if scientists acknowledge non-scientific forms of knowledge.[36]

Experiences with deceased persons are not rare curiosities but rather widespread and are often existentially significant for the experiencer. Surveys in Western countries have shown that around a quarter of those asked, admit to having had these kinds of experiences.[37] The effects are quite predominantly described as positive: love, comfort, support, happiness, peace and inspiration.[38] The widespread preconception that these experiences are based on wishful thinking has not been established. On the contrary, longing for them seems rather to hinder their occurrence.[39]

Astonishingly, contacts with the afterlife were and are disputed not only by representatives of a scientifically-inspired world view, but also by Christianity.[40] This hostile attitude probably dates back to the influence of the Old Testament. In it, the cult of the dead—apparently in favor of Yahweh's sole worship—is suppressed and contact with the deceased is even punishable by death.[41] Apart from the post-mortem experiences of Jesus of

---

33. See Schwenke, *Transzendente Begegnungen*, 171–76; see also, already a hundred years ago, Bergson, "Psychical Research," 87: "[I]t is of the essence of mental things that they do not lend themselves to measurement."

34. See Schwenke, *Transzendente Begegnungen*, 182–84.

35. See Schwenke, *Transzendente Begegnungen*, 181–82.

36. See Schwenke, *Transzendente Begegnungen*, 180–84, 187–91; see also below, p. 160.

37. See Schwenke, *Transzendente Begegnungen*, 26–27.

38. See Schwenke, *Transzendente Begegnungen*, 34–140, 160–67.

39. See Arcangel, *Afterlife Encounters*, 288.

40. See also Schwenke, *Transzendente Begegnungen*, 231–65.

41. See Schwenke, *Transzendente Begegnungen*, 238–39, 251–53, and above, p. 28 with n. 3.

Nazareth, contacts with other deceased played an important role in Christian piety. Augustine of Hippo, who, relying on the Old Testament, seeks to prove that the deceased are fundamentally unaware of us and unable to help us,[42] is forced to allow the knowledge and help to some martyrs of the Christian faith. But he attempts to establish a kind of otherworldly two-tiered society for martyrs and the (normal) dead:

> We are not to think then, that to be interested in the affairs of the living is in the power of any departed who please, only because to some men's healing or help the Martyrs be present: but rather we are to understand that it must needs be by a Divine power that the Martyrs are interested in affairs of the living, from the very fact that for the departed to be by their proper nature interested in affairs of the living is impossible.[43]

In Catholicism, a dichotomy of the saints and the dead is maintained even today. Saints are distinguished from the dead as if they are a separate group.[44] This obscures the fact that the cult of saints is an attempt to contact deceased persons.

If one accepts the error of Jesus to be as I have described, and for that reason abandons—along with the concepts of a physical resurrection and eternal afterlife in an earthly kingdom of God—a deification of Jesus and the pivotal doctrine of redemption of humanity by his death, it raises the question of alternative leitmotifs in Christianity.[45] In connection with the previous considerations, I would like to sketch a suggestion that picks up on and links two ideas from earliest Christianity. The problem of Lessing's ditch will be narrowly contained.

The first leitmotif of my proposal is following Jesus, the so-called imitation of Christ. It was, from the very beginning, an ideal of Christian life.[46]

---

42. See Augustine, *Cur.* 16; for Augustine on contacts with the deceased see Schwenke, *Transzendente Begegnungen*, 246–50.

43. Augustine, *Cur.* 19 (trans. *NPNF*1 3:549).

44. Thus, in the Catechism of the Catholic Church first the "communion with the saints" is described and then the "communion with the dead" (*CCC* 957–58). It is the equivalent of, in a zoological book, dealing first with the falcons and then with the birds.

45. It is my impression, at least in German-speaking Christianity, that at present there is a certain cluelessness when it comes to Christian leitmotifs. Amongst other things, one can observe tendencies to focus on ethical, psychological, social, and political issues, to hold on to traditional theological teachings without more profound intellectual debate and, in the field of spirituality, to favor approaches from non-Christian traditions.

46. On the history of and on the many variations of the concept of following Jesus, see Luz et al., "Nachfolge Jesu."

But how should one follow Jesus today? Perhaps by doing that which most distinguished him from his contemporaries. Judging by the sources, this seems most likely to have been his work as a healer.[47] As healing is a praiseworthy behavior from an ethical point of view, I suggest that the imitation of Christ should focus on Jesus the healer. In multiple sources, not only does Jesus himself heal but he also instructs his disciples to heal the sick.[48] The power to heal physical diseases with simple words or laying on of hands, as it is reported that Jesus of Nazareth did, is (perhaps) not given to everyone. Yet all people are capable of healing in the broader sense, alleviating and freeing others from physical, psychic, and spiritual distress. In Christian history, there is a significant tradition in which this healing, in the broader sense, is central to the way of life.[49]

The second leitmotif is a mystical communion of this-worldly and otherworldly persons. This idea is, as we have seen, also anchored in early Christianity.[50] The initial idea of an afterlife communion with Jesus was soon extended to the concept of *communio sanctorum*, the "Communion of Saints." The expression can be found already in the Apostle's Creed.[51] Often "saints" here is understood to mean all Christians, both living and deceased. The members of the communion of saints help and support each other.[52] This is mainly concerned with remedying acute earthly and otherworldly difficulties for the members themselves.[53] If the concept of

---

47. See above, pp. 124, 148. Jesus' work as a healer seems historically certain. Niebuhr, "Jesus," 422, writes, few traits of the work of Jesus are as well attested in the sources as his acts of healing and their success.

48. See Popkes, *Krankenheilungsauftrag Jesu*, 12 with reference to Mark 6:13; Matt 10:1, 8; Luke 9:1-2, 6; 10:9; Gos. Thom. 14:4-5.

49. See, e.g., Biser, "Christentum," 36: "Christianity is a therapeutic religion." On the Christian history of healing in the narrower sense, see Keener, *Miracles*, 1:359-507.

50. See above, pp. 149-50.

51. See Denzinger, *Compendium*, 27 (D 30). On the uncertain origin and significance of the term the "Communion of Saints," see Kruse, 'Gemeinschaft der Heiligen.'"

52. See CCC 946-48, 954-59, 962, as well as the Encyclical *Mirae caritatis* of Leo XIII of May 28, 1902: "The communion of Saints is nothing . . . but the mutual communication of help, expiation, prayers, blessings, among all the faithful, who, whether they have already attained to the heavenly country, or are detained in the purgatorial fire, or are yet exiles here on earth, all enjoy the common franchise of that city whereof Christ is the head, and the constitution is charity" (trans. Denzinger, *Compendium*, 683 [D 3363]). From this list it is clear that Christians in hell are not counted among the communion of saints. In Protestant theology, the communion of saints is more often thought of as confined to the earthly church (see Müller, "Gemeinschaft der Heiligen," 434).

53. Typically, in earthly persons these are diseases that are healed by the intercession of otherworldly people (by saints in the narrower sense), and in otherworldly persons

the communion of saints were slightly modified it could be a meaningful element of Christian spirituality, even to a modern mind. It would then cooperate with the first leitmotif of the imitation of Christ. In this modern version of the communion of saints, Christians would not be primarily concerned with their own plight, but rather supporting a way of life that is dedicated to healing in the broader sense. Following Jesus would not be a lonely undertaking but be inspired and supported through a mystical communion with others.[54] Others—similarly to the traditional concept of the communion of saints—could be both people living on earth and deceased (and other otherworldly) persons.[55] The idea that Jesus of Nazareth is the undisputed "head"[56] of this mystical communion appears implausible, not least in the light of what I suspect to be a serious eschatological error on his side. In my eyes, this error does not permit the placing of Jesus above all others. It therefore makes sense to give up the hierarchical conception of the communion of saints and to regard them as a communion of fundamentally equals. Jesus of Nazareth would then, in this case, be a member of this communion and its origin, but not its head. A further modification

---

torments in purgatory are mitigated and abbreviated by the prayers of earthly persons (see *CCC* 956, 958). Here we see the already identifiable tendency of Augustine to allow only an indirect help between the living and the deceased, namely through intercessory prayer to God. According to accounts of experience, however, it is not unusual for the saints to appear, communicate, and participate directly in healing events (see, e.g., Schamoni, *Wunder sind Tatsachen*, 27, 80, 130–32, 134, 138–39, 142, 154, 157, 166, 172–73, 199; Ruffin, *Padre Pio*, 380–82, 385, 388–89).

54. One can of course ask whether good actions necessitate the support of others. A knowledge of ethical norms, in any case, does not seem to be sufficient. An empirical investigation concluded that professors of ethics behave no better than representatives from other subject areas (see Rust and Schwitzgebel, "Ethicists' and Nonethicists'").

55. As suggested here, some theologians see the essence of Christianity, or at least its future, as being in mysticism. According to Eugen Biser, Christianity is not an ethical but a mystical religion (see "Christentum," 37). Karl Rahner tended towards the opinion that "the Christian of the future will be a mystic or will not exist at all" ("Christian Living," 15). Albert Schweitzer wrote: "Our religion, in so far as it proves to be specifically Christian, is [. . .] not so much a Jesus-cult as a Jesus-mysticism" (*Quest*, 486). One might see Schweitzer's vote for Jesus mysticism as an attempt to overcome Lessing's ditch. He also brought Jesus mysticism into connection with the imitation of Christ (see *Quest*, 487). The mysticism I have proposed will probably be considered by some theologians to be an inferior one, as Christian mysticism is often understood as a form of God mysticism, in which God is seen as a being among other beings. As a consequence, the mystical orientation towards other beings competes with the orientation to God. This competition would not occur in the context of a panentheism where God is not a being beside others but is rather in everything. Then the sentence from Martin Buber would hold: "[T]he man who turns toward him [God] need not turn his back on any other I-Thou relationship" (*I and Thou*, 182).

56. *CCC* 947.

of the traditional communion of saints is that the mystical communion that I have in mind would not depend on formal characteristics such as baptism, but on sentiments and actions.[57] Those who devote themselves to healing in the broader sense can belong to it.

But what would the experiencing of a mystical communion in the imitation of Jesus concretely look like? On this point I quote a simple contemporary account that has no explicit Christian context. The earthly person in the example, however, devotes herself unequivocally to healing in my sense, and the experience with an otherworldly person gives her the strength for this:

> In the Vietnam War, an American surgical nurse whose father had died five years previously, was subjected to a severe rocket attack on her hospital, shortly after arriving in the war zone. As, filled with fear, she crawled under the bed in her room, she had a special, formative experience: "All of a sudden, my father was with me! I felt his presence and his emotional warmth— my father's caring and love enveloped me. I felt wrapped in the security of his strength, and had an overwhelming sense of peace. [. . .] He was there several minutes, and then he left. The experience strengthened my spirituality and took away my fear of death. Throughout my tour, I dealt with a lot of young men who were severely wounded and others who went on to die. The war didn't stop—the casualties just kept coming. I sat with many who were dying because I couldn't imagine them dying alone in a foreign country. My experience with my father contributed to my ability to do that."[58]

Experiences with otherworldly persons can have different levels of intensity and clarity. The spectrum comprises sensations of inspiration and support that are difficult to assign, clear experiences of a presence, as in the case quoted above, broad visions in altered states of consciousness including dreams, and hyper real encounters with otherworldly persons in the context of an otherworld journey during out-of-body experiences.[59] It is my impression that everyone of us has the capacity for this kind of mysticism.

---

57. The idea of a communion of saints that is founded on intentions and acts can be heard in a note from former UN Secretary-General Dag Hammarskjöld: "Yet, through me there flashes this vision of a magnetic field in the soul, created in a timeless present by unknown multitudes, living in holy obedience, whose words and actions are a timeless prayer.—'The Communion of the Saints'" (*Markings*, 84).

58. Guggenheim and Guggenheim, *Hello from Heaven*, 33.

59. See Schwenke, *Transzendente Begegnungen*, 58–70, 83–136.

The practicing of mindfulness and focus could allow more subtle sensations to enter the consciousness more clearly.

Experiences of a cross-world mystical communion can also be found in non-religious contexts, inter alia, in the context of creativity and art. As an example, I invoke the account that pianist Hélène Grimaud gives of her experience while she is playing the piano. Although this concerns art and not religion, she describes very clearly the fundamental concept of my version of a modern communion of saints: that the experience of transcendent assistance can contribute to the realization of something wonderful on earth. Grimaud says that while she is playing she does not feel alone, she is protected.[60] She also sometimes perceives the presence of the composer of the work she is playing.[61] In this presence she experiences a heavenly inspiration and love that she attempts to transpose to earth through her playing:

> [W]hen I step out of myself and watch myself as I'm playing, sometimes I see a light come down that envelops the entire piano. I know that they [the composers] are that light. At that instant, I know that I am there to receive this heavenly song and, inasmuch so I am its vehicle, to conduct this gentle lightning bolt of love through the core of the tree to the center of the earth, the heart of the earth, this throbbing star.[62]

---

60. Grimaud, *Wild Harmonies*, 230.
61. See Grimaud, *Wild Harmonies*, 230, and Ullmann, "Hélène Grimaud."
62. Grimaud, *Wild Harmonies*, 230.

Appendix: Miracles and Science

Introduction

SO-CALLED MIRACLES ARE OFTEN dismissed as unhistorical fictions because they seem to contradict scientific knowledge and are thus seen as impossible.[1] The question of the objective reality of miracles is, however, irrelevant for our investigation. The influence of so-called miracles on the thinking of persons depends only on whether people believe that they have experienced extraordinary phenomena. Nevertheless, I would like to discuss the relationship between miracles and science, so that one does not prematurely assume that Jesus and those around him, due to their miraculous beliefs, had uncommonly numerous and intense hallucinations or suffered from extreme simple-mindedness.[2]

It cannot be proved that an experience contradicts science as a whole

The view that the miracles of Jesus contradict the results of modern science is widespread.[3] However, upon closer examination this cannot be soundly substantiated.[4] It falls down already on the cognitive limitations of humans. A contradiction between the assertion of the reality of miracles and a particular scientific proposition may be easy to detect, but not a contradiction

---

1. The alleged contradiction between the miracle stories of the New Testament and science has often been overcome by understanding the miracle accounts figuratively. According to Ruben Zimmermann, the texts leave no doubt that they are intended to be historical and can be clearly distinguished from fictional texts such as, e.g., Parables (see "Wut des Wunderverstehens," 35).

2. For the view that people who believe in miracles exhibit cognitive deficits, see Lawrence, "Apparitions," 251–53.

3. So, e.g., Bultmann, "New Testament and Mythology."

4. This section is based on Schwenke, *Transzendente Begegnungen*, 178–79.

between the former assertion and science as a whole. The reason is that it is impossible to prove whether science as a whole is consistent. Already the verification of the consistency of a system of considerably less than two hundred propositions seems to overwhelm the best computer imaginable.[5] But scientific literature contains billions or trillions of propositions. This means that at least for the time being it is impossible to ascertain whether science as a whole is consistent.[6] But the consistency of science would be the precondition of an assertion that a particular statement contradicts science. Because if the system of scientific propositions is inconsistent, it would be compatible with any statement.[7]

Causal closure of the physical world not scientifically provable

Most of Jesus' miracles—healings, multiplication of loaves, the changing of water into wine, the abrupt leaving of a fig tree to wither, or the calming of the storm—have the appearance of something non-physical, namely Jesus' ideas and intentions, having an influence on the physical world. By physical, I understand here something that can be measured or observed with intersubjective methods. Ideas and intentions, like consciousness in general, are non-physical, because they cannot be reached by such methods.[8] Often the principle of causal closure of the physical world is invoked against the influence of the non-physical on the physical.[9] According to this principle, there are no non-physical causes for physical events.[10] The closure of the whole of the physical world is, however, not scientifically provable. One would have

---

5. See Cherniak, *Minimal Rationality*, 93–94, 143; see also Charpa, *Wissenschaftsphilosophie*, 63.

6. On inconsistencies in the fundamental statements of physics, see Rothman, "Physik."

7. The relevant logical principle is: *ex contradictione sequitur quodlibet*.

8. See Schwenke, *Transzendente Begegnungen*, 172–176.

9. See also, quite nuanced, Müller, "Welt kausal geschlossen?" I content myself in the following with two theoretical arguments in close connection to Schwenke, *Transzendente Begegnungen*, 177–78.

10. See Falkenburg, *Mythos Determinismus*, 29. If one does not permit acausal spontaneous events, the principle of the closure of the physical world leads to causal determinism, according to which every state of the cosmos is a consequence of the previous one, determined by strict laws of nature (see *Mythos Determinismus*, 23, 29). A causal determinism of this kind is, however, not demonstrable experimentally, nor can it be shown that it is a premise of science (see Ludwig, "Determinismus"; see also Hartmann, *Philosophische Grundlagen*, 322–28).

to put the whole of the physical world to the test.[11] This is impossible for the simple reason that scientists and their instruments are part of the physical world. A scientific investigation consists of many physical (and mental) events. The events that constitute a scientific investigation cannot be the research object of the same investigation.

A causal closure of the physical world would anyway make scientific action impossible.[12] For the methodical execution of scientific investigations and for the functioning of scientific discourses we must accept a determination of the physical actions of scientists by their ideas and intentions, that is, non-physical factors. The scientist who accepts a causally closed, physical world is not conscious of their own scientific actions.[13]

Is no extraordinary influence of the non-physical on the physical possible?

Let us assume that a critic of miracles acknowledges the influence of ideas and intentions on the intersubjective observable behavior of people. Let us also assume they would likewise accept that not only tiny but also macroscopic, yes even global changes, go back to the ideas and intentions of people and could not be explained using the methodology of an intersubjective science. But they could then argue that ideas and intentions only influence one's own body and do not act directly on anything outside of one's own body, as is supposed to have been the case with Jesus' food and nature miracles. The problem with this position is that ideas and intentions are in no way provable using intersubjective methods. Therefore, with such methods, not even the influence of ideas and intentions on one's own body can be determined. Consequently, science can neither argue for or against the claim that ideas and intentions can have direct effects on something physical outside one's own body.

---

11. The theory of the causal closure of the physical world is often justified by the law of conservation of energy. Because the law of conservation of energy only holds for isolated systems (see Dorfmüller et al., *Mechanik, Relativität, Wärme*, 144), one can, however, not use it to prove the causal closure of the physical world. See also, critically, Müller, "Welt kausal geschlossen?" 98–100, where he contests the necessary relationship between causation and energy by means of examples from quantum physics.

12. See on this also, Ludwig, "Determinismus," 60.

13. This self-forgetfulness of the scientist is unwittingly illustrated by psychologist Wolfgang Prinz, when he says that the idea of a free human will is irreconcilable with science. Science assumes, Prinz claims, that everything has a physical cause. For Prinz it is incomprehensible that someone who practices empirical science can believe that free, non-determined actions are possible (see "Mensch," 22).

Miracle accounts as anecdotes

A critic of miracles could now change strategy and not oppose miracles to scientific knowledge and deny their possibility, but rather argue that there is not a single scientific proof of the existence of miraculous incidents. Accounts of them are non-scientific anecdotes, which an epistemically responsible person should not believe because one should accept nothing that is not scientifically proved. In other places I have extensively argued that a scientist is obliged to accept many facts that are not scientifically proved.[14] Otherwise he could neither survive everyday life, nor could he find his way in his research activities, nor would he have the necessary basic knowledge to be able to carry out intersubjective science. Moreover, it is essential for a scientific discourse that the participants simply believe each other about their respective self-ascriptions of beliefs and questions without the truth of these self-ascriptions being scientifically scrutinized. Otherwise the discourse would be obstructed by an infinite regress of checks. Without the recognition of non-scientific knowledge, science would be impossible.

Furthermore, scientific knowledge is built on facts that cannot be verified by the vast majority of humanity but have to just be believed.[15] I refer to the facts that constitute a scientific investigation. Only a vanishingly low fraction of humanity participates in a particular scientific investigation. Even if all investigators involved in an investigation are being filmed at every turn by cameras, it would seem utopian to scientifically determine in retrospect whether the investigation was actually carried out and proceeded in the way that the researchers later reported in their publication. Protocols can be written carelessly or forged, photographic material edited, data invented or omitted. Often months or even years lie between investigation and publication. It is practically impossible after such a long time to reliably reconstruct every relevant detail with intersubjective methods.[16] It would be possible thus to call into doubt every unwelcome report of a laboratory investigation or a field observation. The classification of miracle accounts as scientifically non-verified anecdotes would consequently have to be expanded to reports of scientific investigations. Some miraculous events—among them, for example,

---

14. See Schwenke, "Wissenschaftliche Methode"; Schwenke, *Transzendente Begegnungen*, 180–84.

15. See Schwenke, *Transzendente Begegnungen*, 187–88; Schwenke, "Außersinnliche Wahrnehmung als Erleben," 120–21.

16. Not the reports of a single scientific investigation but rather more general statements, which can be supported by a great number of such reports, could represent intersubjective scientific knowledge; see Schwenke, *Transzendente Begegnungen*, 190–91; Schwenke, "Wissenschaftliche Methode."

ecstatic flights of Joseph of Copertino,[17] experienced by hundreds of people at the same time, comprising even heads of state[18]—are probably better attested than the course and outcome of the average scientific investigation of our time. It would be selective scrutiny to question only miracle accounts and not accounts of scientific investigations.

Do miracles not exist because they are not reproducible using an intersubjective method?

Scientifically oriented critics of miracles could be inclined to argue against their existence in that they are not reproducible using an intersubjective method.[19] Reproducibility is, however, not an appropriate criterion for the existence of an individual incident but only for the reliability of the production of a particular kind of phenomenon with a particular method. The (pointless) attempt to reproduce a *particular* event (here: a miracle) consists of actions in another point in spacetime than the original incident. Statements about such an attempt refer to an incident other than the original one and could thus not contradict statements about the existence of the original incident. Reproducibility is about a relation between two or more given results. By questioning the validity of one of these results, one would take the ground out from under the judgment of reproducibility. Only with the never provable supplementary assumptions that performing the same method always brings forth the same results and that the absolute similarity of the methods used can be guaranteed could it be concluded from the findings of non-reproducibility with all certainty that one of the events did not take place as described, although it would still remain unclear which one. There can be various reasons for insufficient reproducibility. For example, the description of the method and results could be false or not sufficiently clear. Non-reproducibility can also be due to the fact that an object behaves indeterministically despite all methodological efforts of standardization. For example, the behavior of the water jet of a fountain is not reproducible even if one could precisely standardize the water supply.[20] In life it is the rule that one cannot even *produce* the phenomena using a

---

17. Franciscan monk born in 1603, as Guiseppe Maria Gesa in Copertino in Apulia, died in 1663 in Osimo (Ancona).

18. See Grosso, *Man Who Could Fly*, 69–90; Schamoni, *Wunder sind Tatsachen*, 328–32.

19. This paragraph follows very closely, Schwenke, "Außersinnliche Wahrnehmung als Erleben," 118–19, 121–22; Schwenke, *Transzendente Begegnungen*, 188–90.

20. See Ludwig, "Determinismus," 62.

certain method. How can one, for example, produce a conversation with a neighbor, a dog walk in nature, or a football game with an intersubjective method? But if a phenomenon cannot be *produced* then it cannot be *reproduced* either. Purely mental miracles like telepathy or clairvoyance evade science's grasp from the outset because they cannot be recorded using intersubjective methods. With intersubjective methods one cannot measure sensations, perceptions or thoughts, and thus can neither measure the transmission of thoughts or unusual forms of perception.[21]

---

21. See also Schwenke, *Transzendente Begegnungen*, 172–75; Schwenke, "Außersinnliche Wahrnehmung als Erleben," 113–17.

Bibliography

Ahn, Gregor. "Resurrection: I. Resurrection of the Dead; 1. History of Religions, a. Resurrection as a Religious Category." In Betz, *Religion Past and Present*. http://dx.doi.org/10.1163/1877-5888_rpp_COM_01264. Consulted April 4, 2018 First published online 2011.

Albrecht, Felix, and Reinhard Feldmeier, eds. *The Divine Father: Religious and Philosophical Concepts of Divine Parenthood in Antiquity*. Themes in Biblical Narrative 18. Leiden: Brill, 2014.

Alexander, Eben. *Proof of Heaven: A Neurosurgeon's Journey into the Afterlife*. New York: Simon & Schuster, 2012.

Allison, Dale C., Jr. *Constructing Jesus: Memory, Imagination, and History*. Grand Rapids: Baker Academic, 2010.

———. "The Eschatology of Jesus." In Collins, *Origins of Apocalypticism*, 267–302.

———. *The Historical Christ and the Theological Jesus*. Grand Rapids: Eerdmans, 2009.

———. "How to Marginalize the Traditional Criteria of Authenticity." In Holmén and Porter, *Historical Jesus* 1:3–30.

———. "It Don't Come Easy: A History of Disillusionment." In *Jesus, Criteria, and the Demise of Authenticity*, edited by Chris Keith and Anthony Le Donne, 186–99. London: T. & T. Clark, 2012.

———. *Jesus of Nazareth: Millenarian Prophet*. Minneapolis: Fortress, 1998.

———. *Night Comes: Death, Imagination and the Last Things*. Grand Rapids: Eerdmans, 2016.

———. *Resurrecting Jesus: The Earliest Christian Tradition and Its Interpreters*. London: T. & T. Clark, 2005.

———. "Seeing God (Matt. 5:8)." In *Studies in Matthew: Interpretation Past and Present*, 43–63. Grand Rapids: Baker Academic, 2005.

———. "The Scriptural Background of a Matthean Legend: Ezekiel 37, Zechariah 14, and Matthew 27." In *Life beyond Death in Matthew's Gospel: Religious Metaphor or Bodily Reality?* edited by Wim Weren et al., 153–88. Biblical Tools and Studies 13. Leuven: Peeters, 2011.

Althaus, Paul. "Auferstehung. Dogmatisch." In *Die Religion in Geschichte und Gegenwart: Handwörterbuch für Theologie und Religionswissenschaft*, edited by Kurt Galling, 1 (1957) 696–98. 6 vols. 3rd. ed. Tübingen: Mohr, 1957–65.

———. *Die letzten Dinge: Lehrbuch der Eschatologie*. 5th ed. Gütersloh: Bertelsmann, 1949.

Alvarado, Carlos S. "Out-of-Body Experiences." In *Varieties of Anomalous Experiences: Examining the Scientific Evidence*, edited by Etzel Cardeña et al., 183–218. Washington, DC: American Psychological Association, 2000.

Andersson, Rani-Henrik. *The Lakota Ghost Dance of 1890.* Lincoln, NE: University of Nebraska Press, 2008.

Anklesaria, Behrangore Tehmuras, ed. *Zand-Ākāsīh: Iranian or Greater Bundahišn.* Transliteration and Translation in English. Bombay: s.n., n.d. [1956].

Arcangel, Dianne. *Afterlife Encounters: Ordinary People, Extraordinary Experiences.* Charlottesville, VA: Hampton Roads, 2005.

Aristotle. *On the Heavens.* Translated by W. K. C. Guthrie. Loeb Classical Library 378. Cambridge,: Harvard University Press, 1939.

Atwater, Phyllis M. H. *The New Children and Near-Death Experiences.* Rochester, VT: Bear, 2003.

Aune, David E., ed. *The Blackwell Companion to the New Testament.* Malden, MA: Wiley-Blackwell, 2010.

Avery-Peck, Alan J. "Resurrection of the Body in Early Rabbinic Judaism." In Nicklas et al., *Human Body in Death and Resurrection*, 243–66.

Aviam, Mordechai. "The Book of Enoch and the Galilean Archeology and Landscape." In Charlesworth and Bock, *Parables of Enoch*, 159–69.

Ballou, Adin. *An Exposition of Views Respecting the Principal Facts, Causes and Peculiarities Involved in Spirit Manifestations: Together with Interesting Phenomenal Statements and Communications.* 2nd ed. Boston: Bela Marsh, 1853.

Barrett, William. *Deathbed Visions: How the Dead Talk to the Dying.* 1926. Reprint, Guildford, UK: White Crow, 2011.

Bartelmus, Rüdiger. "Ez 37,1–14, die Verbform w^e qatal und die Anfänge der Auferstehungshoffnung." *Zeitschrift für die Neutestamentliche Wissenschaft* 97 (1985) 366–89.

Bauckham, Richard. "Chiliasmus. IV. Reformation und Neuzeit." In Müller, *Theologische Realenzyklopädie* 7 (1981) 737–45.

Becker, Carl B. "The Centrality of Near-Death Experiences in Chinese Pure Land Buddhism." *Anabiosis: The Journal of Near-Death Studies* 1 (1981) 154–71.

Berger, Klaus. "Das Buch der Jubiläen." *Jüdische Schriften aus hellenistisch-römischer Zeit* 2.3, 272–575. Gütersloh: Gütersloher Verlagshaus, 1981.

Berger, Klaus, and Christiane Nord, eds. and trans. *Das Neue Testament und frühchristliche Schriften*, 7th ed. Frankfurt: Insel, 2003.

Bergson, Henri. "'Phantasms of the Living' and Psychical Research." In *Mind-Energy: Lectures and Essays*, translated by H. Wildon Carr, 75–103. New York: Holt, 1920.

Berlejung, Angelika. "Die Makkabäerbücher." In Gertz, *Grundinformation Altes Testament*, 569–84.

Berner, Ulrich, and Johann Figl. "Christentum." In *Handbuch Religionswissenschaft: Religionen und ihre zentralen Themen*, edited by Johann Figl, 411–35. Innsbruck: Tyrolia, 2003.

Betz, Hans Dieter, et al., eds. *Religion Past and Present: Encyclopedia of Theology and Religion.* 14 vols. Leiden: Brill, 2007–13.

Beuken, Willem A. M. *Jesaja 13–27.* Herders Theologischer Kommentar zum Alten Testament. Freiburg: Herder, 2007.

Biesalski, Hans Konrad. *Der verborgene Hunger: Sattsein ist nicht genug.* Berlin: Springer Spektrum, 2013.

Bird, Michael F. "Passion Predictions." In Evans, *Encyclopedia of the Historical Jesus*, 442–46.

———. "Who Comes from the East and the West? Luke 13.28–29 / Matt 8.11–12 and the Historical Jesus." *New Testament Studies* 52 (2006) 441–57.

Biser, Eugen. "Wird das Christentum noch Prägekraft entfalten? Aus den spirituellen Wurzeln des Abendlandes erwächst eine neue Zukunftsperspektive." *Die politische Meinung* No. 367 (June 2000) 35–45.
Blackburn, Barry L. "The Miracles of Jesus." In *The Cambridge Companion to Miracles*, edited by Graham H. Twelftree, 113–40. Cambridge: Cambridge University Press, 2011.
Blenkinsopp, Joseph. *Isaiah 1–39. A New Translation with Introduction and Commentary*. Anchor Bible 19. New York: Doubleday, 2000.
Blum, Georg Günter. "Chiliasmus. II. Alte Kirche." In Müller, *Theologische Realenzyklopädie*, 7 (1981) 729–33.
Blümel, Wolf-Dieter. *Wüsten: Entstehung—Kennzeichen—Lebensraum*. Stuttgart: Ulmer, 2013.
Böcher, Otto. "Chiliasmus. I. Judentum und Neues Testament." In Müller, *Theologische Realenzyklopädie*, 7 (1981) 723–29.
Bock, Darrell L. "Dating the *Parables of Enoch*: A *Forschungsbericht*." In Charlesworth and Bock, *Parables of Enoch*, 58–113.
Boutelle, Luther. *Sketch of the Life and Religious Experience of Eld. Luther Boutelle. Written by Himself*. Boston: Advent Christian Publication Society, 1891.
Boyarin, Daniel. *The Jewish Gospels: The Story of the Jewish Christ*. New York: New Press, 2012.
Boyarin, Daniel, and Seymour Siegel. "Resurrection." In Skolnik and Berenbaum, *Encyclopedia Judaica*, 17:241–44.
Boyce, Mary. *A History of Zoroastrianism*, vol. 1: *The Early Period*. Leiden: Brill, 1975.
———, ed. and trans. *Textual Sources for the Study of Zoroastrianism*. Chicago: The University of Chicago Press, 1984.
———. *Zoroastrianism: Its Antiquity and Constant Vigour*. Cosa Mesa, CA: Mazda, 1992.
———. *Zoroastrians: Their Religious Beliefs and Practices*. London: Routledge & Kegan Paul, 1979.
Boyce, Mary, and Frantz Grenet. *A History of Zoroastrianism*, vol. 3: *Zoroastrianism under Macedonian and Roman Rule*. Leiden: Brill, 1991.
Brandenburger, Egon. "Himmelfahrt Moses." *Jüdische Schriften aus hellenistisch-römischer Zeit* 5.2, 56–84. Gütersloh: Gütersloher Verlagshaus, 1976.
Braun, Hans-Jürg. *Das Jenseits: Die Vorstellungen der Menschheit über das Leben nach dem Tod* Zürich: Artemis & Winkler, 1996.
Buber, Martin. *I and Thou*. Translated by Walter Kaufmann. 1923. Reprint, New York: Scribners, 1970.
Büchner, Karl. "Einleitung." In Marcus Tullius Cicero, *Der Staat*, edited and trans. by Karl Büchner, 5th ed., 281–351. Munich: Artemis & Winkler, 1993.
Buhlman, William. *Adventures beyond the Body: How to Experience Out-of-Body Travel*. New York: HarperOne, 1996.
Bukovec, Predag, and Barbara Kolkmann-Klamt, eds. *Jenseitsvorstellungen im Orient: Kongreßakten der 2. Tagung der RVO (3./4. Juni 2011, Tübingen)*. Hamburg: Dr Kovač, 2013.
Bultmann, Rudolf. "New Testament and Mythology." In *Kerygma and Myth: A Theological Debate*, edited by Hans Werner Bartsch, translated by Reginald Fuller, 1–44. London: SPCK, 1953.

Butterweck, Christel. "Tertullian, Quintus Septimius Flores." In Müller, *Theologische Realenzyklopädie*, 33 (2002) 93–107.

Bynum, Caroline Walker. "Death and Resurrection in the Middle Ages: Some Modern Implications." *Proceedings of the American Philosophical Society* 142 (1998) 589–96.

———. *The Resurrection of the Body in Western Christianity, 200–1336*. New York: Columbia University Press, 1995.

Campenhausen, Hans von. *Der Ablauf der Osterereignisse und das leere Grab*. Sitzungsberichte der Heidelberger Akademie der Wissenschaften: Philosophisch-Historische Klasse; 1952, 4 Abteilung. Heidelberg: Winter, 1952.

Capps, Donald. "Beyond Schweitzer and the Psychiatrists: Jesus as Fictive Personality." In Charlesworth and Rhea, *Jesus Research*, 399–435.

Charlesworth, James H. "The Date and Provenience of the *Parables of Enoch*." In Charlesworth and Bock, *Parables of Enoch*, 37–57.

———. "Did Jesus Know the Traditions in the *Parables of Enoch*? ΤΙΣ ΕΣΤΙΝ ΟΥΤΟΣ Ο ΥΙΟΣ ΤΟΥ ΑΝΘΡΩΠΟΥ; (Jn 12:34)." In Charlesworth and Bock, *Parables of Enoch*, 173–217.

———. "Where Does the Concept of Resurrection Appear and How Do We Know That?" In *Resurrection: The Origin and Future of a Biblical Doctrine*, edited by James H. Charlesworth et al., 1–21. London: T. & T. Clark, 2006.

Charlesworth, James H., and Darrell L. Bock, eds. *Parables of Enoch: A Paradigm Shift*. London: Bloomsbury, 2013.

Charlesworth, James H., and Brian Rhea, eds. *Jesus Research: New Methodologies and Perceptions; The Second Princeton-Prague Symposium on Jesus Research, Princeton 2007*. Grand Rapids: Eerdmans, 2014.

Charpa, Ulrich. *Grundprobleme der Wissenschaftsphilosophie*. Paderborn: Schöningh, 1996.

Cherniak, Christopher. *Minimal Rationality*. Cambridge: MIT Press, 1986.

The Church of Jesus Christ of Latter-Day Saints. *The Doctrine and Covenants of the Church of Jesus Christ of Latter-Day Saints*. Salt Lake City, UT: The Church of Jesus Christ of Latter-Day Saints, 2014.

Cicero, Marcus Tullius. *On the Nature of the Gods. Academics*. Translated by H. Rackham. Cambridge: Harvard University Press, 1933.

———. *On the Republic and On the Laws*. Translated with introduction, notes, and index by David Fott. Agora Editions. Ithaca, NY: Cornell University Press, 2014.

———. *Cicero's Tusculan Disputations, also, Treatises on The Nature of the Gods, and on The Commonwealth*. Translated by C. D. Yonge. New York: Harper & Brothers, 1877.

Collins, Adela Yarbro. "The Book of Revelation." In Collins, *Origins of Apocalypticism*, 384–414.

Collins, John J. *Daniel: A Commentary on the Book of Daniel*. Hermeneia. Minneapolis: Fortress, 1993.

———. "From Prophecy to Apocalypticism: The Expectation of the End," Collins, *Origins of Apocalypticism*, 129–61.

———, ed. *The Origins of Apocalypticism in Judaism and Christianity*. New York: Continuum, 1998.

Cook, John Granger. "The Use of ἐγείρω and ἀνίστημι and the 'Resurrection of a Soul.'" *Zeitschrift für die Neutestamentliche Wissenschaft* 108 (2017) 259–80.

Crookes, William. *Researches in the Phenomena of Spiritualism*. London: Burns, 1874.
Crowell, Eugene. *The Identity of Primitive Christianity and Modern Spiritualism*. vol. 2, 2nd ed. New York: Published at the Office of "The Two Worlds," 1881.
Dante Alighieri. *The Divine Comedy*. Translated by Henry F. Cary. The Harvard Classics 20. New York: Collier & Son, 1909.
Davies, W. D., and Dale C. Allison Jr. *A Critical and Exegetical Commentary on the Gospel according to Saint Matthew*. 3 vols. International Critical Commentary. Edinburgh: T. & T. Clark, 1988–97.
Dawson, Lorne L. "Prophetic Failure in Millennial Movements." In *The Oxford Handbook of Millennialism*, edited by Catherine Wessinger, 150–70. Oxford: Oxford University Press, 2011.
de Jong, Albert. *Traditions of the Magi: Zoroastrianism in Greek and Latin Literature*. Religions in the Graeco-Roman World 133. Leiden: Brill, 1997.
DeCicco, John M., et al. "Carbon Balance Effects of U.S. Biofuel Production and Use." *Climatic Change* 138 (2016) 667–80.
DeMallie, Raymond J., ed. *The Sixth Grandfather: Black Elk's Teaching Given to John Neihardt*. Lincoln, NE: University of Nebraska Press, 1985.
Denzinger, Heinrich. *Compendium of Creeds, Definitions, and Declarations on Matters of Faith and Morals*. Revised, enlarged, and in collaboration with Helmut Hoping, edited by Peter Hünermann for the original bilingual edition and edited by Robert Fastiggi and Anne Englund Nash for the English edition. 43rd ed. San Francisco: Ignatius, 2012.
Doering, Lutz. "God as Father in Texts from Qumran." In Albrecht and Reinhard, *The Divine Father*, 107–35.
Dorfmüller, Thomas, et al. *Mechanik, Relativität, Wärme*. Vol. 1 of *Bergmann / Schaefer: Lehrbuch der Experimentalphysik*. 11th ed. Berlin: de Gruyter, 1998.
Doyle, Brian. *The Apocalypse of Isaiah Metaphorically Speaking: A Study of the Use, Function and Significance of Metaphors in Isaiah 24–27*. Bibliotheca Ephemeridum Theologicarum Lovaniensium 151. Leuven-Louvain: Leuven University Press, 2000.
Drößler, Rudolf. *2000 Jahre Weltuntergang: Himmelserscheinungen und Weltbilder in apokalyptischer Deutung*. Würzburg: Echter, 1999.
Duling, Dennis C. "The Gospel of Matthew." In Aune, *The Blackwell Companion to the New Testament*, 296–318.
———. "Millennialism." In *The Social Sciences and New Testament Interpretation*, edited by Richard L. Rohrbaugh, 183–205. Peabody, MA: Hendrickson, 1996.
Eadie, Betty J. *Embraced by the Light*. Placerville, CA: Golden Leaf, 1992.
Edwards, William D., et al. "On the Physical Death of Jesus Christ." *The Journal of the American Medical Association* 255 (1986) 1455–63.
Eliade, Mircea. *From Primitives to Zen: A Thematic Sourcebook of the History of Religions*. London: Collins, 1967.
———. *The Quest: History and Meaning in Religion*. Chicago: University of Chicago Press, 1969.
Emmons, Henry. "Letter from Bro. Emmons." *The Day-Star*, vol. 8, nos. 2 & 3 (October 25, 1845) 6–7.
Enea di Gaza. *Teofrasto*. Edited by Maria Elisabetta Colonna. Naples: Salvatore Iodice, 1958.

Engberg-Pedersen, Troels. *Cosmology and Self in the Apostle Paul: The Material Spirit.* Oxford: Oxford University Press, 2010.

Evans, Craig A. "Death and Burial of Jesus." In Evans, *Encyclopedia of the Historical Jesus*, 143–50.

———, ed. *Encyclopedia of the Historical Jesus.* New York: Routledge, 2008.

———. "Jesus and the Extracanonical Works." In Charlesworth and Rhea, *Jesus Research*, 634–62.

Evans, Hilary. *Seeing Ghosts: Experiences of the Paranormal.* London: John Murray, 2001.

Evers, Dirk. "Chaos im Himmel: Die Entwicklung der modernen Kosmologie und ihre Tragweite für die christliche Rede vom Himmel." In *Der Himmel*, vol. 10 (2005) of *Jahrbuch für Biblische Theologie*, 33–58. Neukirchen-Vluyn: Neukirchener Verlag, 2006.

Falkenburg, Brigitte. *Mythos Determinismus: Wieviel erklärt uns die Hirnforschung?* Heidelberg: Springer, 2012.

Feld, Helmut. *Franziskus von Assisi.* 2nd ed. Munich: Beck, 2007.

Feldmeier, Reinhard. "Der zweite Petrusbrief." In Niebuhr, *Grundinformation Neues Testament*, 333–37.

Fenwick, Peter, and Elizabeth Fenwick. *The Art of Dying: A Journey to Elsewhere.* London: Continuum, 2008.

———. *The Truth in the Light: An Investigation of over 300 Near-Death Experiences.* London: Headline, 1995.

Findlay, Arthur. *The Way of Life.* 1953. Reprint. Stansted Mountfitchet: SNU, 1996.

Fischer, Alexander A. *Tod und Jenseits im Alten Orient und im Alten Testament: Eine Reise durch antike Vorstellungs- und Textwelten.* Leipzig: Evangelische Verlagsanstalt, 2014.

Förster. Hans. "Selbstoffenbarung und Identität: Zur grammatikalischen Struktur der 'absoluten' Ich-Bin-Worte Jesu im Johannesevangelium." *Zeitschrift für die Neutestamentliche Wissenschaft* 108 (2017) 57–89.

Fox, W. Sherwood, and R. E. K. Pemberton, trans. *Passages in Greek and Latin Literature Relating to Zoroaster and Zoroastrism Translated into English.* K. R. Cama Oriental Institute Publications 4. Bombay: Taraporevala, s.d. [1928?].

Frenschkowski, Marco. "Beatitudes." In Betz, *Religion Past and Present.* http://dx.doi.org/10.1163/1877-5888_rpp_SIM_124812. Consulted online April 4, 2018. First published online 2011.

Frenschkowski, Marco. "Vision. V. Kirchengeschichtlich." In Müller, *Theologische Realenzyklopädie*, 35 (2003) 137–47.

Freund, Stefan. "Einleitung." In Laktanz, *Divinae Institvtiones*, 1–82.

———. "Kommentar." In Laktanz, *Divinae Institvtiones*, 199–620.

Gardet, Louis. "Djanna." In *Encyclopaedia of Islam, Second Edition*, edited by P. Bearman et al. http://dx.doi.org/10.1163/1573-3912_islam_COM_0183. Consulted online April 6, 2018. First published online 2012.

Gathercole, Simon. *The Gospel of Thomas: Introduction and Commentary.* Leiden: Brill, 2014.

———. "'The Heavens and the Earth Will Be Rolled up'—The Eschatology of the Gospel of Thomas." In *Eschatologie—Eschatology: The Sixth Durham-Tübingen Research Symposium; Eschatology in Old Testament, Ancient Judaism and Early*

Christianity (Tübingen, September, 2009), edited by Hans-Joachim Eckstein et al., 280–302. Tübingen: Mohr Siebeck, 2011.

Gauger, Jörg-Dieter. "Einführung." In *Sibyllinische Weissagungen*, edited and trans. by Jörg-Dieter Gauger, 333–459. Darmstadt: Wissenschaftliche Buchgesellschaft, 1998.

Gavin, Frank S. B. "The Sleep of the Soul in the Early Syriac Church." *Journal of the American Oriental Society* 40 (1920) 103–20.

General Conference of Seventh-Day Adventists. *28 Fundamental Beliefs*. 2015 edition. http://szu.adventist.org/wp-content/uploads/2016/04/28_Beliefs.pdf.

Gertz, Jan Christian, ed. *Grundinformation Altes Testament*. 5th ed. Göttingen: Vandenhoeck & Ruprecht, 2016.

———. "Tora und vordere Propheten." In Gertz, *Grundinformation Altes Testament*, 193–312.

Gibson, Arvin S. *Glimpses of Eternity*. 6th ed. Bountiful, UT: Horizon, 2001.

Gillman, Neil. "Death and Afterlife, Judaic Doctrines of." In *The Encyclopedia of Judaism*, edited by Jacob Neusner et al., 1:593–609, 2nd ed. 5 vols. Leiden: Brill, 2005.

Goforth, August, and Timothy Gray. *The Risen: Dialogues of Love, Grief, & Survival Beyond Death*. New York: Tempestina Teapot, 2009.

Goodacre, Mark. "Scripturalization in Mark's Crucifixion Narrative." In *The Trial and Death of Jesus: Essays on the Passion Narrative in Mark*, edited by Geert van Oyen and Tom Shepherd, 33–47. Contributions to Biblical Theology and Exegesis 45. Leuven: Peeters, 2006.

Goppelt, Leonhard. *Theology of the New Testament*. Translated by John E. Alsup, edited by Jürgen Roloff. 2 vols. Grand Rapids: Eerdmans, 1981–82.

Gräßer, Erich. *Die Naherwartung Jesu*. Stuttgart: Katholisches Bibelwerk, 1973.

———. *Das Problem der Parusieverzögerung in den synoptischen Evangelien und in der Apostelgeschichte*. 3rd ed. Berlin: de Gruyter, 1977.

Greenberg, Moshe. *Ezechiel 21–37*. Herders Theologischer Kommentar zum Alten Testament. Freiburg: Herder, 2005.

———. "Resurrection." In Skolnik and Berenbaum, *Encyclopedia Judaica*, 17:240–41.

Grenet, Frantz. "Zarathustra's Time and Homeland. Geographical Perspectives." In Stausberg et al., *Companion to Zoroastrianism*, 21–29.

Greyson, Bruce. "Incidence and Correlates of Near-Death Experiences in a Cardiac Care Unit." *General Hospital Psychiatry* 25 (2003) 269–76.

———. "Near-Death Experiences and Spirituality." *Zygon* 41 (2006) 393–414.

———. "Western Scientific Approaches to Near-Death Experiences." *Humanities* 4 (2015) 775–96.

Greyson, Bruce, and Surbhi Khanna. "Spiritual Transformation After Near-Death Experiences." *Spirituality in Clinical Practice* 1 (2014) 43–55.

Grimaud, Hélène. *Wild Harmonies: A Life of Music and Wolves*. Translated by Ellen Hinsley. New York: Riverhead, 2006.

Grintz, Yehoshua M. "Immortality of the Soul—In the Bible / In the Talmud." In Skolnik and Berenbaum, *Encyclopedia Judaica*, 19:35–36.

Grosso, Michael. *The Man Who Could Fly: St. Joseph of Copertino and the Mystery of Levitation*. Lanham, MD: Rowman & Littlefield, 2016.

Guggenheim, Bill, and Judy Guggenheim. *Hello from Heaven! A New Field of Research, After-Death Communication, Confirms That Life and Love Are Eternal*. New York: Bantam, 1996.

Hagemann, Ludwig. "Eschatologie im Islam." In Khoury and Hünermann, *Weiterleben— nach dem Tode?* 103–19.

Hammarskjöld, Dag. *Markings*. Translated from the Swedish by Leif Sjoeberg and W. H. Auden. New York: Knopf, 1964.

Haraldsson, Erlendur. *"Miracles Are My Visiting Cards": An Investigate Report on the Psychic Phenomena Associated with Sathya Sai Baba*. London: Century, 1987.

Haraldsson, Erlendur, and Loftur Gissurarson. *Indridi Indridason: The Icelandic Physical Medium*. Guildford, UK: White Crow, 2015.

Harpprecht, Klaus, "Wer glaubt schon an Auferstehung?" *Die Zeit* 15, April 4, 2012. http://www.zeit.de/2012/15/Auferstehung-Christen-Bibel.

Harrill, J. Albert. "Stoic Physics, the Universal Conflagration, and the Eschatological Destruction of the 'Igorant and Unstable' in 2 Peter." In *Stoicism in Early Christianity*, edited by Tuomas Rasimus et al., 115–40. Grand Rapids: Baker Academic, 2010.

Hartmann, Dirk. *Philosophische Grundlagen der Psychologie*. Darmstadt: Wissenschaftliche Buchgesellschaft, 1998.

Heineberg, Heinz. *Einführung in die Anthropogeographie / Humangeographie*. Paderborn: Schöningh, 2003.

Hellholm, David. "Apocalypse. I. Form and Genre." In Betz, *Religion Past and Present*. http://dx.doi.org/10.1163/1877-5888_rpp_COM_00862. Consulted online February 1, 2018.

Henriksen, Jan-Olav, and Karl Olav Sandnes. *Jesus as Healer: A Gospel for the Body*. Grand Rapids: Eerdmans, 2016.

Henslow, George. *The Religion of the Spirit World: Written by the Spirits Themselves*. Chicago: Marlowe, 1920.

Henze, Matthias. *Jewish Apocalypticism in Late First-Century Israel: Reading Second Baruch in Context*. Texte und Studien zum antiken Judentum 142. Tübingen: Mohr Siebeck, 2011.

Herzer, Jens. *4 Baruch (Paraleipomena Jeremiou)*. Translation with an introduction and commentary. Writings from the Greco-Roman World 22. Atlanta: Society of Biblical Literature, 2005.

Hesiod. *Theogony and Works and Days*. Translated with an introduction and notes by M. L. West. Oxford: Oxford University Press, 2008.

Hiebel, Janina Maria. *Ezekiel's Vision Accounts as Interrelated Narratives: A Redaction-Critical and Theological Study*. Beihefte zur Zeitschrift für die Alttestamentliche Wissenschaft 475. Berlin: de Gruyter, 2015.

Hintze, Almut. "Frašō.kərəti." In Yarshater, *Encyclopaedia Iranica* 10 (2000) 190–92.

———. "On the Literary Structure of the Older Avesta." *Bulletin of the School of Oriental and African Studies* 65 (2002) 31–51.

———. "Treasure in Heaven: A Theme in Comparative Religion." In *Irano-Judaica: Studies Relating to Jewish Contacts with Persian Culture throughout the Ages*, edited by Shaul Shaked and Amnon Netzer, 9–36. Jerusalem: Ben-Zvi Institute for the Study of Jewish Communities in the East, 2008.

———, ed. *Der Zamyād-Yašt*: Edition, Übersetzung, Kommentar. Beiträge zur Iranistik, 15. Wiesbaden: Ludwig Reichert, 1994.

———, ed. *Zamyād Yašt*. Text, Translation, Glossary. Iranische Texte 7. Wiesbaden: Ludwig Reichert, 1994.

———. "Zarathustra's Time and Homeland." In Stausberg et al., *Companion to Zoroastrianism*, 31–38.

Hoffmann, Paul. "Auferstehung. I/3. Neues Testament." In Müller, *Theologische Realenzyklopädie*, 4 (1979) 450–67.

Holden, Janice Miner et al., eds. *The Handbook of Near-Death Experiences: Thirty Years of Investigation*. Santa Barbara, CA: ABC-CLIO, 2009.

Holmén, Tom. "The Alternatives of the Kingdom. Encountering the Semantic Restrictions of Luke 17,20–21 (ἐντὸς ὑμῶν)." *Zeitschrift für die Neutestamentliche Wissenschaft* 87 (1996) 204–29.

Holmén, Tom, and Stanley E. Porter, eds. *Handbook for the Study of the Historical Jesus*. 4 vols. Leiden: Brill, 2011.

Holmes, Michael William, ed. *The Apostolic Fathers: Greek Texts and English Translation*. Grand Rapids: Baker Academic, 2007.

Homer. *The Odyssey: Books 1–12*. With an English translation by A. T. Murray, revised by George E. Dimock. Loeb Classical Library 104. Rev. 2nd ed. Cambridge: Harvard University Press, 1998.

Hoping, Helmut. *Einführung in die Christologie*. 3rd ed. Darmstadt: Wissenschaftliche Buchgesellschaft, 2014.

Hoppe, Brigitte. "Sublunar / translunar." In Ritter, *Historisches Wörterbuch der Philosophie*, 10 (1998) 477–81.

Hornschuh, Manfred. *Studien zur Epistula Apostolorum*. Patristische Texte und Studien 5. Berlin: de Gruyter, 1965.

Horsley, Richard A. "Jesus and the Politics of Palestine under Roman Rule." In Charlesworth and Rhea, *Jesus Research*, 335–60.

———. *Revolt of the Scribes: Resistance and Apocalyptic Origins*. Minneapolis: Fortress, 2010.

Hultgård, Anders. "Persian Apocalypticism." In Collins, *Origins of Apocalypticism*, 39–83.

Jaffé, Aniela. *Geistererscheinungen und Vorzeichen: Eine psychologische Deutung*. Zürich: Rascher, 1958.

James, William. *The Varieties of Religious Experience. A Study in Human Nature*. 2nd ed. New York: Longmans, Green, 1902.

Jentzsch, Werner, et al., eds. *Evangelischer Erwachsenenkatechismus: Kursbuch des Glaubens*, On behalf of the Catechism Commission of the United Evangelical Lutheran Church of Germany. 3rd ed. Gütersloh: Gütersloher Verlagshaus, 1977.

Jones, John. *The Natural and Supernatural: Or, Man Physical, Apparitional and Spiritual*. London: Bailliere, 1861.

Jones, Lindsay, ed. *Encyclopedia of Religion*. 2nd ed. 15 vols. Detroit: Macmillan Reference USA, 2005.

Jörns, Klaus-Peter. *Notwendige Abschiede: Auf dem Weg zu einem glaubwürdigen Christentum*. 5th ed. Gütersloh: Gütersloher Verlagshaus, 2010.

Judd, Wayne R. "William Miller: Disappointed Prophet." In Numbers and Butler, *The Disappointed*, 17–35.

Kaiser, Otto, and Eduard Lohse. *Tod und Leben*. Stuttgart: Kohlhammer, 1977.

Karrer, Otto, ed. *Franz von Assisi: Legenden und Laude*. Zurich: Manesse, 1945.

Kasturi, Narayana. "Bala Sai." In *Sathyam Sivam Sundaram (The Life Story of Sathya Sai Baba).* http://askbaba.helloyou.ch/sathyamsivamsundaram/s1007.html.

———. "For You and Me." In *Sathyam Sivam Sundaram (The Life Story of Sathya Sai Baba).* http://askbaba.helloyou.ch/sathyamsivamsundaram/s1017.html.

———. "Rain Cloud." In *Sathyam Sivam Sundaram (The Life Story of Sathya Sai Baba).* http://askbaba.helloyou.ch/sathyamsivamsundaram/s1012.html.

Kee, Howard Clark. "Testaments of the Twelve Patriarchs. A New Translation and Introduction." *OTP* 1:775–828.

Keen, Montague, et al. *The Scole Report: An Account of an Investigation into the Genuineness of a Range of Physical Phenomena Associated with a Mediumistic Group in Norfolk, England.* 2nd ed. Thornton-Cleveleys, UK: Saturday Night, 2011.

Keener, Craig S. *Miracles: The Credibility of the New Testament Accounts.* 2 vols. Grand Rapids: Baker Academic, 2011.

Kelber, Werner H. "The Works of Memory: Christian Origins as MnemoHistory—A Response." In *Memory, Tradition, and Text: Uses of the Past in Early Christianity*, edited by Alan Kirk and Tom Thatcher, 221–48. Atlanta: Society of Biblical Literature, 2005.

Kelly, Emily Williams, et al. "Unusual Experiences Near Death and Related Phenomena." In *Irreducible Mind: Toward a Psychology for the 21st Century*, edited by Edward F. Kelly et al., 367–421. Lanham, MD: Rowman & Littlefield, 2007.

Kemmerich, Max. *Die Brücke zum Jenseits.* München: Langen, 1927.

Khoury, Adel Theodor, and Peter Hünermann, eds. *Weiterleben—nach dem Tode? Die Antwort der Weltreligionen.* Freiburg: Herder, 1985.

Kiel, Nikolai. *Ps-Athenagoras De Resurrectione: Datierung und Kontextualisierung der dem Apologeten Athenagoras zugeschriebenen Auferstehungsschrift.* Vigiliae Christianae, Supplements 133. Leiden: Brill, 2016.

Kittel, Gerhard, et al., eds. *Theological Dictionary of the New Testament: Abridged in One Volume.* Grand Rapids: Eerdmans, 1985.

Klijn, Albertus Frederik Johannes. *2 (Syriac Apocalypse of) Baruch: A New Translation and Introduction.* OTP 1:615–52.

Knoblauch, Hubert, and Ina Schmied. "Berichte aus dem Jenseits: Eine qualitative Studie zu Todesnäheerfahrungen im deutschsprachigen Raum." In *Todesnähe: Wissenschaftliche Zugänge zu einem außergewöhnlichen Phänomen*, edited by Hubert Knoblauch and Hans-Georg Soeffner, 187–215. Konstanz: UVK Universitätsverlag, 1999.

Kobel, Esther. *Dining with John: Communal Meals and Identity Formation in the Fourth Gospel and Its Historical and Cultural Context.* Biblical Interpretation Series 109. Leiden: Brill, 2011.

Kollmann, Bernd. "Jesus and Magic. The Question of the Miracles." In Holmén and Porter, *Historical Jesus* 4:3057–85.

Kollmann, Bernd, and Ruben Zimmermann, eds. *Hermeneutik der frühchristlichen Wundererzählungen: Geschichtliche, literarische und rezeptionsorientierte Perspektiven.* Tübingen: Mohr Siebeck, 2014.

Kongregation für die Sakramente und den Gottesdienst. "260A—De Symbolo Apostolico—Zum Apostolischen Glaubensbekenntnis—14.12.1983." In *Dokumente des Apostolischen Stuhls: 4.12.1983–3.12.1993*, vol. 3 of *Dokumente zur*

Erneuerung der Liturgie, edited by Martin Klöckener, 33-35. Kevelaer: Butzon & Bercker, 2001.

Kreyenbroeck, Philip G., and Shehnaz Neville Munshi. *Living Zoroastrianism: Urban Parsis Speak about Their Religion*. Richmond, UK: Curzon, 2001.

Kruse, Heinz. "'Gemeinschaft der Heiligen': Herkunft und Bedeutung des Glaubensartikels." *Vigiliae Christianae* 47 (1993) 246-59.

Kühn, Dagmar. "Totenkult (Israel)." In *Das Wissenschaftliche Bibellexikon im Internet*, edited by Michaela Bauks et al. https://www.bibelwissenschaft.de/stichwort/36094/. First published 2011.

Kurdzialek, Marian, and Gregor Maurach. "Empyreum." In Ritter, *Historisches Wörterbuch der Philosophie* 2 (1972) 478-80.

LaGrand, Louis E. *Messages and Miracles: Extraordinary Experiences of the Bereaved*. St. Paul, MN: Llewellyn, 1999.

Laktanz. *Divinae Institvtiones, Buch 7: De Vita Beata*. Introduction, Text, Translation, and Commentary by Stefan Freund. Texte und Kommentare 31. Berlin: de Gruyter, 2009.

Lang, Bernhard. *Himmel und Hölle: Jenseitsglaube von der Antike bis heute*. Munich: Beck, 2003.

———. Jahwe, der biblische Gott: Ein Portrait. Munich Beck. 2002.

———. "A Zoroastrian Prophecy of Resurrection: A New Reading of Ezekiel 37." In *Hebrew Life and Literature: Selected Essays of Bernhard Lang*, 83-91. Farnham, UK: Ashgate, 2008.

Lang, Bernhard, and Colleen McDannell. *Heaven: A History*. New Haven, CT: Yale University Press, 1988.

Lapide, Pinchas. *Auferstehung: Ein jüdisches Glaubensbekenntnis*. 5th ed. Stuttgart: Calwer, 1986.

Larsson, Edvin. "Heil und Erlösung III. Neues Testament." In Müller, *Theologische Realenzyklopädie*, 14 (1986) 616-22.

Lawrence, Tony R. "Apparitions and Kindred Phenomena: Their Relevance to the Psychology of Paranormal Belief and Experience." In *Hauntings and Poltergeists: Multidisciplinary Perspectives*, edited by James Houran and Rense Lange, 248-59. Jefferson, NC: McFarland, 2001.

Lehtipuu, Outi. *The Afterlife Imagery in Luke's Story of the Rich Man and Lazarus*. Leiden: Brill, 2007.

Lessing, Gotthold Ephraim. *Theological Writings*. Translated by Henry Chadwick. Stanford, CA: Stanford University Press, 1957.

Lindemann, Andreas. "Herrschaft Gottes / Reich Gottes. IV. Neues Testament und spätantikes Judentum." In Müller, *Theologische Realenzyklopädie*, 15 (1986) 196-218.

Litwa, M. David. *We Are Being Transformed: Deification in Paul's Soteriology*. Beihefte zur Zeitschrift für die Neutestamentliche Wissenschaft 187. Berlin: de Gruyter, 2012.

Lommel, Herman. *Die Gathas des Zarathustra*. Edited by Bernfried Schlerath. Basel: Schwabe, 1971.

———. *Die Religion Zarathustras nach dem Awesta dargestellt*. Tübingen: Mohr, 1930.

Lona, Horacio E. *Über die Auferstehung des Fleisches: Studien zur frühchristlichen Eschatologie*. Beihefte zur Zeitschrift für die Neutestamentliche Wissenschaft 66. Berlin: de Gruyter, 1993.

"Loving Legend—Living Legacies: Episode 7: The Letter to the Brother." *Heart2Heart* 8 No. 10 (2010). http://media.radiosai.org/journals/Vol_08/01OCT10/05-L4_07.htm.

Ludwig, Günter. "Ist der Determinismus eine Grundvoraussetzung für Physik?" In *Determinismus, Indeterminismus: Philosophische Aspekte physikalischer Theoriebildung*, edited by Wolfgang Marx, 57–70. Frankfurt: Klostermann, 1990.

[Luther, Martin]. *Biblia: Das ist: Die gantze Heilige Schrifft: Deudsch*. Auffs new zugericht. D. Mart. Luth. Wittemberg: Lufft, 1545.

———. *The Small Catechism of Dr Martin Luther*. Translation revised and corrected by H. Wetzel. s.l.: s.n., 1872.

Luz, Ulrich. "Warum zog Jesus nach Jerusalem?" In *Der historische Jesus: Tendenzen und Perspektiven der gegenwärtigen Forschung*, edited by Jens Schröter and Ralph Brucker, 409–27. Berlin: de Gruyter, 2002.

Luz, Ulrich, et al. "Nachfolge Jesu." In Müller, *Theologische Realenzyklopädie*, 23 (1994) 678–713.

Macaskill, Grant. "Matthew and the *Parables of Enoch*." In Charlesworth and Bock, *Parables of Enoch*, 218–30.

Markschies, Christoph. "Origenes: Leben—Werk—Theologie—Wirkung." In *Origenes und sein Erbe: Gesammelte Studien*, 1–13. Texte und Untersuchungen zur Geschichte der altchristlichen Literatur 160. Berlin: de Gruyter, 2007.

Mattiesen, Emil. *Das persönliche Überleben des Todes*. 3 vols. Berlin: de Gruyter, 1936–39; repr. 1987.

McAffee, Matthew. "Rephaim, Whisperers, and the Dead in Isaiah 26:13–19: A Ugaritic Parallel." *Journal of Biblical Literature* 135 (2016) 77–94.

McDonald, Lee Martin. "The Scriptures of Jesus: Did He Have a Biblical Canon?" In Charlesworth and Rhea, *Jesus Research*, 827–62.

McKenzie, Keisha. "The New Earth under Construction." *Adventist World* 5 (May 2009) 20–21.

Meiser, Martin. "Der theologiegeschichtliche Standort des lukanischen Doppelwerks," In *Beiträge zur urchristlichen Theologiegeschichte*, edited by Wolfgang Kraus, 99–126. Beihefte zur Zeitschrift für die Alttestamentliche Wissenschaft 163. Berlin: de Gruyter, 2009.

Merkel, Helmut. "Sibyllinen." *Jüdische Schriften aus hellenistisch-römischer Zeit* 5.8, 1039–1140. Gütersloh: Gütersloher Verlagshaus, 1998.

Metzger, B. M. "The Fourth Book of Ezra: A New Translation and Introduction." *OTP* 1:517–59.

Meyer, Marvin W., ed. *The Nag Hammadi Scriptures*. The Revised and Updated Translation of Sacred Gnostic Texts. New York: HarperCollins, 2007.

Mikulasch, Rodolpho H., ed. "Das Medium Mirabelli. Die Wahrheit über seine 'Wunder' und seine umstrittene, unter Beweis gestellte Medialität. Ergebnis einer Untersuchung durch die Akademie für Psychische Studien 'Cesare Lombroso.'" Translated by Eugen Engling. In *Das Medium Carlos Mirabelli: Eine kritische Untersuchung*, edited by Hans Gerloff, 15–89. Bayerisch Gmain: s.n., 1960.

Miller, William. *Views of the Prophecies and Prophetic Chronology: Selected From Manuscripts of William Miller with a Memoir of his Life by Joshua V. Himes*. Boston: Himes, 1842.

Modi, Jivanji Jamshedji. *A Catechism of the Zoroastrian Religion*. s.l. [Bombay]: s.n. [Petit Parsi], s.d. [1911].

Mohler, Albert. "Do Christians Still Believe in the Resurrection of the Body?" https://albertmohler.com/2006/04/07/do-christians-still-believe-in-the-resurrection-of-the-body/.

Moltmann, Jürgen. *The Way of Jesus Christ: Christology in Messianic Dimensions.* Translated by Margaret Kohl. London: SCM, 1990.

Moody, Raymond A., Jr. *The Light Beyond.* New York: Bantam, 1988.

Moody, Raymond, Jr., and Paul Perry. *Glimpses of Eternity: Sharing a Loved One's Passage from This Live to the Next.* New York: Guideposts, 2010.

Mooney, James. "The Ghost-Dance Religion and the Sioux Outbreak of 1890." *Fourteenth Annual Report of the Bureau of Ethnology to the Secretary of the Smithsonian Institutions 1892–93*, by J. W. Powell, Part 2, 641–1136. Washington, DC: Government Printing Office, 1896.

Moore, Lauren E., and Bruce Greyson. "Characteristics of Memories for Near-Death Experiences." *Consciousness and Cognition* 51 (2017) 116–24.

Morgenstern, Matthias. "Die künftige Welt, die Auferstehung der Toten und die Hoffnung auf den Messias. Eine Skizze zur Diskussion über die eschatologischen Vorstellungen im rabbinischen Judentum nach dem babylonischen Talmud." In Bukovec and Kolkmann-Klamt, *Jenseitsvorstellungen im Orient*, 351–77.

Mosis, Rudolf. "Ezechiel 37,1–14: Auferweckung des Volkes—Auferweckung von Toten." In *Schöpfungsplan und Heilsgeschichte: Festschrift für Ernst Haag zum 70. Geburtstag*, edited by Renate Brandscheidt and Theresia Mende, 123–73. Trier: Paulinus, 2002.

Müller, Gerhard, et al., eds. *Theologische Realenzyklopädie*, 40 vols. Berlin: de Gruyter, 1976–2007.

Müller, Gerhard Ludwig. "Gemeinschaft der Heiligen," In *Lexikon für Theologie und Kirche*, edited by Walter Kasper, 4:433–35. 11 vols. 3rd ed. Freiburg: Herder, 1993–2001.

Müller, Tobias. "Ist die Welt kausal geschlossen? Zur These der kausalen Geschlossenheit des Physischen." *Zeitschrift für philosophische Forschung* 67 (2013) 89–111.

Mumm, Peter-Arnold, and Susanne Richter. "Die Etymologie von griechisch ψυχή." *International Journal of Diachronic Linguistics and Linguistic Reconstruction* 5 (2008) 33–108.

Musamian, Farnaz. "World Religions and Near-Death Experiences." In Holden et al., *The Handbook of Near-Death Experiences*, 159–84.

Nahm, Michael. "Außerkörperliche Erfahrungen." In *An den Grenzen der Erkenntnis: Handbuch der wissenschaftlichen Anomalistik*, edited by Gerhard Mayer et al., 151–63. Stuttgart: Schattauer, 2015.

Neihardt, John G. "Black Elk Speaks: Being the Life Story of a Holy Man of the Oglala Sioux; as Told through John G. Neihardt (Flaming Rainbow)." Albany, NY: Excelsior Editions, 2008.

Nestle-Aland. *Novum Testamentum Graece.* Edited by Barbara Aland et al. 28th ed. Stuttgart, Deutsche Bibelgesellschaft, 2012.

Nickelsburg, George W. E. *1 Enoch 1: A Commentary on the Book of 1 Enoch, Chapters 1–36; 81–108.* Edited by Klaus Baltzer. Hermeneia. Minneapolis: Fortress, 2001.

———. "Four Worlds that are 'Other' in the Enochic Book of Parables." In Nicklas et al., *Other Worlds*, 55–77.

Nickelsburg, George W. E., and James C. VanderKam, trans. *1 Enoch: The Hermeneia Translation.* Minneapolis: Fortress, 2012.

———. *1 Enoch 2: A Commentary on the Book of 1 Enoch, Chapters 37–82.* Edited by Klaus Baltzer. Hermeneia. Minneapolis: Fortress, 2012.

Nicklas, Tobias, et al., eds. *The Human Body in Death and Resurrection.* Deuterocanonical and Cognate Literature Yearbook, 2009. Berlin: de Gruyter, 2009.

Nicklas, Tobias, et al., eds. *Other Worlds and Their Relation to This World: Early Jewish and Ancient Christian Traditions.* Supplements to the Journal for the Study of Judaism 143. Leiden: Brill, 2010.

Niebuhr, Karl-Wilhelm, ed. *Grundinformation Neues Testament: Eine bibelkundliche Einführung.* 4th ed. Göttingen: Vandenhoeck & Ruprecht, 2011.

———. "Jesus." In Niebuhr, *Grundinformation Neues Testament*, 408–36.

Nitsche, Bernhard. *Christologie.* Paderborn: Schöningh, 2012.

Noratuk, Vicki. "A Blind Woman's Near-Death Experience." http://ndestories.org/vicki-noratuk/.

Novakovic, Lidija. "Jesus' Resurrection and Historiography." In Charlesworth and Rhea, *Jesus Research*, 910–33.

Noy, Dov. "Elijah—In Jewish Folklore." In Skolnik and Berenbaum, *Encyclopedia Judaica*, 6:335.

Noyes, Russell, Jr., et al. "Aftereffects of Pleasurable Western Adult Near-Death Experiences." In Holden et al., *The Handbook of Near-Death Experiences*, 41–62.

Numbers, Ronald L., and Jonathan M. Butler. *The Disappointed: Millerism and Millenarianism in the Nineteenth Century.* Bloomington, IN: Indiana University Press, 1987.

Ó hÓgáin, Dáithí. *The Sacred Isle: Belief and Religion in Pre-Christian Ireland.* Woodbridge, UK: Boydell, 1999.

Oberdorfer, Bernd. "Visio Dei." In Betz, *Religion Past and Present.* http://dx.doi.org/10.1163/1877-5888_rpp_COM_125359. Consulted online April 4, 2018. First published online 2011.

Oberlinner, Lorenz. "Die Verkündigung der Auferweckung Jesu im geöffneten und leeren Grab: Zu einem vernachlässigten Aspekt in der Diskussion um das Grab Jesu." *Zeitschrift für die Neutestamentliche Wissenschaft* 73 (1982) 159–82.

Oegema, Gerbern S. "Apokalypsen." *Jüdische Schriften aus hellenistisch-römischer Zeit* 6.1.5, 1–208. Gütersloh: Gütersloher Verlagshaus, 2001.

Öhler, Markus. *Elia im Neuen Testament: Untersuchungen zur Bedeutung des alttestamentlichen Propheten im frühen Christentum.* Beihefte zur Zeitschrift für die Neutestamentliche Wissenschaft 88. Berlin: de Gruyter, 1997.

Owens, Justine E. et al. "Features of 'Near-Death Experience' in Relation to Whether or Not Patients Were Near Death." *The Lancet* 336 (1990) 1175–77.

P., M. [John Delaware Lewis]. *Hints for the "Evidences of Spiritualism."* London: Trübner, 1872.

Parnia, Sam, et al. "A Qualitative and Quantitative Study of the Incidence, Features and Aetiology of Near Death Experiences in Cardiac Arrest Survivors." *Resuscitation* 48 (2001) 149–56.

Partin, Harry B. "Paradise." In Jones, *Encyclopedia of Religion*, 10:6981–86.

Pennington, Jonathan T. *Heaven and Earth in the Gospel of Matthew.* Supplements to Novum Testamentum 126. Leiden: Brill, 2007.

Peres, Imre. *Griechische Grabinschriften und neutestamentliche Eschatologie.* Wissenschaftliche Untersuchungen zum Neuen Testament 157. Tübingen: Mohr Siebeck, 2003.

Pezzoli-Olgiati, Daria. "Millenarianism / Chiliasm: I. Religious Studies." In Betz, *Religion Past and Present*. http://dx.doi.org/10.1163/1877-5888_rpp_COM_02896. Consulted online April 4, 2018. First published online 2011.

Philaret, "The Longer Catechism of the Orthodox, Catholic, Eastern Church." In *The Creeds of Christendom: With A History and Critical Notes*, edited by Philip Schaff, 2:445–542. 3 vols. New York: Harper & Brothers, 1877.

Pierce, Seth. "An Old World Made New." In *Signs of the Time* 13, No. 9 (September 2012). http://www.signstimes.com/?p=article&a=40076836864.692.

Pines, Shlomo. "Soul, Immortality of—In Medieval Jewish Philosophy." In Skolnik and Berenbaum, *Encyclopedia Judaica*, 19:36–38.

Poirier, John C. "God." In Evans, *Encyclopedia of the Historical Jesus*, 225–31.

Polkinghorne, John. *The God of Hope and the End of the World*. New Haven, CT: Yale University Press, 2002.

Popkes, Enno Edzard. *Das Menschenbild des Thomasevangeliums: Untersuchungen zu seiner religionsgeschichtlichen und chronologischen Einordnung*. Wissenschaftliche Untersuchungen zum Neuen Testament 206. Tübingen: Mohr Siebeck, 2007.

———. *Der Krankenheilungsauftrag Jesu: Studien zu seiner ursprünglichen Gestalt und seiner frühchristlichen Interpretation*. Neukirchen-Vluyn: Neukirchener Verlagsgesellschaft, 2014.

Porter, Katherine Anne. "Pale Horse, Pale Rider." (1939) In *Pale Horse, Pale Rider: Three Short Novels*, 179–264. New York: Harcourt, Brace & World, 1964.

Priest, John. "Testament of Moses. A New Translation and Introduction." OTP 1:919–34.

Prinz, Wolfgang. "Der Mensch ist nicht frei: Ein Gespräch," In *Hirnforschung und Willensfreiheit*, edited by Christian Geyer, 20–26. Frankfurt: Suhrkamp, 2004.

Rahner, Karl. "Anschauung Gottes." In Rahner and Darlap, *Sacramentum Mundi*, 1:159–63.

———. "Christian Living Formerly and Today." In *Theological Investigations*, vol. 7, translated by David Bourke, 3–24. New York: Herder and Herder, 1971.

———. "Erlösung." In Rahner and Darlap, *Sacramentum Mundi*, 1:1159–76.

———. "Eschatologie." In Rahner and Darlap, *Sacramentum Mundi*, 1:1183–92.

———. *Foundations of Christian Faith: An Introduction to the Idea of Christianity*. Translated by William V. Dych. London: Darton, Longman & Todd, 1978.

———. "Letzte Dinge." In Rahner and Darlap, *Sacramentum Mundi*, 3:220–23.

Rahner, Karl, and Adolf Darlap, eds. *Sacramentum Mundi. Theologisches Lexikon für die Praxis*. 4 vols. Freiburg: Herder, 1967.

Recheis, Athanas. *Engel, Tod und Seelenreise: Das Wirken der Geister beim Heimgang des Menschen in der Lehre der alexandrinischen und kappadokischen Väter*. Rome: Edizioni di Storia e Letteratura, 1958.

Regnerus, "Resurrecting the Dead in America" (September 9, 2014). *First Things*. https://www.firstthings.com/web-exclusives/2014/09/resurrecting-the-dead-in-america.

[Reimarus, Hermann Samuel]. *Fragments from Reimarus, consisting of Brief Critical Remarks on the Object of Jesus and his Disciples as Seen in the New Testament*. Translated from the German of G. E. Lessing; edited by Charles Voysey. London: Williams and Norgate, 1879.

———. "Fünftes Fragment: Ueber die Auferstehungsgeschichte." In *Zur Geschichte und Litteratur, Vierter Beytrag*, edited by Gotthold Ephraim Lessing, 437–94. Braunschweig: Waysenhaus, 1777.

———. *Von dem Zwecke Jesu und seiner Jünger: Noch ein Fragment des Wolfenbüttelschen Ungenannten*. Edited by Gotthold Ephraim Lessing. Braunschweig: s.n., 1778.

Rein, Matthias. "Das Johannesevangelium." In Niebuhr, *Grundinformation Neues Testament*, 143–72.

Retief, Francois P., and Louise Cilliers. "The History and Pathology of Crucifixion." *South African Medical Journal* 93 (2003) 938–41.

Reynolds, Benjamin E. "The Enochic Son of Man and the Apocalyptic Background of the Son of Man Sayings in John's Gospel." In Charlesworth and Bock, *Parables of Enoch*, 294–314.

Richter, Julius. "Die 'konsequente Eschatologie' im Feuer der Kritik." *Zeitschrift für Religions- und Geistesgeschichte* 12 (1960) 147–66.

Righelato, Renton, and Dominick V. Spracklen. "Carbon Mitigation by Biofuels or by Saving and Restoring Forests?" *Science* 317 (2007) 902.

Ring, Kenneth, and Sharon Cooper. "Near-Death and Out-of-Body Experiences in the Blind: A Study of Apparent Eyeless Vision." *Journal of Near-Death Studies* 16 (1997) 101–47.

Ring, Kenneth, and Evelyn Elsaesser Valarino. *Lessons from the Light: What We Can Learn from the Near-Death Experience*. 2nd ed. Needham, MA: Moment Point, 2006.

Ringgren, Helmer. "Resurrection." In Jones, *Encyclopedia of Religion*, 11:7762–68.

Riskas, Thomas J., Jr. "New Heaven and New Earth." In *The Encyclopedia of Mormonism: The History, Scripture, Doctrine, and Procedure of the Church of Jesus Christ of Latter-day Saints*, edited by Daniel H. Ludlow, 3:1009. 5 vols. New York: Macmillan, 1992.

Ritter, Joachim, et al., eds. *Historisches Wörterbuch der Philosophie*. 13 vols. Basel: Schwabe, 1971–2007.

Rogo, Scott. *Miracles: A Scientific Exploration of Wondrous Phenomena*. New and updated ed. London: Aquarian, 1991.

Rooker, Mark F. *Leviticus*. New American Commentary, 3A. Nashville, TN: Broadman & Holman, 2000.

Roose, Hanna. "Ich-bin-Worte." In *Das Wissenschaftliche Bibellexikon im Internet*, edited by Michaela Bauks et al. https://www.bibelwissenschaft.de/stichwort/46917/. First published March 2013.

Rothman, Tony. "Die Physik—ein baufälliger Turm von Babel." *Spektrum der Wissenschaft* (February 2012) 61–65.

Rowe, David L. "Millerites. A Shadowy Portrait." In Numbers and Butler, *The Disappointed*, 1–16.

Ruffin, C. Bernard. *Padre Pio: The True Story*. Rev. ed. Huntington, IN: Sunday Visitor, 1991.

Russell, D. S. *The Method and Message of Jewish Apocalyptic. 200 BC–AD 100*. London: SCM, 1964.

Rust, Joshua, and Eric Schwitzgebel. "Ethicists' and Nonethicists' Responsiveness to Student E-Mails: Relationships among Expressed Normative Attitude, Self-Described Behavior, and Empirically Observed Behavior." *Metaphilosophy* 44 (2013) 350–71.

Sabom, Michael. *Light and Death: One Doctor's Fascinating Account of Near-Death Experiences*. Grand Rapids: Zondervan, 1998.
———. *Recollections of Death: A Medical Investigation*. New York: Harper & Row, 1982.
Sanders, E. P. *Jesus and Judaism*. London: SCM, 1985.
Sattler, Dorothea. *Erlösung? Lehrbuch der Soteriologie*. Freiburg: Herder, 2011.
Scafi, Alessandro. *Mapping Paradise: A History of Heaven on Earth*. Chicago: University of Chicago Press, 2006.
Schamoni, Wilhelm. *Wunder sind Tatsachen: Eine Dokumentation aus Heiligsprechungsakten*. 2nd ed. Würzburg: Johann Wilhelm Naumann, 1976.
Schmid, Konrad. "Himmelsgott, Weltgott und Schöpfer: 'Gott' und der 'Himmel' in der Literatur der Zeit des Zweiten Tempels." In *Der Himmel*, vol. 10 (2005) of *Jahrbuch für Biblische Theologie*, 111–48. Neukirchen-Vluyn: Neukirchener Verlag, 2006.
———. "Hintere Propheten." In Gertz, *Grundinformation Altes Testament*, 313–412.
Schmithals, Walter. "Zu Ignatius von Antiochien." *Zeitschrift für antikes Christentum* 13 (2009) 181–203.
Schnelle, Udo. *Paulus: Leben und Denken*. 2nd ed. Berlin: de Gruyter, 2014.
Scholem, Gershom. "Soul, Immortality of—In Kabbalah." In Skolnik and Berenbaum, *Encyclopedia Judaica*, 19:38–39.
Schöpflin, Karin. "The Revivification of the Dry Bones: Ezekiel 37:1–14." In Nicklas et al., *The Human Body in Death and Resurrection*, 67–85.
Schreiner, Josef. "Das 4. Buch Esra." *Jüdische Schriften aus hellenistisch-römischer Zeit* 5.4, 289–412. Gütersloh: Gütersloher Verlagshaus, 1981.
Schröter, Jens. "The Gospel of Mark." In Aune, *The Blackwell Companion to the New Testament*, 273–95.
Schwaninger, Janet, et al. "A Prospective Analysis of Near-Death Experiences in Cardiac Arrest Patients." *Journal of Near-Death Studies* 20 (2002) 215–32.
Schweitzer, Albert. "Jesus und wir." In *Vorträge, Vorlesungen, Aufsätze*, edited by Claus Günzler et al., 271–84. München: Beck, 2003.
———. *The Kingdom of God and Primitive Christianity*, edited, with an introduction, by Ulrich Neuenschwander; translated by L. A. Garrard. New York: Seabury, 1968.
———. *Die psychiatrische Beurteilung Jesu: Darstellung und Kritik*. Tübingen: Mohr, 1913.
———. *The Quest of the Historical Jesus*. First complete ed. Translated by Susan Cupitt et al. Minneapolis: Fortress, 2001.
Schwenke, Heiner. "Außersinnliche Wahrnehmung als Erleben. Warum die Wissenschaft außersinnliche Wahrnehmungen nicht erreichen und eigene Erfahrungen nicht ersetzen kann." *Zeitschrift für Parapsychologie und Grenzgebiete der Psychologie* 47/48/49 (2005/2006/2007) 111–28.
———. "Einleitung: Was sind und zu welchem Ende erforscht man transzendente Erfahrungen." In *Jenseits des Vertrauten: Factten transzendenter Erfahrungen*, edited by Heiner Schwenke, 11–22. Freiburg: Alber, 2018.
———. "Eschatology of the Synoptic Jesus: Based on a Misinterpretation of Otherworld Experiences?" *Biblical Theology Bulletin* 44 (2014) 202–13.
———. *Transzendente Begegnungen: Phänomenologie und Metakritik*. Basel: Schwabe, 2014.
———. "Wissenschaftliche Methode und die Grenzen der Naturwissenschaften." *UniversitasOnline* 3/2005. http://www.heidelberger-lese-zeiten-verlag.de/archiv/online-archiv/Schwenke1.pdf.

Schwöbel, Christoph. "Resurrection: I. Resurrection of the Dead, 5. Dogmatics." In Betz, *Religion Past and Present.* http://dx.doi.org/10.1163/1877-5888_rpp_COM_01264. Consulted online April 4, 2018. First published online 2011.

Scriba, Albrecht. *Echtheitskriterien der Jesus-Forschung: Kritische Revision und konstruktiver Neuansatz.* Hamburg: Dr. Kovač, 2007.

Sedlmeier, Franz: *Das Buch Ezechiel: Kapitel 25–48.* Neuer Stuttgarter Kommentar, Altes Testament 21 / 2. Stuttgart: Katholisches Bibelwerk, 2013.

Segal, Alan F. *Life after Death: A History of the Afterlife in Western Religion.* New York: Double Day, 2004.

Seils, Martin. "Weltende; Weltuntergang." In Ritter, *Historisches Wörterbuch der Philosophie,* 12 (2004) 464–69.

Sekanek, Rudolf. *Mutter Silbert: Ein Opfergang.* Remagen: Otto Reichl, 1959.

Shaked, Shaul. "Eschatology i. In Zoroastrianism and Zoroastrian Influence." In Yarshater, *Encyclopaedia Iranica,* 8 (1998) 565–69.

Sharp, Harold. *Animals in the Spirit World.* 1966. Reprint, Thornton-Cleveleys, UK: Saturday Night, 2018.

Shushan, Gregory. *Conceptions of the Afterlife in Early Civilizations: Universalism, Constructivism, and Near-Death Experience.* London: Continuum, 2009.

Silverman, Jason M. *Persepolis and Jerusalem: Iranian Influence on the Apocalyptic Hermeneutic.* Library of Hebrew Bible / Old Testament Studies 558. London: T. & T. Clark, 2012.

Skjærvø, Prods Oktor. "Afterlife in Zoroastrianism." In Bukovec and Kolkmann-Klamt, *Jenseitsvorstellungen im Orient,* 311–49.

Skolnik, Fred, and Michael Berenbaum, eds. *Encyclopedia Judaica.* 2nd ed. 22 vols. Detroit: Macmillan Reference USA, 2007.

Smith, Morton. *Jesus the Magician: Charlatan or Son of God?* San Francisco: Harper & Row, 1978.

Solomon, Grant, and Jane Solomon. *The Scole Experiment: Scientific Evidence for Life After Death.* London: Judy Piatkus, 1999.

Spieckermann, Hermann. "The 'Father' of the Old Testament and its History." In Albrecht and Feldmeier, *The Divine Father,* 73–84.

Sprandel, Rolf. "Die Seele der Analphabeten im Mittelalter." In *Die Seele: Ihre Geschichte im Abendland,* edited by Gerd Jüttemann et al., 97–103. Weinheim: Psychologie Verlags Union, 1991.

Stausberg, Michael. *Die Religion Zarathustras: Geschichte—Gegenwart—Rituale.* 3 vols. Stuttgart: Kohlhammer, 2002-4.

Stausberg, Michael, et al., eds. *The Wiley Blackwell Companion to Zoroastrianism.* Chichester, UK: Wiley, 2015.

Steltenkamp, Michael F. *Nicolas Black Elk—Medicine Man, Missionary, Mystic.* Norman, OK: University of Oklahoma Press, 2009.

Stemberger, Günter. "Auferstehung. I / 2. Judentum." In Müller, *Theologische Realenzyklopädie,* 4 (1979) 443–50.

———. *Der Leib der Auferstehung: Studien zur Anthropologie und Eschatologie des palästinischen Judentums im neutestamentlichen Zeitalter (ca. 170 v. Cr.[sic]—100 n. Chr.).* Rome: Biblical Institute, 1972.

Storm, Howard: *My Descent into Death.* New York: Doubleday, 2005.

Stowasser, Martin. "Jesu Konfrontation mit dem Tempelbetrieb von Jerusalem—ein Konflikt zwischen Religion und Ökonomie?" In *Das Heilige und die Ware: Zum*

Spannungsfeld von Religion und Ökonomie, edited by Martin Fitzenreiter, 39–51. London: Golden House, 2007.

Strobel, August. "Die Ausrufung des Jobeljahrs in der Nazarethpredigt Jesu. Zur apokalyptischen Tradition in Lc 4,16–30." In *Jesus in Nazareth*, edited by Erich Gräßer et al., 38–50. Beihefte zur Zeitschrift für die Neutestamentliche Wissenschaft 40. Berlin: de Gruyter, 1972.

———. "Die Passa-Erwartung als urchristliches Problem in Lc 17,20f." *Zeitschrift für die Neutestamentliche Wissenschaft* 49 (1958) 157–96.

Stückelberger, Alfred. "Ekpyrosis." In Ritter, *Historisches Wörterbuch der Philosophie*, 2 (1972) 433–34.

Stuckenbruck, Loren T. "The 'Otherworld' and the *Epistle of Enoch*." In Nickels et al., *Other Worlds*, 79–93.

Theissen, Gerd. "Historical Scepticism and the Criteria of Jesus Research: Or, My Attempt to Leap across Lessing's Yawning Gulf." *Scottish Journal of Theology* 49 (1996) 147–76.

———. "Wunder Jesu und urchristliche Wundergeschichten. Historische, psychologische und theologische Aspekte." In Kollmann and Zimmermann, *Hermeneutik der frühchristlichen Wundererzählungen*, 67–86.

Theißen, Gerd, and Annette Merz. "Gerichtsverzögerung und Heilsverkündung bei Johannes dem Täufer und Jesus." In Gerd Theißen, *Jesus als historische Gestalt; Beiträge zur Jesusforschung; Zum 60. Geburtstag von Gerd Theißen*, edited by Annette Merz, 229–53. Forschungen zur Religion und Literatur des Alten und Neuen Testaments 202. Göttingen: Vandenhoeck & Ruprecht, 2003.

———. *The Historical Jesus: A Comprehensive Guide*. Translated by John Bowden. Minneapolis: Fortress, 1998.

Thompson, R. Campbell, ed. *The Epic of Gilgamish: A New Translation from a Collation of the Cuniform Tablets in the British Museum Rendered Literally into English Hexameters*. London: Luzac, 1928.

Thonnard, Marie, et al. "Characteristics of Near-Death Experiences Memories as Compared to Real and Imagined Events Memories." *PLoS ONE* 8(3) (2013) e57620.

Thurston, Herbert. *The Physical Phenomena of Mysticism*. Edited by Joseph Hugh Crehan. London: Burns Oates, 1952.

Tornau, Christian. "Die neuplatonische Kritik an den Gnostikern und das theologische Profil des Thomasevangeliums." In *Das Thomasevangelium: Entstehung—Rezeption—Theologie*, edited by Jörg Frey et al., 326–59. Beihefte zur Zeitschrift für die Neutestamentliche Wissenschaft 157. Berlin: de Gruyter, 2008.

Treece, Patricia. *The Sanctified Body*. New York: Doubleday, 1989.

Twelftree, Graham H. "The Message of Jesus I: Miracles, Continuing Controversies." In Holmén and Porter, *Historical Jesus*, 3:2517–48.

———. "Miracle Story." In Evans, *Encyclopedia of the Historical Jesus*, 416–20.

Uhlig, Siegbert. "Das äthiopische Henochbuch." *Jüdische Schriften aus hellenistisch-römischer Zeit* 5.6, 461–780. Gütersloh: Gütersloher Verlagshaus, 1984.

Ullmann, Bettina. "Hélène Grimaud: Limiten gibt es nur im Kopf." *Coopzeitung*, No. 32, August 7, 2012, 86–87.

van der Horst, P. W. *Ancient Jewish Epitaphs: An Introductory Survey of a Millennium of Jewish Funerary Epigraphy (300 BCE–700 CE)*. Contributions to Biblical Exegesis and Theology 2. Kampen: Kok Pharos, 1991.

van Lommel, Pim. *Consciousness beyond Life: The Science of Near Death Experience*. Translated by Laura Vroomen. New York: HarperOne, 2010.

van Lommel, Pim, et al. "Near-Death Experiences in Survivors of Cardiac Arrest: A Prospective Study in the Netherlands." *The Lancet* 358 (2001) 2039–45.

Vetter, Dieter. "Leben nach dem Tod im Judentum." In Khoury and Hünermann, *Weiterleben—nach dem Tode?* 85–102.

Viviano, Benedict T. *The Kingdom of God in History*. Eugene, OR: Wipf and Stock, 2002. Previously published by Michael Glazier, 1988.

Walck, Leslie. "The *Parables of Enoch* and the Synoptic Gospels." In Charlesworth and Bock, *Parables of Enoch*, 231–68.

Wan, Sze-kar. "Where Have All the Ghosts Gone? Evolution of a Concept in Biblical Literature." In *Rethinking Ghosts in World Religions*, edited by Mu-chou Poo, 47–76. Numen Book Series 123. Leiden: Brill, 2009.

Ward, Peter, and Donald Brownlee. *The Life and Death of Planet Earth: How Science Can Predict the Ultimate Fate of Our World*. London, UK: Piatkus, 2003.

Watchtower Bible and Tract Society of Pennsylvania. *What Does the Bible* Really *Teach?* New York: Watchtower Bible and Tract Society of New York, 2005.

Watts, John D. W. *Isaiah 1–33*. WBC. Waco, TX: Word, 1985.

Weder, Hans. *Gegenwart und Gottesherrschaft: Überlegungen zum Zeitverständnis bei Jesus und im frühen Christentum*. Neukirchen-Vluyn: Neukirchener, 1993.

Weiss, Johannes. *Die Predigt Jesu vom Reiche Gottes*. 2nd ed. Göttingen: Vandenhoeck & Ruprecht, 1900.

Wiebe, Philip H. *Visions of Jesus: Direct Encounters from the New Testament to Today*. New York: Oxford University Press, 1997.

Wiggermann, Frans. "Magic, Magi. I. Ancient Orient, A. General." In *Brill's New Pauly: Encyclopaedia of the Ancient World*, edited by Hubert Cancik et al. 22 vols. Leiden: Brill, 2002–2010. http://dx.doi.org/10.1163/1574-9347_bnp_e716750. Consulted online on April 8, 2018. First published online 2006.

Wilk, Florian. "'Vater . . . ' Zur Bedeutung der Anrede Gottes als Vater in den Gebeten der Jesusüberlieferung." In Albrecht and Feldmeier, *The Divine Father*, 201–31.

Williams, A. V. *The Pahlavi Rivāyat—accompanying the Dādestān ī Dēnīg. Part II: Translation, Commentary and Pahlavi Text*. Historisk-filosofiske Meddelelser 60:2. Copenhagen: Det Kongelige Danske Videnskabernes Selskab, 1990.

Wills-Brandon, Carla. *Heavenly Hugs: Comfort, Support and Hope from the Afterlife*. Pompton Plains, NJ: New Page, 2013.

Wiltse, A. S. "A Case of Typhoid Fever with Subnormal Temperature and Pulse." *The St. Louis Medical and Surgical Journal* 57 (1889) 281–88, 355–64.

Winston, David. "The Iranian Component in the Bible, Apocrypha, and Qumran: A Review of the Evidence." *History of Religions* 5 (1966) 183–216.

Witetschek, Stephan. "Ein weit geöffnetes Zeitfenster? Überlegungen zur Datierung der Johannesapokalypse." In *Die Johannesapokalypse: Kontexte—Konzepte—Rezeption*, edited by Jörg Frey et al, 117–48. Wissenschaftliche Untersuchungen zum Neuen Testament, 287 Tübingen: Mohr Siebeck, 2012.

Witte, Markus. "Schriften (Ketubim)." In Gertz, *Grundinformation Altes Testament*, 413–533.

———. "Die Weisheit Salomos (Sapientia Salomonis)." In Gertz, *Grundinformation Altes Testament*, 540–50.

Wright, N. T. *Surprised by Hope: Rethinking Heaven, the Resurrection, and the Mission of the Church.* New York: HarperOne, 2008.
Yamauchi, Edwin M. "Magic, Sorcery." In Evans, *Encyclopedia of the Historical Jesus*, 383–84.
Yarshater, Ehsan, ed. *Encyclopaedia Iranica.* London: Routledge & Kegan Paul, 1982–.
Zander, Vera. *Seraphim von Sarow: Ein Heiliger der orthodoxen Christenheit (1759-1833).* Düsseldorf: Patmos, 1965.
Zimmermann, Ruben. "Von der Wut des Wunderverstehens: Grenzen und Chancen einer Hermeneutik der Wundererzählungen." In Kollmann and Zimmermann, *Hermeneutik der frühchristlichen Wundererzählungen*, 27–52.

Ancient and Medieval Writings Index

Ancient Near Eastern Texts

Epic of Gilgamesh

12.85–87	14

Classical Greek and Latin Authors

Aristotle

De caelo

1.9 (278b14–15)	103
2.1 (283b26–84a14)	102

Cicero

De natura deorum

2.43	102
2.56	102

De re publica

6.15(11)	103
6.18(14)	106
6.20(16)	102
6.21(17)	102–3
6.24(20)	103
6.27(23)	102
6.29(25)	102
6.30(26)	105

Tusculanae disputationes

1.42	106
1.43	106
1.51	106
1.65	106

Diogenes Laertius

De clarorum philosophiorum virtis

1.8–9	21

Herodotus

Historiae

3.62.4	21

Hesiod

Opera et dies

167–72	14

Homer

Odyssee

4.563–68	14
11.204–8	17

Plato

Phaedo

70a5	17
77d8	17
80b8–81e2	105
80d10	17
112d4–14c6	105

Phaedros

245a5–49d2   105

Respublica

10.13–16 (613e6–21d2)   105

Plutarch

De Iside et Osiride

47 (370 C)   24, 26

Zoroastrian Scriptures

Gathas (= Yasna 28–34, 43–51, 53)

29.10	20
30.9	19
30.10	20
31.6	19
31.21	19
33.8	19
34.1	19
34.11	19
34.13–14	19
34.14	20
34.15	19
43.16	20
44.17–18	19
45.5	19
45.10	19
47.1	19
48.8	19
48.11	20
49.5	19–20
49.8	19
50.11	19
51.1	19
51.7	19

Zamyād Yašt (=Yašt 19)

19.11	21
19.19	21
19.89	21
19.92	20
19.94	21
19.96	21, 26

Ayādgār ī Jāmāspīg (Pāz.)

6   23, 25

Ayādgār ī Jāmāspīg (Pers.)

6   22–23

Greater Bundahišn

34.4	22
34.5	22
34.7	22
34.8	25
34.23	23
34.24	24, 26
34.32	23

Pahlawī Riwāyat

48.53	23
48.55	22
48.59	26
48.60	26
48.67	22
48.99	26
48.101	23
48.103	25
48.105	26
48.106	26
48.107	25

Wizīdagīhā ī Zādspram

22.11	24
34.1–2	24
34.3	22
34.4	23
34.5	23
34.7–19	22
35.50–51	24
35.51	23
35.54	25

35.56	25
35.59	25
35.60	25–26

Hebrew Bible / Old Testament

Genesis

2:4—3:24	15, 61
2:24	61
8:22	72

Exodus

12:25 LXX	68

Leviticus

19:23	68
23:15–21	81
25:1–7	143
25:8–24	144

Numbers

15:2	68
20:24	68
33:54	68

Deuteronomy

1:8	68
4:1	68
4:21	68
6:18	68
16:20	68
27:3	68
30:4–5 LXX	58
34:5–7	123

Joshua

1:6	68

Judges

18:9	68

1 Kings

10:1–13	59
17:22	91

2 Kings

2:9–12	123
4:34	91
13:21	91

Psalms

11:7	75
17:15	75–76
22	139
37:9	68
37:11	57, 68
37:22	57, 68
37:29	95, 68
37:34	68
102:25–27	100
107:2–3	58
132:13–14	103

Isaiah

2:11	53
2:17	53
2:20	53
11:6–8	111
13:10	72
24–27	32–33
24:23	33, 103
25:8	33
25:8 LXX	33
26:19	32
26:19 LXX	32
27:12–13	32
27:13	33
34:4	72, 114
35:10	59
40:3–4	103
43:5–6	58

Isaiah *(continued)*

51:6	72
51:11	59
52:8	103
57:13	57
60:5–6	107
60:10	107
60:11	107
60:17	107
60:19–20	76
61:5	107
61:7	107
65:9	57
65:17	72
65:17–25	33, 72–73
65:25	111
66:22	33

Jeremiah

36:4–32	43
38:7–13	43
52:28–30	31

Ezekiel

13:9	68
20:38	68
32:7–8	72
36:24	31
36:28	31
37	44
37:1–12	30–31
43:7	103
43:9	103

Daniel

2:34–35	34
2:44	34
7:13–14	144
7:14	34
7:18	34
7:27	34
8:13–14	34
8:14	34
9:27	34
10:5–6	124
11:31	34
12:2 TH	33
12:2–3	33
12:3	34, 61, 75
12:11	34
12:11–13	34

Hosea

2:18	53

Joel

2:10	72, 114
2:31	72
2:32	73
3:4	72, 114
4:2	109
4:15	72
4:16–17	103
4:21	103

Amos

8:3	53
8:9	53

Micah

4:7	103

Zechariah

1:17	103
2:10	103
8:3	103
8:7–8	59
9:9	132
14:4–5	44

Malachi

4:5–6	135

Deuterocanonical Works and Septuagint

2 Maccabees

7:9 LXX	39
7:11 LXX	38
7:14 LXX	39
7:22 LXX	39
7:23 LXX	39
7:28 LXX	39
7:36 LXX	39
14:46 LXX	38

Sirach / Ecclesiasticus

48:9	135
48:10–11	135
49:14	136

Tobit

4:12	68

Wisdom of Solomon

3:1–3 LXX	45

Other Ancient Jewish Sources

Assumption of Moses

2,1	68
10:9–10	42

2 Baruch
(Syriac Apocalypse)

4:3–4	42
30:2–5	63
30:4–5	41
44:12	41
44:15	41
46:7	136
50:2	54, 94
50:2–4	41
51:1	42
51:1–3	94
51:3	42, 94
51:5	41, 94
51:6	41
51:8–11	42
51:9–10	94
76:2	136

4 Baruch
(Paraleipomena Jeremiou)

6:3–7	43

1 Enoch
(Ethiopic Apocalypse)

1–36	35
10:17	36
22	63
22:1	35
22:1–4	35
22:3–4	35
22:5–7	35
22:8–13	35
24:1	36
24:3	36
24:4	36
25:3	36
25:4	36
25:4–5	36
25:6	36
37–71	35
38:2	38
38:4	37–38
45:3	61
45:5	37
48:6	130, 145
48:10	143
50:1	38
51:1	37
51:3	61
51:5	37
52:4	143
55:4	61
58:3	37–38

1 Enoch (continued)

58:6	38
61:5	130
61:8	61
62:2–3	61
62:5	61
62:6–7	130, 145
62:14	37, 144
62:15–16	37
62:16	38
69:27	61
69:29	61
70–71	136, 145
90:20–38	35
92:3–5	35

4 Ezra

6:26	136
7:31	40
7:32	40
7:36	40–41
7:78	40
7:78–99	63
7:88	41
7:97	41
7:100	40
7:113	40
7:125	41
14:9	136

Josephus

Antiquitates judaicae

4.219	138

Jubilees

23:30–31	45

Liber antiquitatum biblicarum (Pseudo-Philo)

3:10	42

Psalms of Solomon

3:12 LXX	39

Babylonian Talmud: Sanhedrin

91a–b	44

Mishnah Sanhedrin

10:1	44

Sibylline Oracles

4.179–92	44

Testament of Abraham

20	45

Testament of Benjamin

10:6–10	40

Testament of Judah

25:1	40
25:4	40

Testament of Levi

12:5	68

Testament of Simeon

6:7	40

Testament of Zebulun

10:1–2	40

New Testament

Matthew

1:24	50
2:9	52
2:13–14	50

2:20–21	50	10:1	153
3:1–12	61	10:7	55
3:2	55, 141	10:8	49, 124–25, 153
3:16–17	128	10:15	56
4:1–11	48	10:23	56, 142
4:11	128	10:28	62, 69
4:17	55, 141	10:32–33	128
4:23–25	126–27	11:2–6	125
5:3	55, 68, 74	11:5	124
5:4	75	11:11–12	55
5:5	57, 68	11:14	135
5:8	75	11:19	149
5:10	55, 68	11:22	56
5:18	71	11:24	56
5:19–20	55	11:27	128
5:20	67–68	11:28	149
5:22	69	12:9–13	126
5:29	68	12:11	50
5:29–30	69	12:13	126
6:10	57	12:15	127
7:14	74	12:28	70
7:21	55, 67–68	12:36	127
7:22	53	12:41	51
8:1–17	126	12:41–42	51, 59
8:3	126	12:42	49
8:5–10	127	13:11	55
8:11	53, 55, 58–59	13:24	55
8:13	127	13:31	55
8:15	50, 126	13:33	55
8:16	127	13:39	147
8:23–27	126, 148	13:41	130
8:25	50	13:41–42	56, 68, 130
8:26	50, 127	13:41–43	54
8:27	127	13:42	69
8:28	127	13:43	55, 61, 75
9:1–8	126	13:44–45	55
9:5–6	49	13:47	55
9:6	126	13:49–50	147
9:7	50	13:50	69
9:9	51	13:52	55
9:9–13	149	14:2	50
9:11–12	149	14:15–21	126
9:18	126	14:19	127, 148
9:19	50	14:23	128
9:20–22	127	14:26	62
9:25	50, 126	14:27	62
9:27–34	126	14:34–36	127
9:29	126	15:28	127

Matthew *(continued)*

15:29–31	126
15:32–39	126
15:36	127, 148
16:9–10	126
16:13	130
16:14	135
16:19	55
16:20	130
16:21	49, 131–32
16:21–22	132
16:27	56, 130
16:27–28	54, 56, 142
16:28	56, 66
17:1–9	75, 128
17:7	50
17:9	49
17:12	131–32
17:12–13	135
17:22	132
17:23	49, 131
18:1	55
18:3	68
18:3–4	55
18:8	74
18:8–9	68–69, 74, 142
18:9	69
18:20	149
18:23	55
19:5	61
19:12	55
19:14	55
19:16–17	74
19:17	68
19:23	55, 68
19:24	55
19:27–28	58
19:28	61, 72, 113, 130–31
19:28–29	130
19:29	68, 74
20:1	55
20:18	131
20:18–19	131
20:19	49
20:21	130
20:22–23	131
20:23	130
20:29–30	126
20:34	126
21:1–11	132
21:9	52
21:12–16	132
21:19	127, 148
21:31	55, 149
21:33–46	133
21:43	55
22:2	55
22:23–33	60
22:24	51
23:1–36	133
23:13	55, 67
23:15	69
23:33	69
23:34–35	142
23:37	133
24:3–29	128
24:5	130
24:7	50
24:11	50
24:24	50
24:24–27	130
24:29	72, 114
24:29–31	54
24:30	56, 130
24:30–31	130
24:31	130
24:34	54, 142
24:35	71
24:36	53
24:36–51	141
24:37–41	54
24:37–44	130
24:40–41	147
24:44	56
25:1	55
25:1–13	141
25:7	50
25:31	56, 61, 130–31
25:31–34	56
25:31–46	54, 130
25:34	68
25:41	56, 74
25:46	56, 69, 74
26:2	131

26:21	131
26:21–24	133
26:29	53, 55, 110
26:32	49
26:36–46	133
26:39	132, 134
26:42	132, 134
26:44	134
26:45	131
26:46	49
26:47–56	133
26:51–54	133
26:53	128, 130, 147
26:56	131, 138
26:57–68	133
26:61	59, 133
26:62	51
26:64	56, 130, 142–43
27:11–14	133
27:26	136
27:27–30	133
27:32	136
27:37	58
27:40	133
27:44	64
27:46	134, 136, 139
27:46–50	135
27:50	134, 136, 139
27:51–53	84
27:52	50
27:55–56	138
27:57—28:8	84
27:63	49
27:63–64	50
27:64	85
27:65–66	85
28:1	79
28:1–6	84
28:6	84
28:6–7	50
28:9	79, 84
28:9–10	79
28:16–20	79
28:17	80
28:20	149–50

Mark

1:3–8	61
1:10–11	128
1:13	128
1:14–15	55
1:15	125, 141
1:25	127
1:29–34	126
1:31	50, 126
1:32–34	127
1:35	51, 128
1:39–44	126
1:41	126
2:1–12	126
2:9	49
2:11	49, 126
2:12	50
2:14	51
2:15–17	149
2:16–17	149
3:1–6	126
3:3	49
3:5	126
3:7–10	127
3:7–12	126
3:26	51
4:27	50
4:35–41	126, 148
4:38	50
4:39	127
4:41	127
5:8	127
5:22	90
5:23	126
5:24–34	127
5:41	49, 90, 126
5:42	51
5:43	90
6:5	126
6:13	153
6:14	50
6:16	50
6:30–44	126
6:41	127, 148
6:45	52
6:46	128
6:49	62

Mark *(continued)*

6:50	62
6:53–56	127
6:54–56	126
6:56	127
7:23	126
7:25–30	127
7:31–37	126
7:33	126–27
7:42	51
8:1–9	126
8:6	127, 148
8:18–20	126
8:22–26	126
8:23	126
8:25	126
8:28	135
8:29–30	130
8:31	51, 131–32
8:31–33	132
8:31–38	130
8:38	56, 130
9:1	55, 66, 142
9:2–9	75, 128
9:9	51
9:11–13	135
9:12	131–32
9:25	127
9:27	50–51, 126
9:31	51, 131–32
9:43	68–69, 74
9:43–48	54, 142
9:45	68–69, 74
9:47	55, 67–69
9:48	74
10:1	51
10:7–8	61
10:14	68
10:14–15	55
10:15	67
10:16	126
10:23–25	55, 67
10:30	74
10:32	52, 131
10:33	131
10:33–34	131
10:34	51
10:37	130
10:38–40	131
10:40	130
10:46–52	126
10:49	50
10:52	126–27
11:1–11	132
11:9	52
11:14	127, 148
11:15–17	132–33
12:1–12	133
12:18–27	60
12:23	51
12:25	51, 60
12:26	49, 60
12:34	55
12:35–40	133
13:3–25	128
13:8	50
13:22	50
13:24–25	72
13:26	56, 130
13:26–27	54, 130
13:27	58, 130
13:30	142
13:31	71
13:35–37	141
14:17–21	133
14:21	131
14:25	53, 55, 110
14:28	49, 52
14:32–42	133
14:36	132, 134
14:39	134
14:41	131
14:42	49
14:43–50	133
14:50	131, 138
14:53–65	133
14:57	51
14:58	59, 133
14:60	51
14:61–62	130
14:62	56, 130, 142–43
15:1–5	133
15:15	136
15:15–20	133
15:21	136

15:26	58	6:19	127
15:29	133	6:20	53, 55, 68
15:32	64	6:20–21	75
15:34	134, 136, 139	6:21	53
15:37	134, 136, 139	6:23	53, 75
15:40–41	138	6:25	53
15:42—16:8	84	7:1–10	127
15:43	55	7:1–15	126
16:1	79	7:12	90
16:6	50, 84	7:14	49, 126
16:9	51, 79	7:14–15	90
16:9–20	80	7:15	90
16:12	79	7:18–23	125
16:14	79	7:22	49, 124
16:14–19	79	7:27	135
		7:28	55
		7:36–50	149
Luke		8:10	55
1:39	51	8:22–25	126, 148
2:9	123	8:24	127
3:2–18	61	8:40–56	126
3:21–22	128	8:43–48	127
4:1–13	48	8:54	49, 126
4:16	51	8:55	51
4:16–30	144	9:1–2	153
4:29	51	9:2	55
4:33–41	126	9:6	153
4:35	127	9:7	50
4:38	51	9:8	50
4:39	51	9:11	55, 126
4:40	126	9:11–17	126
4:41	130	9:16	127, 148
4:43	55	9:19	50, 135
5:12–14	126	9:20–21	130
5:13	126	9:22	49, 131–32
5:16	128	9:26	56, 130
5:17–26	126	9:27	55, 66, 142
5:23–24	49	9:28	126
5:24	126	9:28–36	75, 128
5:25	51	9:31	123, 131–32
5:27–32	149	9:32	123
5:28	51	9:44	131–32
5:30–31	149	9:51	131
6:6–11	126	9:60	55
6:8	51	9:62	55
6:10	126	10:9	55, 153
6:12	128	10:11	55
6:17–19	126–27	10:12	53, 56

Luke (continued)

10:14	56
10:18	128
10:22	128
10:25	51, 68
10:25–28	74
11:7–8	51
11:8	50
11:20	70, 125
11:31	49
11:31–32	51, 59
11:32	51
11:50–51	142
12:5	69
12:8	130
12:8–10	130
12:31	55
12:35–48	141
12:40	56
12:43	64
12:49	56, 130
12:50	132
13:10–17	126
13:13	126
13:25	50
13:28	59
13:28–29	53, 55
13:29	58
13:33	131, 133
14:1–4	126
14:13–23	149
14:14	60
14:15	53, 55
15:18	51
15:20	51
16:17	71
16:19–31	63
16:31	51, 63
17:11–19	126
17:14	127
17:19	51
17:20	55
17:20–21	125
17:21	69
17:22–25	130
17:22–37	70
17:24	130
17:25	131–32
17:26–36	130
17:30	130
17:31	53
17:34–36	147
18:7–8	142
18:8	56
18:16–17	55
18:18	68
18:24–25	55, 68
18:30	74
18:31	131
18:32–33	131
18:33	51
18:35–43	126
18:39	52
18:42	126
19:1–10	149
19:11	55, 131, 142
19:17	107
19:19	107
19:28–40	132
19:45–46	133
20:27–40	60
20:36	74
20:37	49, 60
21:9	142
21:10	50
21:10–26	128
21:25	72
21:27	56, 130
21:31	55
21:33	71
21:34	53
21:36	130, 141
22:16	55
22:18	53, 55
22:21–22	133
22:28	138
22:28–30	58
22:29	55, 128
22:30	53, 55, 72, 130–31
22:39–46	133
22:42	132, 134
22:43	128
22:45	51
22:46	51
27:47–53	133, 138

22:49–51	126	3:16	65
22:51	126, 133	3:18	65
22:63–71	133	3:18–19	65
22:67–70	130	3:36	64–65
22:69	56, 130, 143	4:34	134
23:1	51	4:46–53	126–27
23:3	133	5:1–9	126
23:6–11	133	5:8	49, 126
23:26	136	5:19	128
23:34	138	5:21	49, 64
23:38	58	5:24	64–65, 71
23:43	63, 138	5:25	64
23:46	137	5:27	71
23:49	64, 138	5:28	65
23:50—24:12	84	5:28–29	60, 64–65
23:51	55	5:29	65
24:3–7	85	6:1–13	126
24:6	50	6:11	127, 148
24:10	79	6:14–15	127
24:12	51	6:26	126
24:15–29	79	6:39–40	51, 60, 71
24:15–31	79	6:40	60
24:21	130–31	6:44	51, 60, 71
24:31	79, 130	6:46	123, 128
24:31–36	84	6:47	65
24:33	51	6:54	51, 60, 65, 71
24:34	50	6:56	65, 150
24:36	84	6:64	133
24:36–51	79	7:31	127
24:37	62	7:33	70
24:39	62, 83, 86	7:34	70
24:39–40	79	8:52	66
24:41–43	79	9:1–12	126
24:46	51	9:6	126
		10:17	134
		10:24–25	130
		11:11	64

John

1:18	123, 128	11:14–44	124, 126
1:21	135	11:17	90
1:29–34	128	11:23	51
2:1–10	126, 148	11:23–25	64
2:6–10	127	11:24	51
2:19	49	11:24–26	60, 71
2:19–22	71	11:25	65
2:22	50	11:27	64
3:3	71, 123	11:29	50
3:5	65, 71	11:31	51
3:13	123	11:33	64

John *(continued)*

11:38	64
11:39	90
11:43	126
11:43–44	91
12:1	50, 65
12:9	50, 65
12:12–19	132
12:17	50, 65
12:23	130
12:27	134
12:34	130
12:48	71
13:2	133
13:4	50
13:11	133
13:21	133
13:26–27	133
13:33	70
13:36	70
14:2–3	71
14:3	70
14:12	70
14:18	70
14:28	70
14:31	49
15:4–5	150
16:5	70
16:10	70
16:28	70
17:3	130
18:1–9	133
18:9	138
18:10–11	133
18:11	132, 134
18:19–23	133
18:36	55, 71
18:36–37	133
19:1	136
19:1–3	133
19:8–11	133
19:19	58
19:25–27	138
19:26–27	138
19:30	137
19:38—20:15	84
20:1	79
20:1–9	65
20:2	85
20:5–7	85
20:8–9	85
20:9	51
20:11–22	79
20:13	85
20:14–16	80
20:15	85
20:17	79
20:19	79, 84–85
20:19–23	79
20:26	79, 84–85
10:26–29	79
20:27–28	79
21:4–7	80
21:4–22	79
21:14	50
21:15	79
21:20–23	71
21:25	124

Acts

1:1–11	79
1:4–9	79
1:6	131
1:7–8	49
2:2–4	81
2:20	72, 114
3:6	50
3:7	50
3:8	126
3:15	50
4:2	60
4:10	50
4:31	81
5:30	50
7:55–56	130
9:1–21	2, 150
9:3–7	2
9:3–8	79
9:8	50
9:12	126
9:34	126
9:40	51, 91, 126
9:41	51
10:26	50

10:40	50
10:41	79
11:16	49
12:7	50
13:30	50
13:31	79
13:37	50
14:10	126
17:18	60
17:32	60
20:10	91
20:35	49
22:3–16	2, 150
22:6–11	79
22:11	123
23:6	60
24:15	60
24:21	60
26:8	50
26:9–20	2, 150
26:12–18	79

Romans

4:17	60
6:4–5	60
6:8	60
8:11	60, 89, 97
13:11	50

1 Corinthians

7:10	49
9:14	49
11:24–25	49
15	49
15:3–7	97
15:5–7	79
15:5–8	79
15:12–57	60
15:35–36	97
15:35–37	98
15:38	98
15:40–41	123
15:42	97–98
15:44	50, 96–98
15:50	98
15:51–52	97
15:52–53	98

2 Corinthians

3:7	123
5:6	97
5:8	97
12:2–4	97

Ephesians

5:14	50

Philippians

1:17	50
2:8	134
3:11	60
3:20–21	98

Colossians

1:18	150
3:1	98

1 Thessalonians

4:13–14	60
4:16–17	98
5:2	141

Hebrews

6:2	60

1 Peter

2:23	133
2:24	136

2 Peter

3:8	111
3:10	141
3:10–13	114
3:17	114

Revelation

6:12	72
6:12–13	72, 114
6:13	72
11:1	50
13:1–4	109
18:1	123
19:11	109–10
19:14–15	109–10
19:19—20:6	109–10
20:4–6	60
20:12–13	60
21:1	113
21:1—22:5	117
21:2–3	76
21:18–20	107
22:3–5	76
22:6–7	114
22:10	114
22:20	114

Other Ancient Christian Sources

1 Clement

26.3	87

Epistle to the Apostles

2.3	85
11.1—12.2	85–86
12.1	85
16.4	108
24.2	92
24.3	92
51.3	86
51.5	86

Gospel of Peter

12.50–51	79

Gospel of Thomas

Prologue	66
1	66
3.3	70
11.1–2	67
14.4–5	153
18	66
19	66
22.4–5	66
42	66
49.1—50.2	66
50	66–67
56	66
79.3	66
80	66
85	66
87	66
111	67
112	66
113.4	70
114	66

Ignatius, *To the Smyrnaeans*

3.1–3	86

Infancy Gospel of Thomas

2	49
9–18	49

Syriac Apocalypse of Daniel

30–40	117

Treatise on the Resurrection

7.3	99
9.2–3	99

Ancient and Medieval Christian Authors

Aeneas of Gaza

Theophrastus (ed. Colonna)

64.8–10	21

Athenagoras

De resurrectione

2–3	92
7	92
8	92

Augustine

De civitate Dei

13.18	95
20.6	87
20.9	112
20.16	115
20.18	95–96, 115
20.24	115
20.30	115
21.2–9	95
21.2	95
21.4	95
21.5	95
21.6–8	95
22.4	95
22.11	95

De cura pro mortuis gerenda

16	106, 152
19	152

Bede

Historiam ecclesiasticam gentis anglorum

5.12	7

Cyril of Jerusalem

Procatechesis et Catecheses ad illuminandos

18.2	91–92
18.3	92
18.16–17	91
18.18–19	94

Dante Alighieri

La Divina Commedia

Inferno 5.84	105
Paradiso 11.50	150
Paradiso 33	76

Eusebius

Historia ecclesiastica

4.3.1–2	90

Gregory the Great

Dialogi de vita et miraculis patrum Italicorum

4.37.8	7

Irenaeus

Adversus Haereses

2.29.2	94
5.3.2	93
5.13.1	91
5.15.1	88
5.23.2	111
5.28.2	111
5.30.4	110–11
5.31.2	106
5.32.1	111
5.33.1	110
5.33.4	111
5.34.2	107, 111
5.34.4	107
5.35.1	107, 111
5.36.1	94, 115
5.36.2	111

Josephus

Antiquitates judaicae

4.219	138

Justin

Apologia maior

20	114–15

Lactantius

Divinae institutiones

7.17.9–11	140
7.17.10–11	111
7.18.2	140
7.19.5	111
7.19.7	111
7.21.3	95
7.24.2	111
7.24.2–4	112
7.24.6–8	112
7.26.2–3	115
7.26.5	94, 115

Epitome divinarum institutionum

72	94, 115

Methodius of Olympia

De resurrectione

1.22–23	91

Minucius Felix

Octavius

34.1–5	115
34.9–10	93

Origen

Fragmenta in Psalmos

1.5	91

De principiis

2.10.3	98
2.11.2	107–8
2.11.6–7	104

Tertullian

De anima

9.1	105
9.4	105
9.7	105

De resurrectione carnis

11	93
55	88

De spectaculis

30	115

Thomas Aquinas

Summa Theologiae

Suppl., q. 74, a. 1, ad 3	117
Suppl., q. 74, a. 2–9	115
Suppl., q. 74, a. 8, co.	117
Suppl., q. 77, a. 1, co.	117
Suppl., q. 79, a. 1, co.	96
Suppl., q. 81, a. 4, co.	96
Suppl., q. 83, a. 1, co.	96
Suppl., q. 84, a. 1, co.	96
Suppl., q. 85, a. 1, co.	96
Suppl., q. 88, a. 4, arg. 1	109
Suppl., q. 88, a. 4, s. c.	109
Suppl., q. 88, a. 4, co.	108–9
Suppl., q. 88, a 4, ad. 1	109
Suppl., q. 91, a. 5, co.	117

Ancient and Medieval Christian Doctrinal Documents

Ancoratus	86–87
Apostle's Creed	87, 89, 153
Armenian Church, Great Creed of the	87
Benedictus Deus	100
Congratamulur vehementer	88
Fides Damasi	88
Inter innumeras sollicitudines	147
Lateran, 4th Council	88
Lyon, 2nd Council of	88
Ne super his	100
Niceno-Constantinopolitan Creed	87, 112, 146
Statuta Ecclesia Antiqua	88
Toledo, 4th Synod of	88
Toledo, 11th Synod of	88
Toledo, 16th Synod of	88

Author Index

Ahn, Gregor, 1
Alexander, Eben, 7–8
Allison, Dale C., Jr., 4–5, 10, 44, 47–48, 53–59, 61–62, 66–76, 79–80, 84, 88, 93, 97, 100, 124, 128–32, 134–35, 137–39, 141–43, 149
Althaus, Paul, 89, 115–16
Alvarado, Carlos S., 3
Andersson, Rani-Henrik, 119–20
Anklesaria, Behrangore Tehmuras, 22–26
Arcangel, Dianne, 4, 151
Atwater, Phyllis M.H., 11
Avery-Peck, Alan J., 44
Aviam, Mordechai, 144

Ballou, Adin, 81
Barrett, William, 10
Bartelmus, Rüdiger, 31
Bauckham, Richard, 112
Becker, Carl B., 5
Berger, Klaus, 45, 85, 99
Bergson, Henri, 151
Berlejung, Angelika, 38
Berner, Ulrich, 146
Beuken, Willem A. M., 32
Biesalski, Hans Konrad, 149
Bird, Michael F., 59, 132
Biser, Eugen, 153–54
Blackburn, Barry L., 124
Blenkinsopp, Joseph, 33
Blum, Georg Günter, 112
Blümel, Wolf-Dieter, 149
Böcher, Otto, 109
Bock, Darrell L., 36
Boutelle, Luther, 129

Boyarin, Daniel, 44, 130, 143–44
Boyce, Mary, 18–20, 24–25, 47
Brandenburger, Egon, 42, 124
Braun, Hans-Jürg, 14
Brownlee, Donald, 2
Buber, Martin, 154
Büchner, Karl, 102
Buhlman, William, 3, 8, 16
Bultmann, Rudolf, 157
Butterweck, Christel, 93
Bynum, Caroline Walker, 87–88, 91, 100

Campenhausen, Hans von, 84
Capps, Donald, 122
Charlesworth, James H., 31, 33, 36, 143–44
Charpa, Ulrich, 158
Cherniak, Christopher, 158
Cilliers, Louise, 136
Collins, Adela Yarbro, 109
Collins, John J., 33–35
Cook, John Granger, 52
Cooper, Sharon, 12
Crookes, William, 81
Crowell, Eugene, 82

Davies, William David, 53, 57–59, 62, 71–72, 74–75, 124, 132, 137, 139, 143
Dawson, Lorne L., 129
DeCicco, John M., 149
de Jong, Albert, 21
DeMallie, Raymond J., 120–21
Denzinger, Heinrich, 146–47, 153
Doering, Lutz, 128
Dorfmüller, Thomas, 159

Doyle, Brian, 32–33
Drößler, Rudolf, 72
Duling, Dennis C., 47–48

Eadie, Betty J., 8
Edwards, William D., 136
Eliade, Mircea, 14–15
Elsaesser Valarino, Evelyn, 12
Emmons, Henry, 129–30
Engberg-Pedersen, Troels, 96
Evans, Craig A., 49, 133
Evans, Hilary, 17, 80–81
Evers, Dirk, 108

Falkenburg, Brigitte, 158
Feld, Helmut, 150
Feldmeier, Reinhard, 114
Fenwick, Elizabeth, 6–7
Fenwick, Peter, 6–7
Figl, Johann, 146
Findlay, Arthur, 82
Fischer, Alexander A., 34
Frenschkowski, Marco, 53, 76
Freund, Stefan, 111–12, 115

Gardet, Louis, 1
Gathercole, Simon, 49, 66–67, 70
Gauger, Jörg-Dieter, 43
Gavin, Frank S. B., 106
Gertz, Jan Christian, 28
Gibson, Arvin S., 8
Gillman, Neil, 28, 32, 45
Gissurarson, Loftur, 81
Goforth, August, 80
Goodacre, Mark, 139
Goppelt, Leonhard, 133, 139
Gräßer, Erich, 141–43
Gray, Timothy, 80
Greenberg, Moshe, 28, 31–33, 45
Grenet, Frantz, 18–19
Greyson, Bruce, 3, 6–7
Grimaud, Hélène, 156
Grintz, Yehoshua M., 45
Grosso, Michael, 161
Guggenheim, Bill, 4, 9–10, 81, 155
Guggenheim, Judy, 4, 9–10, 81, 155

Hagemann, Ludwig, 1

Hammarskjöld, Dag, 155
Haraldsson, Erlendur, 10, 81, 127
Harpprecht, Klaus, 88
Harrill, J. Albert, 114
Hartmann, Dirk, 158
Heineberg, Heinz, 149
Hellholm, David, 47
Henriksen, Jan-Olav, 148
Henslow, George, 81–82
Henze, Matthias, 42
Herzer, Jens, 43
Hiebel, Janina Maria, 30–31
Hintze, Almut, 18–21, 26
Hoffmann, Paul, 60
Holden, Janice Miner, 6
Holmén, Tom, 70
Holmes, Michael William, 86
Hoping, Helmut, 84–85
Hoppe, Brigitte, 102
Hornschuh, Manfred, 85
Horsley, Richard A., 34, 58, 73
Hultgård, Anders, 20

Jaffé, Aniela, 13
James, William, 4
Jones, John, 82
Jörns, Klaus-Peter, 134
Judd, Wayne R., 129

Kaiser, Otto, 35
Karrer, Otto, 150
Kasturi, Narayana, 125
Kee, Howard Clark, 39
Keen, Montague, 81
Keener, Craig S., 153
Kelber, Werner H., 134
Kelly, Emily Williams, 3, 6
Kemmerich, Max, 17
Khanna, Surbhi, 3
Kittel, Gerhard, 132
Klijn, Albertus Frederik Johannes, 41
Kobel, Esther, 65
Kollmann, Bernd, 126
Kreyenbroek, Philip G., 18
Kruse, Heinz, 153
Kühn, Dagmar, 28
Kurdzialek, Marian, 108

LaGrand, Louis E., 4
Lang, Bernhard, 28, 44, 100, 110, 115, 118, 123
Lapide, Pinchas, 138
Larsson, Edvin, 147
Lawrence, Tony R., 157
Lehtipuu, Outi, 63–64
Lessing, Gotthold Ephraim, 149, 152, 154
Lewis, John Delaware [M. P.], 81–82
Lindemann, Andreas, 69–70
Litwa, M. David, 96, 106
Lohse, Eduard, 35
Lommel, Herman, 19–20
Lona, Horacio E., 87
Ludwig, Günter, 158–59, 161
Luther, Martin, 70, 134, 146
Luz, Ulrich, 130, 133, 152

Macaskill, Grant, 144
Markschies, Christoph, 98
Mattiesen, Emil, 17, 82
Maurach, Gregor, 108
McAffee, Matthew, 32
McDannell, Colleen, 28, 110, 115, 118
McDonald, Lee Martin, 61
McKenzie, Keisha, 118
Meiser, Martin, 48
Merkel, Helmut, 43
Merz, Annette, 124, 131–33, 138, 141, 149
Metzger, Bruce Manning, 40
Meyer, Marvin W., 99
Mikulasch, Rodolpho H., 80
Miller, William, 129
Modi, Jivanji Jamshedji, 18
Mohler, Albert, 88–89
Moltmann, Jürgen, 139
Moody, Raymond A., Jr., 6–7, 11, 24
Mooney, James, 121
Moore, Lauren E., 7
Morgenstern, Matthias, 44
Mosis, Rudolf, 31
Müller, Gerhard Ludwig, 153
Müller, Tobias, 158–59
Mumm, Peter-Arnold, 17
Munshi, Shehnaz Neville, 18
Musamian, Farnaz, 5

Nahm, Michael, 3
Neihardt, John G., 121
Nickelsburg, George W. E., 35–38, 143
Niebuhr, Karl-Wilhelm, 148, 153
Nitsche, Bernhard, 134
Noratuk, Vicki, 11
Nord, Christiane, 85, 99
Novakovic, Lidija, 97
Noy, Dov, 136
Noyes, Russell, Jr., 3

Ó hÓgáin, Dáithí, 14
Oberdorfer, Bernd, 76
Oberlinner, Lorenz, 84
Oegema, Gerbern S., 41–42
Öhler, Markus, 135
Owens, Justine E., 6

P., M. [John Delaware Lewis], 81–82
Parnia, Sam, 3
Partin, Harry B., 15
Pennington, Jonathan T., 55
Peres, Imre, 35, 101
Perry, Paul, 6
Pezzoli-Olgiati, Daria, 47
Philaret Drozdov, 89, 99, 134, 146
Pierce, Seth, 118
Pines, Shlomo, 45
Poirier, John C., 128
Polkinghorne, John, 116
Popkes, Enno Edzard, 49, 66, 153
Porter, Katherine Anne, 24
Priest, John, 42
Prinz, Wolfgang, 159

Raei, Shahrokh, 24
Rahner, Karl, 76, 100, 116, 147–48, 154
Recheis, Athanas, 104
Regnerus, 88
Reimarus, Hermann Samuel, 131, 140–41
Rein, Matthias, 48, 65
Retief, Francois P., 136
Reynolds, Benjamin E., 144
Richter, Julius, 141
Richter, Susanne, 17
Ring, Kenneth, 12
Ringgren, Helmer, 25

AUTHOR INDEX

Riskas, Thomas J., Jr., 118
Rogo, Scott, 150
Rooker, Mark F., 143
Roose, Hanna, 62
Rothman, Tony, 158
Rowe, David L., 129
Ruffin, C. Bernard, 154
Russell, David S., 31, 34
Rust, Joshua, 154

Sabom, Michael, 6, 8, 11
Sanders, Ed Parish, 58, 70, 77
Sandnes, Karl Olav, 148
Sattler, Dorothea, 134
Scafi, Alessandro, 15
Schamoni, Wilhelm, 10, 154, 161
Schmid, Konrad, 31–32, 103
Schmithals, Walter, 86
Schnelle, Udo, 97
Scholem, Gershom, 45
Schöpflin, Karin, 30–31
Schreiner, Josef, 40
Schröter, Jens, 48
Schwaninger, Janet, 3
Schweitzer, Albert, 52, 77, 122, 136–37, 150, 154
Schwenke, Heiner, 2, 4–6, 13, 80, 83, 150–52, 155, 157–58, 160–62
Schwitzgebel, Eric, 154
Schwöbel, Christoph, 89
Scriba, Albrecht, 143
Sedlmeier, Franz, 31
Segal, Alan F., 45
Seils, Martin, 114
Sekanek, Rudolf, 10
Shaked, Shaul, 18, 20, 24
Sharp, Harold, 81
Shushan, Gregory, 5
Siegel, Seymour, 44
Silverman, Jason M., 18, 31, 44
Skjærvø, Prods Oktor, 18–19
Smith, Morton, 126
Solomon, Grant, 81
Solomon, Jane, 81
Spieckermann, Hermann, 128
Sprandel, Rolf, 105
Stausberg, Michael, 18

Steltenkamp, Michael F., 120-21
Stemberger, Günter, 29, 36–41
Storm, Howard, 11
Stowasser, Martin, 133
Strobel, August, 69, 143–44
Stückelberger, Alfred, 114
Stuckenbruck, Loren T., 35

Theißen, Gerd, 124, 131–133, 138, 141, 149
Thompson, R. Campbell, 14
Thonnard, Marie, 7
Thurston, Herbert, 10
Tornau, Christian, 66–67
Treece, Patricia, 10
Twelftree, Graham H., 124, 126

Uhlig, Siegbert, 35–36
Ullmann, Bettina, 156

van der Horst, Pieter Willem, 64
VanderKam, James C., 35–38, 143
van Lommel, Pim, 3, 6–7, 10–11
Vetter, Dieter, 44
Viviano, Benedict T., 101

Walck, Leslie 144
Wan, Sze-Kar, 28
Ward, Peter, 2
Watts, John D.W., 33
Weder, Hans, 70, 125
Weiß, Johannes, 70
Wiebe, Philipp H., 150
Wiggermann, Frans, 126
Wilk, Florian, 128
Wills-Brandon, Carla, 81–82
Wiltse, A. S., 8, 15
Winston, David, 18
Witetschek, Stephan, 109
Witte, Markus, 33–34, 45
Wright, Nicholas Thomas, 88, 116, 116

Yamauchi, Edwin M., 126

Zander, Vera [Valentine], 10
Zimmermann, Ruben, 157

Lightning Source UK Ltd.
Milton Keynes UK
UKHW011028290319
340143UK00005B/262/P